I0777711

When the memories won't let go...

THE LAST ONE YOU LOVED

WRITER'S DIGEST AWARD WINNING AUTHOR

LJ EVANS

When the memories won't let go…

The Last One You Loved

L J Evans

Published by LJ EVANS BOOKS

www.ljevansbooks.com

Cover Design: © Emily Wittig Designs

Content & Line Editor: Evans Editing

Copy Editor: Jenn Lockwood Editing Services

Proofing: Karen Hrdlicka

ISBN: 978-1-962499-09-5

Library of Congress Cataloging in process.

Listen now on Spotify: https://spoti.fi/3Pp12T5

For all the cowboys who didn't ride away.

For Leisa who is the reason this book exists.

And for the gang at TWSS who took a gamble on a lost cause.

I'll forever be grateful.

Prologue

Maddox

AIN'T ALWAYS THE COWBOY

Performed by Jon Pardi

The lake shimmered in the moonlight. The warm breeze stirred up tiny waves, sending white sprinkles shifting across the surface as it drifted toward the shore where we were parked.

We were on the tailgate of my beat-up Bronco with our hands and limbs joined. McKenna's jean-clad legs were flung over my lap, and her head rested on my shoulder. Her cowboy boots were off, lost somewhere behind me in the chaos of blankets and food wrappers. I ran the fingers of my free hand over the gentle arch of her foot, and she jerked it away, laughing.

"Don't you dare tickle me unless you want to end up with a busted nose," she teased, her soft voice washing over me.

It wasn't like I hadn't known she'd pull away. Ten years of knowing her meant I knew just how ticklish her feet were, but I'd done it anyway in an attempt to lighten the mood. But the sound and scent and feel of her made it almost impossible to feel anything but sorrow. It might be the last time I would hold her like this, and my heart screamed as if it could change what was happening by merely twisting inside my chest.

"Wanna go for a swim?" I asked.

It was still humid outside, even though the sun had set hours ago. Long enough that the twilight sounds of the bugs and wild animals had almost disappeared. Instead, a quiet had taken over the space, a preview of what would happen once she drove down the road tomorrow and my life was forever changed.

In answer to my question, she slid off of me and started discarding clothes. She was wearing a string bikini under her jeans and floaty blouse, as if she'd known I'd ask for this—us in the water. I swallowed hard at the gentle curves I'd spent years getting to know as well as my own. I glanced down at my sinewy body toughened from years of working on the ranch. She'd always said my muscles were the very best kind—built from hard work. Would anyone else ever care about them the way she had?

I hadn't been as prepared as she'd been for a swim, so my boxer briefs were going to have to do. Once I'd stripped down, I recaptured her hand, determined to touch her for as long as possible, and led us toward the water, picking our way through the twigs and rocks as we went.

As soon as we hit the cool water, I shivered. It was a soothing relief to the heat and heaviness of the day. If only it could lift the weight inside me as easily as it chilled my skin.

We swam toward the makeshift dock someone had fastened to the middle of the lake decades ago. We didn't pull ourselves up on top. Instead, we hid in the shadows. She wrapped her long limbs around my waist, and I looped an arm through one of the ropes hanging off the wooden slats to hold us steady while my hands continued to touch her.

She kissed me. Wet and wild. Slow and torturous. Love and goodbyes blended into the movements as we rejoined our bodies in the way we'd been doing over the last couple of months. Like a flame on the wick of a firecracker, burning, burning, burning until it finally ignited into a shower of light and sound.

Until it became nothing but us.

She moaned into my mouth when my fingers slid under her bikini, touching pieces of her that were aching for me. I wanted to cry out as well, but with a different ache. I wanted to let my tears wash into the lake.

But it would be selfish because I wouldn't be crying for her. I'd only be crying for me, and that didn't seem fair. McKenna deserved the future she was heading toward—her dream of becoming a doctor finally starting. But her desire to escape this town and her mother hurt because it meant she was escaping me and my family as well—the people who'd loved and sheltered her.

Knowing it was coming hadn't eased the pain of its arrival. As much as I wanted to follow her, I couldn't. My life was here with my family, and the ranch, and my own dreams of serving my community. Even if everything at home had been perfectly fine, I wasn't sure I'd want to leave our small town for a place where you couldn't see the stars. Here, they were so bright it seemed like you could grab them, put them in your pocket, and take them with you. If I was forced to live in a city, I'd burn out just like those faraway suns. If you forced her to stay, she'd wither like the roses I'd given her last week. Dust into dust.

We loved each other more than I'd ever thought was possible, especially considering we were just two kids, barely legal. I knew her smiles and looks and moods better than she knew them herself, and vice versa. But this was where the road we were on finally divided after a decade of running side by side. A bitter taste rose inside me because I wasn't sure our roads would ever cross again.

"I'll come visit," I told her, breaking my mouth from hers. "Thanksgiving or spring break. Whichever works."

Could I get through to spring without seeing her? Touching her? Loving her? How would I even come up with the money for the trip?

She rested her forehead on my shoulder, placed a gentle kiss there, and then looked up at me with sad, tormented eyes.

"Maddox…between college, medical school, and a residency, it'll be at least eleven years before I'm done. I'll always be your friend. I'll always love you…but…I just…" A choked sob broke free from her, and my throat bobbed, eyes watering.

"You want to break up. You don't even want to try?" I asked, that bitterness coating my tongue and my mouth growing. She had choices. She could have applied to Tennessee State. She could have kept us closer, but even as I said it, I knew she couldn't. McKenna needed to put her childhood behind her…even if that meant giving me up along with it.

She put her hands on my cheeks, cupping them and kissing my lips sweetly.

"You're my favorite thing. My favorite memory. My favorite gift. My favorite person," she said quietly.

I could no longer hold the tears back. I didn't know how to let her go. But I'd have to because it wasn't always the cowboy who ran away.

Sometimes, it was the golden-haloed woman with a future so bright the gods had to be jealous.

That was my McKenna.

And tomorrow, she'd be gone.

No longer mine, but the world's instead.

Chapter One

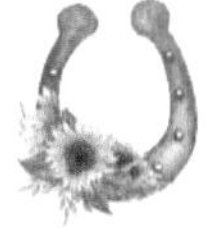

McKenna

YOU ALL OVER ME

Performed by Taylor Swift with Maren Morris

TEN YEARS LATER

Bouncing on my bed woke me. I forced my eyes open and then slammed them shut upon seeing Sally's glowing face. It was too early for this kind of over-the-top happiness.

"Happy birthday, McKenna!" she practically screamed, forcing me to look at her again.

I groaned and tried to bury my head under the covers, but my roommate wouldn't let me. Instead, she ripped the blankets back with surprisingly strong hands and shoved a heavy present at me. Her large, mahogany eyes twinkled in her light-brown face as her pink-tipped waves swung around her sharply defined cheeks and chin.

I hated birthdays, while Sally was from a family who celebrated them like they were a bigger deal than Christmas. In the three years I'd been living with her, she'd made sure I had cake, presents, and whatever I wanted for dinner. Last year, she'd even thrown a surprise party for me at the nurses' station. I'd wanted to run as soon as I'd turned the corner, and I'd made her promise never to do it again.

Growing up, my birthdays had been a painful reminder of what had gone wrong in Mama's life, and she'd done everything to make sure her worst day would also be mine. Only one person besides Sally had ever tried to make this day something different.

I pushed aside the memories that threatened to weigh me down and groused without any real heat, "It's too early for presents and celebrations, Sal."

"Shut up and open it!" she said, ignoring my grumpiness and shoving the box at me with her wide smile fixed permanently in place.

I sat up, and my naturally blonde hair tumbled around me in knots. I'd regret going to bed with it wet, but I'd been exhausted after my twelve-hour shift at the hospital had turned into a sixteen-hour one. I'd barely been able to shower, let alone worry about my hair.

I pulled the bulky gift onto my lap and shot Sally a frown. "I hope you didn't do something stupid, like spend some of your car money on me. I don't want to be the reason you can't get it in January!"

She flicked my shoulder. "Just open it and stop being ridiculous."

I slowly undid the ribbon and pulled off the lid. Inside was a DVD collection of *Buffy the Vampire Slayer*. Every season. I swallowed hard. The DVDs weren't new, but they still had to have cost her a pretty penny to get the entire set. With both of us barely scraping by due to the enormous college debt resting on our shoulders, this wasn't a little gift.

Tears hit my eyes for real, but I refused to let them out, like I'd learned to do early in life by biting my cheek and clenching my nails into my palms. But my voice was still clogged with emotions when I choked out, "Dang it, Sal."

She hugged me to her, and I did my best not to stiffen, letting my head land briefly on her shoulder.

"Now, you'll always have Buffy when you need her," she said softly.

"I need her less these days because I have you," I responded. She was the best female friend I'd ever had. I'd say she was my best friend ever, but there was a teeny-tiny place inside my heart that knew it would be a lie. But I wouldn't hear from him today. I'd shoved him out of my life for a dream—a mirage—that had disappeared in the shimmer of the hot sun.

My gut twisted.

I couldn't think of that today. Of him. Of my mistakes.

I had to get my head on straight, put on my white jacket, and head to the ER—to the real dream I was mere months away from finalizing.

Once my residency was over, I'd be one-hundred-percent official. I'd not only be a doctor, but I'd also be able to call the shots. Goosebumps covered my arms. Ten-year-old me would hardly be able to believe it. That I'd actually escaped and made it happen.

"Get dressed. Your birthday breakfast awaits," Sally said and basically pushed me out of the bed. I stumbled, barely catching myself on the dresser.

"Geez, if this is how you treat a friend on her birthday, I don't want to see how you treat your enemies," I teased.

She headed for the door. "If you're not out in five minutes, I'm going to shove your pancakes—whipped cream and all—in your face. Dickwad Gregory is in charge today, so neither of us can afford to be late."

My stomach knotted thinking of the head of the ER department. He was obnoxious, and egotistical, and thought everyone should swoon over his fifty-year-old, married self. Worse, some people did. Made me pukey even thinking about it.

"McK, I'm not kidding. Five minutes," Sally said, bringing me out of my thoughts.

"Okay, okay."

I slipped into the bathroom, washed up, and pulled on my scrubs. As I fought to drag my messy hair into a high ponytail, the shadows under my hazel eyes caught my attention. They'd pretty much become a permanent feature since starting my residency and were almost as black as my heavy brows. My hand stalled as it hit me suddenly—I looked like Mama.

That scared me. My tired expression wasn't from drugs and alcohol, but it was from running fast and furious for too many years.

"McK!" Sally hollered.

I shoved my phone, water bottle, and keys into a small backpack and hurried out of the room before coming to a complete stop, mouth dropping open.

The entire apartment was full of balloons and streamers.

I bit my cheek hard, tasting blood, and blinked rapidly to hold back the waterworks. Sally was all but dancing around me, excitement on her face from the pure joy of doing this for me.

I didn't care about my birthday. But I thanked the universe for the day Sally had found me on the bench outside the hospital, in a rare fit of tears, and befriended me. It was almost as important as the day Maddox Hatley had found me cowering in a shed behind his uncle's bar when I was eight.

Too bad I didn't have Maddox anymore.

It made this, what I had with Sally, that much more important. So, I'd celebrate today because she wanted me to. Because she was literally the only soul left on this planet who would care if I disappeared tomorrow.

Chapter Two

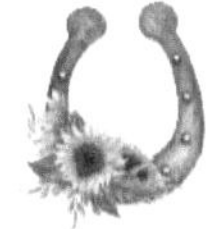

Maddox

SLOW BURN

Performed by Zac Brown Band

I pulled back just in time, letting the fist barely graze my chin. The movement was enough to send my Stetson flying, landing amongst the straw where it was going to get trampled. It was the sight of my hat on the ground that pissed me off more than the fist or Willy Tate's drunken, angry snarl as he lunged for me again.

I ducked the second shot and shoved my shoulder into his gut, taking him down to the ground with me. The music had stopped, the customers in the bar quiet as they watched two burly men wrestle. Several chairs were tipped over, tables were bumped, and drinks were spilled as we rolled around. It took me one too many moves before I finally had him pinned facedown with his hands behind his back and my knee holding him in place.

"Damn it, Willy, you owe me a new hat!" I growled.

Clapping filled the air along with hoots and hollers that made my eyes roll.

"Thanks for the show!" someone in the back yelled as someone else shouted out, "Brings me back to my sheep-tying days!"

"Thanks for the help, y'all," I said sarcastically, eyeing my brother sitting calmly on a stool at the bar with a crooked grin.

"Why, Sheriff Maddox, no one would ever presume to think you needed help." Ryder's grin grew, and then he had the audacity to wink at me as he raised a beer in my direction. I barely resisted flipping him the bird as laughter erupted from him, causing his blue eyes that matched mine to crinkle at the corners. He brushed a hand over his perfectly tousled dark-brown hair that should have been smashed flat after wearing a hat all day but instead looked like he'd stepped off the page of a damn magazine.

I was not anywhere near picture-perfect. My dark-blond hair was standing up in places, and the stubble on my chin—a day past trendy—was dripping and sticky from the whiskey Willy had thrown at me. The alcohol had stained my tan shirt, and our scuffle had snagged the ends of my olive-green tie, almost ripping it from my neck.

"She left me, Maddox. For a goddamn suit from Knoxville." Willy was crying now, and it almost looked ridiculous on the six-foot-three mechanic with the hair and beard of someone who'd been lost in the wild for one too many years.

"Taking it out on everyone here isn't going to make the pain go away, shithead," I grumbled. "You gonna start swinging again if I get up?"

Willy shook his head. I stood and then helped the man to his feet. His sad, puppy-dog eyes were full of tears that tumbled down his cheeks.

"You going to arrest him for hitting a lawman?" Gemma asked, trying not to giggle. My sister was sitting next to Ryder at the bar. Her long hair was the same color as mine, but her hazel eyes were full of our brother's laughter. Ryder tapped her elbow with his in appreciation of the taunt she'd thrown my way.

Willy hunched his enormous shoulders. "Fuck. I forgot you're the sheriff now."

"I've been an officer of the law for damn near six years, Willy. Hitting me before or after I'd been elected wouldn't change a damn thing." I leaned down and picked up my hat, brushing it against my thigh and shoving him toward the door of McFlannigan's. It was the only bar in town and normally looked as Irish as my uncle who owned the place, but on Thursdays, they had two-dollar beers, line dancing, and a live band. Uncle Phil brought hay in from the ranch to make it more *Tennessee barnyard* than *Dublin dive*.

I'd told him more than once the hay was a hazard, but as he was friends with the county health inspector, who just happened to be in one of the booths tonight with his wife, my uncle clearly didn't have to worry about being fined. That was the way everything in this town worked, and while I'd been able to turn a blind eye to some of it as a deputy, since I'd been elected, it had been harder to do.

The people of Winter County had put their trust in me. Maybe it was because Sheriff Haskett had thrown his hat in my direction when he'd stepped down, or maybe it was because the Hatley family had been in Willow Creek since its inception. Regardless, they'd taken a chance on a green twenty-seven-year-old last year, and I'd spent twelve months proving to them it had been the right choice.

Willy and I were at the door when Ryder called out, "Going to come back and have a beer with us after you get him home?"

I shook my head.

"Come on, Maddox, one drink!" Gemma called.

I had no desire to sit at the bar, shooting the shit with my siblings, after the long day I'd had. If the bar hadn't been mere blocks from my house when the call had come in as I walked out the station door, I would've let one of my deputies handle the call. Now that I'd done my civic duty for the night, I had only one goal, and that was getting home to my girl.

I directed Willy into the passenger seat of my ancient green and rust-covered Bronco, wishing I'd driven my sheriff truck instead. But the Bronco had called to me this morning—the date dragging at me as it did every year.

The date I tried to ignore and failed miserably to do.

I got Willy tucked into the small apartment above the garage his family had owned almost as long as mine had owned the ranch and then headed to my 1950s-style bungalow two streets over. After three years of hard work, the house was pretty much how I wanted it. The wood siding had a fresh coat of pale-yellow paint, new black shutters edged the multi-paned windows, and a burnt-orange custom door invited you in, just like the swing tucked in the corner of the front porch.

An antique lamp on the hall table cast a gentle light onto the dark plank floors as I let myself in, and the murmur of the television in the open-space living area greeted me. Rianne looked up from the cushy, leather couch I'd spent a small fortune on as I hung my destroyed hat on the rack by the door.

Her bright-red lips curved upward in greeting, and her dark-brown face was just starting to show signs of wrinkles even though she was as old as my grandparents. Her black-and-white corkscrew hair was tucked beneath a vivid-blue scarf littered with pictures of baby ducks. She had so many head wraps I thought she could wear a different one every day of the year and still have more.

"How is she?" I asked.

"Like always. Pretending to sleep but really waiting for you," she said, turning off the TV and rising. She was wearing soft jeans and a long tunic top, looking far more casual than she ever had as my third-grade teacher. When I'd been a rowdy eight-year-old, I'd adored her, and now that she'd turned in her teacher badge and taken on helping me, I loved her almost as much as I loved my mama.

"You smell like a liquor cabinet." Rianne's nose squished up, but there was a smile on her lips.

I sighed, ran my hand over my half-assed, alcohol-soaked beard, and grimaced.

"Had to pull Willy out of McFlannigan's before he tore it apart."

Rianne's face fell. "Aw, he's taking the loss of his woman pretty hard."

I nodded. It was why I'd tucked him at home instead of locking him up in a cell at the station. I knew what it felt like to watch your woman drive away. The agony I'd felt didn't make me want to bleed out on the floor anymore, but the reminder on this day, more than any other, made the hurt tumble through me as if it had happened yesterday instead of a decade ago.

Rianne gathered her things, and I walked her to the door.

"Try to get some rest tomorrow, and I'll see you on Sunday," she said before leaving.

I was technically off the clock for a whole day, but that never meant much when you were one of only twelve people holding down the only law enforcement agency in the county. We didn't have a lot of crime in Willow Creek, but we did have a lot of work. On any given day, I might be helping round up stray chickens one moment and taking beer from underage kids at the lake the next. The biggest pain in my ass was the motorcycle club, The West Gears, who used their headquarters up in the mountains right at the county line to deal drugs and store stolen merchandise. The Gears were the reason I was dead on my feet tonight after a day of hunting them down.

I headed down the hall, feet stalling as I passed Mila's door. She'd expect me to crawl into bed with her, and I didn't want to do that smelling like whiskey, so I continued on to the one room I hadn't let Mama or my sisters help decorate. Instead, the main bedroom reflected me like almost no other part of the house. It was full of dark woods, navy linens, and black-and-white photographs of the lake and the ranch.

I locked my weapon away in the gun safe, showered in the bathroom filled with teak woods and blue linens, and then changed into sweats and a long-sleeve T-shirt before padding on bare feet back to Mila's room. I turned the knob as quietly as possible in a vain hope that she might actually be asleep but chuckled to myself when I saw her dart her head under the covers.

Her room looked like a rainbow had thrown up in it. She was obsessed with them. She'd even convinced me to paint her white headboard in rainbow stripes. Between that, her four pastel-colored nightlights, and the pile of stuffed unicorns that filled an armchair in the corner, it felt like walking into a cartoon world. I crossed the faux-fur white rug and stood looking down at the rainbow comforter that shed glitter like it was a cat changing seasons.

"Oh good, Mila is asleep. I don't have to read *The Day the Unicorns Saved the World* for the one-thousandth time," I said softly.

The covers were thrown back, and beautiful wheat-colored eyes stared at me under thick brows that were almost black and contrasted with the honey-blonde hair spiraling in waves around her round face. "I'm not sleeping, Daddy! You *have* to read it, or I'll be up all night."

There was a little whine to her sweet voice and a pout to her lips that made my mouth twitch. I sighed dramatically, looked up at the ceiling, and pretended to contemplate the fate of my life before pulling the book from her nightstand.

"Scootch over," I said as if this wasn't our nightly routine.

She pulled back her covers and moved to the side as I slid in with her. Her tiny, five-year-old body curled up against me, and I put one arm around her, holding her tight. She smelled like the berry shampoo Mama had bought for her birthday, and she had on a pair of fuzzy, pink-striped pajamas that had been from my sister. Her body was warm and her tiny hand soft as she placed it on my arm. My heart filled to near bursting just by having her there.

"How was your day?" I asked.

"I learned that the letter L says *lllll* like in lion, and that five and two more is seven. Seven is my birthday number, so Mrs. Randall let me use the butterfly pointer and lead the class in the alphabet song."

Kindergarten. My baby had started kindergarten at the end of August. I hadn't expected it to be as hard as it had been to drop her off at school and walk away. I mean, I'd been leaving her every day for the four years of her life that she'd been mine. But there was something different about leaving her with Rianne versus taking her into a classroom full of kids who I couldn't guarantee would be nice and adults who were strangers. I'd run the name of the principal and every teacher at the school to make sure there weren't any scumbags hiding in the system, even when I knew the state wouldn't have given certificates to criminals. I'd sort of gone off my rocker for a day or two. The only thing that made it easier was knowing Mila liked being there.

"That sounds like a really good day," I told her.

"Yeah. But Missy wouldn't give me a turn with the hula hoop." She pouted, and every vein in my body tightened. The need to protect her, even from other five-year-olds, was a strange sensation. There was a time in my life when I hadn't wanted to be a dad, when I'd promised another blonde-haired girl that we wouldn't have kids because she was adamantly opposed to having them.

"I'll buy you your own damn hula hoop tomorrow," I told her, voice gruff with emotions. She giggled.

"You cussed again, Daddy. You owe me another dollar for the cuss jar."

I smiled with my lips against her hair. She'd have enough money in that jar to go to college if I wasn't careful. The thought of her being grown up and going away to college threatened to rip some more at the scars that had already cracked open today.

I pushed the pain away, opened the book, and started reading as my girl snuggled deeper into my chest. My heart expanded until it was quadruple the size it should have been. This was perfect. I didn't need anything else in my life but this.

Chapter Three

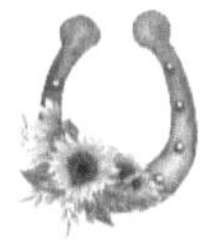

McKenna

My eyes were blurry from another twelve-hour shift as I headed toward the doctors' lounge with nothing but my bed and sleep in mind. As I came around the corner, I almost ran into a lanky, red-haired teen. I put out a hand to stop us from colliding, and it hit his chest. He groaned, almost doubling over on himself, and my eyes grew wide. I'd barely touched him, definitely not enough to cause pure agony.

My heart pounded viciously as I recognized Dr. Gregory's son. Concern swept away my tiredness, and I asked, "Layton, what's wrong?"

He pulled back, wrapping an arm around his middle and trying to straighten to his full height, which easily met my five-foot-ten. Layton leaned against the wall for a moment, breathing heavily.

"Nothing. I'm fine," he said, grunting through the pain.

"You're not fine. At all. Shall I call your father?" I whipped out my phone, and his eyes grew rounder until they took over his whole face with sheer panic.

"For fuck's sake, don't call him," he hissed.

I hesitated, and when he saw it, he looked down and away, throat bobbing as he swallowed hard.

"Dad knows," he said quietly, still avoiding looking at me. All my senses went haywire. A shiver went down my spine for no reason that I could name except a gut instinct and a well of memories that threatened to overtake me if I didn't push them away.

"Do you mind me asking what happened?" I asked softly, keeping my tone as neutral as possible in an attempt to be soothing without raising Layton's red flags.

He still wouldn't meet my gaze and was running the toe of his shoe over the lines in the tile flooring.

"Got hurt climbing," he said. "It's just a bruise."

But as he talked, his breathing remained shallow in an attempt to keep the pain at bay.

"Your dad looked you over?" I pushed, warring with myself. It wasn't my business. He was a minor. His dad was my boss and a well-respected man at the hospital and in the community. My stomach clenched, unsubstantiated thoughts based on nothing more than instinct filled me, and I knew—with a panicked sense of certainty—that this was exactly what I'd spent the last ten years of my life working and waiting for. And yet, now that it was here, I was terrified because it came in a form I couldn't be sure would end well for me.

"It's just a bruise," Layton insisted, and this time, he raised his chin defiantly at me, as if daring me—or begging me—to say something different.

Half of me was screaming to just let it go—to walk away. The other half of me, the girl from nowhere who'd promised herself she'd be a shield for those who needed it, was yelling at me to push him into one of the ER beds and demand an X-ray.

He pushed off the wall, took two steps away from me, and then listed sideways as his knees started to crumble. I caught him under the arm with my shoulder so he wouldn't hit the ground, and he yelped.

We darted looks in both directions down the hall, and I knew I was right. I hated that I was. I hated that I was going to have to do this, but I didn't have another choice.

"Let's get you into a bed so I can take a look," I said quietly.

He didn't argue. He could barely stand, breathing so erratically I thought he might actually pass out, and I'd have to call for a gurney. If I did that, his father would be called, and this kid wouldn't stand a chance.

I opened the door of the closest hospital room, breathing a sigh of relief when I saw it was empty. I got him over to the bed, and he sat down, whimpering again as I helped him lie back. When I went to move away, he grabbed my hand, clutching it so tightly his nails almost broke the skin before he dropped it.

"Please, don't call my dad."

I swallowed hard, pulled the rolling stool from the corner, and sat next to him.

"Did you really get hurt climbing?" I asked, but I already knew he hadn't.

He closed his eyes. "Don't ask me that."

"How old are you?"

"Fifteen."

Crap on a cupcake. I debated one last second before saying, "Normally, I can't conduct an exam or provide any medical care without getting permission from one of your parents, but there are certain circumstances that allow me to sidestep that rule," I said gently, wanting to reassure him I could look at him if I suspected there was abuse without actually saying the words and scaring him off.

If I found what I thought I'd find, I'd also have to report it. I'd have to report the head of my department, and I already knew that would bring hell down on me. Roy Gregory was a narcissistic ass who I'd already gone toe to toe with several times after I'd wounded his pride by discouraging his sexual overtures.

Layton's mouth turned grim, jaw clenching.

"Do you want me to call your mom?" I asked, tightening my ponytail and pushing my toes up and down like a ballerina, which sent my knees into a seesaw motion. Both moves were old tells. Ones I'd thought I'd gotten past. Ones that had irritated my mother. But then, any movement I'd made had irritated her.

He shook his head and bit his lip. "She knows."

My heart fell. Having one parent who filled your life with fear was bad enough. Being afraid to tell the other parent was a different kind of torture that I knew acutely. But I couldn't even imagine having the second parent find out and do nothing.

My dad, Trap, had turned vicious when he'd found out about Mama. But it hadn't been his fists he'd used, even when he was known in three counties for doing just that—for being a violent man you didn't want to cross. It had still been too little, too late.

Painful memories threatened to overwhelm me in a day full of them as I scooted the stool over to the room's computer. I typed in my ID and password and then asked Layton for his social security number. I was officially crossing the line—the right line, but still one that wasn't easy to step over.

I eyeballed his file, my stomach growing tauter with each entry I read. Fractured wrist from a tee-ball injury. Displaced shoulder from a climbing accident. Bruised cheekbone from a fall off a skateboard. I wondered how many of those sports Layton actually participated in. I'd heard Dr. Gregory bragging about his extreme-sports addict of a son, but maybe it was all a ploy to cover the abuse.

I donned gloves from the box by the door and took Layton's temp and blood pressure when normally a nurse would have done it for me. I could have called Sally. She was still on duty in the ER. But there was no way I was bringing her into this.

I gently probed Layton's chest and ribs, and his eyes rolled back.

"Stay with me, Layton. Tell me about your favorite sport."

He drew his gaze back to me, brows furrowing as he concentrated on his motocross escapades. After the exam, I placed an order for an in-room X-ray. I didn't want to wheel him about the hospital. Hopefully, the name on the file wouldn't send someone scurrying to ask Dr. Gregory about it, but it couldn't be helped. I had to have a name to log the request under, and I wasn't prepared to make one up. I had to keep as many of the I's dotted and the T's crossed as I could if I wasn't going to lose my residency over this.

It was at least an hour later before the tech had come and gone and I'd received the results—cracks to ribs seven and eight, but nothing that would endanger his heart or lungs. It would hurt like hell for weeks, but he'd recover. I explained what I saw to Layton and what he needed to do to take care of himself. Then, I sat at his side on the rolling stool, moving silently back and forth as I pushed my toes against the ground, first one and then the other.

"Want to tell me what really happened?" I asked.

He looked toward the window. "I already told you."

"Bullshit." I pulled the sleeve of my white coat up to reveal my forearm. "These were from *boiling water*," I told him, showing off a dozen faded-brown scars that were perfectly round. I could still feel the butt of the cigarette as it singed and the smell of burning flesh. I dragged up the other sleeve to reveal a jagged scar running from my elbow almost to the wrist. "This time, I fell out of a treehouse we didn't have."

His eyes grew wider, but he still didn't say anything.

I pointed under my chin, lifting it so he could see the faded-pink line. "This one was the last one. I supposedly fell skateboarding. At seventeen. When I didn't own a skateboard and never had. That was the one that finally allowed them to pull me away. I was lucky. I had a…friend…whose family took me in until I graduated."

My throat clogged with emotions and memories, recalling Maddox and his anger that day. My body relived the utter despondency I'd felt and the pure joy when he'd said he'd never let me go back.

The screech of tires and the roar of Maddox's 1972 Ford Bronco filled the street outside my house, and I did the only thing I could. I ran for it.

The screen door crashed shut behind me as Mama screamed my name followed by curse words that were all slurred together from the drink in her hand. My heart was slamming against my rib cage, a violent struggle going on inside me, but I didn't stop until I was pulling myself into the passenger seat.

"Go!" I screamed.

Maddox obliged, hitting the pedal so hard my head flew back against the vinyl seat as the wind swirled around me. He had the hardtop off, and my long hair whipped into my face, sticking to the blood on my chin, as we drove away at a speed that was sure to get him a ticket if he wasn't careful.

We were halfway to the lake before he finally spoke, drawing my eyes to his newly muscled body, dark-caramel tousled hair, and bright-blue eyes that glimmered in the fading sunlight. What he saw made his hands jerk the wheel, and we almost went off the road before he corrected, straightening the tires back onto the pavement.

"You're bleeding!" he growled.

My stomach churned, acid burning. I hated that Maddox knew about this part of my life—the drunken mother who hated me enough to strike out when I breathed the wrong way. But he'd been the first to know. The only one I'd ever risked telling the truth to since the day he'd found me hiding as my mother screamed obscenities from the door of our shitty duplex.

"Do I need to take you to the ER, McK?" His voice cracked, worry and heartache in every syllable.

"No," I told him, pushing a kitchen towel that I'd grabbed against my chin. Another thing for her to hate me for. Another thing I'd cost her.

We were quiet the rest of the way. The lake was where we'd spent most of our free time since he'd gotten his license. Maddox four-wheeled out to the edge of the water, and I climbed into the back of the Bronco. The insides of the vehicle were still a mess with torn seats and rusted sides, but the engine was strong and steady. Maddox had spent every last dime he'd earned schlepping hay and horse manure and bussing tables at Tillie's to save money for a paint job and new seats. The entire thing would be redone soon.

I reached for a fuzzy blanket Maddox kept in the back, and it revealed a small cooler. I stretched the blanket out as Maddox joined me. He turned on our favorite radio station, using the ancient boombox he'd found in the shed at his uncle's that was stuffed with memorabilia from his great-grandmother's time on sets in Hollywood.

When Maddox opened the cooler, it held two beers he'd likely swiped from his older brother's refrigerator. He opened them both and handed me one.

Was it a problem to be drinking when my mama was an alcoholic? Probably. Did I care at the moment? No. I needed to relax. I needed to escape her violent words. I needed to pretend I didn't have to go back there when the night was done.

Maddox lay down, reaching for me and tugging me up against him.

My body tingled at every single touch, the heat of him pushing away the cold and heartache. My body yearned to feel more than just these sweet touches. I wanted to feel his lips on mine. I wanted his hands sliding over my skin, making me feel alive.

But he was my best friend, and I didn't dare risk his friendship for a chance at something more. I didn't know what I'd do if I lost the one beautiful light in my world. We'd been Maddox and McKenna, M&M, to everyone who knew us since we'd been in the third grade. There hadn't been a day since then that I hadn't talked to him, even when he'd had to sneak over and throw rocks at my window to do it. He was the one stable, good, perfect thing in my life.

"Do you want to talk about it?" he asked.

The feel of Mama's hand shoving my face into the sink, and the splintering pain rushing through my jaw hit me all over again as if it had just happened, and I closed my eyes against it. I'd made the mistake of asking her for grocery money. That was all, but it had been enough to remind her I was there. That she wasn't the free-spirited, no-responsibilities thirty-two-year-old she wanted to be.

I shook my head, opening my eyes to stare up at the sky as the colors faded from it. The hazy pink and orange slowly blended into gray and then finally black as we drank our beers and comforted each other by just being together.

A trail of light shot across the sky—a shooting star. Of course, it wasn't really a falling star, but rather bits of dust and rock colliding with the Earth's atmosphere and burning up. Still, I liked thinking of them the way I had when I was a child and hadn't known better. I liked pretending I could wish on them and that those wishes might just come true. I sent my two secret desires out into the universe and hoped with all my heart that one of them would become a reality.

When I looked over at Maddox, he'd moved so his body hovered slightly over mine, and his eyes were scouring my face.

"What did you wish for?" he asked in a deep gravely tone that had become his in the last few years. The tone that made my stomach quiver with want and need.

"You know I can't tell you. It won't come true, then."

"I wished…" he started and then shook his head. "Why don't I just show you."

And before I could even think about it, he laid his lips on mine. A soft kiss that wasn't weak as much as it was hesitant, as if he thought I might shove him away. Instead, I wrapped my arms around his neck and tugged so his body collided with mine like the meteor had with the earth. Light and fire and burning particles. Every warning skipped from my head as his tongue slid along my mouth, and I opened it, letting him in, forgetting everything but the all-consuming need to be closer to Maddox than we'd ever been before. He groaned, and my body seemed to think it was a call, because it arched into him automatically. Too many days of wanting this had the simple kiss turning ragged and raw in mere seconds.

Lost in the moment, the bottle I still held tilted and sent a stream of beer over his neck and back, causing us to jerk apart.

"Oops," I said, smiling up at him as he chuckled. He pulled the bottle from my hand, setting it with his on top of the cooler, and then turned back to me.

"Tell me you wished for it, too," he said.

There was a beg in his voice that I responded to by pulling him back to me, placing my mouth on his and mumbling, "I've been wishing for years."

His eyes crinkled at the corners as an enormous smile took over his face, transforming him from a bright star to a supernova. We lost ourselves to kisses and hands and skin.

Beautiful touches that turned breaths into pants that trailed up to the sky and the stars. We spent hours exploring the last parts of each other that we hadn't yet learned. Bodies we'd only partly seen in swimsuits at the lake. Bodies that had filled out in muscles and curves.

Hours later, we were still touching. Eventually, the batteries on the boombox died, the moon crossed above us, the crickets went to sleep, and an owl hooted somewhere in the dark.

He pulled his lips from mine with a sigh but didn't let me go. His arm was wrapped firmly about my waist, holding me against him. I placed my head on his chest.

"It's late. We should probably head back," he said reluctantly, and for the first time in hours, my stomach clenched, the burning acid returning.

"One more minute," I begged. I didn't want to let him go. I didn't want to lose the love I felt flowing between us to walk into a cold house filled with hatred.

"Okay, one more minute, but then you're coming home with me," he grunted.

Tears hit my eyes. It wasn't possible, and he knew it. I shook my head.

"I'm not taking you back there, McK. Not ever."

For the next few minutes, I let myself believe that both my wishes had come true. I let joy overtake the fear and worry. I let us both stay in the bubble world we'd created where nothing but stars and kisses existed.

Lost in my memories, I didn't hear the hospital-room door open or the curtain being yanked aside until it was too late.

"What in the hell do you think you're doing?" a deep, angry voice boomed.

All I could do was wish, as I had a decade ago, that Layton and I had one more minute. One more wish to keep our worlds from tumbling down around us.

Chapter Four

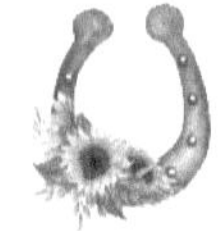

Maddox

MEMORY I DON'T MESS WITH

Performed by Lee Brice

Mila fell asleep when I was only halfway through the book. It was too late for her to have been up anyway, but as tomorrow was Saturday, it would be fine. We'd sleep in, make pancakes, and go find her a damn hula hoop.

I eased out of her bed, pulled the blankets up, tucked them tight around her little body, and then just stared. She was a small miracle. Not only because she'd survived the first year of her life in horrifying conditions, but because she'd changed my life. Made me a better person. Given me an even bigger purpose.

I placed a kiss on her forehead and left the room with her rainbow of nightlights casting a million shimmers along the walls.

I made my way to the kitchen and blessed Rianne silently one more time when I found a plate of meatloaf and mashed potatoes in the microwave. I heated it up and then sat down on the sofa with my plate and a beer I rarely drank to watch a hockey game that couldn't keep my attention.

My phone buzzed with a message from Ryder in a group text that included our two sisters.

DIPSHIT: You should have come back. Mary Beth almost stripped on the dance floor, and Chuck had to toss her over his shoulder to get her to leave.

I chuckled, imagining the scene. Mary Beth and Chuck owned the feed store everyone in the county used to place their orders. She was renowned for her antics when she let loose, and Chuck was renowned for reeling her in and keeping her safe.

ME: Thank God I missed it. I don't want to see someone as old as Mama getting naked.

Sadie came back the fastest. Our little sister was in her last year at the University of Tennessee, Knoxville getting a pre-law degree I didn't think she'd ever use. Instead, I was ninety-nine percent sure she'd end up making waves on the professional dart circuit.

SASSY PANTS: There's our little monk.

Gemma came to my rescue.

GEM MINE: I kind of have to agree with Mads here. I don't want to see Mama, Daddy, or anyone their age naked.

SASSY PANTS: You just don't want to see anyone naked. You're as bad as Mads. Thank God Ryder and I are around to balance you out by rejoicing in the human flesh.

DIPSHIT: Damn it, Sadie. Do not make me drive to UTK and beat the hell out of someone. You are not allowed to have sex, think about having sex, or even look at the other sex.

SASSY PANTS: Too late, big brother.

I groaned.

> *ME: Can we stop talking about sex and family at all? I just ate Rianne's magnificent meatloaf, and I don't want to toss it back up.*

> *SASSY PANTS: Have you even had sex, Maddox? Besides with your hand?*

> *GEM MINE: ***puke GIF*** Please STOP TALKING. I'm changing the subject. How are you doing today, Mads?*

I glanced over to the side table Mama and my sisters had loaded with picture frames. They contained years of childhood memories as well as ones of Mila and me since we'd become a family. My eyes settled on the photo of sixteen-year-old me with the Bronco when I'd first bought it in worse shape than it was now. Tucked against my side, grinning like she'd been the one to buy the vehicle, was McKenna Lloyd. Her skin was golden from the days we'd spent at the lake. Her honey-blonde hair glowed with natural highlights the sun had been responsible for, and her wheat-colored eyes were sparkling. The tip of her slim nose turned up just the tiniest bit, and her full lips were spread wide.

Pain, ragged and sharp, drew down the middle of me, taking my breath for a second.

It seemed impossible that, even a decade later, it could still hurt so much—barely having her and then losing her.

I shook my head. I'd had her for ten years. We'd pretty much become inseparable from the time I'd found her hiding from her mama's hateful words. We'd been side by side, playing at school or escaping her mama to run wild in town, and, whenever my family could convince her mama to let her come, exploring the ranch.

All my best memories had McKenna tangled and twined in them, like vines growing through a magnolia tree.

Memories I didn't mess with. Memories I kept locked up deep inside me and took out to relive and cherish whenever I was feeling strong enough. That wasn't today—her birthday and also the day I'd lost her for good.

The day she'd told me she was engaged and to stop calling.

I hadn't even known she'd been dating anyone.

We'd communicated solely by texts and video chats since my one and only ill-advised trip to California. Even though she'd told me not to come back, not to wait, I'd stupidly gone on doing just that.

But I shouldn't have waited, because I'd known she'd never come back to Willow Creek, just like she'd known I'd never leave. Our friendship that had flared, briefly, into something more had been forced back into what it had started as—two people who simply wanted the best for each other.

> *DIPSHIT: Do we need to stage an intervention,*
> *Sheriff Hatley?*

The text loosened the hold the memories had on me. They might hurt, but I'd never regret my past, because if I hadn't had McKenna, I never would have had Mila, and she was the best thing in my life.

> *ME: No, asshole. I'm just exhausted. Arrested*
> *a bunch of the West Gears and wrestled with*
> *Willy. I'm going to bed.*

> *DIPSHIT: Wah-wah-wah. I worked all day,*
> *gutting the cabins. Do you see me whining?*

> *ME: Did you have a gun pulled on you and*
> *fight off a knife attack? Come talk to me when*
> *it was your life on the line, and I'll show you a*
> *whine.*

GEM MINE: Maddox! You did not almost get shot and stabbed, did you? Mama's going to shit a brick.

ME: Don't tell her, Gems. You know she'll just worry. I shouldn't have said anything to any of you, but Dipshit pissed me off, as usual.

SASSY PANTS: This is double the proof you need to get laid, Maddox. Life is too short. You could be gone tomorrow. You want to hand your V card over at some point.

I choked on the beer as I read it.

ME: Jesus, Sadie. I'm not a fucking virgin.

SASSY PANTS: Years ago, one time, with one person, doesn't exactly mean you've lost it, monk.

ME: I'm not talking about my sex life with any of you. I'll just say that I'm completely happy and satisfied, sexually and otherwise.

GEM MINE: This conversation is making me uncomfortable. BTW, I'm leaving Ryder at the bar with a redhead who can't take her eyes off him. I don't know her. I think she's new in town.

My protective instinct jerked back to life.

ME: What's her name?

DIPSHIT: Even if I knew, I wouldn't tell you. I don't need you running my sexual partners through the system.

> *ME: But you're okay with me running Gemma's and Sadie's?*
>
> *DIPSHIT: Absolutely.*
>
> *SASSY PANTS: You're both male chauvinist pigs. Gems, we need a nefarious and irreversible plan to get even with them.*

When there was no response from Gemma in five minutes, I assumed she'd left the bar and was driving herself back to our parents' house where she still lived after finishing her degree online. Her life goals were all tied up around a screenplay she never let anyone read while passing the days working at the jewelry store in town.

I put my home phone on vibrate, threw the empty beer bottle away, cleaned the kitchen, and headed to bed. I placed my work phone on the nightstand, with the volume up to make sure it woke me if the dispatcher called, and stripped down to my briefs before climbing into the king-size bed— a bed I'd never had a woman in, regardless of the texts with my siblings.

I'd had sex beyond McKenna, beyond the fumbling but emotional moments we'd shared before she'd left for good or the heat-seared weekend we'd shared in her dorm room. But since Mila had come into my life, I hadn't brought anyone into the house. Instead, I'd gone to their place. In truth, I'd kept the dates and women down to a minimum, not only because of my daughter but because of my career. Running for sheriff so young meant I'd needed a squeaky-clean reputation.

What I barely admitted to myself—and would never admit to my nosey siblings—was that the time I'd spent with other women had been forgettable. Interchangeable events that had given pleasure and release but had never carved a spot on my soul. Probably because I'd lost the piece of my heart that could love a woman. It had been cut out the day McKenna had told me to stop calling, fading away just like the five-percent chance I'd ridiculously held on to of her coming back to me.

I closed my eyes, pushed beyond the tortured phone call she'd placed on her birthday five years ago, and gave in to the sweet memories that laid beyond it.

The moonlight on the water shifted, breaking apart and then reassembling itself as the wind kicked up and sent waves across the lake. The sound of the trees rustled outside the Bronco. Spring had finally kicked in, sending away the long days of snow we'd had that year and filling the air with the scent of new growth.

McKenna lay below me in a white summer dress with gold strands woven through it.

The taste of her skin was on my tongue. Like RC Cola and MoonPies.

My fingers found their way over her curves and valleys.

The feel of her peaked nipples on the pad of my finger.

My aching hard-on pressed into her cotton underwear.

Her breathy gasps.

Her palm as it skimmed my tip.

The torturous pleasure of slowly sliding into her tight wetness.

I was snatched out of the memory when my work phone clanged softly, breaking the silence of my room. My dick was hard, pushing against the fabric of my boxers just like in my memories. I fought to get it under control before I answered.

"Hatley."

"Sorry to wake you, Sheriff, but Deputy Adams picked up Sybil Lloyd again, and you know she won't calm down until you see her."

I sighed. The last thing I needed tonight was more memories. More pained moments.

Every time Sybil blew back through town, my chest was a bundle of knots until she breezed out again.

"Let me get someone here for Mila, and then I'll be over."

I hung up, dragging a hand down my face. Rianne had just left mere hours ago, and I knew she'd come right back if I called, but I didn't want her to have to. These were the times when being a single dad with a job like mine were the hardest.

I hated not being there when Mila bounced out of her room in the morning.

So many smiles I'd missed.

But I'd go because Sybil held a rock over my head that would crash down and wreck my world if I didn't. I might have lost McKenna because of Sybil, but I sure as hell was never going to lose my daughter because of her.

Chapter Five

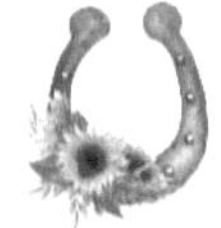

McKenna

HUMBLE QUEST

Performed by Maren Morris

"You're fired!" Dr. Roy Gregory snarled, gray eyes flaming and spittle jumping from his mouth as he spoke. He was a dark-haired, smooth-skinned man with spray-tanned skin and muscles he earned in a high-dollar gym. "Pack your things and get the hell out before I have security throw you out."

I stood up from the stool, lifted my chin, and crossed my arms. Normally, the sterile smell of the hospital soothed me, but it could do nothing to calm the waves of panic rushing through me now. "I was well within my rights."

There was a rustling of fabric at the door, and Sally appeared behind him in scrubs with a pissed-off look on her face. Behind her was the hospital's chief medical officer, Dr. Selena Gomez. Dr. Gomez stood with her hands across her chest and concern flitting through her brown eyes. I'd had limited interactions with the short, serious woman, but she'd always seemed direct, professional, and fair. I wasn't sure I could count on that today with Dr. Gregory throwing his venom in my direction.

"Any minor, but especially *my* minor son, will not receive care in this hospital without parental consent." He stormed past me, eyes flashing at Layton who seemed to shrink into the bed further. "Get up."

Layton's eyes darted toward me before attempting to swing his feet over the edge of the bed. A groan escaped his lips, and I stepped closer to him.

"You don't have to go," I told the teen, but I wasn't sure he'd even heard me as alarm spread over his face.

Dr. Gomez moved past Sally and into the room farther, a small furrow appearing between her brows. "Are you hurt, Layton?" she asked.

"If he's going to take risks like he does, he's going to get injured. A lesson he learned. The pain will be a good reminder," Dr. Gregory barked.

Dr. Gomez moved into my space, and I backed away so she could assess the teen. "Did your dad already check you out?" she asked.

Layton's face paled, but he nodded.

"And did you ask Dr. Lloyd for care?"

"It doesn't matter if he did or not. As a minor, she shouldn't have agreed," Dr. Gregory said tersely, the fury barely contained.

"I was sort of passing out. Dr. Lloyd just helped me lie down," he said so quietly it could hardly be heard.

"You have a problem with her helping your son if he passed out?" Dr. Gomez sent the question toward Dr. Gregory with narrowed eyes.

"I have a problem with her not sending for me before she ordered X-rays and issued prescriptions, yes. And the board will agree with me."

"I'm filing a report," I finally found my voice. I sent a reassuring gaze toward Layton because I hadn't been able to get to this point in our conversation when we'd been interrupted. "I'm calling Child Protective Services."

Technically, as a mandated reporter, I didn't have any obligation to tell the parent. It was actually better if I remained anonymous, but no way was that happening now, and I didn't want this asshole to think he'd gotten away with what he'd done once again.

Dr. Gregory's face turned purple, and he stepped toward me but couldn't reach me with Dr. Gomez between us. "You little piece of shit. How dare you!"

"How dare I? How dare you?!" I tossed back, moving forward so that poor Dr. Gomez was sandwiched between two angry individuals.

"If you both don't step off, I'll call security," she growled.

I took a shaky breath before easing backward. Dr. Gomez met my gaze. "You sure you want to do this?"

"Absolutely," I said.

Dr. Gregory went deadly still, carefully tucking his anger and hate behind an impassive wall until it was only his eyes that were still shooting daggers at me and Layton.

"You do that, and your career is over. Your name will be on every banned list from the East Coast to the West," he said. The deadly calm was way more terrifying than his anger.

"Do no harm. I guess the oath you swore doesn't apply to your family," I tossed back, shivering as my memories assaulted me. The helplessness. The fear.

His hands clenched, and I knew with a certainty built from years of ducking my mama's hands that he wanted to hit me. He wanted to take his fury out on my flesh just like he'd taken it out on his son's.

He looked down at Dr. Gomez with barely veiled contempt. "Selena, this is retaliation. McKenna got her hand slapped for misreading an intake and putting a patient and their family through unnecessary tests. The mark will be on her record, so she's striking back."

I paled. That mistake hadn't been mine. It had been his. We'd argued about it just like we'd argued about a suspected abuse report I'd filed. He hadn't liked my disagreeing with him even less than he'd liked my rejection of his advances.

"Everybody out! Everybody except Layton," Dr. Gomez said as if she was suddenly tired of all the accusations. "Dr. Lloyd, go home. I'll contact you later. Roy, call your wife to come and pick up Layton, and Sally, don't you have a job to do?"

Nobody moved.

"Now!" she commanded.

Dr. Gregory's jaw ticked, and his teeth ground together.

"I'll leave when he does," I said quietly.

"You little bi—"

Sally pulled on my arm. "She's leaving. I'll clock out, Dr. Gomez. It's slow in the ER at the moment, and I was only an hour from the end of my shift anyhow."

I tried to pull away, but Sally's grasp was fierce, and I would've hurt one or both of us if I fought it. I turned my head to look back at Layton, and his face was crumpled in a resigned look I recognized. It was the realization that you were walking back into the viper's den where no one was going to save you.

My determination grew. Roy Gregory was not going to get away with this—not any longer than he already had.

Once we were out the door, Sally didn't let go. Instead, she hauled me down the hallway toward the doctors' lounge. My heart was filled with pain for Layton. For me. The farther we got from the hospital room, the looser her grip got until I could finally drag my arm away. My pace increased until I was almost jogging, determined to get my stuff and place the call I knew needed to be made.

Sally barely kept up, her bright-pink hair spinning about her face. "McK, what the hell just happened?"

"I have to call CPS, now, Sal. I don't have time to give you the lowdown."

I grabbed my backpack, stuffed my stethoscope and jacket inside it, and was literally running down the hall to the exit as my finger found the number I'd saved in my phone. The wait time was ten minutes when it finally connected, and I groaned.

Outside, the heat hit me. It was November, but the Northern California sunshine didn't seem to know it. If I'd been in Tennessee, the leaves would have changed color by now, and it would be brisk if not downright cold. Some days, I missed the weather almost as much as I missed the man I'd left behind when he'd been nothing more than a boy.

My heart twisted and turned not only from the flicker of Maddox that had gone through my brain but at the knowledge I was likely going to lose everything I'd worked for. I'd already given up everything once to start this future, and now, I was going to lose it, too. The pain in my gut at the thought jerked me to a stop. I leaned over, trying to catch my breath, trying to inhale, and it brought a wave of nausea with it.

Sally's hand was on my back, rubbing soothingly.

I closed my eyes, and Layton's fearful eyes filled my vision.

If I could only save one, I would. I had to.

I stood up, and Sally and I walked the rest of the way to our apartment while I waited for the line to be picked up by an actual human being.

When we walked in the door, my feet stalled, remembering the balloons and presents Sally had filled our apartment with this morning. My heart grew heavy. Just another crappy thing to have happened on my birthday. Maybe Mama was right. Maybe this day really was jinxed. Maybe I really was nothing but a bad omen.

♫ ♫ ♫

Four hours later, I'd finished the paperwork, sent it off to Child Protective Services, and tried to pull together the personal documentation and reviews I had from my two and a half years of residency at Hearld Community Hospital. I wasn't perfect, but I was a damn good doctor. Emergency medicine was my whole world, and I had a knack for it. That was what every report said—even asshole Gregory's.

After I'd hung up with CPS, I'd spilled my guts to Sally, even though I wasn't supposed to talk about the situation. But I had to tell someone. I had to feel like I wasn't losing my damn mind. That my past wasn't creeping in and making me see demons that weren't there. I needed someone who believed in me.

My mind filled with an image of a wide grin and a black cowboy hat tipped down low over eyes so bright a blue you thought you'd drown in them. He'd believed in me. I could almost hear his deep voice, saying, "One hundred percent of the time, McK. I'll always have your back."

Belatedly, Kerry's face came to my mind, and I wondered if he would have sided with me or Dr. Gregory. His black hair and brown eyes were completely different than the image of the man in the cowboy hat. Kerry was all dress shirts and ties and Dockers. Even in medical school, he'd been the consummate professional. We'd been engaged for three years… We'd slept together, and shared an apartment, and planned a life together, and yet his hadn't ever been the face that had come to mind when my life was in turmoil.

That said something. Too much.

Kerry had simply been one of the many ways I'd tried to escape the memories of an ugly childhood.

But today, my past, present, and future had collided together.

The knot in my chest was so big and painful I could barely breathe around it. As I assembled my files on the coffee table, Sally watched with worried eyes.

"The first time I met you, you were crying," she said quietly.

I shot her a glance. "Those were tears of relief and joy. Hearld had just accepted me for their residency program."

"You were crying because that jerkwad, Kerry, had left you for a residency in Boston," Sally countered.

How bad was it that the wound of his leaving didn't come close to the scars of me choosing to leave Maddox? From not hearing once from Maddox after I'd caved to Kerry's ultimatum and told him to stop calling. It should have been a sign. I should have known that it wouldn't work when Kerry hadn't trusted me…had placed demands he knew would cause me heartache.

But I'd wanted so badly the life I'd envisioned with him—two well-respected doctors, hands held at the charity drives, serving a community. I'd had delusional images of his pediatric-surgeon father and psychologist mother looking over at us with pride when, in truth, they'd never been anything but tolerably polite to the girl who'd never been wanted.

Except, that wasn't completely true. Maddox had always wanted me.

His family had also.

Pain twisted and groaned inside me, but I just buried it.

"Technically, he didn't leave me. He wanted me to go with him," I told her.

"And not start your residency for another year!"

"It wasn't his fault I hadn't applied in Boston. I knew he had. I just assumed he'd take the Davis position over the Boston one if he was accepted to both."

"And not join his family's legacy in Boston?" she scoffed.

"I thought we were starting our own legacy," I said quietly, and there was the pain, the warped feeling of rejection. "Is there a reason you're reminding me of this now?"

"I'm more worried about you today than I was then. You're not crying or ranting and raving, but this… It's worse, McK."

I swallowed hard, shoving my toes into the carpet and tugging on my ponytail. "I know."

But then Layton's shamed, pale face shifting with agony reminded me that I'd done the right thing. I couldn't have made a different choice.

My phone rang, a local number I didn't recognize, but I picked up anyway.

"Hello."

"Dr. Lloyd, this is Dr. Gomez."

"Hey."

Silence for a moment before she continued, "I'm afraid I have more bad news than good."

"I kind of figured," I told her. I didn't want her to feel guilty for simply telling me the consequences of my actions. I'd brought this on myself.

"We've suspended you, pending further investigation. The board will review the findings and make a ruling, but it's going to take some time."

I swallowed hard, biting my cheek and pushing my nails into my palms.

"Is Layton safe?" I asked.

She hesitated. "We had to release him into his mother's custody."

"Which means he'll be home with his dad."

"Did you call CPS?" Dr. Gomez asked.

"Yes."

"He's accusing you of false reporting. Says it's retaliation for his bad review."

"He didn't give me a bad review. We did butt heads a couple of times, but the case he mentioned today was his case," I told her.

"I have multiple infractions listed in your record by him."

My brain stalled for a moment. There was no way. My heart started to pound.

"That's not possible. I…" I didn't know what else to say.

"He and Shirley, from IT…they're…friendly," Dr. Gomez said softly.

Shit. Shit. Shit. I was screwed beyond anything I'd even considered. Even if I'd been let go by Hearld, I could have found somewhere else to finish my residency. It would have been hard, almost impossible, but I could have. But if he filed a report with the medical board and the police, I could lose my license. I could be fined. In the worst scenario, I could be facing jail time.

I closed my eyes, willing back the tears, grinding my teeth and trying not to choke on the lump in my throat. "I did the right thing, Dr. Gomez," I croaked out. "If that boy had come in off the street, I would have done the exact same thing. I stand by my call."

"There's nothing else I can do for you at the moment. I did convince them to suspend you with pay, if that helps at all. I can tell you that Layton was adamant he hurt himself climbing."

God, my whole life was gone, washed away in mere hours.

"It was the right call. I'd do it a thousand times over," I told her in a fierce whisper.

"Okay. Well. It's going to get rocky, but I'll do my best to make sure you have a hospital advocate and attorney at your disposal as we would in any other case of false reporting. Is this the best number for them to reach you?" she asked.

"Yes. And…thank you."

She paused before saying, "You repeated the Hippocratic Oath today, Dr. Lloyd. Do no harm. It's a shame the newer versions of the oath don't have it in there quite the same way. But if that was your intention, then I can only hope your good deed will be rewarded."

Then, she hung up, and I sat with tears pooling, body rigid, wondering if I'd ever get any of my dreams back, or if they were all gone in the blink of an eye. Wondering if the mountain of debt I had would ever be paid off. Wondering if I'd have to get a minimum-wage job because I had no other career path open to me.

My breath became uneven. My eyes grew spotty, and I forced myself to lie back down on the couch before I passed out. Sally sat next to me on the floor, head pressed into my thigh.

"I'm so sorry, McK."

There was nothing else to say. Not a damn thing.

♫ ♫ ♫

Two days later, an article appeared in the local paper, spewing Dr. Gregory's side of the story along with a host of fake data on the number of false CPS reports made each year. Instead of going underground with shame at abusing his son, Roy Gregory was flaunting his standing in the community and telling everyone he was determined to be the mouthpiece for parents who couldn't speak for themselves.

The next day, our apartment door was tagged with hateful words that couldn't simply be washed away. Our landlord had needed to paint it a stark black to make it disappear. My social media accounts were flooded with both positive and negative comments. I disabled them all because even the positive ones still wanted me to share my side of the story. I wouldn't. I couldn't. If I talked about the CPS report, I could face charges. Even telling Sally had been a risk.

For nearly a week, Sally went to work, facing the rumors on her own because everyone knew we were friends. Every day, I fought my old fight-or-flight instincts that were slamming back into existence as strong as if Mama was screaming a slew of nasty names at me. Except, now I had nowhere to hide. There'd only been one place…one person…I'd ever run to, and I couldn't go there.

I'd burned that bridge.

I'd burned it and thrown myself into the gorge off the other side.

For a man and a future that had all been a mirage wavering in the heat of the sun.

On Wednesday, after a particularly nasty article I was tormenting myself by reading, my brain finally remembered the key I had tucked in a dresser drawer.

Growing up, my dad had been nothing more than a thirty-second advertisement in my life, and I'd thought I'd never see him again after I'd moved out of the duplex. But then Trap had shown up at the ranch my last day in Willow Creek and given me the key as an unspoken apology for a life he couldn't change.

I'd forgotten about it for a good reason—because going back wasn't a possibility.

I reminded myself that nothing had changed in that regard.

No, I'd have to stick it out here.

But thoughts of the key returned the next day.

I was watching *Buffy the Vampire Slayer* and wishing I could turn Dr. Gregory into a vampire who I could make go poof with a stake when Sally came home. She looked more exhausted and worn out than I felt, but she'd still stopped for food. The greasy bags were a splurge we rarely allowed ourselves with the strict budgets we kept while trying to pay off our college debt.

I scrambled for my backpack, took out the only cash I had left without leaving the apartment to get more, and handed it to her.

"Keep it," she said.

"Sal," I protested.

"Don't argue with me. I've had a shit day," she said, face serious, and so I didn't.

We ate in a depressed silence, watching Buffy and Spike flirt on screen.

My phone rang, and I silenced it when I saw it was just another unknown number. I'd been hounded with requests for interviews. This time, a text popped up a moment later from the same number.

> *1-530-555-8205: They thought they could make me leave my house. MY HOUSE. The one I fucking paid for with MY MONEY. If you don't fix this, if you don't admit your mistakes, I'll come for you. Every hour I spend dealing with this will be marked on your skin, and by the time I'm done with you, they won't even find a molecule of your DNA.*

Chills went up my spine, fear cutting through me even more than the time I'd accidentally shattered a glass in the kitchen when I was eleven. Every time I'd picked up a shard, Mama had pushed it into my hand. My fingers had been littered with cuts and blood by the time she was done making her point.

This…this was almost worse.

There was a chance he was all talk, bluster from a man who prided himself on power and control, lashing out because he'd lost some. But what if it wasn't? What if the evil hiding behind the calm face of a doctor the community trusted meant he wasn't afraid to come after me? I'd known there was a good chance my career was over, but I hadn't felt like my life had been threatened. God, would he hurt Sally, too?

I swallowed hard, putting down my burger as the little appetite I'd had completely dried up.

"What is it?" Sally asked, reading my expression and glancing down at the phone.

I deleted the text and shook my head. "Just another interview request."

For a moment, she looked like she'd challenge me but then just put down her burger also looking suddenly nervous.

"I'm taking a few vacation days," she announced. "I'm going home for a long-overdue visit with Dad. Wanna come?"

She was having to leave because of me. Because she was being harassed. Guilt wrapped around my rib cage, squeezing. "Sal…I'm so sorry."

"Don't you dare apologize for standing up for that boy. I just wish he was big enough to stand up for you, too." Her tone was fierce, protective of me in a way only a handful of people had been in my lifetime.

"He's fifteen, Sal. Give him a break. He's scared—no, terrified of both staying and being pulled away." The text I got made a shiver crawl over me again. If Dr. Gregory had reacted this way to me, I couldn't imagine what Layton had been through once he'd gotten home. "I can't blame him." I swallowed hard, trying not to show my fear. Sally knew some of my history but not everything. Only one person had ever known it all.

"Come with me?" she repeated, skipping over my defense of Layton.

Sally had a ginormous extended family, but it had been just her and her dad living in the California coastal town of Avalyn Beach growing up. Their home was a tiny cottage where he created his art, giving up the luxury of space in order to have the beach right outside their door. When Sally had been little, he'd slept on a pullout couch in the cramped living room so she could have the only bedroom in the house. Sally didn't let him do that these days when she visited, but if I was there as well, he'd insist the two of us stay in his room while the seventy-year-old man took the couch. I didn't want that. And I couldn't afford a hotel right now. Neither could Sally.

Plus, if I was with her and Dr. Gregory really did come after me, there was a chance she'd get hurt as well. No. I couldn't go with Sally.

But…I did have the key. I had a place… My temples pounded, and my lungs seized just thinking about using it. I'd sworn I never would because going back would be too painful. Too many bad memories…and good. It was the good ones that I'd once thought would derail me from my goals. I'd doubted my ability to leave again if I found my feet back outside his door, so I hadn't gone. Not once.

I looked at Sally's tired face, and guilt squeezed tight again.

I could use the key. Should use it. Trap had told me I was welcome any time. That it was a place I could land if I ever needed somewhere safe. He'd said he didn't use the house, even when he was in Willow Creek, because he stayed at the motorcycle club's headquarters. In the ten years since I'd left Willow Creek, I'd only heard from Trap three times, and each time, he'd reiterated that the place was there if I needed it.

I frowned, trying to recall how long it had been since he'd last texted. It had to have been four years or more. It was definitely before Kerry had left for Boston, demanding his family's heirloom engagement ring back.

My chest tightened until I thought I couldn't breathe. It had nothing to do with Kerry and everything to do with the fleeting idea of going back to Tennessee, of seeing Maddox with a wife and kids—who blended into the Hatley gang perfectly—in the only place he'd ever wanted to call home. I'd wanted to fly, and he'd wanted to take root. He'd wanted Willow Creek, and I'd wanted anywhere else.

And now, it had been years since I'd talked to him.

Years I could only blame on myself.

Me and that damn fictional story I'd created in my head with Kerry, a man who'd never once made me feel the way I'd felt with a mere brush of Maddox's hand, but whom I'd convinced myself I wanted anyway.

I could have called Maddox after Kerry and I had gone our separate ways, but what would I have said? It's okay to talk to me now that my jealous fiancé isn't in the picture? Worse…Maddox would have…because that was Maddox for you. Even if he'd had a wife and kids, he would have still allowed me back in because we'd been more than boyfriend and girlfriend. We'd been best friends. He'd been my confidant. My hero.

And I'd hurt him.

Not just by leaving Willow Creek. I'd hurt him more when he'd come to see me in the spring of our freshman year. We'd spent an entire weekend lost in each other's skin, and it had been a jagged relief. A beautiful and exquisite homecoming. I'd almost begged him to stay, even though I knew he couldn't, not with the ranch in the state it was in. But worse…scarier…I'd almost thrown in everything here and gotten on the plane with him. So, in self-defense, I'd asked him not to come back. I told him we couldn't be anything more than friends.

And I'd believed it at the time. I'd believed it when I'd told him I didn't want him waiting eleven years for me to become a doctor and that I was never going back to Willow Creek. I'd told him to find someone who would love him, his family, and the town as much as he did, but that it wouldn't be me.

After he'd left, everything had been different between us, a barrier up because he'd been hurt and because I was desperate to hold on to my goals, to become a person who was worth something…anything. Our calls and texts after that had been stilted, as if for the first time in our lives, we couldn't bare our souls to each other.

But at least we'd had those awkward conversations until I'd stuck the final stab in our wounded relationship. I'd taken away any contact because Kerry had been jealous of me maintaining a friendship with an ex.

Could anyone ever forgive someone who'd hurt them so many times?

I wasn't the person to ask. I couldn't ever forgive Mama.

"Hey? Where you at?" Sally said, flicking her finger into my shoulder, and I realized the credits had long ago ended for the episode of *Buffy* without me even reacting to it. Her question about going with her had spiraled into questions about every decision I'd ever made.

"I think…" I took a deep breath. "I think I'm going to go back to Tennessee."

Her eyes grew wide. "No…really?"

I nodded. Maybe it was just my flight instinct finally winning out over hiding, but it would put me farther away from Dr. Gregory and keep Sally out of harm's way. Maybe it would be a chance for me to do what my therapist had been wanting me to do for ages. She wanted me to face my past when I much preferred shoving those monsters right back under the bed and trying to forget about them.

"Maybe I'll be able to lay some of my demons to rest," I said softly.

"Or maybe you'll finally find your way back to your guardian angel."

I snorted. "Not likely."

The most I could expect was that Maddox would allow me to apologize, to selfishly ease some of my guilt for cutting not only him but the entire Hatley gang out of my life. It had been the only way I'd survived—by pretending they didn't exist at all, by burying my good memories along with the bad.

The thought of seeing Maddox again—of seeing all the Hatleys—sent a flurry of something I thought might be hope wafting through my veins. Hope I damn sure couldn't afford. Just like the hope I'd had as a little girl that Mama would change, Trap would somehow see the truth, or we'd become a "real" family. Hope had only ever done one thing, and that was to splinter me in two every time reality ripped it away.

Chapter Six

Maddox

THE BEST PART OF ME

Performed by Lee Brice

My stomach cringed as I headed down the hall of the women's rehab clinic in the next county over. I didn't want to be here, and I damn sure didn't want to talk to Sybil, but I always felt like I had a knife at my throat when it came to her. While my sensible brain knew there was no way I could lose Mila to her, my panicked heart always made me jump when she snapped her fingers so I didn't rock the boat. It was easier this way.

When I'd gone to pick her up after the dispatcher had called me a week ago, she'd been handcuffed to an ER bed, screaming profanity at anyone and everyone around her. Her ugly expression and wild eyes, high from drugs and alcohol, were the norm. What hadn't been normal was her clean body, expensive haircut, and designer clothes. Instead of being dirty and grimy, she'd been layered with enough real jewelry to buy a car, reeking of money she'd never had before. It had raised the hair on the back of my neck, and I was ninety-five percent sure her newfound wealth didn't bode well.

When she'd faced the judge on Monday for her drunk and disorderly charge, he'd let her slide with a stint in mandated rehab when he could have ordered prison time for violating her parole from her last encounter with the courts. Since then, I hadn't heard a word from her until today. Even if I'd been inclined to ignore her call, my police-officer instincts were nagging at me to figure out where her sudden inflow of cash had come from.

I knocked on the door of her room and opened it when she called, "Come in."

When I entered, she was eerily calm. With her serene expression, she looked so much like McKenna it hurt. If I squeezed my eyes and washed away Sybil's age and weathered skin, I could see McKenna in every line. The slim nose with the slight curve upward at the end, the large wheat-colored eyes that flashed green, and the straight black brows that were a contrast to the blonde hair. They even had the same slim frame with full, round curves. They were so much alike that when McKenna had been a teen, people used to mistake them for sisters. I supposed having had McK when Sybil was only fifteen herself had a way of doing that.

Mila shared their hair, eyes, and brows, but that was it. The rest of her had come from a father who'd never been identified—a father who would be able to reclaim his parental rights he hadn't knowingly given up if he chose to. That was the real threat that hovered over me like a noose. The real reason I was there.

"Maddox Hatley, looking stern and saintly as always," Sybil said, fidgeting with the intake bracelet on her wrist and tugging at a silk shirt she shouldn't have been able to afford.

I could read it in her already—the desire to leave, to get a hit, to have a drink.

Some days, deep in the dark, secret spots of my heart, I wished she'd pass out and never wake back up. I hated that she could make me feel that way, make me feel less human. Less of a cop. Make me feel like I was a bit of the monster I'd always considered her to be.

"What do you want, Sybil?" I asked, tossing my cowboy hat from hand to hand.

"Besides out of this hellhole?" She laughed as if she'd said something hilarious, and when I didn't join her, she pouted. "How's Mila?"

"You don't care. That's not why I'm here," I said, refusing to talk about my daughter with her.

She gave me a grin, and I swore it was the evilest thing I'd ever seen. "Just checking in and making sure that bitch isn't back in town."

"By bitch, you mean your eldest child? The one you abused until she had to be taken away?"

Her eyes narrowed in on me. Her fingers fidgeted as if she was uncomfortable without the ever-prevalent cigarette she'd had in her hands since the first moment I'd met her. I'd only been eight to her twenty-three, but I'd already been able to see her fiery ending written in the darkness around her.

"Don't take that tone with me," she said, glaring. "I'm just holding you to your word so I don't have to make a call."

"Nothing's changed, Sybil. Nothing at all," I said before thinking, *including your abusive ways.*

"I need outta here," Sybil said when I didn't add on anything else.

"You'll have to take that up with your court-appointed attorney and the judge."

"But you can make the charges go away. It was your dumbass deputy who arrested me. If that shithead at the bar had just done what I'd asked, none of this would have happened. He insulted me when I had good money to spend."

She'd broken a glass and threatened the bartender with the jagged edge if he didn't let her buy another round—a round for the entire house—on her. Ted knew Sybil didn't normally have that kind of money. I didn't blame him for thinking she wouldn't be able to cover the bill. He certainly hadn't known she'd had five thousand dollars on her when we'd arrested her.

My bullshit meter was clanging loudly.

"I can't do that, and you know it," I told her, trying to keep my patience intact while every vein in my body screamed to get the hell out.

"My mind's awful clear now that you've made me wipe away all the alcohol haze. Five years ago…I can see his face now as we created that little fleabag."

I snorted, and her eyes narrowed. "Something funny about me suddenly remembering who my baby daddy is? Mila's *real* father? The one who *hasn't* given up his parental rights?"

"Nothing funny except the fact that you don't even know how old the child you gave birth to is."

"My daughter," she returned with a smug smile.

Every ounce of protective instinct flared to life in my chest, and I took a step toward her. "*My* daughter. She never was and never will be yours. You were never a mother. You were an incubator. A test tube. A place she grew and then had to be cleansed of. The monster…" I trailed off, limbs shaking, heart hammering, as I fought to take back control.

Sybil's eyes narrowed. "Fuck you."

"No, thanks."

I turned on my heel and headed for the door.

"You'll regret your words, *Sheriff* Hatley. You'll regret them just like every single person who's even blinked at me, including that bitch who took my youth and ate it up with her whines and her tears and her goddamn need to breathe."

I kept going, the door shutting her out, muffling her voice.

My pace picked up until I was almost sprinting out to my work truck. I needed to call my attorney. But first, I needed to hold my daughter.

I almost turned on the siren and lights in my department-issued F-150, but instead, I simply raced back toward Willow Creek at a speed that wasn't safe for anyone. I drove wildly, passing people on the wrong side of the road as anxiety bloomed, consuming me. I skidded up alongside the curb at the house, not wanting to block Rianne's vehicle in the drive, and jumped out.

I bounded up the steps and burst into the house like I was after an escaped convict. It felt like I was. Like I could lose my life. Like everything could crumble.

Rianne's and Mila's heads jerked up as the door slammed. They were at the counter, making cookies, a tray of little round balls in front of them. Mila was standing on a step stool, and it made her almost as tall as Rianne. God…she'd grown so much.

It hit me all over again how much she looked like her mother and sister. But the smile on her face was because of me. Because I was there, walking through the door when I wasn't due back for hours.

In two strides, I was in the kitchen, pulling her to me and hugging her so tight she giggled and then groaned, "Daddy! You're squishing me!"

I met Rianne's eyes over the top of my daughter's head. My old teacher's expression was one of shock and worry.

Mila squirmed against me, but I wasn't sure I could let go.

"Daddy! I'm getting cookie dough on your uniform!"

I finally eased up, looking down into her face and over at her hands holding a smooshed ball. Half of it was on my shirt and badge, and I didn't even give a shit. Holding her this way, I knew she was real. She was mine, and I'd be damned if anyone would ever take her away.

"It'll wash," I said, voice deep and gravelly with emotions I couldn't ever explain to a five-year-old.

I put her back down on the stool, and she patted me on the arm. "Are you going to stay and make snickadoodles with us?"

"Snick-er-doodles," Rianne corrected.

Mila shrugged. "That's what I said. Snickadoodles."

It jerked a laugh out of my tightly coiled chest. Leave it to Mila to insist she was saying it right. Sassy and full of spunk, my girl was everything McKenna would have been if she'd been raised in a loving home. It made tears prick at my eyes.

Rianne raised the tray and put it in the oven before turning back to us. "That was the last batch, chick-a-dee. Why don't you go wash up?"

Mila climbed down off the step stool and attempted a poorly formed skip toward the bathroom. She looked back at me and smiled. "My skip is getting better, isn't it, Daddy?"

"Sure is, Bug-a-Boo." I smiled back, but it was a wavery one, and even she seemed to sense it, because she halted before running back to me. I bent down so I was at eye level with her, and she kissed my cheek.

"I'm glad you're home early! That means we can have pizza *and* popcorn tonight, right?"

I chuckled again, chest loosening even more.

"Maybe."

She patted my shoulder. "That means yes."

And then she turned and ran off toward the bathroom.

It took me a minute to gather myself, and when I stood back up, Rianne was looking at me with concern etched over her brow.

"Want to talk about it?"

"I can say it all in one word—Sybil."

She shook her head. "That woman is the devil."

I wouldn't argue with that.

"I'm going to call Stephanie," I said.

"She's going to tell you the same thing she does every time that woman flies through Willow Creek. You have nothing to worry about. Mila is yours," Rianne said, but I was already walking toward my study.

Rianne was right. My lawyer had assured me many times that no judge would ever pull Mila from me completely, even if her biological dad showed up in the picture. But the thought of having to even share Mila was enough to make my heart forget to pump.

I needed all the reassurances I could get.

Then, I'd spend the night eating pizza, popcorn, and snickerdoodles while watching *Scooby-Doo* with my adventurous little queen. Nothing else on earth was better to help me forget everything bad that had happened today.

Chapter Seven

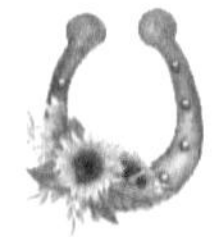

McKenna

IF I DIDN'T LOVE YOU

Performed by Jason Aldean and Carrie Underwood

Between the flight, rental car, and paying my regular bills, I'd pretty much emptied my savings. I had just enough money left to put some food in my belly before my next paycheck—assuming I got one. Dr. Gomez had insisted they were paying me while they investigated, but what happened if they finished early? If they fired me?

Ripples of apprehension washed over me in waves, making the fast-food burger I'd eaten threaten to come back up.

This was stupid. I shouldn't have wasted the money to come back.

I should have just continued hiding out in the apartment like I'd been doing all along.

The town's sign appeared, glowing in the sunset and making my heart hammer.

Willow Creek—home of football heroes, rock stars, and ranchers.

My lips curled upward. Our little town was as proud of their celebrities as Bell Buckle was of their RC Cola and MoonPies. The football stadium at my high school had been named after a dead football star, and the area behind the lake was well-known as "Watery Reflection Hill" because the famous band had built several homes at the top of it. Famous was normal in Willow Creek. I'd almost forgotten that in the years I'd been gone.

Memories assaulted me as I drove into town—running down the sidewalks with Maddox, ice cream sticking to our hands that we'd taunted each other with, fishing with string and worms at the creek. The good memories twined with the ugly screams, broken bones, and bruises that had chased me out of a house and into his arms.

I pushed all the visions aside, trying to see Willow Creek through a grown-up's eyes. I'd forgotten the plethora of church steeples that peeked from the town's rooftops, but not the quaint feel of Main Street. It was as if nothing had changed in all the years I'd been gone. It still resembled a Hallmark Christmas card with its old-fashioned lampposts, cobbled streets lined with magnolia and willow trees, and ancient brick buildings with columns and wood-encased storefronts. The sun was setting, and the light glinted off the bicycles parked, unlocked, along the sidewalk because no one dared steal them. The lead-glass windows of the mom-and-pop shops sparkled, turning the street into a mass of gold and crystalized rainbows.

I didn't know if I was happy or sad about the lack of change. Like some reverse version of *Rip Van Winkle* where the entire town had been asleep for a decade, and I was the only one who'd moved on, grown up, and become an alternate version of the teen who'd sped away as fast as she could.

My map app told me to turn left just after the jewelry store. I barely remembered the names of any of the roads. As a kid, growing up here, I'd never needed them, so I'd had to look up the address. Turning now meant I wouldn't have to drive by the bar and the duplex across from it on my first day in town. Maybe I'd work up to going by it. Maybe I wouldn't. Maybe I'd join Rip and the entire town in their deep sleep, dozing for another decade without ever leaving my bedroom.

I parked the subcompact rental on the curb and stared at the house the navigation had sent me to. It was in much better shape than I'd expected. I'd thought it would have peeling paint, old carpet, and dust balls crowding the floors, but Trap must have had someone maintaining it, because it felt almost…charming.

There was a sheriff's vehicle parked in front of it by a quaint mailbox shaped like a barn with the number emblazoned on the side, so I knew it was the right address. I frowned, the first note of apprehension sneaking in. Nothing about the house screamed Trap. My dad was not charming or into barn-shaped mailboxes. The yard wasn't overgrown with weeds but was carefully mowed with a large weeping willow off to one side and bushes lining a picket fence that would likely be full of color in the spring.

Only two things kept me from driving away—the fact that the house was dark, with no sign of movement inside, and the key I had in my pocket. Trap had said it would always be waiting for me if I needed a place to land. And I desperately did. He'd promised, and my dad had never promised me anything else.

I swallowed back my unease, climbed out of the car, stretched my tight muscles from the drive, and then pulled my two bags from the back. They'd barely fit in the car's trunk because it was so tiny. I dragged them up the walk and hesitated again, seeing a porch swing with a brightly patterned cushion and pots of what looked like rosemary and basil growing inside a wrought-iron stand shaped like a bicycle.

This was wrong.

Everything felt wrong.

But where else did I have to go? I was here—with a hundred dollars to my name until I got paid in a week. That was barely enough for the gas back to the airport in

Nashville. What could I do? Go back and try to change my flight home? Pay the difference on a credit card already screaming? My residency came with a decent wage, but I'd been shoving as much of my salary as I could stand at my loans, living off the bare minimum.

I juggled the key in my hand while I debated. If the key didn't work, I'd know something had changed, that the house was no longer Trap's. And if it opened, and I found Trap had set up a girlfriend there, and she was maintaining the place for him, I'd beg to stay until I got paid at least.

Shoulders back, I inhaled and stuck the key in the lock. When it clicked open, I let out my breath shakily. Thank God.

The smell of cinnamon hit me, like someone had baked recently. Shit.

I dragged my rolling suitcase inside and set my other bag down.

"What did you forget?" a deep voice asked from inside, and I froze as it wafted through me, colliding with all the memories from the drive into town.

The hall light was flicked on, and I felt the color drain from my face. I had to put a hand out on the door behind me to keep from falling over. The last person I'd expected to see tonight was standing in front of me.

He wore an old Henley with a tattered hem and jeans that looked like they'd been washed a hundred times, and his long feet were bare. He'd been smiling, the edges of it showing new laugh lines around his eyes and at the edges of his mouth, but it slipped away as our gaze met. His blue eyes seemed more vivid, squinting as if trying to focus on the image of me in his doorway.

"McKenna?" He seemed confused, rubbing a hand through a hefty amount of growth on his chin.

What the hell was he doing in Trap's house, looking like I'd just pulled him from a cozy snuggle on the couch?

"Mad-Maddox?" I said his name in a stunned, breathy whisper.

I'd known I'd see him while I was in town. But there was no way I was prepared for it tonight, not after days of hell, Dr. Gregory's threats, the long drive, and the loss of my dreams that had followed me back to my childhood nightmares.

As I watched, his expression changed from startled surprise to pure panic.

"You can't be here!" he growled. "You have to fucking leave."

My heart slammed against my chest, and tears pricked my eyes, causing me to bite my cheek and clench the handle of my bag tighter. I deserved his response. Deserved the harshness—the anger—but damn did it still hurt.

"I don't understand," I said, hand pulling on my ponytail, bouncing up on my toes and back down. He watched the movements, closed his eyes, and swallowed hard.

"You have to go!" he said.

"Daddy! You're missing the best part!"

A little body ran from the open archway down the hall and slammed into his legs. He didn't even budge. He just reached a large hand down to surround a head of hair the color of hay drenched in sunshine. The little girl's face was buried in the back of his jeans, but I could still tell she wasn't more than four or five.

My chest exploded with pain.

I'd known he'd be married with kids.

I'd known he'd have moved on. I'd told him to. Begged him to. So why did it seem to rip my soul in half? Why did I hate the knowledge that his lips had kissed someone else, that his fingers and tongue had coasted along someone else's skin? That he'd made someone else cry out and shudder as he sank into them. That he'd made them belong to him just as he had once made me.

He'd created another human being with that person, and it caused a surprising ache in my ovaries I never would have expected. Not in a million years. I didn't want kids. I didn't want to try and be a mother when all I'd learned from mine was what not to do.

"Who's she, Daddy?" the little girl asked, peeking out at me. Her eyes were hazel, a mix of gold spiked with a pale green that was eerily similar to the ones that greeted me in the mirror every morning.

"No one." His voice was gruff, the panic still there. "She has the wrong address. She's leaving."

I swallowed hard, dread filling me. Where was I going to go?

Maddox knelt, meeting the little girl's eyes. "Go get another snickerdoodle, and then wait for me on the couch."

The little girl's face lit up. "Another cookie! Yes!" She pumped her little arm inward as if in victory and danced away on light feet.

The entire exchange was so sweet it made my already knotted heart squeeze even tighter. I could barely breathe.

As soon as the little girl had disappeared, Maddox rose and stepped toward me. "You have to leave," he repeated. "How did you even get in here?"

"I...I have a key," I said, frustrated that I was still stammering, but the entire thing had taken me by surprise. I was having trouble regaining my balance and control.

He eyed my luggage, and his jaw tightened.

"I don't know how or why you're here, but I won't say it again. You need to leave."

It hurt so damn much. His anger. The one person I'd always turned to had become just another person to hate me. I was pretty pathetic because there was only one person left in this world who saw me as a human being, and I'd just put her through the wringer.

I turned, opened the door with hands that shook, and then fumbled with my suitcases. Once I finally had them, I yanked them out of the house and nearly tripped down the steps in my hurry to get back to the car. He was watching me from the door. I could feel his stare cutting through me just like I had as a teen. Scouring me. Assessing me for damage. Yearning for me. God, did he still?

Every single molecule of my being was clamoring to run back to him. To throw my arms around his neck and beg for forgiveness. To feel those firm lips possess mine. To make me feel seen and loved. To feel safe.

When was the last time I'd truly felt that way? Like nothing could hurt me? Since I'd left Willow Creek a decade ago.

I threw the luggage in the trunk and dared a look at the door. It was shut, but I swore I could still feel his gaze on me.

I got in the driver's seat, pulled on the seat belt, started the car, and then did nothing. Where was I going to go? I rested my forehead on the steering wheel, eyes and fists clenched tight, but I couldn't stop the tears this time. They fell, silently traveling a slow path down my face and then gaining speed as I lost control completely.

I'd come back to Willow Creek, knowing it was likely a mistake. But I'd let that damn demon called hope win again. And for what? An ideal of Trap swinging me into his arms like he'd done whenever he'd blown through town when I was little? Tickling me until I screamed? Or had I really hoped Maddox would knock on my door and sweep me back into his arms and his life?

In the ER, I was known for my calm, for making quick, decisive decisions. I prided myself on it, and yet I was stuck in a wasteland here. I was an idiot for coming back.

So, I sat here doing nothing except letting the tears come, wracking sobs that scored through my entire body. Tears I hadn't shed since that day Sally had found me outside the hospital.

My world had crumbled, and there truly was nothing left.

Chapter Eight

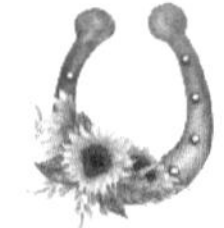

Maddox

LET IT HURT

Performed by Rascal Flatts

Fuck, fuck, fuck!

She hadn't moved from in front of the house.

A swarm of mixed emotions blew through me, panic being the loudest. I couldn't afford to have her there. Not with Sybil one town over and on a rampage after I'd lost my temper. Not when it could mean losing the best thing in my life. The most important.

But underneath the panic and anger was a tiny flick of joy and relief. She was here. For years, I'd hoped she'd stroll back into Willow Creek. That she'd ask me to forgive the hurtful words and the way she'd pushed me aside. For months after she'd told me not to ever contact her again, I'd pretty much shut down emotionally, losing myself in my job, waiting for her to bring me back to life. But it hadn't been her who'd returned me to the land of the living. It had been Mila.

McKenna's shocked, exhausted expression in my entryway flashed in front of my eyes. She'd looked worn in a way her mother normally did—dark circles under her lashes, pain in her eyes. She'd been too thin, as if no one had been watching over her to make sure she remembered to eat.

She had to be in trouble if she'd actually come back to Willow Creek. Nothing but a threat of hellfire and damnation would have brought her back otherwise.

She'd had a key to my house.

That made me frown.

The house had changed hands several times in the couple years before I'd bought it. The local real estate management group had owned it last, and I hadn't changed the locks. In hindsight, that was pretty stupid, but it was Willow Creek, for God's sake. Break-ins were rare, and everybody knew I was the sheriff. It wasn't like they were just going to waltz into my place.

Except, McKenna Lloyd had.

Shit. Why? Why was she here now?

"Daddy!" Mila's little voice was demanding and impatient.

I made my way back into the family room, kissed her on the top of her head, and made a comment about Scooby that satisfied her. But then, I was drawn to the diamond-paned window looking out at the street.

She was still there. The sun had barely set, so there was enough light for me to see she had her forehead on the steering wheel and her shoulders were shaking. She was crying. McKenna was crying…and she never cried. She'd been fierce and brave. Taking the beatings. Taking the verbal abuse. Hiding away all the pain with a face that showed nothing.

Goddamn, it sent swirls of emotions through me. Guilt. Protectiveness. A desire to comfort her. I clenched my teeth together so tight I was sure they were going to break.

A little hand slipped into mine, and I looked down at my daughter and nearly burst into tears myself. The relief I'd felt this afternoon when I'd come home and found her baking with Rianne had been overwhelming. The feel of her tiny body hugging me had righted everything in my world.

There was no way in hell I was letting anyone take her from me. I'd run away to some non-extradition country if I had to. I now understood, completely, parents who kidnapped their kids, because I'd do the same. She was *my* little girl.

"She's still here? Why didn't you invite her in? She was pretty. How do you know her?" The barrage of questions hit me one after another.

Answers I couldn't give her. Answers I'd never be able to tell McKenna either, not without risking Mila.

"I used to know her a long time ago. But she was looking for a different house," I said, settling for half-truths.

"She looks sad," Mila said, and her happy voice filled with dejection at the thought of someone else hurting. She'd always been that way, easily feeling others' emotions. My mama called her an empath, said her life would be full of emotions. I wasn't sure I liked that idea. I wanted her to only have one emotion—happiness.

I looked back out at the street. McKenna was still crying.

I sighed, warring with myself, the urge to go to her and the urge to send her packing still swimming together.

"Stay here," I said to Mila. "Don't leave this room. Don't get another cookie. Don't budge from the couch. Do you understand?"

"Okay, Daddy," she said, pulling Chester the Unicorn to her chest, sitting on the couch, and nibbling on the corner of her thumb. It was progress from sucking it, but it was still a habit I needed to break her of eventually.

I slipped on a pair of sneakers I'd left by the door after my run that morning and headed down the walk toward the street. McKenna didn't see me coming, not even when I was standing by the driver's side door. I knocked on the glass, and she jumped a mile, putting a hand to her chest.

I motioned for her to roll down the window with my heart hammering so hard I could barely hear anything but the thudding in my eardrums. My gut twisted as I stared at her beautiful face splotched with red and eyes that were still streaming. I didn't want to help her—for more reasons than I could count. Because she'd hurt me in ways no one ever had. Because I couldn't risk her being here. But even knowing both those things, I ached to reach out and pull her to me and try and soothe away her pain. To put those lips that had haunted my dreams for years up against mine and slide home. To feel joined again to the person I'd thought made up my other half and who'd been missing for a decade.

Not missing, I reminded myself. Missing implied they hadn't wanted to be gone.

"You're still here," I said, trying to keep all the emotions out of my voice.

"Y-yes," she hiccupped. "Sorry. Was melting down. Give me a minute to figure out where to go, and then I'll be out of your hair. Your wife probably freaked out. Some random woman showing up with her luggage."

My gut twisted, but I didn't correct her misunderstanding.

"Why were you at my place?" I asked.

"Trap. Trap gave me the key ages ago. Told me I could come here anytime I need a place to stay."

So many things about those sentences bothered me. The fact she was still in touch with her father, the previous leader of the West Gears, when she'd refused to stay in contact with me was only one of them. Her needing a place to land, seemingly exhausted and on the run, bothered me even more.

How could I still care what happened to her? Why did my heart slam against my chest, worrying about what trouble she was in? It was ridiculous. She'd left. She'd left and told me not to come back when I'd gone to see her. She'd gotten engaged while I'd waited for her to come home. She'd told me to stop calling and hung up on me the one and only time I'd tried to contact her after that.

I looked down at her hand that was resting on her chest. There was no ring there. No strip of white that said the ring had disappeared recently. Stupid hope flared that I squashed with a vicious fist. I couldn't want her, not only because of what she'd done but because having her here would risk Mila, and fuck if I'd let that happen.

I finally found my voice after pushing through the storm of thoughts and feelings that had assaulted me at her side. "Trap sold the house to cover his lawyer fees when he was arrested," I told her. "Elizabeth at Gold Lake Realty bought it, and then she sold it to me."

McKenna burst into a bitter laugh that was filled with more tears.

"Of course he did. Why the hell did I think he'd ever keep the one damn promise he'd ever made?" She closed her eyes, and I watched as pain etched itself across her face. Her cheeks were hollow, as if stress and worry had marked them. "He's in jail, then?"

I shook my head. "He got out on parole about six months ago. Last I heard, he was in Knoxville."

She dragged a hand over her ponytail, fighting for control, and all I could think was she needed to go before I asked her to stay.

"I'm sorry, but you really need to leave. There's…you just can't be here," I said, my voice turning gruff. "But I'm sure there's room at the Beehive, or there's a Heartland in town now."

The Beehive was a lodge from the 1800s that had been one of the first buildings built in town. It had been renovated and improved over the years into a five-star boutique hotel. The Heartland was a bland chain hotel that satisfied the tourists and fans flocking Willow Creek in hopes of catching sight of a Watery Reflection band member.

"The weekend before Thanksgiving?" she asked doubtfully before shaking her head. "It doesn't matter. I couldn't afford either, anyway."

She grimaced as if she hadn't meant for the words to slip out.

She had to have been in her third year of residency, and I wasn't quite sure, but I suspected those doctors made some big cash. If she was broke, something bad really had happened, something that had derailed her goals. And as much as I didn't want to, I felt heartbroken for her—that she'd lost the one dream she'd given everything else up to achieve.

My jaw clenched. I had my arms spread across my chest, and my fingers dug into my biceps to keep me from reaching for her.

She leaned her head against the seat back and sighed. "I'll figure something out. Go back inside. Your family must be wondering why you're even talking to the lady losing it in your yard."

I glanced up at the house and saw Mila's little face in the window. She ducked back when I caught her looking. It made my lips quirk upward. Her curiosity was a beautiful and troublesome thing.

"The unit above the barn is vacant at the moment." I'd said the words before I'd fully processed them and instantly regretted the hope that filled the eyes she turned to me. I crushed it by adding, "But you can't stay longer than a night or two."

My chest tightened, stomach acid churning. Even a night or two was a risk. But Sybil was in rehab. No one from here was going to go running to see her. I doubted she'd have any visitors other than me, and I wasn't going back again. McKenna could stay for a day, do whatever the hell it was she had to do, and leave again without Sybil being any the wiser.

"Ryder isn't living there anymore?" McKenna asked.

"He's not twenty-one anymore, McK. He's a grown-ass man with a house and a life." My words were sharp and bitter, but I couldn't help it. What had she expected? Everyone to be exactly the same while she was the only one who'd moved on, grown up, changed?

Her face shuttered, a hand fluttering to her forehead. "Of course. That was stupid of me." Tears filled her eyes again, but I could tell she was biting her cheek to keep them at bay now. "I'm not normally this addle-brained. I just…there's a lot…coming back… never mind."

"Let me get my keys and Mila, and you can follow us to the ranch," I said, knowing I'd regret it, feeling in my soul that somehow today everything in my world had shifted. I'd pissed off Sybil, and McKenna had shown up on my doorstep. It was like the Fates were laughing at me.

"I know my way to the ranch. You don't have to show me," she said quietly. "But are you sure your family won't mind? I promise to figure things out tomorrow."

There was no way I was letting McKenna Lloyd show up at the ranch without warning. Without reminding everyone they absolutely could not tell her the truth about Mila. That it would cost me everything. Cost my parents their first grandchild and my siblings their niece.

"It's better this way. Give me a minute or two," I said and turned away. I barely heard the thank-you she sent out the window. I jerked my chin in her direction as I made my way back toward the house, wondering just how much I was going to regret this.

Chapter Nine

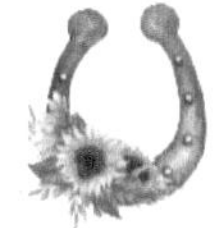

McKenna

I NEVER SAID I'M SORRY

Performed by Ryan Hurd

I watched Maddox as he walked back through his front door, emotions spinning through me. Regret. Heartache. Disappointment. At myself…and Trap…and even Maddox.

I should have known I couldn't count on Trap.

It wasn't like he'd been there at any point in my life when I needed him. But I thought his remorse had been legitimate. I thought he was trying to make amends for leaving me with Mama and her fists and vile words. But Trap would always put himself first. It was why he'd never stayed with us long. He didn't want to be a husband or a father. He wanted his gang of motorcycle cronies and the excitement of his criminal lifestyle. I was disappointed I'd let myself believe in him when I'd had years of experience proving I shouldn't.

And Maddox… The realization hit me hard in the chest that I was goddamn disappointed in him, too. For years, I'd blamed myself, but the truth was, Maddox had walked away easily. I'd asked him not to come back to Davis after that first trip he'd scrounged up enough money to make, and he hadn't. I'd asked him not to call after I'd gotten engaged, and he hadn't—except once, two years later, which had ended badly for all of us. It was as if I'd been all too easy for him to give up. Somewhere deep in my heart, maybe I'd wanted—needed—him to fight for me a little harder. I'd needed to know I was worth keeping.

Tears hit me again that I tried to brush away. My therapist was right. The wounds of my childhood had never really healed, not even with the shiny new life I'd tried to give myself.

At the end of the day, I had to live with the fact that I'd never truly been wanted. Just for a brief period by a boy who'd looked at me as if I was the entire universe of stars contained in one body. And now he'd grown up and found out the truth—that the stars were a mirage, a dull glow on the outside hiding the emptiness inside.

When Maddox came out of the house, he had the little girl in his arms. She had a stuffed unicorn clutched to her chest and was wearing a puffy coat with a glittery rainbow on the front. Maddox had a black cowboy hat on his head, looking so much like the man I'd known last that it carved a line of pain through my chest. Except, he wasn't the same. His muscles seemed to have doubled, and he might have even grown another inch or two. He'd seemed mammoth when he'd been in the tiny entryway with me, but I'd thought it was just the tightness of the space. Now, I could see that he really was a much larger man than he'd ever been as a teen.

He disappeared with the girl into a detached garage, and when the door rolled up, I was surprised to see his old Bronco backing out. A wave of happiness washed through the layers of sadness. I was glad he'd kept it all these years. While Maddox had changed, the Bronco had not. It looked like it still needed a paint job, the forest-green paint giving way to rust here and there, in the exact way it had when he'd bought it.

We'd made so many memories in that vehicle.

We'd lost our virginity together in the back of it.

Heat and longing settled low in my belly, remembering fingers and hands and mouths coasting over bare skin while the moonlight peeked through the windows.

His little girl flashed a smile in my direction from her car seat in the back, shattering those memories. They headed toward the cross street, and I put my rental in gear to pull out behind them. We made our way out of town as the sun completely disappeared, and dark settled over the landscape. As we passed the turnoff to the lake, a whole new wave of memories assaulted me before we hit the sprawling fields, rolling hills, and ancient trees of ranch territory.

When we got to the Hatleys' driveway, I was surprised to see enormous stone pillars and a wrought-iron gate with a bucking bronco twined into the metal. The words "Welcome to Hatley Ranch" were scrolled across the top, and my heart skipped a beat. It looked so…prosperous…wealthy, even. The last time I'd been here, they'd been hanging on to the ranch by the skin of their teeth. There had been no gate, every building had needed repair, and the dairy equipment had barely worked.

As the gates rolled open and we started down the lane, I was suddenly relieved Maddox had brought me. Arriving at the entrance and having to explain my presence over an intercom, would have been nearly impossible.

The trees stretching along the winding drive to the farmhouse seemed taller and fuller. The paved road was asphalt instead of the dirt, hole-pocked path it had once been. Yet another sign that the ranch I'd once known had disappeared into some alternate-universe version of it.

When the house finally came into view, I was overwhelmed with more memories—Maddox chasing me along the wraparound porch, sitting on the roof outside his bedroom window, climbing trees, riding the horses—but then, the memories disappeared into shock at the changes time had brought. My headlights flashed, giving a glimpse of the once gray house with peeling paint that was now a gorgeous light blue with white trim and a slate gray tiled roof.

When we drove around it, toward the barn, I was surprised to see a large addition tacked onto the back of the house, jutting out like an L. In the middle of the addition was a pair of golden oak doors etched with stained glass and a sign I couldn't read while I focused on keeping up with Maddox.

He parked by the enormous barn that had once dwarfed the main house, and there I found even more changes awaited me. In the past, the dull-red barn doors had always hung open, giving visitors a view of the horses, cows, tractors, and farm equipment that had bled into the yard. Now, the barn was painted in colors that matched the farmhouse, with the doors sealed shut, and not a hint of equipment anywhere. The only similarity was the smell of hay and animals that still assaulted me even with the windows rolled up as I came to a stop next to Maddox's Bronco in a paved parking spot.

The alterations were disconcerting, as if I'd somehow missed something enormous…something important.

My heart pounded fiercely, and my hands shook, but I forced myself out of the car and to the trunk. I left my roller bag, just pulling my carry-on out. I wasn't staying. I'd spend the night, calm my nerves, and make a new plan. I could always go back to California and either stay at the apartment or drive down the coast to Avalyn Beach with Sally and her dad. They'd accept me. Welcome me. My gut twisted at the thought. I didn't really want to bring my shit back to them.

When I turned around, Maddox had helped his little girl out of the back of the Bronco. She danced over to me, swinging the unicorn.

"Hi! I'm Mila, and this is Chester," she said, pointing to the stuffed animal.

"It's very nice to meet you, Mila and Chester," I said, trying to pull myself together and attempting my friendly doctor voice that usually calmed kids down in the ER. It was much more of a struggle than I expected, because she was beautiful. And she was his. And both those thoughts left me breathless.

Her hair was lighter than Maddox's, her face rounder, eyes bigger, but her smile was wide and full. It hit me that she didn't really look anything like him, but she had the gregarious friendliness that had always been Maddox's as a child.

"I'm McKenna," I told her belatedly.

She nodded. "Daddy told me. He said you used to be friends a long time ago."

My eyes met Maddox's, and he glanced away, lifting his cowboy hat, running his hand through his hair, and then replacing it. A tell as much as my tugging my ponytail had ever been. He was nervous. He didn't want me there. He'd told me to *fucking* leave and had meant it.

I swallowed hard.

"Come on, Bug-a-Boo, let's get her set up, and then we need to get you back to the house before it's way past your bedtime."

He grabbed her hand and turned, heading toward the back of the barn and the outside stairs that would lead to the apartment atop it, stuffed into the rafters. At one point, it had housed the farm's business manager, but Ryder had taken it over when he'd left college and the Hatleys had no longer been able to afford the extra employees.

Mila skipped awkwardly next to Maddox, trying to keep up with his long stride, and once he realized it, he slowed his pace. The simple action—the sweetness of it—made my heart twirl and spin again, yearning for things I'd never wanted.

I wondered where his wife was. I wondered what she was thinking about him bringing his old "friend" out to his parents' house to stay.

The old wooden slate stairs had been replaced with a beautifully ornate, wrought-iron set that was smooth and cool under my hand. At the top, Maddox unlocked the door that now had a fancy stained-glass insert, stepped inside, and turned on a switch to light the apartment up.

I swallowed hard. It looked like a five-star hotel instead of the bare-bones bachelor pad Ryder had kept. It was furnished with brown leather chairs, warm woods, and brightly colored linens. The cream-colored walls were littered with black-and-white shots of the ranch. Views you only found when riding on horseback across the hills and valleys they owned. Places I'd ridden with Maddox.

"Wow," I said, hesitating at the door. "Everything looks so…different."

Maddox looked around, jaw tightening. "It's one of the guest units now."

My brow furrowed. "Guest units?"

He sighed, as if not wanting to explain it, or as if the words pained him. "We're a boutique, dude ranch now. Open April to September. You could have stayed in one of the cabins out back, but they're all torn up at the moment with some big renovation Ryder's trying to wrap up before next season."

My lips twitched. "A dude ranch?"

"Sounds worse than it actually is," he said with a slight grimace.

Mila was spinning in the small kitchen off to the side. It didn't have an oven, just a two-burner stove and a minuscule refrigerator that, once upon a time, Maddox and I used to steal beer from. It was no longer the cheaply thrown together kitchenette it had once been. Instead, it had teal-colored, fifties-style appliances with white, farmhouse-chic cabinets.

When I turned back from the little girl and the kitchen, Maddox's hooded gaze was resting on mine. My heart leaped, the pace increasing as awareness shifted over the air between us. I had to fight every single fiber in me that wanted to hug him, wanted to push my head against his chest and ask a thousand questions about his life. Mila had to be at least four, if not five, which meant he'd met her mom not very long after I'd told him to stop calling. I frowned, the math being almost too close to make sense of, but then I pushed it aside. It wasn't my business.

He'd made it perfectly clear I was nothing more than a nuisance tonight.

A little hand slipped into mine, and I almost pulled away reflexively before Mila's fingers tightened. "Come on, I'll show you the bedroom. Auntie Sadie says she's going to live here when she guaduates."

"Graduates," Maddox corrected her.

"That's what I said, guaduates."

Mila tugged me down the short hall to the open bedroom door. It certainly looked different than the last time I'd been there, done up in luxurious lines of purples and forest greens instead of the gray tones Ryder had used. Maddox and I had lost ourselves in each other here whenever Ryder went out of town. We hadn't dared make love in the house because his mama would catch us. The woman had the ears of a barn owl, but here, I'd been able to moan and cry out, and he'd done the same.

My eyes pricked, and my skin burned with the memories. When I glanced behind us at Maddox, I could have sworn his ears were pink, and I didn't know how it made me feel to know he was recalling our same moments.

Mila let go of my hand and sat on the bed, pointing to the side table. "That's the drawer that is o-f-f, off-limits!

Auntie Sadie says she has a right to some privacy, even if her brothers think she doesn't."

I couldn't help it. My lips curved upward, thinking about what could be in the bedside drawer. When I glanced at Maddox, he'd definitely turned red and was looking up at the ceiling like he was trying to count backward and ignore every thought that had entered his mind about his sister. A little chortle escaped me that drew his eyes back to me and my lips.

My breath caught, my glance darting to his firm mouth. A mouth that had commanded and possessed even as a teen. A mouth that had brought me to heights I'd never experienced again. Not with Kerry. Not with any man who'd been in my bed.

"Mila!" The warning that burst from him had me looking over to Mila as her hand pulled back from the drawer handle, and my chortle burst into full-on laughter. It eased the tension in my chest and body.

"Okay, okay!" Mila said, picking up Chester and coming to stand next to her father. "Can we go say hi to Nana and Papa?"

God, she was too sweet. Thinking of Eva and Brandon as grandparents made me weepy again. They'd be perfect grandparents, just like they'd been perfect parents. I bet they spoiled Mila silly when they had her, sending her back to Maddox hyped up on sugar and gifts.

"It's late. We'll see," he said, and when she pouted, I could already see he was going to give in. She had him wrapped around her finger like a ring she could twist, and it only made my smile grow.

Maddox backed out of the room, taking Mila with him, and I followed.

He pulled a key from his keychain, handing it to me. I hesitated and then reached for it. Our fingers collided, and the jolt of energy that shot through me had me jerking back without the key. He inhaled sharply, eyes closing briefly, and then set the key on the counter nearby.

At least I wasn't the only one feeling the draw, the pull of everything we'd once been trying to raise its head and scream at us. Then, I reminded myself that, somewhere out there, he likely had a partner who wouldn't appreciate any feelings wafting between us.

"You can just drop the key in the box by the back steps. It's where the guests leave theirs when they're checking out," he said.

Another stab ripped into my bleeding heart. He wanted me to scuttle away without seeing anyone. He wanted me gone as quickly as I'd come, but the gentlemanly, Southern protector in him hadn't allowed him to wash his hands of me completely when I'd accidentally slipped that I had no place to go.

He headed for the door, and Mila skipped behind him.

He turned back, as if unsure what to say, so I spoke first. "Thank you, Maddox, for letting me stay. I'll be out of your hair as soon as I can."

He stared for a moment, gave a curt nod, and then left without even saying goodnight. It tore at me, the laughter of a moment ago disappearing until there was only bitter disappointment left.

I wasn't sure what I'd expected to find coming back to Willow Creek. Ridiculous wishes that had never been true. Ridiculous thoughts of reconciliations, of washing away the painful memories of this town by making new ones, maybe? A place to lay my head down and forget the investigation, the threats, and the debt I'd have nothing to show for if Dr. Gregory got his way.

I was exhausted. I wanted to scrub away the tears, the travel, and the guilt and just lie down and sleep for a week. So, I picked up my bag and headed for the small bathroom, promising myself I'd figure everything out in the morning.

Chapter Ten

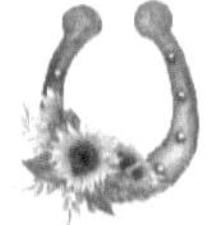

Maddox

I STILL MISS YOU

Performed by Keith Anderson

I couldn't get out of the apartment fast enough. The memories of McKenna and me there were too strong—us tangled together on the couch, the bed, the kitchen counter. Ryder's apartment had been one of our safe spots, hidden away from Mama. We hadn't dared sleep together in Ryder's old bedroom in the main house where McKenna had stayed our senior year.

My family had taken her in even when they could hardly afford another mouth to feed amid the ranch's decline. They'd taken her in like they'd been wanting to do for years but had no legal means of doing so. None of the CPS investigations had ever resulted in proof of Sybil's abuse because Sybil was a good actress, and McKenna was good at keeping their secrets. At least, she had been until the day she'd had her chin split open and undeniable finger-sized bruises along her neck and arms. Wounds that were the third in a month.

I'd kissed her that day, changing everything between us and refusing to take her back to Sybil. When I'd brought McK home, Mama had tried to make everything better. She'd taken her shopping, bought her new clothes and school supplies, and made her feel like she belonged, while

Dad hadn't even blinked an eye at the cost. What both my parents had done was threaten me with a bed in a horse stall if I even thought of sneaking into McK's room at night.

"Daddy, McKenna still looks so sad. What do you think we should do to make her happy?" Mila asked as we made our way back to the Bronco.

It made the acid in my stomach churn some more. Once upon a time, that was all I'd wanted to do—bring a smile to McKenna's face, lighten her day, even if it was just a little bit.

"It isn't our job to make her happy, Bug-a-Boo. She'll be gone in the morning. Just passing through," I said.

Mila was shaking her head. "I don't think so." Her brows drew together. "I think she'll be here a while."

My heart jerked for a different reason as my feet came to a halt, and my breath left my body. I looked down into her sweet face and asked, "What makes you say that?"

Mila's eyes were wide, and she was staring out at the dark expanse of fields and pastures beyond the barn. When she came back to me, her smile returned. "Don't know. Can we please, please, please, go say hi to Nana and Papa?"

I needed to get her home and into bed. Even if it was Friday, if she was up too late, she'd be cranky all the next day, but there was no way I could leave McKenna Lloyd in the unit above the barn and not warn them. Plus, I had to tell Mama she might want to have a look at what Sadie had moved in there before any of our guests discovered it.

"Let's go," I said.

"Yes!" she cried and took off at a dead run past the restaurant that had been added to the house seven years ago.

She'd already burst through the back door by the time I caught up. The kitchen was lit up with Gemma at the family's private dining room table in front of her laptop and Mama at one of the large counters in the renovated kitchen. In our busy season, the place was packed with staff and activity, but now it seemed to echo its emptiness. Mama pulled a lid off a blender full of what looked to be margaritas, and there was loud country music coming from the living room. It all meant Dad wasn't there.

"Baby girl!" Mama called out as my daughter ran straight for her. "Isn't this a surprise?"

"Nana! Guess what?"

"What?"

"Daddy's friend is staying in Aunt Sadie's apartment!"

Shit. Well, that was one way to break it to them. I took my hat off, hung it on the rack at the back door, and slid onto a stool while Mila and my mama hugged it out. Gemma slammed her laptop shut and joined me at the counter. Her lips were twitching.

"This should be way more interesting than reading my script for the fifty-millionth time."

She shoved my shoulder, and her hazel eyes twinkled. She was the only one of us who didn't have blue eyes, and sometimes, they reminded me of McK's, the light golds and green mixing together.

"Who's this, Maddox?" Mama asked, brows furrowing.

I opened my mouth to answer, but Mila beat me to it. "Her name's McKenna, and Daddy says they were friends a long time ago."

My heart throbbed hearing McK's name coming out of Mila's mouth. It caused a renewed wave of fear to coast through me. No one could know she was in town, and she had to leave as fast as she'd shown up.

My eyes dropped to the blender and the two margarita glasses sitting next to it.

"I think I'm going to need one of those," I told her.

Gemma gurgled, and even Mama's lips twitched.

"Why don't you go look in your playroom and see if you can find what's new?" Mama suggested to Mila, kissing her cheek and letting her go.

"This may be the best day I've ever had," Mila said. "Rianne and I made snickadoodles, Daddy let me have three cookies after pizza, I watched *Scooby*, met a new friend, and now I get a present!"

Mila twirled out of the kitchen, heading for what used to be my bedroom and had now been converted into her playroom. It had a pink canopied twin bed for the times she spent the night and looked like a toy store had blown up inside it.

"That should keep her busy for at least fifteen minutes," Mama said, reaching behind her to pull out a third glass. "So…this is a surprise."

I dragged my hand through the stubble that I had to admit was now the start of a damn beard and spilled my guts about how McKenna had walked into the house with a key. "She can't stay," I said. "Sybil's back. The judge has her holed up at the women's rehab clinic after Bruce arrested her."

"Well, hell," Mama said.

"There's nothing Sybil can do, Mads. No matter how much she blusters, she can't take Mila from you," Gemma said, putting her arm around me and resting her head on my shoulder.

I swallowed hard. "I can't risk her suddenly remembering who the father is and having to fight for my girl all over again."

My jaw clenched as I fought the tears that pricked my eyes.

"Did you tell her?" Gemma asked quietly.

My eyes widened. "About Mila? Hell, no."

"She's going to figure it out," Mama said. "Just looking at them together will be proof."

"Mila only has their eyes and their hair coloring. Nothing else. And you forget, I tried to tell McKenna. I tried and got my heart and soul stomped on for the effort."

Mama slid a margarita over to me, and I took a huge swallow. There wasn't nearly enough alcohol in it.

"You don't know what was going on in her life at that moment," Mama said gently.

"She was engaged, Mama. That's hardly a terrible place."

"When you tried to contact her about Mila, it had been, what, a year since she'd first told you to stop calling? How do you even know she was still engaged? Is she married? She's here alone, right? What's that all about?" Mama pushed.

I thought back to McKenna's ringless hand in the car, the dark circles under her eyes, and the way her body screamed exhaustion. No matter what her life had been like four years ago, when I'd first found Mila screaming in filth and squalor with Sybil passed out in her own vomit, it was clear that McKenna's life wasn't a happily ever after at the moment. She was running. Running hard enough that she'd thought she'd use her father's house as an escape. A father who'd barely been in her life and who she'd told me she'd never trust.

I took another sip of the margarita and shot my sister and Mama a severe look. "No one tells her. She says she's leaving tomorrow, so it shouldn't matter, but send one of your bat-signals out to all our family and friends to make sure they know."

"So, what *are* you going to tell her?" Gemma asked.

"Nothing. I won't likely even see her again. I told her to put the key in the guests' drop slot on her way out tomorrow," I said, and hell if that didn't twist my gut in a different way. I wanted to know what was eating at McKenna. I wanted to know why she was exhausted and running, but I couldn't afford to find out, not only for Mila's sake but for the sake of my heart and soul, which had taken one too many hits at her hands.

"Well, damn," Mama said, brow scrunching. "If Ryder hadn't torn up all the cabins, we'd have plenty of room, but with Sadie and all her friends showing up on Monday, we're full up, even in the barn unit."

"McKenna isn't staying," I said firmly. She couldn't, and she'd agreed. But then I frowned, trying to recall what words McKenna had actually used. Surely, she wouldn't stay now that Trap's house—my house—wasn't available.

A scream of little-girl joy tore through the air, and I frowned at my mother. "What did you do now?"

Mila's feet pounded down the stairs, and she twirled into the room with not one but two unicorns in her hands. Chester had been a dying breed when we'd found him in a shop in Knoxville when Mila and I had dropped Sadie off at college two years ago. The toymaker had retired the line, but ever since we'd bought him, and Mila had seen the tag on him that named each of his unicorn friends from that damn book she loved, she'd been clamoring to find the rest of the herd and bring them all together, which is exactly what my mama had done. She'd found Chester's friend, Charlotte.

"NANA!!! You are the best grandma on the face of this planet. Chester is so very happy." She hugged my mother and then ran to me, shoving the two unicorns up into my face. "Look, Daddy, Charlotte returned home to Chester just like McKenna returned home to you."

My stomach plummeted while Mama and Gemma burst out laughing.

"Okay, Bug-a-Boo, say thank you and goodnight so we can get you home and to bed."

"Can I stay the night, Daddy? Pretty please?"

I eyeballed the margaritas. "Not tonight, Mila. Nana had other plans."

"Puh-lease. Having my grandbaby is always better than any other plans I've made. Besides, you were going to drop her off in the morning to help with the Thanksgiving pies anyway."

"Where's Dad?" I asked.

"Went with Ryder to Nashville for a Tennessee Dude Ranchers' Association meeting. They'll be back tomorrow."

Mila jumped from foot to foot, hugging the two unicorns to her chest. "Please, Daddy?"

She got her way too damn much, but it lifted my heart to make her happy, to give her the simple pleasures of a family who loved her.

"I guess I'll have to finish watching *Scooby* by myself," I said, forcing all the fake despair I could into my voice, and Mila giggled.

"You're funny, Daddy. You know you won't watch it without me."

"Give me hugs," I said.

She did, squeezing me as tight as her little arms could and kissing my cheek. "I love you, Bug-a-Boo," I told her, voice gruff and full of emotions.

"Love you, too, Daddy!" And then she ran back to Mama. "Can we have a dance party?"

"Anything you want!"

"She's going to be a grouchy mess tomorrow, so good luck with the pies," I said with a smirk.

"She's only cranky with you," Gemma said.

My smile widened at that thought. It didn't bother me at all. It meant she felt safe enough to be herself with me.

I hugged Mama and Gemma, said goodnight, picked up my hat, and headed for the door. The music had already switched to Mila's latest Disney pop obsession before I'd even closed it behind me. It eased the worry coasting through me.

When I reached the Bronco, I looked up at the unit above the barn to find it dark. Maybe it had all been a dream. Maybe McKenna wasn't back in Willow Creek. But her rental car parked next to me told me otherwise. My entire chest ached from worry. It wasn't just for my daughter. It was for the person who I'd thought was the other part of my soul before she'd left. The person who looked like she'd run herself into the ground.

I climbed in, started the ignition, and drove down the drive.

At the turnoff to the lake, my body seemed to take control, heading toward the water instead of back into town. There were a handful of cars parked in the lot. A bonfire going on the shore and the rowdy noise of teens and music competed with the sounds of the crickets. It was a gathering I was sure I could bust up, but I had no desire to do so while out of uniform.

Instead, I strode toward the path winding its way to the top of the cliff overlooking the lake. The worn trail was steep, but I was hardly out of breath by the time I reached the top. The water sparkled below, drawing me to it as it had my entire life. McKenna and I had found peace out here— escape from her mama for her and escape from the heavy burden of the ranch's failure that had weighed on me.

My phone buzzed. It was Ryder, not in the group chat with our sisters, but a private message. Eighty percent of the time, we texted as a group, leaving the solo chats for more serious discussions.

DIPSHIT: Just checking to make sure you haven't driven your Bronco off a cliff.

I rolled my eyes.

ME: I can't believe Gem-Mine told you already.

DIPSHIT: Actually, it was Mama who sent Dad a message. Seriously, though, are you okay?

The cold feeling of dread inside me eased a little with the warmth of Ryder's concern.

ME: She'll be gone tomorrow.

DIPSHIT: Yeah, but if I'd had to see Ravyn even for ten minutes, you might have had to lock me up for murder.

ME: Totally different situation. I might have to lock myself up for murder if Ravyn showed up.

DIPSHIT: Drinks tomorrow night.

ME: Maybe.

DIPSHIT: I wasn't asking, Mads.

I couldn't help the wry grin that hit my lips.

McKenna might have torn open my painfully healed scars by showing up, but my family would be there to help me cover them back up. I'd lose myself in my job and my daughter, and I'd forget she'd ever blown through town.

At least, that was what I hoped.

Chapter Eleven

McKenna

COMING HOME

Performed by Keith Urban with Julia Michaels

Something was poking my cheek that felt oddly like a finger, and it dragged me out of fitful dreams. Ones filled with memories of punishment at my mama's hands, which had turned into Dr. Gregory's fists, until Maddox had stormed in to save me. He'd never had to physically save me growing up. I'd always escaped on my own. But he'd saved me emotionally, kept me from going off into a deep abyss.

"Miss McKenna?" It was a breathy, childish whisper that joined the pressure on my cheek, and my eyes flew open.

Maddox's daughter was standing before me. She now had two unicorns clutched under one arm, but she was wearing the same grin as the night before. One that was infectious as much as it stabbed at me with the reminder that she was Maddox's. That he'd fathered a child with someone.

"Hey," I finally croaked out.

"Nana says you need to come to the house for berry craps."

I choked out a laugh. "Craps?"

Her dark brows furrowed, and it hit me in the gut how much like my own they were—dark and thick compared to her much lighter hair. Something twisted in my stomach, a niggling thought that left me before I could tie it down.

"Do you not like craps?" she asked.

The smile stayed on my face as I said, "I'm not sure I've ever had them."

"Oooooh. They are soooooooo good, and Nana makes the best ones. They are like pancakes but skinnier, and she stuffs them with strawberries and covers them in whipped cream. Daddy says they make me hyper, but Nana always lets me have them when I ask."

"Oh, you mean crepes," I said, finally catching on.

"That's what I said, craps."

My chest filled with another chortle that I barely held back.

I sat up, and the little girl plopped down on the bed near my feet. "Auntie Gemma said you and Daddy were best friends."

My heart squeezed, and I nodded.

"My best friend is Missy, but she's mean to me sometimes, so Daddy says she isn't a real friend and that it takes time to find the right person to be your bestie. But Missy invited me to her birthday party at the teahouse next Friday. That's after Thanksgiving, in six days. Did you know there are actually seven days in a week? I learned that in kindergarten. I'm in kindergarten because I'm five. I won't be six until August seventh. When's your birthday?"

The chatter should have been annoying in my half-asleep state, but it was oddly addicting, like I could listen to it for days.

"My birthday is November seventh," I told her.

"That's the same number as mine! Wait. Does that mean you just had a birthday?" she screamed. "You're so lucky. What did you get? I want Chester and Charlotte to find their friends, Chantelle and Chin, for my birthday." She shoved the unicorns in my direction again. "But Daddy says they're improbable to find." She danced the girl unicorn in front of my face as I bit my lip, trying not to laugh at her saying *improbable* instead of *impossible*. "But look at what Nana found! She gave me Charlotte last night when we went to tell her you were here."

Her cheerful attitude was something I needed in my life. A positive outlook I wasn't sure I'd ever owned because hope had always failed me. Even now, coming back to Willow Creek, I'd had it slammed out of me before it could even start to really grow.

Her smile faded as she glanced at the clock on the bedside table.

"Oh no. How long have I been here? Nana told me that if we weren't back in ten minutes, she'd start without us. I don't know how to tell time yet. Do you?"

My lips twitched. "Yes, I know how to tell time, but as I don't know when you got here, I'm not sure how long it's been."

"You better get up, then." She darted to the door. "Nana said just come as you are because we're all in our pj's."

She glanced down at her thermal pajamas peeking out below a white fluffy robe covered in rainbows and a pair of fuzzy slippers with hard soles.

My gut twisted at the thought of seeing Eva. I wasn't sure I was ready to see any of the Hatley family again. They had to hate me, not only for hurting Maddox but for leaving and not keeping in touch with them. My cheeks burned when I thought about the care packages Eva had sent me when I'd first gone to college that I hadn't known how to say thank you for. Each package had been a painful reminder of what I'd left, and I'd simply wanted to forget it all. It had been selfish and cruel, trying to focus on only me and my dreams.

It made my chest ache more, tears threatening to come. The fact I only had Sally in my life was my fault. I could have had the Hatleys, and I'd thrown them away.

"Thank you for inviting me, Mila, but I'm thinking I need to head out soon," I said because I wasn't sure I could face any of them, wasn't sure they really wanted me there. Maddox surely hadn't. *You need to fucking leave*, reverberated through my head.

Mila was nodding at my words. "Nana said you'd say no, and she told me to tell you she'd be crushed if you didn't come and have breakfast. She says it's been *ten years* since she saw you."

The little girl said ten years as if they were a hundred, as if it was beyond her comprehension. Then, her smile went away, and her eyes looked sad.

"I don't want Nana to be sad, so you have to come." She shifted her head as she assessed me. "You're sad, too. Maybe Nana's craps will make you feel better because they always make me feel like I can jump from the tire swing in our yard to the porch. I haven't been able to do it yet, but soon I will."

Surprise settled through me, leaving me a bit speechless that this little child could somehow sense the shadow of sorrow hovering around me. A sorrow that was tinged with fear and regret.

Mila jumped down and pulled on my hand. "Come on. We don't want to miss the craps, Miss McKenna."

"It's just McKenna. You don't need the Miss."

She nodded and then pulled harder on my hand. I let her drag me up and out of the bed. I looked down at my body, thankful I'd fallen asleep in a pair of yoga pants and an old UC Davis tee rather than my underwear and a tank top like I normally wore to bed.

I tugged her to a stop outside the bathroom. "I have to, uh, use the bathroom first."

"Okey-dokey, I'll just wait here."

I stared at the little bundle of energy as she hopped from foot to foot and then went in, shutting the door behind me and locking it because I wasn't entirely sure she wouldn't burst inside. I used the toilet and washed my hands before my image in the mirror caught my gaze. I was a wreck. My hair was tangled, and the dark circles I was unable to escape were even more pronounced.

I slipped the hair tie from my wrist where it lived semi-permanently and pulled my blonde waves up into a messy bun. Then, I made quick work of brushing my teeth. I'd much rather the Hatleys see me after I'd had time to shower, put on some makeup and actual clothes, but I knew I didn't have that kind of time.

Proving me right, a knock on the door was followed by Mila's tiny voice, "How long has it been, Miss McKenna? Will we have missed the craps already?"

I chuckled, and the smile reflecting back at me in the mirror surprised me so much I dropped my toothbrush. I couldn't remember the last time I'd seen myself smile—a real smile, not the doctor smile I pasted on.

I opened the door to see she had a worried frown between her brows again.

"Phew. I thought maybe you weren't ever going to come out, Miss McKenna."

"It's just McKenna," I repeated, and she nodded, picking up my hand and towing me toward the door.

I barely had time to slide into a pair of Crocs that I practically lived in at the hospital before heading out into the chilly November air. Scratch that, not just chilly, downright cold. I shivered, looking out at the mist that had settled down low over the frost-covered fields beyond the barn. The sun hadn't cleared the horizon yet, barely tinting the sky pink, but clouds were hanging above us, indicating a storm would be hitting soon. I wanted to stop and drink it in—the quiet of the early day and the scenes from my childhood where I'd felt safest—but Mila kept a tight grip on my hand as she directed me toward the farmhouse.

As she skipped beside me, I had a chance to take in the new addition. It had old oak doors, stained-glass windows, stage-coach-type lanterns, and red brick swarming with ivy. It was graceful and elegant while still blending in with the ranch somehow. The sign above the door read *Sweet Willow Restaurant*, but on the glass, it said, *Closed until April*. Maddox had said something the night before about the ranch being closed for the season, and I guessed that applied to the restaurant as well.

As we got closer to the farmhouse, I fought waves of dread and anticipation. I wasn't sure what waited for me inside. Would Maddox be there with his family? His little girl was there. She'd clearly spent the night. Did that mean he'd left her and gone back to his partner? Maybe they'd had a date night and lost themselves in each other without their little girl hovering around them. The knots inside me grew.

"Do you know how to skip?" Mila's voice brought me back to her. "I love, love, love to skip, and Daddy says I'm going to be a world champion skipper someday."

We'd reached the wraparound porch and the back door, and it was Eva Hatley's voice that answered Mila instead of mine. "Skipping is pure joy, Bug-a-Boo. But maybe you can take it down a notch so you don't burst our guest's eardrums."

My heart squeezed tighter as my eyes met Eva's. She'd called me a guest and had a smile on her face as she took me in that made those damn tears threaten to leak out again. Made me want to rush into her arms, spill all my worries, and tell her how much I'd missed her.

Mila dropped my hand and ran past her grandmother into the house as I mounted the steps. Without another word, Eva moved forward and wrapped me in a hug. As hard as I tried, I couldn't help my normal reaction that had me stiffening in her arms, but she didn't seem to care. She just hugged me tighter while I kept my arms at my sides, hands balled into fists. I bit my cheek, refusing to shed tears that never changed anything.

When Eva let go, her hand went to my face as she assessed me with blue eyes just like Maddox's. Ones that saw more of me than anyone, except her son, had ever been able to see. Her brown hair was woven with gray, and her face was lined with a few more wrinkles, but she still exuded an air of energy and liveliness that matched all of her children's.

"You look like shit," she said, and the tension in me eased with a laugh that burst from me.

"Tell me how you really feel, Eva," I said, and this caused her smile to dim.

"Not now, but if you stick around, you know I probably will."

My throat squeezed tight because, in those words, I could hear the hurt she felt and the reproach. She'd taken me in, made me part of her family, and I'd abandoned them all for my dreams, thinking I couldn't keep them without keeping the nightmares of my youth as well. I'd given it all up because I didn't know how to keep only the good parts without wanting to run back to them.

She stepped away and opened the door. "Come on, let's get you fed. It looks like you haven't eaten in a month."

I followed her and continued to be astounded by the changes that had been wrought in my absence. If I'd thought Willow Creek had been lost in a *Rip Van Winkle* time warp, the ranch was the opposite—so much change it was hard to keep up. The kitchen was enormous now instead of the cozy offshoot it once had been. Multiple commercial stoves, ovens, and refrigerators were mixed in with huge quartz counters that went on forever. The cabinets were white on the top and gray on the bottom with elegantly lighted glass displays.

Tucked off to the side in a smaller space was a large oak table I remembered eating and playing cards at more times than I could count. Mila had taken a seat there next to a woman who I thought must be Gemma. She had the blonde hair and hazel eyes that had once made me feel like maybe I fit in here, but she'd also changed so much that it was hard to believe she was the awkward teen I'd left behind when she was only thirteen. She smiled at me, and it was her brother's smile, so it stabbed at my heart.

"Hi, McKenna. It's really good to see you," Gemma said. I wondered how they could all be so nice when I'd done nothing to deserve their kindness. I'd left, ignored them, and never come back.

"Hey, Gemma," I returned, feeling suddenly awkward.

"You ready for some berry craps?" Gemma asked, winking toward Mila.

It made my lips twitch again. "I have to say, it was a bit confusing."

Eva laughed and waved me toward a chair. The plates of crepes lined up at each place setting looked like they were from a five-star restaurant, perfectly formed, decorated, and garnished. Eva had always loved to cook, experimenting with new things, and it made me wonder what the restaurant's menu looked like when it was open.

"Coffee or tea?" Eva asked as I sat down.

"Coffee would be great if you have some made, but please don't go out of your way. I certainly didn't expect to be asked to breakfast," I said.

"What nonsense is this? Have you ever known me to have a guest and push them out the door without a meal?" Eva asked. She filled a mug that read *Cows Do Cud Best,* and my mind flashed back to all the times I'd used the same damn mug a decade ago. I swallowed hard over the lump in my throat as I took it from her.

"Thank you."

"Cream? Sugar?"

"No, thanks. Between med school and my residency, I basically IV'd the stuff, and there was never time to add anything to it." The thought of my career and the shambles that remained of it brought another round of unexpected tears to my eyes. I closed them, trying to hold them in. When I opened them back up, three sets of eyes were staring at me.

"How long are you in town for?" Gemma asked.

"I'd hoped to be here for a few weeks, but I think I'll be heading out today or tomorrow. I just have to figure a few things out." Like how to pay for the changed flight on my nearly maxed-out credit card.

"You can't go yet. You'll miss Thanksgiving!" Mila cried. "It's pie-making week, and Nana makes the best pies in three counties—at least that's what Papa says. And Auntie Sadie is bringing her friends from college, and there will be a big trivia challenge that Daddy says he'll be damned if he lets the girls win again."

"Don't cuss, Bug-a-Boo," Eva said with a slight laugh.

"I made Daddy add two dollars to the cuss jar just yesterday. I think there are, like, a million dollars in there now. What do you think we could buy with a million dollars? Could we buy Disneyland? I want to go to Disneyland, but Daddy says I'm still too little to go on some of the rides, and that I'll appressiate it more when I'm taller."

"Appreciate. And breathe, Mila," Eva said with a laugh.

"That's what I said, appressiate."

The little girl dug into the crepes with a grin. Gemma and Eva did as well, and I just sat there, staring, for a moment. It felt right to be there…and wrong. Like I'd come home when I'd never allowed myself to make the ranch one.

Every time I'd visited as a child, I'd known I'd have to leave again, and it killed me a little more each time. Being here and then having to return to Mama had been like slicing off layers of skin. And then, when I'd moved in my senior year, I'd protected myself from the heartache of loving and losing them to chase my dreams. Only Maddox had broken through my shield, forcing his way in with his smile, his charm, and hands that made me feel stronger and braver and more loved than I'd ever known. And then, when I'd left, I'd taken the tiny piece of my heart I'd kept alive only for him and shut it down, too. Kerry certainly hadn't brought it back to life. I'd thought it was dead.

But sitting there in the Hatleys' kitchen, I could feel it spasming, trying to beat again.

And it scared the shit out of me.

I finally picked up my fork, savoring the burst of flavors that slid along my tongue. I never had time to cook, which meant I slammed together a lot of half-assed sandwiches after my long shifts or ordered out with Sally when we weren't near the end of the month. This breakfast…it was some of the best food I'd had in…I wasn't sure how long.

The adults were fairly quiet as we ate, but the room was never silent because Mila chattered nonstop. Once she found out I was a doctor, she peppered me with questions and showed me the scar she had above her eyebrow that had been the result of one of her attempts to jump from the tire swing to the porch.

"Daddy almost took the tire swing down." She frowned slightly. "But Uncle Ryder told him he couldn't put me in a bubble and to remember all the times Daddy had fallen while climbing trees. Did you climb trees with Daddy?"

She had whipped cream and strawberries all over her lips and cheeks. It was utterly adorable, and my ovaries clenched again. Having children had always been a hard no for me, so why was this little girl tugging at pieces of me I never thought I'd wanted?

"Why don't you go wash up, and then we'll get started on the pies," Eva said with a smile, taking in her granddaughter with a warmth that shone like a light.

"Are you going to stay and make pies with us?" Mila asked as she got up.

I felt my face heat and looked at Eva, who only smiled and said, "We can always use an extra set of hands on pie-making weekend."

Another memory hit me. This one of all the siblings and me lined up in the kitchen, all working on different parts of the pie-making endeavor. Like Mila had said, Eva was known for her amazing pies and had sold them during the holidays and again in late summer when the wild berries were in season. I remembered hot summer days by the creek, picking the berries with Maddox just so his mom could make them.

I'd blocked so many of these moments out, all because I hadn't wanted to miss them. Any of them.

My phone buzzed, and when I looked down at it, a wave of panic hit. It was from a different number than the last time because I'd blocked that one.

> *1-530-555-8210: This is day three without my family. Do you know what this means for you? Fix it. Before it's too late.*

The crepes turned uncomfortably in my stomach. What I really needed to do today was figure out where I was going and how I was going to pay for it while staying out of Dr. Gregory's sight. When I looked up from my phone, with my heart pounding, it was Eva's concerned expression I saw. I tried to hide the fear, pasting on a watery smile I was sure she could see through.

"You're always welcome in our home, McKenna. Always. You're family," Eva said, even though I hadn't asked a question.

I suddenly wanted to spend the day in her kitchen where the warmth wasn't just from the oven, where it filled the air, and where you were accepted even though your own mother didn't want you. I not only wanted to stay, it was as if my body physically needed it, as if being here could help stabilize my world that was spiraling out of control.

"I'd like that…very much," I found myself saying quietly, and Eva smiled. But I also saw the worried look Gemma sent her mother, and I added on, "If you're sure it won't be a problem."

Gemma started to say something, but Eva cut her off. "It's not a problem."

Those stupid tears I'd let out yesterday and that had been prickling at me all morning tried to escape again. I clenched my fists and bit my cheek. Letting them out wouldn't solve or change anything. I forced an even brighter smile to my lips.

"I'm gonna go help Mila," Gemma said and excused herself, and I could see she was still hesitant about my staying. I couldn't blame her.

Eva started to clear the table, and I joined her.

"I'm not sure how any of you can be this nice to me. I ignored all your calls…your care packages. Why don't you hate me?" I asked Eva once the table was emptied.

She looked up from where she had her hands in the soapy water. "You lived through hell, McKenna, and like anyone who does, you had to find your own way out. A way to heal and live. We were a reminder of those painful events. But I won't deny being hurt or deny I hoped you'd make your way back to us someday."

I bounced on my toes, tugged at my hair, and then looked around the kitchen at the tools and ingredients spread on the counters.

"Where do you want me to start?" I asked.

"I need to get it organized in my head first. Give me about ten minutes, and then I'll put you to work. Why don't you take your coffee into the family room and rest for a moment?"

I grabbed the cow mug and found my way into a room filled with even more memories. At least this space hadn't changed very much. The furniture had been upgraded, but it was almost all newer versions of what had been there before. I'd played video games with Maddox on a similarly overstuffed couch and done homework at a bulky, square coffee table. Maddox and I had run up and down the dark wooden staircase, tracking in mud and dirt from the fields, and Eva had never yelled about it. A large Christmas tree had always sat in front of the huge bay window during the holidays, and I figured it would be up in a matter of days, knowing how much Eva loved Christmas.

Since the moment I'd met the Hatleys, they'd always had a present for me under the tree. I hadn't been able to keep many of the presents because Mama had taken them away when she found them. She didn't want me to have anything new…anything that gave me pleasure. She wanted me to be as miserable as she was. My heart thudded with twisted pain. Being hated so much had made it hard to accept being loved.

One of the walls in the family room had been converted into a gallery of picture frames. I found my way over, surprised to see my face amongst the other Hatley siblings. Mixed in with the pictures of my past and the family were newer pictures of Maddox and Mila.

In one, he was holding her as a tiny little thing, maybe a year old or so. She had a crocheted blanket clutched in her hands below enormous eyes that stuck out of a body that was too thin. She must have been sick… That twisted something in my gut, but in all the later pictures, she appeared healthier and full of smiles. And Maddox… God, every time the camera caught him looking at her, his expression was full of love and awe. I remembered that look directed at me once upon a time. It crawled through my heart, snagging at my veins and ripping more holes in them.

What I didn't see in any of the pictures was Mila with a woman. Just like there were no pictures of Maddox with one either. There were no wedding photos—not that they needed to be married to have a child, but still. There were no images of her at the hospital giving birth or tucked into the table during the holidays. Mila's mother's absence was almost as telling as if she'd been there.

I paused at a picture of Mila sitting on Maddox's lap on the tailgate of the Bronco with its top off. She was laughing at the person taking the picture and had a child-sized fishing rod dangling from her grasp. Right next to it was a picture of Maddox and me taken on the day he'd bought the Bronco. He had his arm around my shoulder, and we were both smiling like goons.

The bright memory unpeeled itself from the vault I'd locked it away in. We'd driven with Brandon two towns over to pick it up. Maddox had been so dang proud of the fact he'd earned the money for it himself by bussing tables, schlepping stables at the Abbots', and even working as a lifeguard at the high school pool during the summers.

The next picture was Maddox and me right after we'd first met. I'd been invited to his birthday party, and the only reason Mama had let me go was because CPS had been at the house the day before, and she was trying to make it look like she was a good mother. I'd been in awe of everything about the Hatley house and family, and I'd shut down a bit, hiding out on the porch, away from all the commotion. Maddox had found me on the steps, and someone had taken the shot of us, knee to knee, with his arm around my shoulder just like in the picture of us with the Bronco. In this photograph, I had messy pigtails that I'd done myself, a checkered shirt that had a hole in the sleeve, and jeans that were too small. I remembered being embarrassed about them because they wouldn't button anymore. Maddox hadn't cared. He was still smiling, but I'd been expressionless.

My eyes went from my non-smiling face in that picture, to me smiling with him behind the Bronco, to Mila smiling with him on the tailgate. And I suddenly saw it. The elusive thought that had hit me earlier. The shape of her eyes, her dark brows and blonde hair, even the shape of her cheeks and jaw. It all slammed into my chest with a gasp. She looked like me. She could almost be a doppelgänger of me as a child. Not only did she look like me, but she also looked like Mama.

Holy shit!

I shook my head. No way...

My chest burned. My eyes watered. I could barely breathe. A ragged gasp escaped me.

Eva was suddenly there, and I turned wide eyes to her.

"Who's her mother?" I choked out through a throat that threatened to close completely.

Eva's expression turned soft with concern. "You need to talk to Maddox about that."

"Eva..."

She cut me off with a wave and a hand on my shoulder. "I can't talk about it, McKenna. Maddox isn't supposed to either, but if you want the truth, that's where you have to go for it."

I turned and nearly ran for the door.

"He's at work."

I turned back at the last moment. "And where exactly is that?" I demanded.

"He's the sheriff, so I expect you'll find him at the station."

I swallowed hard. He'd made his dream come true. He'd wanted to be in law enforcement for as long as I'd wanted to be a doctor. My jaw clenched. Maddox had everything, and I had nothing. I wondered what that said about me. Maybe I really was the worthless nobody Mama had always said I was. I'd thought, with therapy and time, that I'd gotten past her hurtful words, but being here was tearing them all open.

I thought of the pictures on the wall again, and anger replaced the sadness. If Mila was who I thought she was, I had every right to be mad.

Chapter Twelve

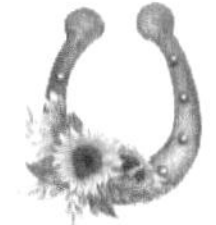

Maddox

I SHOULD PROBABLY GO TO BED

Performed by Dan + Shay

I was exhausted, emotionally and physically, by the time I put on my cowboy hat and headed for McFlannigan's. The morning had been spent rounding up sheep that had escaped through a fence, and the afternoon had been spent questioning two West Gears members who'd been arrested hauling stolen appliances across the county line in a semi-truck that we still weren't sure was theirs. I'd wanted to cut them a deal, find out what the hell was really going on, because we all felt something simmering in the air with the gang, but the district attorney had balked. He'd just won his re-election campaign by promising to remove the Gears from Winter County, and a deal wouldn't satisfy his constituents, which meant I still had to figure out what the hell the West Gears were up to right at the moment McKenna Lloyd had chosen to descend back into my life.

As I pulled my leather jacket tighter against the wind blowing heavily through Main Street, I wished I hadn't caved into Ryder's demands to meet him at the bar. What I really wanted was to spend time on the couch with Mila and let her childish wonder rub off on me. But she was spending her second night in a row at my parents' after helping Mama bake pies all day. According to the texts I'd received from

Gemma, Mama had treated McKenna to her typical five-star service, including crepes, and had even asked her to stay to help with the pies. I didn't know how to feel about it—my family welcoming her after everything I'd been through on account of her and the threat she could mean to Mila.

Gemma said McKenna hadn't stayed to help. Instead, she'd scrambled out of the farmhouse. They weren't sure if she was coming back, but she hadn't left the key to the barn unit either. I wanted to go investigate, see if the apartment was empty and her car was gone, but the thought of seeing her again made my heart beat at a pace that wasn't healthy. I'd barely slept the night before, thinking of her tear-stained face and the sadness that was leaking from her.

I walked into the bar, and a round of, "Evening, Sheriff," greeted me. I tipped my hat and headed for the corner stools. The dark-lacquered bar top, etched-glass mirror behind the counter, and forest-green walls had once given McFlannigan's a classy, Irish vibe, but the entire place was now faded and in need of work. The UTK banners and Tennessee Raven jersey, courtesy of hometown hero, Ty Waters, that Uncle Phil had hung above the bottles of liquor were as dusty as the signed Watery Reflection tour posters. Uncle Phil was nothing if not a supporter of the famous people who littered Willow Creek's history, but someone needed to remind him to clean them.

Ryder was already seated at the bar with a beer in front of him and a second one waiting for me. I placed my new Stetson down, picked up the beer, and downed half of it in one go.

Ryder didn't say anything. He just waited.

"She gone?" I finally asked.

Ryder shrugged. "Haven't been by the house. Dad and I just got back into town. I showered and came here. Figured you'd need a stiff drink."

I finished the beer and waved to Ted, who'd worked for Uncle Phil for as long as I could remember. "I need another beer and a shot of tequila. Make it a double." I looked at Ryder. "Want one?"

He shook his head. "Nah, I think I'm on Maddox duty tonight."

I scoffed but didn't disagree. Instead, I downed the shot Ted slid my way and then pulled the beer closer, letting the liquor burn through me. It took another beer and two more shots before Ryder dared to ask me what I knew was weighing on his mind.

"So, she saw Mila?" Ryder asked.

I nodded, head spinning as the buzz of alcohol hit me.

"Did she ask about her?" he continued to prod.

I shook my head. "She thought I had a wife, and I didn't disabuse her of the notion."

Ryder chuckled. "You'd have to date to have a wife."

"Fuck you. Just because I don't take a woman home every weekend doesn't mean I don't date."

"I wouldn't call what either of us does dating."

I grimaced. He was right. We both had trust issues.

Before I could reply, he shot me his crooked grin and said, "It's more like wild screwing."

"I don't need to know the details of your sex life any more than I need to know about Sadie's."

Ryder's grin was wiped away. "I'm going to show up unannounced in Knoxville and knock heads."

"I think one of the ones coming with her on Monday is the boyfriend, so you won't have to drive to Knoxville. We can toss him into the lake and threaten his balls right here in Willow Creek."

Ryder nodded approvingly. "Bring your badge and your gun. We'll make sure we make him pee his pants."

It brought the first grin to my lips that I'd had all day.

"Shit," Ryder grunted. When I looked at him, he had his eyes trained on the door, and when I glanced in the same direction, my stomach lurched.

McKenna had entered the bar in a pink sweater dress that clung to her frame and put her body on display. She'd never been an overly curvy teen, but the material showed off every one of them and hinted at newfound muscles. The dress ended mid-thigh where a pair of thigh-high boots accentuated long legs. Her hair was down, curling around her shoulders and down her back, and I was suddenly filled with memories of how soft it had been tangled in my fingers while I plundered her mouth with mine.

Even sad and exhausted, she was more beautiful than I remembered, more beautiful than in my dreams, and it ripped open the scabbed wounds of loneliness I'd felt ever since losing her. I'd missed her—not just the woman I'd made love to for the first time, but my best friend.

"Fuck." The quiet word escaped me before I could hold it back.

She was drawing looks, whispers spiraling through the room. She looked exactly like who she was—Sybil's daughter. The dark shadows under her eyes were a little less visible than they had been the night before. I didn't know if it was rest or makeup that made her appear a little less harrowed.

The tiny spark deep inside of me, that had rejoiced on seeing her yesterday, flickered back to life before pure panic filled my chest.

When her eyes found me, there wasn't sadness there anymore. Now, there was anger. Anger that she didn't have a right to. I was the one who deserved to be angry. She'd left me. Pushed me away. Fucking gotten engaged to some other man when she'd known there was only one person she should ever belong to. That thought pushed the hurt I kept buried most days back into the light, but she didn't deserve for me to feel anything for her—anger, hurt, or love. I just needed her to leave so I could keep my daughter at my side.

She stormed across the bar, and if we'd been in a cartoon, there would have been smoke coming from her ears. She stopped in front of me, and for a second, I thought there were two of her. I hardly ever drank more than a single beer in a sitting these days. It wasn't good to have the sheriff drunk in public, so when I did drink, it hit me hard.

"What the hell is going on, Maddox?" she demanded.

My brows drew together in confusion as I glanced from my beer and the empty shot glass, to Ryder with his beer, and back to McKenna. Her lips were bow-shaped, and I remembered, as if it was just yesterday, how they tasted when I'd kissed her. Like devouring MoonPies.

"I'm having a few beers, that's what's going on." I was pretty sure my words were slurred, and I hated that she was seeing me this way. Slightly out of control.

"You owe me an explanation," she said, hands going to her hips.

On the job, I was cool and collected. I rarely let anyone or anything rattle me, but drunk and faced with the idea of losing my daughter all because of the one woman I'd never gotten over, I couldn't keep the fury that flew out of me. "I owe *you* an explanation? I don't think I owe you shit. You made it clear you wanted nothing to do with me. Your fiancé's feelings were way more important than mine."

"Really? You kept her from me out of spite? Revenge? That's what this is?"

My heart fell as her words registered in my inebriated brain. Fuck. She knew. How the hell did she know? The full-fledged panic returned, squashing away any flicker of relief at seeing her.

"Who told you?" I demanded. "You can't know. You can't. She'll tell him. She'll…" I swayed on the stool, my chest tightening until I couldn't breathe. Ryder propped me up.

McKenna's anger turned into wary confusion. "What are you talking about?"

"Go away, McKenna. Go back to your dreamy life, and your dreamy fiancé, and your medical career. Leave us alone. We don't need you. We don't want you," I stormed. "You'll ruin everything."

Behind her confusion, hurt piled in before she locked it away, and I couldn't help feeling a bit remorseful because her mama used to say McKenna had ruined her life. And yet, it was also the truth for me. McKenna had ruined me for other women. She'd ruined me for love. But she'd also brought me the biggest gift. She'd brought me Mila.

All those thoughts muddled together in my hazy brain, making it hard to think clearly. I shook my head, trying to shake off the cloud of alcohol.

"I think you should leave." It was Ryder who said the words to McKenna because I was still full of panic, but it eased my heart that my brother was glowering at her, protecting me. "Being here isn't going to help."

"Nice to see you, too, Ryder," McKenna said, her voice full of sarcasm. "And I'm not going anywhere until I hear the truth. Until I know exactly why my sister is with Maddox, and why the hell no one contacted me."

"I did call you!" I growled. "You hung up on me and then changed your number to make sure I couldn't call you again."

She had the decency to look chagrinned, cheeks flushing, but then she crossed her arms over her chest, tipped her chin up in defiance, and said, "I told you not to call me as Maddox, my ex-boyfriend, but not as the sheriff who had my sister."

"I didn't know for sure she was your sister. Not right away. Not for weeks."

"Please. All you have to do is look at her and know."

"She was one, McKenna. She didn't look like anything but a malnourished baby who'd been living in grime and squalor."

It was as if I'd hit her. She took a step back.

"Do you really want to do this here?" Ryder asked quietly at my back. "Now? Drunk? Maybe you should sober up and have this conversation in private?"

"You don't get to have it both ways, McKenna," I said, ignoring my brother's warning. "You're either here, or you're there. You get your perfect doctor dream world, or you deal with the remnants of your old life, and I know what you'll choose every single time. It will never be this." I waved my hand around the bar, but I meant the town…me.

"She's my family," McKenna said, but it was breathy, as if she didn't know how that word could ever apply to her. The only family who'd ever really wanted her, she'd tossed aside.

I scoffed. "What would you have done with her? Hauled her to class with you? How could you have taken care of her while working sixteen hours a day at some hospital? You would've had to give up your perfect life."

"You had no right to make that choice for me!" she shot back.

My lungs burned, and my stomach was so knotted I thought I might toss the alcohol I'd drunk. By the time we'd finally sorted out the truth about Sybil, and the prosecution had pressed charges, I'd already fallen in love with my daughter.

"Who would she have had if she'd been with you?" I demanded. "Some random daycare provider? People in and out of her life? Here, she has people who care about me and my daughter and surround us with love—who give us what we need. You wouldn't know the first thing about giving her any of that."

It was cruel, but I just needed her to go. I needed her to scurry back to her real life and leave me and Mila alone. McKenna's face shut down, becoming a blank slate like I'd seen her do hundreds of times when her mama was yelling obscenities at her.

"I'm not going anywhere, Maddox Parker Hatley. Not yet. Not until I figure out how the hell you got custody of my sister without the state ever contacting me. Where the hell is Sybil? Why would she even give you custody?"

"She would have given her to anybody but you," I said and hated the sharply inhaled breath she took that proved my barb had landed home. Even though it was the truth, I regretted stabbing at her one more time.

McKenna stepped closer to me, pushing a finger into my chest, and even though it had been years, and she was touching me in anger, I still felt the electricity zap through me at her touch. Awareness of every inch of her made my body lean forward, as if we were going to embrace instead of throttle each other.

"You've let your role as sheriff go to your head, Maddox," she all but growled. "You don't get to dictate everyone else's life for them."

"But I do get to dictate my daughter's, and you can't be a part of hers."

"Mads," Ryder said gently, a warning in his tone that I was too drunk and too agitated to hear.

"We'll see about that," McKenna said, twirling on her heel and storming toward the door.

When she left, there was a low whistle from the table behind us, and someone whispered, "That McKenna sure grew up to be a firecracker."

My heart was on fire, as if she'd thrown the cracker directly at me, fear brushing through me anew. I had all the right paperwork, so I wasn't worried McKenna could take

Mila from me. It was Sybil's threats about the father that worried me.

I was about seventy percent sure Mila's father was one of the West Gears because those were the only people I'd ever seen Sybil with. I didn't think the father was McKenna's dad, Trap, who'd been the head of the motorcycle club for years. He'd washed his hands of Sybil after he'd found out about the physical abuse she'd dealt McKenna. What I did know was that if Mila's father was a Gears member, he would absolutely rejoice in trying to take my daughter from me. They hated me with a vengeance because of the dents I'd been putting in their business.

I slid off the stool, reaching for my hat and having to stabilize myself using the bar. "I gotta go," I said.

Ryder stood up next to me, throwing cash down.

He followed me out, and the cool wind ripped through me just as the rain started. It was icy and bitter, like the cold fingers wrapping themselves around my heart. Dread and fear and anger at myself for letting McKenna rile me up, for being cruel when I prided myself on being anything but.

Ryder's stride matched mine, our hats ducked, rain dripping off the brims as we made our way to my house. I was suddenly glad Mila wasn't home, because I didn't want her to see me this way. Drunk. Torn. Scared.

I fumbled with the lock before letting us in. We stripped our coats and hats and boots, leaving them in the hall as I headed into my study. I opened my safe, took out the paperwork that said Mila was mine, and sat, elbows on the desk, head in my hands, reading through it for what felt like the hundredth time.

Ryder leaned against the desk and put a hand on my shoulder. "Mads, you're stressing over nothing. She's yours. No one is going to take her from you, but…"

My head whipped up. "But what?"

"Maybe you should tell McKenna the whole messed-up story. You know it about kills me to say this, but Mila has a right to know her sister."

"No," I grunted out. "She can't waltz in here, make Mila love her, and then abandon her."

Even the thought made my chest burn.

Ryder rubbed his unshaven jaw. It looked almost as thick as mine did, as if we'd both given up the battle with our facial hair.

"You're the one who is always telling me that what happened with you and McKenna is totally different than what happened with me and Ravyn," Ryder said.

"This isn't about me!" I barked out, shooting daggers at him with my eyes.

"Isn't it?" he said quietly. "If you keep Mila from knowing her now, and she asks about her later, what are you going to tell her? How will Mila feel, knowing you kept her sister from her? Just because you let them get to know each other doesn't mean you have to let her back into *your* heart. Fuck that. You have every right to keep your heart to yourself." Then, he got up and headed for the door. "Just think about it," he tossed back as he left.

I put the paperwork back into the safe and found my feet journeying to Mila's room. The nightlights were on, sending their typical rainbow of color across the walls and ceiling, but it was empty of the person I loved more than anyone in this world. The thought of it being empty permanently, or even semi-regularly if I had to share her with someone, shredded my insides. I lay down on her bed, looking up at the ceiling. Her pillow smelled like her berry shampoo.

Damn Ryder for making sense. I knew it killed him almost as much as it did me to think about McKenna invading our lives. But what would Mila say in a few years if she found out? Was my determination to force McKenna away really about me feeling abandoned rather than what was right for my daughter? What would really happen if I let her into Mila's life?

Ryder was right. Letting them get to know each other didn't mean I had to let McK back into my heart. My subconscious laughed at me because I wasn't sure she'd ever left it. But the girl who remained tucked in my memories, embedded in my soul, was just a mirage. Someone who didn't exist anymore. A teenager who'd faced the abuse of a drunken mother with so much bravery it seemed impossible. A girl who'd laughed and teased and challenged me. Dared me. Pushed me out of my comfort zone.

McKenna was on the back of Shadowfax, the dapple gray stallion she'd ridden since Dad had taught her to ride. Her hair flowed out behind her as the two of them leaped across the fast-moving river, swollen with the heavy winter rains. The day was cold, and there were several inches of snow on the ground, making it hard to see what was beneath it. I'd told her not to jump, but she'd been determined to reach the hollow and its tangle of cavern-like roots from the old oaks on the hill above it as quick as possible.

When they landed gracefully on the other side, she looked back at me with a smile that carved its way into every vein and molecule of my soul.

"Come on, Maddox. Don't chicken out on me now."

I patted Arod, the dark bay I always rode. "What do you think, fella? Are we going to take the chance?"

McKenna pulled Shadowfax to a halt. "Mads...come on...the hollow is calling us. It'll all be melted by the time we come back."

I turned Arod around. We trotted back several yards before I bent low over his shoulders and sent him racing toward the creek. The cold wind bit into my hands and face as we increased our speed, and he didn't even hesitate as I urged him over the rushing water. We landed on the other side not quite as gracefully as McK and Shadowfax, but Arod found his footing again and headed in their direction.

When I drew near her, I pulled on Shadowfax's reins until the horses were so close I could lean into McKenna's space. "You can't take risks like that, McK. If something happened to you…"

And then I was kissing her, hot and fast and heavy like we'd started doing since that day I'd taken her from her mama's house and not allowed her to go back. I groaned when she pulled back, and I felt almost despondent when I saw the smile had disappeared from her face.

She pulled a jar from her saddle bag.

"I need to do this today. I need to bury this so the bad memories won't follow me to California."

I hadn't known exactly what was in the mason jar other than the fact they were little strips of paper she'd been working on for days. It lodged a knot in my chest when I realized she was writing down her darkest memories.

I was trying hard to not let this—a day filled with thoughts of her leaving—to be one of mine.

Because it should have been a sweet memory. The sunlight hitting the snow made the ice crystals glisten and sparkle and was almost as beautiful as her twinkling eyes. Her cheeks were bright pink from the wind and exertion…and maybe my kisses. But instead of being a moment I wanted to hold on to, it was tainted by the knowledge that she was leaving…that she'd be gone in a few months, following her dreams…and I couldn't help the black hole it carved in me.

"Come on, broody boy. Let's go." She pushed away from me, sending Shadowfax into a trot that kicked up the white powder on the ground. And all I could do was follow her. Follow her and wish that I had it in me to follow her farther…all the way to California. But just the thought of *leaving my family when they needed me, of leaving Tennessee and the town I loved, made my stomach twist. I wanted both. I wanted to keep her and my home.*

She wanted to escape, and sometimes, I knew she meant escaping me as well, because, just like me in this moment, her good memories of me were tangled with the dark cloud that was her mama.

McKenna may have buried her worst memories that day and escaped to a brand-new world with dreams and a fiancé and safety, but now Sybil had placed the dark cloud over my head. It had been hovering there for too long. I needed to excise it just as McKenna had tried to do with strips of paper. I needed to call Sybil's bluff because I was fifty percent sure she didn't know who the father was.

But the risk…God. What if I took the risk and the worst happened? I'd have to run. I'd give up the law, my family, everything, to keep Mila with me.

Chapter Thirteen

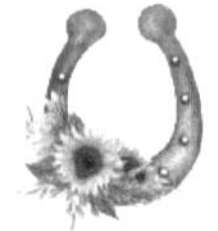

McKenna

FIRE AWAY

Performed by Chris Stapleton

Anger and hurt filled me as I drove back toward the ranch. The rain started coming down in fierce streaks that hit the windshield with a thud that spoke of sleet and hail. My anger took a back seat to nervousness. I'd never had to drive in the snow in California because I was never in the mountains, and as a teen in Tennessee, I'd never had a car. I'd walked to school, and once Maddox had gotten his license, I'd always ridden with him.

I slowed down to an almost crawl and soon had a line of cars behind me—people who were used to the Tennessee weather. Relief filled me when the gates of the ranch appeared. I pulled up and realized I didn't know how to get in. I buzzed the intercom box tucked into one of the pillars, and it was Eva's voice that responded.

"Hey, it's McKenna. Is it still okay for me to crash here for another night?" I sure hoped so because I had a bag of stuff in the apartment. After I'd run out of the farmhouse this morning, I'd showered, changed, and then headed into town and spent hours tracking down Maddox.

He hadn't been at the sheriff's station, and my fury had grown to epic proportions when the deputy there wouldn't tell me where he'd gone. I'd driven by his house and then made the mistake of driving by the bar. That had sent me spiraling when the duplex I'd lived in with Mama came into sight. I'd sat parked across from it for a long time, reliving horrible memories I'd thought I'd buried in a snowy field. Memories my therapist in Davis had tried to help me lay to rest even more.

While I'd sat there, I'd looked at every scar on my body, remembering how I'd gotten each and every one, remembering the nauseating fear I'd felt every time she'd lost control, wondering if that was the time I was going to die. Because of my childhood, I'd sworn I wouldn't be the type of doctor who turned a blind eye. I would absolutely report every case that came in front of me.

And doing so had ended my career and sent more terrifying threats my way.

But there was no way I'd stand by while anyone suffered like I had, especially not my own sister. The thought of Mama having another baby made me want to throw up. I would never have let Mila grow up as I had. If I'd been contacted, I would have done anything to keep her safe. But I hadn't been given that chance, and that filled me with waves of mixed emotions. Gratitude and frustration and fury.

"Of course you can stay," Eva said, drawing me back to the dark and the sleet and away from dark thoughts that had chased me all day. "I'll buzz you in, and I'll meet you at the apartment to give you a key card so you can come and go."

"Thank you so much," I said, meaning it.

I drove up the lane, parked at the side of the barn as I had the night before, and raced up the stairs to the apartment as icy drops poured over me. I was drenched by the time I got inside. I hadn't worn a coat when I'd left, and now the sweater dress was dragging down with the weight of the water. I shed my drenched boots at the door and headed to the bedroom. I rifled through my bag, replacing the dress with a pair of flannel pajama bottoms and a long-sleeved T-shirt.

I'd just wiped the makeup from my face when a knock sounded. I opened it to see Eva covered in rain gear. She stepped through, dripping onto the tiled entry.

She handed me a plastic card. "This will get you in and out as you need, but are you really only staying one more night?"

I looked down and away. My feelings were jumbled. I wanted to get to know my sister. I wanted to know why she was with Maddox, and I truly didn't want to return to the mess of things in California. Dr. Gregory's threats hung over me, twisting my stomach in a way that hadn't happened since Mama had wielded her power over me.

"I don't know."

"Ryder texted me about what happened at the bar. I'm sorry Maddox said such hurtful things. I'm sure it was just the alcohol talking. He rarely drinks these days, maybe a beer now and then. He's devoted his entire life to serving others, but you…you personify his biggest fear…losing her."

I went up and down on my toes, tugging at my hair. Guilt and hurt flew through me in equal measure, remembering his face and his words. I'd let that damn demon—hope—in, and it had stabbed me again.

"I get him hating me," I finally breathed out. "I understand that, but to deny Mila her family…"

I shook my head, trying to shake away the emotions.

"There's more to the story than what he told you tonight, McKenna," Eva said. "I think, when he's sober and in his right mind, he'll tell you."

Silence settled down. It was Eva who broke it.

"Mila was right. You should stay for Thanksgiving. Unfortunately, we've got a crowd of Sadie's friends coming with her from UTK on Monday, and the cabins are a disaster with the renovations. But if I can get Maddox's head out of his ass, he has a guest room. It would allow you to spend some time with Mila."

Back to the house that I'd thought was Trap's? It meant not only being with Mila but with Maddox, and I was damn sure that wasn't a good idea for either of us. There was too much hurt laying between us now. Mine. His. Things we'd both done wrong.

What would I have done if he'd continued to come to California before I'd ever met Kerry? If he'd shown up at my dorm room or my apartment? Would I have been able to close the door in his face? I didn't think so, but he hadn't come. He'd chosen his life here just like I'd chosen my life there. He was as responsible for us drifting apart as I was. By the time Kerry had come into my life, our texts and calls had become awkward and stilted with all the things we could no longer say to each other.

I'd always thought I was completely to blame for everything that laid between us. But he hadn't ever really fought for me…one call that had never become anything more. And to find out that he'd hidden this from me…Mila. It was so much larger than a wounded teen pushing away a boy. This was denying me the one thing he'd known I'd never had.

"I don't think that's going to work, Eva."

She reached over and patted my face with fingers wet from the rain. "Trust me. I know my children. I know what's best."

She whirled around toward the door, sending water in all directions before she looked back. "Did you eat? You look like you never eat."

"I did," I lied, meeting her gaze with a confidence I didn't feel. If I told her I hadn't had anything since the crepes, she'd insist on feeding me again, and I needed to be alone. I needed to process everything that had happened since I'd arrived in Willow Creek.

Her eyes narrowed as if she wasn't sure she believed me.

"Really, I'm good. Thank you."

She nodded. "Breakfast is at nine, but I'll warn you in advance—the entire gang will be here helping out with day two of the big pie-baking adventure."

She left, and I leaned on the door behind her, looking around the quiet space, heart hammering. My phone rang, and Sally's smiling face lit up the screen. God, I missed her already.

"Hey," I said as I answered.

"How's Tennessee?" she asked.

I lay down on the couch and spent the next half an hour explaining everything that had happened, only leaving out the threats from Dr. Gregory.

"Wow," Sally said. "When your life blows up, it really blows up."

I sighed, clutching a throw pillow to my chest. "Yep."

She was quiet for a moment before saying, "It's pretty amazing, though."

"What?" I scoffed.

"He took in your baby sister…made her his. He must have been, what, twenty-three or twenty-four? That isn't something small, McK. That's huge. He became a single dad just to raise her. I don't know many people who would take on that kind of responsibility at any age, let alone such a young one."

It twisted my heart, taking my anger and making it shrivel up to an almost nonexistent, coin-sized ball. Why had he done it? Maddox had to have been only a year or two out of college when he'd taken Mila in. I would have been in medical school, and my hours of class, studying, and work would have been off the charts. I couldn't even imagine what it would have been like to have been handed a one-year-old to care for. Maddox was right. I would have had to give up my dreams.

But they were dreams I was losing anyway. My medical career was over. Dr. Gregory would make sure of it.

"I should have had a say in it," I said softly.

"You're not wrong," she said.

"But I'm not right either?" I asked.

"I don't have a clue. I don't think you will either until you talk to him."

I wasn't sure I could handle talking to him again. Every time I'd seen him, I'd been assaulted with memories. Beautiful ones as well as painful ones. My insides were bruised, as if I'd been pummeled with a thousand clubs on tender organs that never saw the light of day.

"How's your dad?" I asked, changing the conversation.

She didn't try to stop me from switching gears, knowing I wouldn't come to any decisions without hours of quiet contemplation. We talked instead about her dad, their family in Avalyn Beach, and the stunning glass creations he made.

"You're always welcome here," Sally said softly. "If it gets to be too much, hop a plane, and come to us."

"I'm surprised the hospital let you off over the holiday week. We're always short-staffed."

She was quiet again, and something in the silence twisted my gut.

"Sal?"

"Well…about that… I quit."

"What?!" I sat up.

"Before you get your panties all bunched up, it wasn't just because of you. I mean, that's why I took a vacation to start with, because people were being utter assholes, and it would absolutely have sucked to go back. Because no matter what happens with the investigation, there will always be people who'll take his side, and I couldn't stand there and listen to their smack day in and day out. But that isn't what really pushed me to quit. When I got here, Dad didn't even remember me telling him I was coming, even though it had only been hours. And his bills hadn't been paid, even though he'd said he'd done it. I need to be here for him just like he was always there for me."

I hated that my first thought was about what this meant for me. Another loss. Another person I wouldn't have. I wasn't sure how many hits I could take in a row before I collapsed. But I knew this was the right thing for Sally and her dad. They'd been a team her whole life. She wouldn't want to be anywhere but with him when he needed her.

I also realized she was right about the hospital. Even if, by some miracle, everything went my way, my CPS report was proven right, and the hospital took me back, there'd be staff who would never believe me. They'd simply be pissed I'd ruined a family and a career.

"I'm so sorry, Sal. About it all. The hospital. Your dad. Everything."

"I've already got an application in at a hospital nearby. Nurses are still in high demand, so I think I have a good shot. It'll suck to be at the bottom of the seniority list again, but it'll be worth it to be with Dad when he needs me. I only have one regret."

"What's that?"

"You. I don't want you to think I'm abandoning you."

My throat bobbed, stomach clenching.

"I'd never think that," I said, even though I had.

"We're friends for life, McK. A change in job, cities, states…none of it can stop me from being there for you whenever you need me."

My eyes filled for what felt like the thousandth time in the last two days.

We hung up, and I clutched the throw pillow to my chest, wondering why life had to hurt so damn much.

♫ ♫ ♫

My growling stomach forced me out of bed and into the shower the next morning. If I'd stopped and gone grocery shopping, or if there'd been even a scrap of bread in the refrigerator or cabinets, I would have stayed hidden here for the rest of the day. But I also knew if I was still here at nine, Eva was going to insist I eat with them, and I wasn't sure I could handle more of the Hatleys and things I couldn't change. Instead, I decided to splurge by spending some of my tiny cash reserves on breakfast at Tillie's café.

The storm from the night before had left a very light dusting of snow on the ground that was already melting as I stepped out of the apartment. The skies were clear, and the air smelled like hay and rain and teenage memories as I picked my way around the puddles to my rental. It made me want to open the barn doors and see if the dappled gray I used to ride was still in a stall. It made me want to ride out to the hollow that Maddox and I had made our own years ago.

Instead, I drove out the gate, the card Eva had given me to get back in tucked into my wallet. The roads were dripping as the light snow melted, but in the light of day, they didn't seem nearly as terrifying as they had the night before.

The street outside Tillie's was packed with cars, and I belatedly remembered it was Sunday which was why the café was hopping. The brick building the restaurant was in was long and narrow, with ancient lead-paned windows from over a century ago and a sign painted in bright-gold letters. The words below the café's name read *Boots, Hats, and Dogs Welcome*.

The place had been in Tillie's family for generations, like many of the businesses in town. Growing up, Mama had worked at the restaurant off and on. Every time she was sober, Tillie had given her another chance. More than three. More than anybody should rightly be given. Whenever Mama had a job there, I'd actually had a full belly because Tillie fed me while I waited for Mama in a booth at the back.

The bell jingled as I opened the door, and a few heads turned, but most people were too focused on their conversations to pay much attention to a random tourist. The narrowness of the building meant there was only room for one long row of tucked-leather booths on the one side of the restaurant while a black-lacquered counter lined with cowhide barstools took up the other. An antique mirror with gold leaf designs curled around its edges filled one entire wall, reflecting its beginnings as an old saloon that had once competed with McFlannigan's.

A faded sign by the door still read *If there's a seat available, take it*, just like it had a decade ago. My eyes searched the room for a vacant spot that didn't seem to exist, and the longer I stood there, the quieter the restaurant got. I swallowed hard as more and more eyes settled on me. But it was only one pair that shook me to my core, sending curls of awareness across an entire room and dozens of bodies.

Maddox frowned from a stool near the back.

His eyes had shadows under them like mine, and he seemed paler than the day before. He was dressed in his sheriff's uniform, and it accentuated his broad shoulders, muscled chest, and narrow hips. His dark-caramel hair was damp with the ends curling toward his ears, and it made me think indecent thoughts of him in a shower. He was so beautiful it caught my breath and made me ache in places I'd almost thought were dead. Made me remember just how perfect it had felt to be coming apart with him embedded inside me.

We hadn't known what we were doing when we'd made love the first time, notches and grooves barely fitting. But we'd learned each other's bodies slowly and sweetly. He'd made it easy to not be embarrassed as we'd explored with tongues and fingers, finding out what felt good, what made the other gasp and moan.

Kerry had never taken the time to get to know my body in the same way. He'd been skilled but not overly affectionate. We'd found release and then returned to our separate corners of the bed to fall asleep alone. When I'd been with Maddox, we'd always fallen asleep tangled, until we woke with a start, knowing we had to go home to our separate rooms. Untangling ourselves had been painful. I'd never felt that way with Kerry, but I'd just assumed what we'd had was a grown-up kind of love versus teenage infatuation.

"McKenna Lloyd, you get your skinny butt over here and give me a hug," Tillie's voice rang through the diner as she emerged out of the swinging doors at the back.

She was dressed in a long tunic dress with a round collar embroidered with flowers. Her long, gray hair was tied in two low ponytails, and she had a wreath of flowers on her head. She looked like she'd stepped from the pages of a seventies fashion magazine and then aged forty years, even though she hardly looked a day older than the last time I'd seen her.

I took a couple of steps, and she almost floated across the terra-cotta-colored tile floor to meet me halfway. She wrapped me in a tight hug while I stiffened and awkwardly patted her back.

My eyes darted to Maddox again to see his face had turned into a dark scowl.

"How the hell you been, honey?" Tillie asked.

"Good," I said automatically, and she laughed.

"Really? Because you look like shit."

My lips twitched at the honesty she and Eva had in common. No one I knew in California would have dared to be so truthful.

Tillie looked around the restaurant, eyes settling on the only empty stool that was right next to Maddox where his cowboy hat was resting. It was clear from the tightness in his jaw he would not welcome me sitting there, but Tillie didn't seem to notice or care as she dragged me by the elbow to it.

"Move your hat, Sheriff."

He did so, reluctantly, placing it back on his head like many of the people in the restaurant. Tillie took the words on her door seriously.

"Sit, sit. Tell me what you want so I can get it started before I come back and give you the third degree about everything in your life."

"Um…" I looked around for a menu and then up at the specials board behind the counter. It looked like it hadn't changed in the decade I'd been gone. "Biscuits and gravy, please. Bacon crispy."

"Scrambled or fried eggs?"

"Scrambled, thanks."

"Nice to see some things never change." She winked, patted my hand, and headed toward the back, already hollering the order at Javier, who had been her fry cook for as long as I'd known her.

Maddox was squeezing his cup of coffee with such force it was lucky the mug didn't break, and his jaw looked as tight as his fist beneath the beard he'd grown. Even scowling, he was breathtaking. The beard was a good look on him, adding an aura of wisdom to his appearance that his eyes already screamed, adding another layer of sexiness that made me wonder what it would feel like on my skin.

He did his best to ignore me, but it did nothing but continue to build the tension in the air between us. My conversations with Eva and Sally had tempered my emotions from yesterday, and I didn't know if I should apologize for my anger or beg to spend time with Mila.

Tillie came swirling out and put down a cup of coffee in front of me, then she put one hand on Maddox's shoulder and another on mine. "M&M… Gosh dang, it's good to see the two of you sitting here next to each other again."

My stomach clenched at the nickname. Once upon a time, I'd reveled in it. The idea of being tied so closely to the bright light that was Maddox. To the Hatleys.

Maddox rose suddenly, and Tillie's hand fell. "I gotta go, Tillie, hold the breakfast."

"Maddox Hatley, you sit back down and wait for the meal you ordered."

"I forgot I need to stop by Willy's this morning to help him look for his tools," Maddox said, stepping backward, but Tillie caught his arm and darted a gaze between me and him.

"So, the rumors are true. Y'all were at each other's throats last night?"

My cheeks heated. You'd think with the way gossip spread in Willow Creek, I would have been free of Mama much earlier than a week before my eighteenth birthday. You'd think the whole town would have come to my rescue. It just proved how good Mama and I had been at covering her tracks.

Maddox rubbed his jaw.

"You gonna apologize?" Tillie asked Maddox.

"Tillie," I said, desperately wanting to dive below the counter and stay there because I could feel everyone's eyes on us.

"Sit down before I call your mama," she said to Maddox.

"Jesus," he said before doing just that. "I'm not ten, Tillie."

"No, you're an elected official who should know better, so act like it."

She flounced away, heading for the antique cash register and the couple waiting to pay. When I turned back, risking a glance at Maddox as I took a sip of coffee, his eyes were hidden beneath the brim of his hat, but his jaw remained tight.

The stools were so close together that every time I moved, my elbow brushed his arm. It made my skin tingle, sending spirals of electricity through me as if I'd used the crash cart on myself. My breath was shallow and unsteady, and I had to concentrate to get it back in order.

"You're leaving today?" he asked, his voice bland, and I couldn't tell if it was a command or a question, and the knowledge it might be a bit of both stopped the apology I'd wanted to give before I could utter it.

"No. I told you, I want the truth. I want to get to know her," I said, forcing myself to stay calm and using my very best doctor voice—the one that stated the facts but still tried to gentle the sting of the words.

He whirled toward me on the stool, feet and legs tangling with mine and causing more heat and energy to drift through me. My body flushed from head to toe as memories assaulted me of us twined like this without clothes in the back of his Bronco. The best kind of memories that I'd carefully packed away and refused to open for nearly ten years. And now they were pouring from me, causing the ugly demon hope to try and pop back up.

I couldn't help wanting to know if he felt it, too. Did his skin ripple with the pulse and draw that seemed to be yanking us together? Did his belly have the same low ache of desire I had in mine? Was he as confused as I was by having these feelings atop the anger and hurt time had laid between us?

Chapter Fourteen

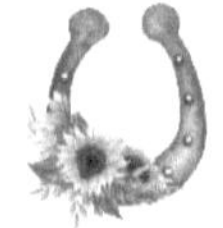

Maddox

EVEN IF I WANTED TO

Performed by Jason Aldean

Even after Ryder had talked me down last night, McKenna's forceful denial did nothing but spark panic, sending it rushing through my veins. I needed her to leave before the teeny voice at the back of my brain screaming how glad I was to see her, how having McKenna in Willow Creek was like a dream come true, got the better of me. Because what would the dream cost me?

She lifted her chin defiantly, as if my lack of response was a challenge.

I'd somehow forgotten how damn stubborn she was. As a teen, I'd begged and pleaded for her to report her mama, just walk out of the duplex and never go back. I'd promised her she'd have a place to stay with me and my family, but she'd refused. Sybil had done a number on her head, instilling not only fear but also making McKenna feel like she was a burden. McK had never wanted to bring the heavy weight of her existence onto my family.

My feet and legs were tangled with hers on the narrow stools, and the touch coasted through me like a lit fuse, growing and racing along the wick. Every nerve ending came alive, and it pissed me off almost as much as her showing up in Willow Creek had, because I didn't want my damn body to remember what it felt like to be wrapped in her embrace. I didn't want McKenna to be the only one who I'd ever felt this overwhelming sense of desire for. It was so strong that, even now, hurt and panicked and needing her to leave, I still wanted to push my lips against hers and remind her just how much we'd always fit.

"It's selfish," I grunted out, tipping my hat back so I could meet her eyes with mine from under its brim.

"Excuse me?" she demanded as her eyes flashed with annoyance.

"Wanting to get to know her. It's selfish," I said, keeping my voice low so our conversation wouldn't be broadcast on the gossip line again.

"Exactly how is it selfish? I'm simply asking to get to know my sister."

How could she not see what the simple request would do to Mila? How knowing McKenna, loving McKenna, and then losing her would destroy her tiny little heart? I wouldn't let anyone hurt my daughter, especially not McKenna, who was brutally good at it.

"It's selfish," I explained, trying to hold back the protective growl I felt growing inside me. "Because it's all about you and has nothing to do with her. We both know that as soon as you've done whatever the hell you're here to do, you'll go back to California. You'll always choose what you want over what's best for her. I'm not going to let you fly in and out of her life, taking pieces of her whenever you leave. She's my daughter, and I damn well have the right to protect her from everything that will hurt her, including you."

She looked away, toes bouncing on the footrest, finger rubbing along a seam in the lacquered countertop, before she looked up at me with eyes so sad and aching it stole my breath. She said quietly, "There may be nothing left for me in California."

My heart stuttered to a stop.

I wasn't sure I could handle even the slightest twinge of hope that McKenna was here for good. My brain and body spiraled, longing and wishes I'd tried to bury unfurling but were cut short by a calm coming over her face and words contradicting her last ones.

"That was stupid. I'm sure I'll be back. I have a little under a year left on my residency." The way she talked was as if she was trying to convince herself as much as me. It pissed me off. The ridiculous flare of hope I'd felt. The fucking stupid desire I still felt. The fear I had for me and Mila and the family I'd built.

I stood abruptly, and it made her tip on the stool because our legs had been tangled. She caught herself on the counter, looking up at me with shock.

"Then go. Go now before you do what you're good at and hurt the people who actually care about you."

I didn't wait for a response. I didn't wait for Tillie to come back with my breakfast and another warning. I just headed for the door, ignoring the looks and the "Morning, Sheriff" greetings tossed my way.

The bell jangled as I slammed the door behind me. I looked up at the sky, inhaling the brittle, cold air that had settled down after the storm. In my head and heart, the storm was still raging.

"You're not applying to any schools in Tennessee?" Shock and waves of fear hit me as I looked up from the laptop where McKenna was clicking away at the form the counselor had given us. It was the fall of our junior year, and we were supposed to list the top three schools we hoped to get into and another three we thought were a sure thing.

"What would be the point?" she asked.

My heart cracked a little.

I pulled her hands from the computer, turning her to face me. We were working on my bed with the bedroom door open as Mama had demanded for as long as I could remember in the rare moments when we got to have McK at the ranch. It was in these fleeting hours with her that my dad had taught her to ride, I'd taught her to fish, Mama had taught her to cook, and Ryder had taught her how to rib a sibling perfectly. And now that I had my license and was close to getting the car I'd saved up for, I'd been hoping to escape them all so we could teach each other a few more things.

"Mck…I don't want…I can't imagine…" I'd never even fucking kissed her. I'd waited too long. Ryder was right. He'd harassed me about McKenna for at least a year now. "Shit or get off the pot," he'd said.

At first, I'd been terrified that if I tried to change our friendship into something more, and she didn't feel the same way I did, it would ruin what we had. And then, I'd wanted to make it perfect when it did happen. At the lake, on our own, with just us and the stars. But now, if I let her leave without kissing her…without ever telling her how much I wanted her to stay, it might end in something even more frightening than her rejecting me. It might end with McKenna disappearing from my life altogether. That thought made the crack in my heart almost splinter completely, pain shooting through me.

"Mads?" she said with a frown, her breath becoming unsteady as she looked down at my hands holding hers.

"I get why you want to leave Willow Creek. I get how bad your life is with your mama, but there are people here who care about you. If you go clear across the country, who will you have? If you're in Knoxville or Nashville, I could get to you in a couple of hours."

She squeezed my hand gently, shaking her head. "Honestly, Mads, you have no clue how bad it is."

"Because you won't tell me."

"*Because if I do, it makes it more real. This way, I can pretend she didn't dump her cigarette ashes onto the only meal I'd had at home in three days, or that she didn't shred the sweater your mama gave me for my birthday.*"

She gulped and closed her mouth into a straight, tight line, as if she'd hated telling me any of it. While all I hated was her mama and the fact every time McKenna walked through the door of a home that should have been a safe haven, it was like walking into a torture chamber. She pulled her hands away.

"*I'm not sure California is even far enough...*"

"*I wouldn't let her hurt you. If you came and stayed with us, she couldn't hurt you anymore. Don't go back tonight, McK. You don't need to. Do you think she'd even care where you were?*"

"*She'd care because she wants me to be miserable. She'd come and find me and drag me back.*"

"*My parents wouldn't let her.*"

She closed her eyes, fighting emotions like she always did. I was the only one she showed them to, and even then, it was rare. If she let Sybil see the fear, it only egged her mama on.

"*I can't...I don't want you and your family to start hating me too.*"

"*They'd never! I'd never.*"

"*They would. She'd call the cops on them. On me. And besides, all I'd be here is another burden. Another mouth to feed. Another drain on their bank account.*"

The ranch had had a couple of bad years. Things were tight, and McKenna knew it, but Dad was working to get some new contracts. He was turning it around, and Mama had started selling her pies. We were going to be okay, but it was also why my list of schools included only the local JC. I was needed here, not at a four-year university, increasing our debt.

"That's your mama's demented thinking, McK," I said. "Don't give in to it."

She got up off the bed, picking up her books. She didn't have a backpack. She carried everything by hand, leaving her things at school or hidden in Uncle Phil's shed because if her mama saw them, she'd ruin them.

"I can't stay in Tennessee, Maddox. But I get why you need to."

Even if my parents weren't struggling, I'd still want to be here. I didn't want to work at the ranch forever, but I also had no desire to live thousands of miles from the family I loved, from the hills and valleys and creeks of my childhood. But I'd do it for McKenna. If it meant we could be together, I'd follow her to California after Dad got the ranch back on its feet.

Except, by the time my parents had started to turn things around, McKenna had asked me not to come. She'd asked me to stay in Tennessee because it was too hard to see me and then have me leave. Really, I thought she'd needed to forget everything about her childhood, including me.

The bitter taste of heartache and disappointment filled my mouth.

I looked back in the window of the café, and I saw McKenna, her golden hair twirling around her finger as Tillie leaned on the counter next to her. They were both smiling, and McKenna's was heartstoppingly beautiful, even when it was fake like it was now. I wondered if she ever smiled her real one anymore, if her fiancé got to see the one that crinkled the corners of her eyes and stretched her cheeks until they almost disappeared into her ears.

I turned and headed down the sidewalk.

I couldn't afford to feel sorry for her or wonder what about her life had momentarily made her think she couldn't go back to California. I couldn't do anything but wish she'd leave as quickly as her mama would.

Chapter Fifteen

McKenna

After breakfast at the café, I'd headed to the grocery store for a few supplies and then back to the ranch because I didn't know where else to go. I was still feeling bruised from memories I'd stirred up the day before in my search for Maddox around town—just like every encounter with Maddox himself had left me feeling. But when I got back into the apartment, it felt stifling. I didn't even have my *Buffy* DVDs to keep me from dwelling on the million things in my life I could have done differently.

I needed escape. I needed air. The sunshine outside the windows was deceptive, making the day look warm when I knew it was still frigid and damp. But my heart suddenly tugged at the thought of exploring the fields and hollows that had once felt like a saving grace to me.

I put on the only pair of tennis shoes I'd brought with me and pulled on a jacket more than warm enough for California's winters but would barely stand up to the winters in Willow Creek. Then, I headed out, walking a path I used to know like the back of my hand.

Once upon a time, I'd crossed the fields on horseback with Maddox at my side. Sweet moments of escape when

Mama was too drunk to realize I'd asked to leave or when she couldn't be found to ask. Moments that lasted until she rang the Hatley home and demanded I be returned to her.

I pushed Mama from my mind and just let myself take in the wet fields, endless skies, and the mix of oak, willow, and magnolia trees sprouting up everywhere as if they were weeds. I crossed the back pasture, finding the creek bubbling slowly before the winter rains got a chance to turn it into a rushing river. Come January, I wouldn't be able to make my way across it without the use of a horse to jump it.

I was out of breath by the time I reached the hidden hollow Maddox and I had called our own. It had been made when part of the hill had slid away, baring the roots of the ancient oak trees surrounding the depression on three sides and making them look like a tangled warren of caves. As kids, we'd crawled over and through the roots, hiding in the dark recesses that had felt strangely safe. As if the trees' giant-sized fingers and hands were holding us in an embrace. The quiet in the cool, damp spaces was only broken by the creek drifting along the last side of the hollow as a natural barrier.

In the early days, we'd played cops and robbers and pirates. As we'd gotten older, we'd brought picnic lunches and pretended to fish while talking about our futures—my dream of being a doctor and his dream of being in law enforcement.

Aching nostalgia filled my chest.

I sat on one of the old roots, closed my eyes, and lifted my face to the sun as it attempted to warm the earth and chase away the vestiges of the storm. The snow was all gone, but the trees and grass were still dripping, and the rocks were still slick. Every inhale brought the dampness of the earth into my lungs.

My phone buzzed, and when I reached inside to pull it out, dread filled me as yet another unknown number popped up. A new one seemed to arrive almost as quickly as I blocked the last.

 1-530-555-8215: You little bitch. Where are you? Come back and fix this.

At the hospital, layered in my white coat with my stethoscope, I'd finally felt like I was something. Someone. An actual valid human being. One who could make a difference. One who wasn't a burden but who could lighten other people's loads by healing their loved ones.

Now, I might have to start over completely—as nothing again.

I tightened my jaw and forced back the tears.

I didn't want to cry. Mama may have been wrong about a lot of things, but she'd been right when she said tears wouldn't change anything. They wouldn't miraculously make everything better.

I turned to look deeper into the web of roots, wondering if my jar was still there. The last year, before I'd left for college, I'd read an article about how if you wrote all your nightmares down and then buried them, they'd leave you. So, I'd done just that. Now, I searched between the snarled wood and found the place where I'd buried it. I didn't have anything to dig it up with, and I didn't really want to. It was better to keep those nightmares in the ground. Instead, I put my hand on the dirt and whispered to my teenage self, "We almost made it, kid."

Then, I turned and headed back the way I'd come.

I was wet and cold by the time I got back to the apartment. I cleaned up, put on a warm sweater and jeans, and was staring at the little fridge, eyeing the food I'd bought, when the phone on the wall rang. The bright-yellow phone with its push buttons brought a smile to my lips. When was the last time I'd seen a landline?

I wasn't sure I should answer it because it wasn't my home, but when it stopped and then started again, I finally picked it up.

"Hello?"

"McKenna! It's Eva."

"Hey."

"So…sweetheart, we have a little problem."

Of course there was. I wanted to laugh at the ridiculousness of my life, but I couldn't. I really was the bad omen Mama had called me.

"Come up to the house for linner, and we'll talk."

I chuckled, memories assaulting me of the first time I'd heard Maddox's family talk about linner. A late lunch or early dinner that often occurred on the Hatley ranch on Sundays when the days were more relaxed, and everyone was determined to enjoy the last few hours of the weekend before it faded away.

"You don't need to feed me, Eva," I said.

"The entire gang is here. One more person won't make any difference. Besides, I'm used to cooking for a mess of people these days when the ranch is full-up," she insisted.

"Eva, the damn bacon is going to burn!" Brandon's deep voice boomed behind her, and my chest twisted with the same melancholy I'd felt out at the hollow. Maddox's dad had done more for me than my real dad ever had.

"Just turn it!" she yelled, but it was muffled by a hand she must have placed over the receiver. Then, she said back into the phone, "Did I mention there's bacon? If I remember right, I could always bribe you with bacon."

I chuckled because it was true. I'd never had bacon before I'd had it at the Hatleys', and I'd fallen in love with it. Now, even knowing as a doctor just how bad it was for me, I still ate it on almost everything.

"I'll be right up," I said.

"Good." And the line went dead.

I didn't give myself a chance to find a reason not to go. Instead, I let the call of the voices chattering away in the background while she'd talked lure me up to the house and away from pained thoughts and aching loneliness. When I neared the house, I saw Maddox's Bronco parked in the yard and almost backed out. Our talk at the café hadn't gone much better than the one at the bar the night before, but I deserved at least a conversation about Mila. I deserved the truth. And he deserved my apology.

Besides Maddox's Bronco, a mammoth pickup was parked as well as three other vehicles. The random cars all had UTK parking permits hanging in the windows, and my chest tightened because I thought Sadie and her friends weren't arriving until the next day. I'd thought I'd have one more night to figure out where to go, and now I knew what Eva had meant about a little problem.

When I knocked on the back door, someone hollered to come in, and when I did, the noise and smells assaulted me. Laughter and music blended together, almost to a fever pitch, while the scent of bacon and barbecue hung in the air. Yesterday, the enormous kitchen had felt empty, and today, it was bursting with people, some trailing into the living room.

Sitting on the counter, licking a wooden spoon covered in chocolate, Mila was all smiles as she chatted up several twenty-somethings who stood in front of her. As soon as her eyes landed on me, she screamed my name, "Miss McKenna!"

A hush settled down over the room as she jumped down from the counter and raced through bodies to get to me. She threw herself at my legs, and I barely had time to stabilize myself on the wall in order to keep us on our feet.

"You stayed!" she said, voice high with excitement. "I thought you'd left without saying goodbye, and I was sad, but now you're here!"

I cleared my throat, shoving aside the emotions clinging to it, and said, "I'm here. And remember, it's just McKenna. No miss."

Over the top of my sister's head, my eyes landed on Maddox, still in his uniform, looking as unfriendly and grumpy as he had when he'd left me at the café.

"Everyone be quiet!" Mila's little voice screamed, even though she hadn't needed to yell because everyone was still hushed. "This is McKenna. She was Daddy's best friend, and I think she'll be my new friend, too."

She dragged me into the room farther and started pointing. "That's Uncle Ryder, and you know Auntie Gemma. Do you know my papa? His real name is Brandon. And that's Auntie Sadie and her friends Misha, Terrance, Gia, Lexi, and Tal."

A sea of faces blurred in front of me, but Sadie's stood out. If I'd been surprised by Gemma's changes the day before, Sadie's were even more startling. She'd only been eleven when I'd left—still a child, really—and now she was a vivacious brunette with a pixie haircut, bright-blue eyes, and tan skin that practically glowed. One of the men Mila had pointed out had an arm thrown casually over her shoulders, but the look on his face as he watched her was one of awe, as if he'd found a winning lottery ticket.

Ryder was glowering at her friend just like he'd glowered at me last night at the bar. At least I didn't have to take it personally.

The person who stepped forward first to greet me was Brandon. Maddox's dad looked like an older version of Ryder—dark hair and tan leathery skin from spending most of his life outdoors. He had on a worn flannel shirt and equally worn jeans, but his face was twisted into a wide smile that was all Maddox.

He hugged me, squishing Mila between us. She giggled as I tried not to stiffen in his embrace.

"McK! It's damn good to see you, kid."

I wasn't a kid, but the word didn't bother me at all. Instead, it tugged at the inner parts of me that had felt alone for too long. The word was the same one I'd unconsciously used back at the hollow in just the way Brandon had always used it. He'd been a dad when I didn't know what it meant. I closed my eyes, heart hammering. Why had I left all of this behind? Why did I think I had to wash it all away to forget the pieces I didn't want to keep? I could have picked through the memories and people and kept the best of them. Couldn't I have?

"Linner is ready. Dish up and find a seat anywhere you want," Eva called out. "But after, I expect all hands on deck to help with the final pie assembly."

There was a mad rush to get to the plates stacked on the kitchen counter—a buffet line of sorts. I loved how informal this house was…had always been. Here, it was more important you had food and company than formal place cards and china settings. I wondered if that carried over into Eva's restaurant and if their guests felt the same sense of family when they came.

Kerry's family had loved formality, and for a brief moment, I'd thought I did, too. His life was a hundred-and-eighty-degree difference from my childhood, and while I'd savored the change, I now knew it had never fit me. Living in their life had felt like I was wearing a skin that wasn't mine, a costume I'd have to shed at some point. Except, Kerry had shed me before I'd been ready to give it up—another person who'd left me behind and easily forgotten me, even after we'd lived together for three years.

I tossed those thoughts aside because I hated wallowing, and it felt like all I'd done since being forced out of the hospital was wallow in things I couldn't change. I much preferred diving headfirst into studies, and tasks, and my patients than sitting around assessing my feelings. *You'll have to face it all at some point, McKenna. You can't push it behind a busy schedule forever*, my therapist's voice rang through my head.

I watched as the others dished up, fidgeting with the hair tie on my wrist, going up and down on my toes, a soothing motion I'd thought I'd abandoned, just like I'd thought I'd left all of them behind. Eva held out a plate in my direction, and I stepped forward to grab it. It placed me behind Maddox and in front of Eva in the dwindling line.

"We didn't expect Sadie and the gang until tomorrow, McKenna," she said loud enough for Maddox to hear. "You're welcome to stay, but we only have the couch here in the living room. Ryder says there's no way any of the cabins are inhabitable, but like I said yesterday, Maddox has a spare room that will work just fine."

"Mama," Maddox's head whipped around, looking from her to me and then grimacing.

"It's the right thing to do, Maddox Parker Hatley, and you know it," Eva said as if it was the end of the discussion.

"It's okay, Eva." I jumped in. "I'll figure something else out."

Mila twirled by, dancing over my foot and then landing next to her father. "Daddy, can I please have two more pieces of bacon?"

He looked down at her, and his expression changed from wary discomfort to adoration. Love. My heart stopped and then started again at a wild pace, the look peppering me with memories of him looking at me just that way.

"How many pieces have you already had?" he asked with a hint of humor.

She hopped from foot to foot. "Two plus three."

"I can add, Bug-a-Boo, so I know exactly how many that is. Why don't you wait until everyone has fixed a plate, and then if there's more, you can have some then."

"That's maybe, right?" she asked, and he nodded with an eye roll that turned into a smile.

Mila leaned toward me and whispered, "Daddy's maybes always mean yes."

Then, she ran off, calling for Ryder, who I had a feeling was as wrapped around her finger as Maddox was…as all of them were. She'd lived a life spoiled in the best possible way. The lump in my throat grew. If she'd come to live with me, she wouldn't have had any of this. She would have had a sister who was working a thousand hours to put food on the table and pay off college debt. A sister who might have turned bitter from giving up her dreams. Would I have ended up like my mom? Taking it out on her?

I shook my head. No way. Never.

I stepped in behind Maddox, reached into the dwindling pile of bacon, took two, and then placed them on Maddox's plate before he could move away.

"She can have mine," I said.

He froze, looking down at me with a frown. "You can't win her over with bacon."

"Be nice," Eva scolded him.

Maddox turned and headed for the living room.

"Ignore him. He's hungover and grumpy because he had to work on his normal day off," Eva said.

She nudged me toward the food, and I piled my plate with a barbecued burger and potato salad before wandering around, looking for a place to sit. The only empty spot was on the couch next to Maddox or the floor near the coffee table. I made my way to the floor. I'd sat there a million times when I was younger, and it brought back more nostalgia. Unfortunately, it also brought me closer to Maddox than was probably wise.

I tried to look everywhere but at him. I listened as one of Sadie's friends told Brandon about how she'd hustled several rough characters while throwing darts at a bar in Knoxville. Ryder was talking to the guy who'd had his arm on Sadie, still glowering. Gemma and Eva were talking pies. The entire atmosphere was relaxed and easy. The way it had always been. I'd forgotten so much…and now all I wanted to do was absorb it all like a sponge and hope the easiness rubbed off on me and the chaos of my life.

Chapter Sixteen

Maddox

LOVE THIS PAIN

Performed by Lady A

McKenna watched everyone with an expression of wonder on her face. It wasn't much different from the look Mila had whenever she watched her favorite shows or experienced something new. My daughter was curious and adventurous and found everything about life fascinating.

Glancing from McKenna to Mila, sitting on Mama's lap, and then back, it was impossible not to see they were related. I'd always thought Mila just had McKenna's and Sybil's hair, eyebrows, and eyes, but there was something about the curve of their cheeks and the turned-up tips of their noses that were the same as well. Mila's face was more oval, and her hair was a wild bushel of curls versus McKenna's gentle waves, but anyone could tell they shared DNA.

Mama had read me the riot act when I'd arrived this afternoon, having heard all about my drunken words to McKenna and the standoff at Tillie's. She'd also insisted the best thing for all of us was to allow McKenna to stay with Mila and me while Sadie's friends took over the apartment above the barn and the guest rooms at the farmhouse.

"She deserves to know her sister no matter what happened between the two of you in the past. I've always said that," she'd told me. I'd started to interrupt, and she'd stopped me. "You know I'm right, Maddox. You've given Sybil Lloyd too much power over your life for too long. Don't let her destroy one more thing of McKenna's."

It had hit me in the gut. Had that been Sybil's intention all along? Another way to manipulate the daughter who'd finally escaped her grasp? Abuse, physical or mental, was all about control and power, and I was giving Sybil too much of it, letting her get off on it, letting her believe she could still pull strings in both her daughters' lives.

But Mama's demand for me to open my home to McKenna flashed stupid ideas in my head. Of us tangled in ways that wouldn't happen. Every time I saw her, the part of my brain freaking out became smaller, and the part of my brain jumping for joy became bigger.

I'd only seen her four times in the last three days, and I was ready to relent and give her what she wanted. What would happen if she was here for a week? Two weeks? Longer… My heart spasmed at the idea of McKenna being here for good.

I shut that rogue thought down.

My eyes landed on her for the hundredth time since she'd walked through the back door. The jeans she had on clung to her hips, and the olive-green sweater made her hazel eyes stand out. She looked as sexy as she had in the pink dress the night before but in a completely different way, as if she was ready for a day spent on the couch at home instead of out at the bar.

The decade she'd been gone had added a layer of mystery to her instead of simply aging her, making me want to know how each line had become a reality. Every tiny movement she made—placing the fork to her mouth, shifting her legs, tilting her head—called to me. My veins were straining toward her, aching for a touch. To reclaim her lips. To see if she would still gasp if I sucked the soft swell of her earlobe.

She turned and caught me staring, and I looked down, fighting a blush and a growing hard-on. I couldn't escape the frustration or surprise I felt at still desiring her after years of heartache. My head and my body were definitely on different planes.

After leaving Tillie's, I'd spent the afternoon at the station, recovering from a hangover and feeling regret for the words I'd sent her way, truthful or not. I'd called her selfish, striking out in fear. I knew enough about human behavior to identify my fight-or-flight instincts. I'd fought—with words instead of a fist, but I'd still fought.

I looked back up at her, cleared my throat, and said words I never thought I'd say to McKenna Lloyd. "I'm sorry." I inhaled sharply and then continued. "About last night and earlier. I was cruel…"

Her eyes softened. I remembered that look. It was the expression she'd held whenever she was trying to convince me she was right. It had never taken much for me to see her way. I would have done anything for her—jump over a snow-covered creek or off a bridge or out of a plane.

"I just want to understand what happened. I just want to know her," she said quietly. "I'm not… I won't…"

She faded off as if unsure of what she wouldn't do.

"She feels too much," I said gruffly, eyes finding Mila again as she danced around my dad. My lips twitched as he handed her his last piece of bacon. My girl would do anything for bacon, and I suddenly remembered, once upon a time, McKenna had been the same way. It launched a dart into my chest. "Mama says she's an empath. I didn't really get what it meant before she came into my life, but she'll take on all your emotions. She'll love you easily and without restraint, and then, when you leave, it will leave a mark like…" I faded off, not wanting to bring myself into this discussion. Like Ryder had said, it wasn't about me.

"Like the one I left on you," she finished for me.

Our eyes met, and I thought I saw regret in hers, but I couldn't afford that any more than I could afford for her to be in Willow Creek. If I knew she regretted pushing me away, it would cause the little flare of hope I'd had spark to life to grow, and that would end as badly for me as it would for my daughter.

I rubbed my hand over the beard I'd grown. I needed to decide soon whether to shave it or go all in. McKenna followed the movement of my hand, and her lips parted slightly, tongue darting out to lick her bottom lip, and it did nothing but make my body tighten more, made the desire to kiss her grow until I thought I might do it regardless of my daughter and family in the room. Regardless of the fact she'd just leave and butcher my heart along with Mila's.

"Why are you really here?" I asked, a tortured growl to my voice I wished I could take back.

She looked away but not before I saw fear flash across her face, raising my alarm bells to a new level.

"Are you in trouble?" I pushed.

Her shoulders went back, and her face became an unreadable mask. "It doesn't matter why, but I'm here now, and what I'd like to do is get to know her." She looked around at Sadie and her friends. "But I don't really have a place to stay, and I definitely don't have the money to try and book somewhere during Thanksgiving week, so you may get your wish. I may have no other choice but to leave."

Mila screeched, and my heart thudded, getting ready to run to her just as she collided with me and looked at McKenna with pained eyes. "Daddy, you can*not* let McKenna leave. She has, has, has to stay! It's important."

My breath disappeared from my body, and when I looked over at McKenna, her face had paled, and her eyes were wide. The room had quieted down, and everyone was staring at us even as they pretended not to. Mila didn't even know McKenna was her sister, and she was already feeling the ties that bound them together. Fuck.

The empty guest room at my house flashed before me as well as Mama's words about it being the right thing. If I invited her, I'd be surrounded by her scent, and her eyes, and her emotions. It was a disaster waiting to happen. Not just because of Sybil, but because of Mila…and me…

The memory that had haunted me the night before, the one of McKenna daring me to jump the creek so she could bury the shadows left by her childhood, swarmed me all over again. It was as if that teenage girl was daring me again, this time to be brave enough to throw off Sybil's darkness just as she had.

I cleared my throat.

"You already have a key. I kind of feel like you were meant to stay with us." My words surprised her, as if she'd never thought I'd agree, and part of me still wished I hadn't. My heart pounded a furious beat. It wasn't just me I was thrusting into an unknown snowbank. I was bringing Mila along with me when I'd vowed to do everything in my power to protect her.

"Yes!" Mila said, her little arm pulling into her side, and then she ran off to Mama, screaming about McKenna staying.

McKenna's eyes grew wide before she said softly, "I won't hurt her, Maddox."

It wasn't just McKenna hurting her worrying me, but I couldn't say those words at the moment with my little barn owl listening in. Instead, I said, "You can't promise that."

"I can. *Do no harm* isn't just part of the Hippocratic Oath. It's how I live my life."

"Now."

She looked confused.

"How you live your life now," I said because she'd hurt me more than any other soul on the planet had ever done.

Understanding blossomed over her face, and she looked down, fidgeting with her fork. "Right…now."

Mila interrupted us by plopping back down next to me and reaching for one of the pieces of bacon McKenna had placed there. I grabbed her hand to halt it. "How many now?"

She looked up at me with huge, pleading eyes. "Five plus two."

I chuckled. "I think that's enough, Bug-a-Boo. You'll end up with a tummy ache if you keep going."

"But bacon is my favorite food," she pouted, crossing her arms over her chest.

"Even above craps?" McKenna asked, and I almost laughed but held it back.

"Even above craps. Although, Nana's apple pie might be tied for my favorite food. Nana?!" Mila bounced over to my mama. "Can we put bacon *in* one of the apple pies? That would be the best pie ever in the entire world."

Mama chuckled. "Maybe, chick-a-dee."

"Yes!" Mila pulled her arm inward in another little victory move.

My alarm on my phone rang out, "Hey, Soul Sister" blaring through the air, and when I looked up from turning it off, McKenna's lips were twitching.

"You're still using that song?" She was trying not to laugh, but it was impossible not to hear it in her tone.

"Damn straight," I said. "It's a good song."

She'd harassed me for making it my alarm a decade ago.

"Daddy! You owe another dollar for the cuss jar!"

I burst of laughter escaped me.

"Wow, how did she even hear you?" McKenna asked, glancing over to my daughter at Mama's side.

"She's just like Mama, got the ears of a barn owl."

I rose and looked down at the woman who'd once destroyed my heart. "So…" I cleared my throat. "Looks like I have to run out to the Jenkins' farm real quick, but I'll be back to pick Mila up. You can come with us then, or you can go over now…it's up to you."

She tugged on her hair. "I'll wait for you. It wouldn't feel right otherwise."

♫ ♫ ♫

I was still debating the wisdom of my mama and my demented self for letting her stay with us when I picked up Mila and drove us back to our house with McKenna following us in her rental car. The doubts had gotten worse when I'd gotten a call from the rehab clinic saying Sybil had walked out the door. It was partly my fault. I'd baited her by ignoring her last two calls demanding I come and see her. But it also meant she'd violated the judge's orders, was going to see the inside of a jail this time, and could show up in Willow Creek at any moment.

My gut was churning over all of it, including whether or not to tell Mila the truth about who McKenna was. So many of the decisions I'd had to make as a parent were not black and white, and this was just one more of them. Sometimes, I wished I had a handbook filled with codes and regulations, like I did at my job, in order to navigate this role better.

"Daddy?" Mila called from her car seat in the back of the Bronco.

"Yes, Bug-a-Boo?"

"Do you *not* like McKenna?"

Now there was a loaded question. Once upon a time, I'd loved her, and then hated her, and now I was terrified of her and the power she held over me and could hold over Mila. I desired her still, which was a fucking nightmare, but did I like her? I didn't know her anymore, so how could I like or dislike her?

"I like her just fine," I finally answered.

Mila was quiet for a moment, and I tried to assemble my emotions so she wouldn't sense them.

"I don't like the dark," she told me as if I didn't know this already. As if we didn't have a dozen different nightlights in the house because of it. Personally, I thought it stemmed from when she'd been a baby, left alone too much, screaming in the dark for her basic necessities. From times encoded in her body before she could even process them. It made my soul hurt to think of her like that. The way I'd found her…

"I know," I said.

"That's how you and McKenna feel. Like I do about the dark."

I glanced at her in my rearview mirror, awed by the way she processed the world. I'd never believed in the whole empath thing until her. When Mama had first told me, I'd scoffed, but Mila amazed me almost daily with an insight into people most adults didn't even have. And now, my daughter was right. I was afraid, and I knew exactly what was making me scared, but I had no idea why McKenna was.

We pulled into the garage as I tried to figure out a response Mila would understand. When I got out of the car and opened the back door for her, she slid out of her car seat but stood next to it, eyes almost even with mine. She placed her hands on my face. "Do you need to borrow my nightlight, Daddy?"

My breath caught at my magnificent little child offering up the one thing that banished her fear so I wouldn't be afraid.

My voice was gruff when I responded. "No, sweetheart, but thank you. McKenna and I…we need to find a different kind of light."

She nodded sagely, as if she understood completely.

Then, she slipped out of the car and headed for the front door at a dead run.

"Watch your step!" I hollered.

When I finally caught up, it was to see McKenna pulling her two bags out of the back of the rental. The same two she'd had with her when she'd arrived two nights ago. But the sight of them was a reminder this was a vacation for her, not a cross-country move. She'd be gone in days, and I'd have to pick up the remains of our life when she left again.

As soon as I unlocked the door, Mila zoomed past me toward the back of the house just as McKenna joined me on the top step. I reached for the bigger bag, and our hands collided. Heat and desire swept through me, flickering at the fuse that had once ignited us, uncontrollable feelings I didn't want to have. When I met her gaze, her lips parted again like at breakfast. Knowing she felt the attraction between us made me want to yank her to me and kiss her as much as it made me want to push her into her car and force her to drive away.

Instead, I pulled the luggage into the house and toward the guest room. "You're just back here."

She followed me. Mila was already there, sitting on the bed, bouncing up and down.

"We've never had a guest stay over other than Miss Rianne," Mila said.

McKenna looked over at me, dragging her eyes down my body and then back to my face, and I wondered who she thought Rianne was. I could have told her she was our ancient third-grade teacher, but for some inexplicable reason, I hoped she was jealous. I hoped she thought Rianne was my girlfriend.

"You need to go get ready for bed," I told Mila.

She sighed and dragged her feet as she got up. "Okay. But can McKenna read *The Day the Unicorns Saved the World* with us?"

My heart squeezed. I'd accused McK of being selfish earlier, but really, I was the selfish bastard because I wanted all of Mila's sweet moments to be mine and mine alone. "That's up to McKenna. She might want some peace and quiet."

Mila turned to face McKenna. "You have to listen to the story. It's about Chester and his friends and how they save the world from a troll who lives in a cave above their valley. He wants to steal their horns because they have magic."

"If you tell her the whole story, she won't need to read it," I said, lips twitching.

McKenna's head was tilted, watching our exchange, and then she said quietly, "I'd love to read the story with you."

"Yes!" Mila did her victory move again and then twirled out of the room. "I'll wash up as quick as I can."

"Don't skip brushing your teeth!" I hollered after her.

"I won't. I won't."

I turned back, and McKenna's face was soft with an emotion I couldn't name.

"You're really amazing with her," she said quietly.

I rubbed my beard. "She makes it easy."

She nodded and then turned serious. "Thank you for letting me stay. For giving me the chance to know her."

I shifted my feet, uncomfortable with everything about her being there. "I don't think we should tell her about your relationship yet. She knows Sybil is her mom, but she hasn't seen her once since the visitations stopped, so I don't think she even remembers her."

"Whatever you think is best."

What I really thought was best was for us to rewind a week or two and never have McKenna or Sybil show up in Willow Creek at all. But a teeny-tiny thought wedged at the back of my brain, calling me a liar, because seeing McKenna in my home—seeing her with Mila—sparked back to life the wishes I'd had when I'd first found my daughter. I'd hoped I'd tell McKenna about her sister, and she'd come running back to Willow Creek. That we could make ourselves a family in a way I'd once dreamed.

I squashed the wish, tucking it back where it had been hiding.

I was one-hundred-percent sure I couldn't afford it.

Chapter Seventeen

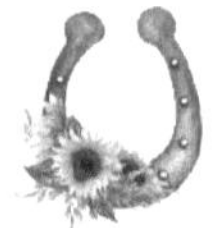

McKenna

THINGS A MAN OUGHTA KNOW

Performed by Lainey Wilson

There was something different in Maddox's eyes this evening other than the anger from last night and the bitterness from earlier in the day. Beyond the fear, it seemed like there was resignation and maybe even a bit of that demon named hope I always tried to banish.

He turned away from me, heading out of the guest room door and saying, "I'm going to get out of my uniform before the queen demands our appearance."

My lips twitched as he left.

I looked around the room. It was bright and feminine with rose-colored toile blending in with mahogany woods and bright-white lace. I couldn't imagine Maddox putting the room together, but then I wondered if Miss Rianne had done it. The thought twisted my gut with a jealousy I had no right to.

He might not have a wife, but there was likely a girlfriend in the mix. A man as attractive and kind and successful as him would draw people to him. He'd had that power even back in high school. He'd been well-liked by all the different cliques at school, but he'd avoided most of them just to hang out with me.

I took off my shoes and opened my luggage just as Mila skipped back into the room.

She had on pajamas covered in rainbows.

"Are you ready for the bestest story in the entire world?" she asked, and I couldn't help but smile at her enthusiasm.

"I'm always ready for a good story," I said as she grabbed my hand with her tiny one and pulled me from the room and down to the next door. I stepped inside, and my feet halted, a laugh escaping my chest. The room was an utter kaleidoscope of color and rainbows. As if a cartoon world had popped like a water balloon and sprinkled the entire space.

"Wow," I breathed out, and the smile she directed at me was so huge I thought it might split her cheeks.

"You like my room? Daddy said it was *over the top*, but then he said it was my space, and I could do whatever I wanted with it as long as I promised he'd never step on another LEGO again."

My laughter grew. I wasn't exactly sure why. The love he showered her with was beautiful. Earlier, I'd thought she was spoiled, but it wasn't the right word. She wasn't bratty. She just seemed like a vivid flame, showering the world with joy…and rainbows. My laughter made her laugh as well, and she had even less understanding of why. I wondered if it was her empathic abilities Maddox had mentioned or just the contagiousness of laughter in general.

"What's so funny?" Maddox's deep voice boomed from behind us.

I spun around, the smile and joy still registering on my face as I took in the most relaxed Maddox I'd seen yet. A soft T-shirt bared his muscular biceps, gray sweatpants hung low on his hips, and when he crossed his arms over his defined chest, I caught a glimpse of tan skin and manly hair that disappeared under the waistband.

My mouth went dry, my laughter disappeared, and I had to force my hands into fists to stop myself from reaching out to touch him. Anywhere. Everywhere. To feel his warmth and his strength encompassing me. To get lost in the glow that was Maddox. To feel truly safe like I only had whenever I'd been tucked in his embrace.

The air between us was charged. His gaze fell to my lips, and I licked them instinctively, as if preparing them for the assault of his mouth on mine. Heat flared in his eyes, and he swallowed hard, shifting on his feet and looking up at the ceiling where rainbows were painted on a blue sky full of puffy clouds.

"Daddy, you need to sit here." Mila's voice pulled us both from the trance we'd lost ourselves in. She was tucked under her blankets, leaning on a pillow up against the headboard, and she was pointing to her left side. "And McKenna, you need to sit here." She pointed to her right.

The bed was a full-sized one rather than a twin, but it was still going to be a tight fit with the three of us. It didn't stop either of us from doing just as she'd instructed, shuffling our feet under the covers and squishing together. Maddox had an arm behind us as he tried to keep himself on the bed, and I could feel the warmth of it along the back of my neck even though he wasn't touching me.

Mila opened the cover of an obviously well-loved book and looked to Maddox.

"All the voices tonight, Daddy. We have to give McKenna the full Chester experience!" she demanded.

Maddox sighed—a fake one, obviously egging her on.

"I don't know, Bug-a-Boo. My voice is pretty tired tonight," he said, trying to keep back a smile as he looked down at her.

"Daddy! This is her first time with the unicorns. You *have* to do the voices."

"Fine, fine. But you have to do all the neighing."

She nodded, scooting down a little, tucking one hand onto his arm, looping the other through mine, and drawing the three of us together even more.

My heart flooded with emotions. The sweetness of it. The mirage that we were a family. It hurt more than anything had hurt me in ages. Maybe since I'd told Maddox to stop calling. Maybe since I'd said goodbye to him on the dorm steps and told him not to come back. I'd been so stupid. I'd given up so much for such ridiculous reasons.

For dreams that were now crumbling and fading away.

As Maddox read the book, I listened as enthralled as Mila. His voice changed inflections and tones with the pace of the story, the different characters, and the emotions the plot demanded. He wasn't the least bit embarrassed I was there listening. It was almost as if he'd forgotten I was there at all as he put on the show his daughter demanded. Mila giggled and sighed, and her fingers got tense at the part where the troll had all the unicorns locked up in his dungeon. She'd obviously read the story a million and one times, but she still felt everything.

I wondered what it was like to feel that much.

I'd purposefully shuttered my emotions for years. First, because if I didn't, Mama used them against me, and then because you had to be calm and sure as a doctor. Friendly but serene. The only person who'd ever seen my true feelings was the man reading to us. He'd gotten my fear and sadness and heartache. He'd gotten my love and joy, too.

When the story was done, Mila clapped and then leaned up to kiss Maddox's cheeks. "Thank you, Daddy! That was the best you've done in *months*." Then, she turned to me and asked, "Wasn't it the dreamiest story ever?"

I nodded, heart in my throat. I cleared it and said carefully, "It was pretty remarkable."

My eyes met Maddox's as I spoke, and something passed between us again. Desire tangled with more. Regret.

Anticipation. I couldn't name it and didn't want to. I just wanted to revel in it for a moment. To enjoy the sensations of being wanted.

That snapped me out of it.

I wasn't wanted. Maddox definitely didn't want me here. He'd given in because Eva had nagged at him.

Maddox and I both got out of her bed at the same time. He put the book on the nightstand, kissed her forehead, squeezed her tight, and said, "Time for sleep."

"Can't we read one more story?"

He shook his head. "No, tomorrow is a school day."

She sighed dramatically. "There's only two days before Thanksgiving break. Can't I just stay home? With you and Miss Rianne and McKenna?"

"You love going to school. You beg to go on your days off, so what's up?" he asked, crossing his arms over his chest and assessing Mila, as if he could ferret out what was wrong by just looking at her. He used to do that to me…and he'd almost always succeeded.

"I love school," she said with a wild nod. "But McKenna is here, and I don't know how long she'll stay, and I just *need* to spend time with her."

My heart wasn't sure it could handle the wave of emotions flowing through me. When was the last time anyone had *needed* to spend time with me? The desperate need that my little sister expressed. God…I had a sister… It kept hitting me at the weirdest moments.

Maddox looked up at me and then down at her again, clearing his throat. "I believe she'll be here until after Thanksgiving. You'll have plenty of time with her."

"Are you? Staying?" Mila asked me, and I found myself nodding.

"I'll be here through Thanksgiving at least," I told her. My original intent when I'd thought I'd have Trap's house to myself was to stay until I heard from the hospital. But now it seemed a risky venture. If I stayed that long with them, would I be able to walk away without hurting Mila…or Maddox…or myself? There was no telling if I'd even have anything to go back to, but if I did, I had the rest of my residency to complete, and I'd had no plans to leave Hearld Community afterward. I'd thought I'd spend my life there in the ER department.

Mila pulled Chester and Charlotte from where they'd been sitting at the bottom of her bed and then burrowed with them under the covers.

"Okay. Tuck me in, Daddy!"

He pushed the covers up along both sides of her so tight you could clearly see the outline of her under the blankets. She giggled.

He kissed her again, they exchanged *I love yous,* and then he headed for the door. I followed, and when Maddox turned off the lights, the room barely dimmed because of the number of nightlights scattered around the room. It was a haze of rainbow shimmers, like sleeping in a cotton-candy cloud.

"McKenna?" Mila asked.

I looked back, and she smiled a tired smile, eyes already drooping. "If you need one of my nightlights so you won't be afraid, you can take one."

My chest tightened again, emotions filling me, and I barely croaked out, "Thank you. I think I'll be okay tonight though."

Her eyes were already closed as Maddox shut her door behind us. An awkwardness suddenly filled the air as we stood with shoulders almost touching in the narrow hallway. Just when I turned toward the door leading to the guest room, he headed down the hall to the main living area and threw back over his shoulder, "Feel like a drink?"

I hesitated and then nodded. I followed him more because I wasn't ready for this dreamlike evening to end than because I actually wanted the alcohol.

The bungalow's living space had been opened up so the living room, dining room, and kitchen were one great big room with old wooden plank floors waxed to a shine, sunny yellow walls, and furniture that was a mix of whites and warm woods. It was modern and yet still held an agelessness to it. The couch looked soft and cozy and had two crocheted blankets thrown over the back, one a rainbow of colors, the other in blues and greens. The kitchen was full of stainless-steel appliances and two-toned cabinets.

"Have a seat," he said, waving me toward the couch as he pulled open the fridge. "I have beer or hard cider."

"A cider sounds good," I said, curling into a corner of the couch.

He came back with an open cider for me and a beer for him. As he handed me the bottle, our fingers grazed, and awareness shot through me once again, curling through my chest and low into my belly. He drew back, sinking into the other side of the couch, leaving two cushions between us.

"I'm sorry I've disrupted your world," I told him.

"Why'd you really come back?" he repeated his question from earlier in the day.

I fidgeted with the label on the bottle and then told him a half-truth. "Some things were going on at the hospital that I needed to get away from."

"There a reason you came here instead of to wherever the fiancé is?"

"I'm not engaged. Haven't been for almost three years," I said. When I risked looking at him, I saw surprise and something else cross his face that I thought might be desire, but before I could really examine it, he'd hidden it away.

"What happened?" he asked.

I shrugged. "He got accepted for a residency at his parents' hospital in Boston. I didn't. He wanted me to move with him anyway, but—"

"You wouldn't give up your dream for him either," he finished for me. Our eyes locked, and I should have been mad at him for making it sound like I was cold-heartedly breaking off relationships to follow my dreams, but his words were justified. They also frustrated me. Why did I have to be the one to give up my dreams to keep the men in my life? Why couldn't they be the ones to give up their dreams for me?

You're nothing. No one will ever really want you. They'll happily toss off the burden of you. Like throwing away a bad penny.

Mama's words were brutal and cruel. But true.

"I shouldn't have said that," he said, looking away. Then, he drank from his beer before setting it on the side table and propping his bare feet up on the coffee table. His feet were long and lean. Like his hands. Like the rest of him. He'd bulked up since I'd seen him the first year of college, but not so much that it countered his overall litheness. Beneath the changes the years and muscles had wrought, there was still the Maddox I'd first explored with my fingers and tongue.

I swallowed hard, turning my thoughts away from him and back to what he'd asked.

"The truth is, even if I'd gone with him or he'd stayed with me, we wouldn't have worked. I was pretending we were something we weren't," I said, voice tight, wondering why I was telling him anything about Kerry and me.

"What was that?" he asked.

"A family," I breathed out. "We were never one. We were just two people who happened to get along and had similar goals for a while."

"But he was enough for you to give me up," he said, and I could tell he was trying to be nonchalant, but there was a layer of hurt to the words after all these years.

I pulled the label from the bottle and started folding it. I thought about the little bubble I'd lived in for so many years, the wall I'd kept myself safe behind…even with him. "I was pretty messed up, Maddox. I didn't even know it for a long time. After Kerry left, I finally got help. Seeing a therapist has made a difference. It's helped me understand how I shielded myself from everyone in my life and why I pushed away those who tried to see behind the shroud. But…I'm still messed up."

My voice bobbled, and I hated it. I didn't want to cry again like I had the other day in the car.

He sat up, feet hitting the ground, and moved as if he wanted to reach for me but then stopped himself just short of touching my arm. Silence settled over us. It wasn't awkward, but it was full of tension. Not just the sexual tension I'd felt wafting between us since arriving, but expectant tension, as if we were both waiting for the other to make the first move.

"Will you tell me how you ended up with Mila?" I asked in an attempt to deflect the brewing desire.

He sighed, raising his hand and scratching the back of his neck as if nervous all of a sudden.

"Janie Withers had been growing herbs out the back of the abandoned Cross farm, and one day, while she was there, she heard a baby crying and glass breaking from inside the dilapidated house. She was too scared to go in and check it out, so she called 9-1-1. I'd been working for the sheriff's department for about two years by then and was sent to check it out. When I arrived, I heard a baby wailing as if it was being tortured, so I busted open the door and found Mila. She was covered, head to toe, in dirt and grime, a disgusting diaper, and was screaming at the top of her lungs. She was so skinny you could see all the bones in her chest as she sat in the middle of a floor covered in mouse droppings. When she saw me, she stopped crying and put her arms up. It was the damndest…"

His voice dropped off, clogged with tears, as if he was right back there finding Mila. It disgusted me and made me hate Mama and myself both a little bit. If I'd been here, would I have been able to stop that from happening to Mila?

Somehow, I doubted it. Once Mama and I had split ways, we'd never seen each other again. She'd taken off, and I hadn't cared to find out where to. Even if I'd been in Willow Creek, I wouldn't have known she was pregnant. I wouldn't have known about Mila until Maddox found her. But it didn't ease the feeling that I should have known. As if the moment the bond had been created, the universe should have informed me. It was ridiculous but true. All I could do at the moment was be glad it was Maddox who'd found her.

Chapter Eighteen

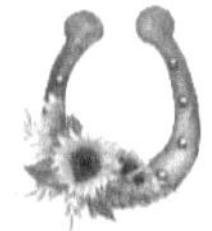

Maddox

I'LL JUST HOLD ON

Performed by Blake Shelton

I was back at the Cross farm, reliving that day, miles away from my living room and McKenna with Mila safe in the room down the hall. Instead, I could smell the pee and vomit and the refuse of the house. The mold from the cracked roof and the rain pouring in. Feeling the cold that had made me shiver when I was fully dressed, and when I'd picked up Mila's tiny body in only a dirty diaper, she'd been so cold she'd almost been blue.

"Where was Sybil?" McKenna prompted, and I continued down the dirty hall of the Cross place in my mind with Mila clutched to my chest and my gun in my other hand.

"I found her in the next room, passed out in her own vomit. For a moment, I thought she was dead." I remembered the relief the thought had given me. I'd felt like such a bastard for having it. For wishing someone dead. But when she'd groaned, anger had filled me instead. "I got them both back to the station and got them cleaned up. When Sybil came to, she denied Mila was hers. Said her friend had left the baby with her while she'd gone to Knoxville to get them some dope."

I finished my beer, not wanting to relive those moments.

"Why didn't CPS take Mila?"

"She wouldn't let go of me. Every time I tried to hand her off or someone tried to take her, she screamed bloody murder, like we were pulling her skin off. We all thought it would be easier—at least for a night."

"You could have just let her scream," McKenna insisted.

The CPS worker had told me the same thing, saying Mila would stop crying eventually. That she was just traumatized. But there'd been something about her that had made it impossible for me to let her go. Contrary to what I'd told McKenna in the bar the night before, I'd seen the similarities even when Mila was fourteen months old. There'd been something in her gaze that had called to me, reminded me of another person who'd looked at me with scared eyes and begged me not to leave.

When I'd found McKenna at age eight, her gaze had pleaded with me without a word to not give away her hiding spot. Sybil had stormed over with a whiskey bottle in her hand, asking me if I'd seen a dirty little girl, and I'd just shaken my head.

And McKenna had been dirty, dressed in an old, ragged nightgown, her feet bare and black from crossing the road, her hair an oily tangle about her face. As little as I'd been, I'd known deep in my soul I would do anything to help her. There'd been no way I was going to tell the woman yelling profanities where she was at.

"It didn't feel right," I finally told McKenna. I suddenly realized she'd moved on the couch so she was right next to me. She picked up my hand and squeezed it.

The touch was painful, slamming through my senses, waking up nerves I'd tried to put to rest ages ago, filling me with a need so great I thought my chest might explode from the desperate longing.

"Thank you," she said quietly, "for looking after her like you looked after me."

I hadn't said any of the words aloud about finding her in the shed, but somehow, just like Mila could read my emotions, McKenna had read my mind, had known where I'd gone. I couldn't speak, just nodded, slowly pulling my hand away because I couldn't keep it there and not try to touch her in other ways.

"When did you find out she was Mama's and not her friend's?" she asked.

"Officially, about two weeks in. We finally found her friend in Knoxville, and she laughed when she heard Sybil had said Mila was hers. The judge forced them both to get DNA tests so we would know which one of them to press neglect and abandonment charges on."

"Officially?" she poked at the word I used, but I didn't respond to her dig. She knew what I meant.

"I called you then," I said, turning to her and trying to keep the hurt out of my voice.

She grimaced. "Kerry was so angry when he saw your name flash across the screen. He thought I'd lied about asking you to stop calling. Thought I'd been talking to you behind his back the whole time. He bought me a new phone with a new number and basically said if I didn't take it, he'd know I wasn't serious about us."

"He sounds like an ass. He sounds like someone I'd never expect to see you with."

She gave me a wry, pained smile. "I think that's what attracted me to him to begin with. I thought I could turn myself into someone completely different. That day…his threat of taking the phone or losing him…it hit all my raw points. I was afraid he'd be just another person who didn't want me enough to stay."

"That's bullshit." The words slipped out before I could help it, anger welling up inside me. I pulled away from her and stood, looking down at her. "You're the one who left, McKenna. You were always enough for me. I always wanted you."

She rose, hands on her hips, glaring at me as she scoffed. "Was I really enough, Maddox? Did you truly want me more than your family or this town? I told you to stay away, and you did. I told you not to call, and you did. You didn't even try to fight for me."

Her voice cracked, tears welling in her eyes, and my anger turned to frustration and maybe some regret as I realized with a slam to my heart that she was right. I hadn't fought to stay in her life when she'd pushed me out, and I certainly hadn't been willing to leave everything I loved in order to keep her.

"Maybe," I said. "Maybe you're right, but I'd been taught my whole life that no means no. That if someone asks you to leave, you do. I didn't think I had to beg you to be a part of my life after everything we'd been through. I didn't know it was some goddamn test."

"A test? I wasn't testing you, Maddox." She shook her head. "I didn't even know I'd done it until my therapist pointed it out to me. It may not have been fair to you, but I was waiting for you to prove Mama wasn't right. That I was worth fighting for. I'd suffered years of abuse, abandonment, and neglect, so pushing you away was a self-fulfilling prophecy. I wasn't enough for you to stay. I didn't deserve you…"

Her words hit us both at the same time, and her face flared with embarrassment. She was still fighting her tears just like she'd fought them whenever I'd found her hurt and bleeding in our past. And I goddamn couldn't take it.

In two strides, I had her in my arms, pulling her against my chest and holding on to her like I had in my dreams a million times. Like I'd wanted to do for a decade. My hand ran up and down her back as heat and the scent of her washed over me, tangling with memories of our childhood. RC Cola and MoonPies. Belonging. Peace.

When she lifted her haunted eyes to me, I wasn't sure which of us moved first, but suddenly, my lips were on hers. The moment they touched, a groan escaped me. Years of missing her twisted with anger and frustration that quickly disappeared into sensations of home and heartache. They flooded my veins, mixing with the acute joy of finding something you lost. Rediscovering every piece of it. Her mouth was pliant but greedy, moving underneath mine and searching for the memories and the past as much as I was. I slid my tongue along her seam, and she let me in, where I lost myself all over again to the taste of her as our mouths danced and pushed and demanded.

I gripped her hair, tugging her head back, exposing the long expanse of her neck and sending my lips on a journey over her sweet skin. I nipped at her earlobe, licking the juncture between it and her neck before sucking and plundering like I'd wanted to do earlier. She gasped just like she had a decade ago, and my body tightened from head to toe, raw need fueling my movements as I continued the assault of kisses and licks down her neck and back up. I took her mouth again with a savage ferocity I'd never felt, not even with her in those early, tentative days of making love.

A buzzing that kept repeating brought us both back to our senses, but it was McKenna who pulled back first, a shaky hand going to my chest. She was breathless, lips red from my teeth and tongue and beard. I wanted to take that flush and place it all over her entire body with my caresses. I wanted to rediscover every curve and valley and erogenous zone I'd once found.

She turned back to the coffee table and her phone vibrating against the wood. When she read the text, her expression chilled me to the bone. Fear and heartache.

I stepped toward her again. "What's wrong?"

Her face became the blank slate she was an expert at making, and she shook her head. "Nothing."

"That wasn't nothing, McKenna. That was fear. I know fear when I see it."

She swallowed and looked away.

"Tell me," I said, the demand in my voice sounding so much like the voice I used on the job that it did the opposite of what I wanted. Instead of easing her mind, it had her lifting her chin in defiance.

"One kiss doesn't mean you can make demands of me. I don't owe you any explanations." She headed for the hallway, and I followed.

"I didn't mean it that way," I said. She hesitated, and I continued. "I just meant, I'm here for you. I can help."

"Unfortunately, at this point, there's nothing anyone can do, but thanks."

She didn't wait for a response. She just ducked into the guest room, shutting the door behind her with a click that rattled through my soul.

I looked up at the ceiling, rubbed my hand over my face, and whispered a quiet, "Fuck." I didn't know what to do. Run after her? Force her to tell me the truth? Or let her go even if it risked her feeling like, once again, she hadn't been enough?

My work phone rang, and I let out another curse before hurrying over to pick it up from the counter.

"Hatley," I barked into it.

"Sheriff, I think I spotted Sybil hitchhiking toward the West Gears' headquarters. When I flipped around to go back, she was gone. I passed a beat-up 1970 Charger heading there that she might have gotten into. What do you want me to do?" Bruce Walker was my best deputy. He was older than me by two years but didn't give a shit about our age difference. There was no hostility about me being in charge.

Bruce said he'd never wanted the headache of being sheriff, and there were days I couldn't blame him.

"Don't go into the Gears' headquarters without backup, Bruce. Let me call Sheriff Scully to see how many of us we can pull together. Park near the turnoff to their place until you hear from me. They might just kick her right back out."

"Will do," he said and hung up.

I placed the call to Scully, the sheriff of the county over from us, asking for help. Neither of us had a whole lot of manpower, and we backed each other up whenever we could afford to do so.

I looked down the hallway, wondering if I should tell McKenna about Sybil, wondering if I should tell her I was leaving. But I didn't want Mila waking up to a practical stranger in her house, and McKenna didn't know Mila's routine. It would be easier to get someone here. So, instead of going down the hall and knocking on her door, I called the first person I always called—Rianne. If she couldn't come by, I'd call Mama. And if that didn't work, one of my siblings would show up. They all had my back when it came to raising my daughter.

Fifteen minutes later, I was back in my uniform, and Rianne had let herself in.

"So…I don't know if she'll be awake before you get Mila off to school, but I wanted you to know McKenna is in the guest room."

Rianne's lips twitched. "I'd heard she was in town, but I didn't know she was staying with you. I honestly heard you'd pretty much sent her scurrying."

Heat coasted over my cheeks, thinking of my drunken words.

"Mila doesn't know they're related. We haven't figured that part out yet."

"What parts have you figured out?" Rianne's eyes twinkled with humor, and the heat in my face grew.

"It isn't what you think." I swallowed hard, thinking of the kiss we'd shared. If McKenna hadn't pulled away because of her phone, I would have taken it further. We'd be naked and tangled in my bed by now.

Rianne chuckled softly. "Just go. I'll handle Mila and McKenna both. Stay safe and come back to your daughter."

My heart clenched.

That was the hardest thing about this job—the idea of something happening to me and leaving Mila without her dad. It would be like hearing her tormented cries that first night. Ripping us apart would be brutal and cruel. She'd never be alone like she'd been when I'd found her, because she'd have my family even if she didn't have me, but it would never be the same. We had a bond, the two of us. And I wanted to be there to see all her firsts. All her successes. All her joys and sorrows.

I didn't say anything else because I couldn't. I just headed for the door with a heavy heart and chest, unsure how to fix them.

Chapter Nineteen

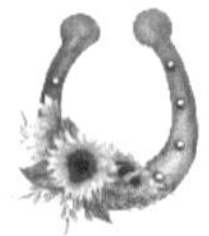

McKenna

DREAMED YOU DID

Performed by Jordan Davis

I scurried into my room, shutting the door with a heart that was clanging fast and furious as much from the raw, torturous kiss that had savaged us as from the recent text from Dr. Gregory. I put my forehead on the door, trying to find the calm I savored, the even keel I needed to get through every day.

The latest nasty message was from yet another unknown number and had been the worst one yet. A huge portion of me had been tempted to tell Maddox, just needing someone to know in case the worst happened—to voice the fact I was getting threats from a vicious man who was making it his mission to destroy me because he no longer had his son at his disposal.

But what could Maddox actually do if I told him? If Dr. Gregory was using burner phones—as I highly suspected because he wasn't stupid—there would be no way to prove the messages were from him. He would have used cash to buy them. This wasn't some television show where they'd find a miraculous connection. No, the only path I had was to wait for the investigations by CPS and the hospital to work themselves out.

I stripped down to my underwear and the tank top I had on beneath my sweater and crawled into bed. I touched my lips, feeling again the stunning kiss that had destroyed not only every memory of any kiss by another man but also the memories of Maddox's kisses from our teen years. This kiss had been full of primal emotions, as if our bodies had been yearning for years to be rejoined, and when we'd collided again, a fire had ignited around us.

That bruised sensation I'd been feeling since arriving remained. My heart felt wrung out and yet still full of emotions all at the same time.

I pictured Maddox's face as he'd told me about finding Mila. He'd fallen in love with my sister the moment he'd picked her up, and it sounded like she'd fallen for him as well. She hadn't let anyone take her from him without screaming. She must have been able to sense he would protect her, like he'd always tried to protect me.

It took me hours to fall asleep, and when I finally did, I dreamed of Maddox, his hands, his lips, and forgiveness. I dreamed we were together, lost in beautiful moments that felt so safe and so peaceful that I didn't know if I was actually alive or if I'd found heaven. It was harsh and painful to come awake and find myself alone in my bed with all the same problems hanging over me that had been there the day before. I hated it. I wanted to go back to those blissful moments and forget the world.

Instead, I pulled myself from the covers and headed into the guest bath, showering and changing into jeans and a blue sweater. I'd have to do laundry soon because I was already running out of clothes. I stared in the mirror for way too long, contemplating what to say to Maddox when I saw him again. Last night, when I'd come to the room, I thought the kiss had been a mistake. It had just been pent-up emotions we'd both needed to express and had burst from us through lips and hands. But after the dream…

After the dream, I wanted heaven again.

I left the room hesitantly. The air was filled with the scent of coffee and cinnamon and the sound of little-girl giggles. It tugged at my heart, and I found myself once again wishing for things I'd never wanted until I'd stepped back into Willow Creek.

When I rounded the corner to the kitchen, I found Mila sitting on a stool at the island. Her hair was done in two long French braids, and she was wearing a sweater, jeans, and rain boots she was pounding against the cabinet as she swung her feet. She was laughing at the person on the other side—a person who tugged at my memories but who I couldn't quite place and was definitely not Maddox.

"There she is. Good morning," the woman said. She was an older woman with dark-brown skin, maybe in her seventies, with wrinkles around her eyes and mouth, and gray in her thick black hair partially hidden below a wrap covered in cartoon turkeys.

"McKenna!" Mila jumped down and ran over to me, wrapping my legs in a hug like she'd done the day before. I bent over and attempted to hug her back even as my fists flexed and my teeth bit down on my cheek. My throat closed, chest aching at the sweetness of her…of hugs that were so freely given. Hugs so similar to ones her father had once given me that it sent me spiraling into my past.

I'd fallen off the monkey bars at school, and my elbow was bloody and swollen. The nurse thought I might have chipped or broken a bone—an injury that, for once, I'd actually been responsible for myself. The school called Mama, and she burst into the office, looking harried with her hair wild, her clothes askew, and chewing gum to hide the scent of the liquor.

"Where's my baby?" she asked the secretary.

She pointed to me, waiting in a chair just inside the open door of the nurse's office. Mama rushed over to me, glancing over her shoulder at the women in the office watching us, and then she threw her arms around me in a hug. Her arms were taut and awkward, and I stiffened, unaccustomed to any sort of affection. She pressed her lips to my hair and whispered so no one else could hear, "If I have to spend even one dollar taking you to some damn doctor, you'll regret it."

She followed the words with a squeeze to my injured elbow that brought tears to my eyes, and I bit down on my lip in order to stop from crying out.

"Let's go, sugar," Mama said, standing up and meeting the nurse's and secretary's eyes with a soft smile. "She is the clumsiest little thing. I wish I could stop her from her daredevil ways. It breaks my heart when she gets hurt."

She even sobbed, as if I was the one causing her pain.

I stood there, wishing I didn't have to go with her. Knowing I was going to get more care where I was at than when I left. Knowing she'd take pleasure in poking at the injury for as long as it took to heal.

Mama grabbed my uninjured hand, nails biting into my palm, and pulled me out of the office.

Outside, Maddox came running up, eyes going wide once he saw Mama's hand gripping mine. He ignored her, surrounding me with a real hug. One that was warm and caring. One I felt in my soul. Mama didn't allow me to savor it. Instead, she yanked us apart, glaring at him.

"Stay away from her," she hissed before dragging me down the street.

"You're awake!" Mila's little voice centered me, bringing me back from the harsh memories.

"Wait? I am? Are you sure I'm not sleepwalking?" I teased, and she giggled.

She took my hand and skipped beside me toward the counter. "This is Miss Rianne. She takes care of me when

Daddy is at work, and she makes the best cinnamon rolls. But do *not* tell Nana I said that, because Nana thinks her cinnamon rolls are *the best*. They actually have a contest sometimes, and we have to vote without knowing whose is whose. Nana always gets upset when Miss Rianne wins."

"Breathe, Mila," Rianne said as she came around the counter and stuck her hand out. "You might not remember me, but I'm Rianne Barry. I was your third-grade teacher."

It all clicked—the headbands, her warm eyes.

"You were in her class?!" Mila all but yelled. "Daddy was in her class, too. You're so lucky. Only, I guess maybe I'm luckier because I get Miss Rianne all to myself and don't have to share her with other students."

I couldn't help smiling at Mila before I took Rianne's offered hand and shook it.

"I remember you," I said, and I did. I was almost certain she'd called CPS on Mama the year I'd been with her— maybe more than once. She'd seen through me to the things I was hiding, and looking into her dark eyes, I was pretty sure she might be able to do the same now if I was around her too long.

"There's coffee in the pot, if that's your morning poison, and cinnamon rolls in the oven, keeping warm," she said, turning toward Mila. "Go get your backpack and coat on."

"Dang it." Mila's little face turned downward. "I didn't even get to show McKenna the picture I drew."

"She can see it when you get home," Rianne said, her tone firm but loving.

Mila sighed heavily but then skipped toward the coatrack by the door. She shrugged into a heavy coat and pulled out a backpack from underneath the stand that, not surprisingly, had rainbows and unicorns on it.

"Will you be here when I get home from school?" Mila came running back to ask me.

"I think so," I told her.

"Yes!" She did her little victory move and then skipped back over to the door where Rianne had put on a thick coat and grabbed an umbrella.

I looked out the window and saw it was dark and cloudy, with more rain or snow on the way.

"Have a great day at school, Mila," I said, heart clenching at her happy smile. She waved at me.

"I'll be back to clean up after I drop this little chick-a-dee off," Rianne said.

I didn't know what to say, and they both left without another word. The house felt very silent once the door closed behind them. The kitchen was a bit of a disaster with mixing bowls and flour all over the counters.

I fixed myself a plate and cup of coffee, but instead of sitting down to enjoy them, I finished them off while cleaning up. It gave me something to do instead of dwelling on things I couldn't change. The past. My future. They were both out of my control. I'd had too much time to think and dwell on both in the last few days. I needed to change that, to busy myself with something, anything, even if it was cleaning.

By the time Rianne came back, the kitchen was pretty much sparkling, and I was on my second cup of coffee. She hung her dripping raincoat on the rack and then stopped as she took in the mess that was no longer there.

"You didn't need to clean up," she said. "But thank you."

She grabbed another cup of coffee for herself and sat down on the stool next to me.

"It must feel strange being back and finding out about Mila," she said.

"Strange isn't the only word I'd use," I said with a wry smile. "So, I take it you're not teaching anymore?"

She shook her head. "No, but I was going a little stir-crazy and wondering if I'd made a mistake in retiring at the same time Maddox took in Mila. Eva and I were at a book club meeting, and she said he was looking for the impossible—someone to work around his ever-changing hours and the ranch schedule, and it felt like it was meant to be. I get plenty of downtime when the family has Mila, but I also can be there whenever they need me."

My chest ached, the knots and pain growing larger. Mila really had the best life here. If I'd taken my sister, her life wouldn't have been anywhere near as full of love as it was in Willow Creek. Maddox had done the right thing by keeping Mila to himself.

Rianne was eyeing me in that all-knowing way.

"He wanted to tell you," she said quietly.

I nodded. "I know. When he called, it wasn't one of my better moments."

She patted my arm. "Life has a funny way of working out the way it should. I've been telling him for years he needed to call Sybil's bluff, and now he doesn't have a choice."

"What do you mean?" I asked with a sense of foreboding washing over me.

One of her eyebrows went up. "He didn't tell you? That boy…" She shook her head. "It's not really my place, but sometimes he tries to protect everyone too much. When he first got Mila, CPS had to follow the rules requiring them to give Sybil a chance to get her life together and get Mila back. She went into rehab, was out on probation, got a job at Tillie's Café, and was checking all the boxes. Then, they started supervised visits, and you know Sybil, she can act with the best of them."

She let it hang for a moment, watching my expression. Yes, I knew how good of an actress my mama was. She'd fooled CPS every single time they'd come to call on us, and

I'd done it right along with her. I'd been afraid not to. Afraid of her retaliation. Afraid of foster care because Mama had filled my brain with the horrors waiting for me there. There were worse things than being hungry. Worse things than the occasional burn or cut. But mostly, after I'd found Maddox, I was afraid of losing him. Mama had made it clear the Hatleys would never, ever see me again, and I'd believed her for too many years.

"Anywhoodle," Rianne continued, "Maddox was beside himself because he just knew she was going to get Mila back, and he'd already fallen in love with that girl. He couldn't abide the thought of her living through what you'd lived through. One day, about a week or two before she was going to get custody, Sybil found Maddox at the sheriff's station and told him she'd sign over her parental rights to him if he promised you'd never know about Mila. That you'd never, ever have any say in her life."

My mouth dropped. I couldn't help it. I hadn't seen Mama since I'd moved out my senior year. So, I was surprised she'd given me even two thoughts, let alone enough to pass down that kind of ultimatum to Maddox.

I cleared my throat. "But he has custody, right? I mean, she can't get it back? So how can she possibly hold it over his head now?"

"Well, she signed away her parental rights, but the father never did."

My stomach fell, visions of Trap's burly beard, black leather, and gold chains filling me. He'd worn a green bandana over his long, thick, brown hair tied back in a ponytail for as long as I could remember. I didn't know if I'd ever seen him without it. He'd never been dirty or oily, but there'd always been a hint of the road on him. A scent of gas and motorcycle tangled with the smell of cigars.

"Do you know…" my voice trailed off.

Rianne shook her head. "Sometimes, she says she doesn't remember who the father is, and some days, she says she knows and if he finds out, he'll take Mila away. Maddox thinks it's one of the West Gears, and he and the Gears are in an all-out war these days, so it wouldn't be a surprise if they did try and take the one thing he loves in the struggle."

A sense of panic washed over me at the thought of joyful, sweet Mila being pulled from her happy home with Maddox, the Hatleys, and Rianne to be tossed into the West Gears' headquarters. I'd been there a few times growing up. It was a dank dungeon. The smell of weed, alcohol, and sweat filled the air between the dark walls and dim lights. There were rooms I'd been told not to go into. Upstairs had been completely off-limits, and downstairs had been a threat held over me by Mama with leather straps and chains.

If I felt this way, full of anxiety and fear at the thought of Mila being lost to a West Gear, I couldn't even imagine what Maddox felt having raised her, having loved her and made her his.

"I don't even know what to say," I said, shaking my head.

"I just want you to understand why he threw those cruel words at you at the bar."

I blushed, realizing that—as normal in Willow Creek—everyone in town must have heard by now what he'd said.

"Whenever Sybil is in town," Rianne continued, "she makes Maddox jump through hoops. She enjoys every moment of the power she has over him, holding the father over his head."

"Does she come into town often?" I asked the question even though I was afraid to know the answer.

"About every six months. She was just here, got arrested and stuck in rehab, but I hear she skipped out. She's violated her probation, and if he finds her, he's going to have to stick her in jail. She'll be pissed, and even more so when she hears about you."

My heart slammed, pulse picking up. No wonder Maddox had screamed at me to get the fuck out. No wonder he'd been panicked and cruel at the bar. I was threatening everything he loved. I closed my eyes, fingers squeezing the mug until I thought it might burst.

Maybe Mama was right. I was a bad omen. Nothing good would happen around me. I'd run away, trying to change my fate, but maybe I could only keep it at bay for so long. Maybe my luck had completely run out.

"If he knows who the father is, what happens?" I asked.

"If he knows, and it's someone the court deems unworthy of being a parent, they can strip the rights away. If it's someone the court thinks deserves a chance, he'll likely have to share custody in some way."

Holy hell…

That feeling I'd had when I'd seen Layton Gregory nearly faint in the hospital hallway filled me again. Like the world was shifting around me. Like my choices could wreck my world. But this time, they could also wreck Mila's and Maddox's and the family they'd built together.

I looked down into my coffee cup with one thought ringing through my ears—I should leave. My lungs forgot to breathe for a moment. If I went back to the apartment in Davis, there was a much better chance of Gregory coming after me. But where else could I go? Sally's face flashed, but I still didn't want to bring this to her door either. I could just go anywhere. Anywhere but here. Max out the credit card. Declare bankruptcy. Get a temporary job until things were resolved.

Mila's happy face after I told her she'd see me after school took over. God, I realized how badly I wanted to be here when she walked through the door. Then, Maddox's expression after our kiss returned, filled with heat and longing, and I was overcome with the desire to continue what we'd started. God, I wanted it all. The hope—the little tiny flare that had burst inside me when I'd thought of coming back to Tennessee—flickered, growing stronger. It was a demon that would destroy me, but I would let it…as long as it didn't destroy them.

There was something between Maddox and me. Had always been. Years and hurt and denial hadn't extinguished it. Maybe instead of expecting someone to come running after me, to fight for me, I had to be the one to fight. Maybe I had to be the one to stay and declare to the world I belonged here…belonged to someone…a whole family.

That thought held me captive for way too long.

When I looked back up from my coffee, Rianne was still watching me with an eyebrow raised.

"It would be better to know, right?" I asked. "Mama wouldn't be able to hold it over him anymore. He wouldn't have to be at her beck and call."

"I think so, but it's never been my call to make. I think Maddox might have finally come to the same conclusion because…well, he let you stay here when he knew what the cost might be."

The cost being Mila…Jesus.

I slid off the stool and looked into her face full of a kindness I wasn't sure I'd ever earned. "Thank you for telling me. If you'll excuse me, I need to make a call."

I didn't wait for an answer. I headed for the guest bedroom, searching for my keys, my shoes, and my phone I'd purposefully left behind because I hadn't felt up to another terrifying text from Dr. Gregory.

My hands shook as I opened my contacts and scrolled down to the T's. I wasn't sure the number would work. I wasn't sure I even wanted to see him, but I thought he might be the one person who could get me answers…get Maddox answers.

It meant facing my past yet again, and maybe that was what the universe was demanding of me. Maybe I'd been meant to stay and fight all along, and now it was giving me the chance to make amends. To do it right.

Chapter Twenty

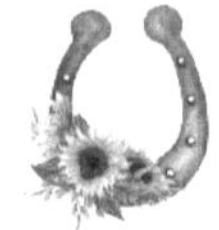

Maddox

The rain was pouring down over us as we huddled beneath a line of trees at the turnoff leading to the West Gears' headquarters. Sheriff Scully and I had scrambled together six officers, including ourselves, which left a handful in each of our stations if things went haywire.

"If they've let her in, they aren't going to let us take her without some encouragement," Scully said.

I nodded.

"You sure you don't want to just wait until she comes back down?"

I wasn't sure at all, but she was a fugitive who'd broken her probation, and we knew where she was at. Even more than wanting to catch a criminal, I wanted her out of my life. I wanted her locked up and unable to rain havoc on me and my family.

"We'll send Bruce and Liam out the back, keep Jones and Stanton out front, and you and I will go in," I told Scully, who nodded with a grim face. I looked at the rest of the men. "I don't want to scare Sybil or any of them into drawing weapons by showing up with a bunch of squad cars. We'll all squeeze into Scully's Escalade, stop short of The Nest, and walk the rest of the way on foot. Everyone good with that?"

They nodded, and we all ducked under our hats and headed for the SUV. We were dripping water over the seats and floor by the time we got in. Scully accelerated up the muddy road to the Gears' Nest atop the mountain. It was part bar, part slum, and part warehouse that many of the gang called home. I'd heard stories about what happened in the basement, but I'd never had cause to go down there and hoped to God I never would. My goal was to systematically put them out of business, hoping the building would eventually just rot away without its members to care for it.

Scully pulled over in a cutout just before we rounded the last corner. We all got out, hands tucked on our weapons as the cold wind and rain blew around us. There was a hint of snow in the air, but I doubted the fires of hell that burned here would ever let the pristine flakes land in this place.

Our men broke off, and Scully and I gave them a moment to get into position before heading for the door covered in bars you might see in the middle of a gang-riddled city block. We didn't knock. We just swung the door open. We were greeted with guns already pointed in our direction—exactly what I'd hoped to avoid. The two burly, leather-clad men welcoming us were the ones who'd dropped off the bail money the other night for the peons we'd arrested with the stolen appliances.

I didn't care about them, their guns, or what may or may not have been downstairs. I was there for Sybil. As my eyes scanned the room, I didn't see her, but that didn't mean anything. The place was a warren of rooms.

"Think you wandered into the wrong place, assholes," Burly One said.

"Maybe we should show them *our* cells," Burly Two chortled. "Give them a taste of what it's like to be held in an actual prison."

"Those guns in your hands legal, shithead? Maybe we should take you down the hill and find out," Scully grunted out.

The men laughed. "I'd like to see you try."

My body was tight, ever synapse on alert, eyes scanning the periphery, watching the three other people in the room and the unwavering guns.

A door leading to a stairwell behind the main room slammed open, and everyone's trigger fingers flexed in a way that didn't bode well.

"Get up off your asses and go after—" The dickhead storming into the bar stopped himself, his instructions trailing off once he saw us. His entire frustrated demeanor changed, cold nonchalance replacing it.

Chainsaw had been the leader of the West Gears ever since Trap had gone to prison. I wasn't sure, but his being enormous might have had something to do with the reason he'd been chosen. Six foot five, with muscles built on top of muscles, he looked like he could swallow anyone whole while not even breaking a sweat. Unlike the rest of the gang, with long hair and equally long facial hair, Chainsaw looked almost like a banker. His dark-blond hair was cut short, and he had a tightly trimmed goatee that bordered on red, but his beady eyes screamed menace rather than numbers. He wore a Rolex on his wrist, tailored gray slacks, and a black button-down shirt opened to show off a mile of chest hair and several gold chains.

"Sheriff Hatley, to what do we owe this unwanted pleasure?" Chainsaw asked. His deep Louisiana accent layered with years of smoking sounded raw.

"You know why I'm here. I'm surprised you let her in the door."

He shot a look back the way he'd just come, and a flicker of rage spread over his face before he hid it. "Sybil isn't here."

My eyes narrowed. "She got something on you, Chainsaw? Is that why you're protecting her?"

He laughed as if the idea was ridiculous, but there was a wariness to him making me think maybe I was right.

"Then, there's no reason for you to hide her. She's in violation of her court-ordered rehab. She's going to prison this time."

The front door of The Nest jerked open, and all the guns in the room, including Scully's and mine, swirled in that direction. Someone was going to get fucking shot if things didn't simmer down. Bruce stepped in, breathing hard, rain pouring from his face. His hat was missing, and his uniform was spattered with muck, as if he'd taken up mud wrestling.

"She left. Slider took her on an ATV down the backside of the mountain," Bruce gasped out. "Ran after them, but the mud pulled me under like quicksand."

I turned to face Chainsaw, whose jaw was ticking.

"I don't know what she has on you. I don't know why you're protecting her, but it's a mistake. Not only because I won't rest until I have her, but because Sybil doesn't know how to be loyal to anyone but herself."

Chainsaw's eyes narrowed. "Ask yourself, Hatley…if she had something on me, do you think your deputy here would have seen her leaving with Slider? Ask yourself if I would have let her walk away at all. The only reason she was here was out of honor for our former leader and for everything Trap once was."

Every time I thought of Sybil being dead because of her lifestyle and her choices, I had to fight the flicker of relief…of almost joy. I wanted her to pay for her crimes against McKenna and Mila, and I wasn't sure I'd have it in me to stop a bullet if it went in her direction.

But it wasn't what he'd said about Sybil that piqued my interest. It was the way Chainsaw had talked about Trap in the past tense, as if he was dead instead of out on parole somewhere in Tennessee.

"I do have a deal to offer you, though," Chainsaw said. My eyes narrowed, but I didn't respond, and it made his smile widen as if he had me in his sights. "You go back to minding your business like Sheriff Haskett used to, and I'll see what I can do to bring Sybil to your door."

My gut twisted. There was no way my mentor had turned a blind eye to the West Gears' crimes. He was as straight of an arrow as you could get. Chainsaw was trying to mess with my head.

He didn't wait for me to respond. Instead, he turned his back to me, sauntered over to the bar, and fixed himself a drink. He swallowed the contents, eyes finding mine in the mirror behind the bottles of alcohol.

"I think that's all we have to say, don't you?" he said calmly. "Better if you leave before someone decides to scratch an itch and accidentally pulls a trigger."

I turned on my heel and walked out the door with Bruce and Scully inching out behind me.

The rain had stopped, but the ground was a muddy mess. We all slogged our way back to the SUV and four-wheeled it down the mountain to where the rest of our vehicles sat. Our men took off, leaving Scully and me looking out at the trees and the clouds that were hanging low over the hilltops, making the scene seem like something from a fantasy novel.

"You believe him?" Scully asked. "About her not having anything on them?"

"They're protecting her for a reason," I said. "That line about honoring Trap was bullshit, but I'll make a call, see if I can scrounge up Trap's location just to make sure he isn't six-feet under somewhere."

Scully nodded and turned the ignition back on.

"Thanks for having my back as always, Scully," I said.

"Anytime, Hatley." He winked and then drove off.

I climbed into my F-150 and pointed it down the windy road to the station with my mood growing from bad to worse.

Amy was at the door as I walked in with a cup of coffee she handed me. She had short white hair, skin so pale it was almost see-through, and gray eyes that could sparkle with humor or ice over with frost depending on the situation. She'd been around the station for almost as long as I could remember and had stuck out the transition between me and Sheriff Haskett even though she threatened to retire every other day.

"Thanks," I grumbled. "I guess you already heard we came up short."

She nodded. "That woman doesn't know how to stay away though. You'll get her."

Which only made my foul mood grow because there was a part of me that still didn't want to find her. A part hoping she'd disappear in a way Chainsaw might appreciate.

"Can you get the Knox County Parole Office on the line?" I asked her. "I need them to do a check-in, preferably a home visit, with Trapper Lloyd. Tell them I have reason to believe he's either skipped town or someone's put a bullet in him."

I started toward my office, but she halted me.

"Change your shoes, Sheriff. I don't need mud all over my station," she scolded.

I looked down at the trail I'd already left and bit back an expletive. I yanked off my boots and headed for my office where I kept a full change of clothes. I closed the door, twisted the blinds shut, and stripped down to my boxer briefs, tossing the wet, dirt-spattered clothes onto a wooden chair in the corner with disgust. I pulled the closet open and snatched a pair of pants off a hanger just as the door rattled open. I flipped around, ready to bite someone's head off, but found my hands stalling as McKenna strode in.

Her eyes went wide, a little gasp escaping, before she slowly took me in from head to toe. My body reacted to the perusal by instantly going on full alert. I knew the moment she saw the semi-hard-on, because her cheeks turned pink, and she glanced away.

She cleared her throat. "Uh. Sorry. Um. What are you doing?"

Her eyes whipped back to mine, locking on my face as if she were afraid of looking anywhere else.

"Changing," I growled, my mood not improving as pent-up desire leaped back to life.

Amy bustled in, head down, staring at a paper in her hand. "Trap's parole officer said he'd call back as soon as he had eyes on him." When she glanced up, her gaze went from me to McKenna's pink face, and instead of being embarrassed at my half-dressed state, a twinkle appeared in her eyes. "Sorry to interrupt," she said, laughing.

McKenna let out a garbled, choked noise, and it did nothing to help my dick's reaction to her or the frustration I was ready to take out on anyone. Anything. But especially her.

"I'll just leave you to it," Amy said, walking out and shutting the door behind her with a loud click before saying loudly, "The sheriff is to be left alone. Anyone going near his door will answer to me."

I rolled my eyes, lips twitching for the first time all morning. When I looked back at McKenna, her cheeks had gone from pink to fiery red. "Jesus, Mads, what are you doing half-naked in your office?"

I hadn't heard her call me Mads in so long I'd almost forgotten what it sounded like. The way the D and the S turned into a whispery breath on her lips was different from how anyone else said it, and it did nothing for the state of my body or my heart.

"What the hell are you doing here?" I demanded, irritation dripping from me as I stepped into my pants. I pulled them up while she watched, and when she swallowed hard, my dick jumped again. I didn't even bother buttoning as I strode toward her.

I was in a bad mood from the entire fucking clusterfuck at The Nest. I was in a bad mood from her being in Willow Creek, making me feel sorry for her, and stirring up old feelings with our earth-shattering kiss the night before. I was pissed I'd jerked off all alone in my bed last night, like I had hundreds of times before, to images of McKenna. Except, these had been new images instead of decades-old ones.

She backed up, hitting the file cabinet, eyes going around the room wildly as she tried to keep them from landing on me in my half-dressed state, and I took a perverse pleasure in making her uncomfortable—because damn if she didn't do the same to me.

"I…" she trailed off as I stepped even closer, my bare chest grazing breasts barely hiding behind her tight sweater. "Can you finish dressing so we can talk?"

My hands went to either side of her on the file cabinet. "Why are you here, McKenna?"

It was a question I'd asked her several times and never gotten a straight answer, but today, I didn't mean in Willow Creek. I meant in my office.

She crossed her arms, and it pushed her breasts up, causing the swell to peek above the scooped neckline. A goddamn temptation I couldn't stop myself from taking. I placed one hand on the bare skin, thumb sliding along the curve. My body slowly burned from head to toe at the simple touch, an aching need to reclaim her lips filling me. A raw, all-consuming passion to repeat our kiss from last night.

A kiss that had been better, deeper, fuller than any we'd shared as teens, and it only made me wonder what it would be like if we were fully tangled, with me inside her. Would the absolute oneness I used to feel when we were joined become something greater? Would we find another plane of existence altogether?

Her eyes closed briefly, but then she opened them again and pushed my hand away. I set it back on the file cabinet, squeezing the metal viciously in an attempt not to touch her. What I really wanted to do was ignore everyone outside my office door, take her down to the floor, and pound out a decade's worth of longing.

"Why are you trying to find Trap?" she asked, her voice deep and husky.

Her nipples were hard, poking through her sweater, and I suddenly wondered if she had a bra on at all. There were no visible lines. That singular thought only added fuel to the fire threatening to overtake me.

"Why do you care?" I grunted out a response, bending until my nose could brush aside her hair and my breath coasted over her cheek. She shivered.

"I…I wanted to see if I could help. I…" She swallowed hard, and then her chin came up, defiance in her eyes. She placed both her palms on my chest, pushing as if to create a distance between us. The touch scorched me, heat spiraling through every vein. "Can you back up?"

"No," I grumbled. "Not until I get answers."

Her eyes squinted in a disapproval her body didn't feel. She was breathing rapidly, little pants proving she was as affected by our nearness as I was. I shifted, moving closer instead of farther away, until I could feel the outline of her against my hips and legs. The hard length of me pressed into her belly.

Her fingers on my chest moved tantalizingly slow, and then she twisted a nipple—hard.

"Fuck!" I said, taking a step back and putting a hand on the bruised skin.

She grinned, and damn, if that didn't do me in as much as her bated breath. Pure guts and determination radiated from her as she put me in my place just like she'd done as kids. She'd never let me have the upper hand for too long before she flipped the balance back.

"That was hardly fair," I said, rubbing my chest and practically shattering from the desperate need to have her back in my arms.

"And you were being fair?" she tossed back. She started toward the door, but there was no way I was letting her go yet. I caught her arm and hauled her back until we collided again. Chests, hips, shoulders. The frantic pace of her heart matched mine, and I suddenly had no desire to ever be fair again.

I kissed her, immediately thrusting my tongue between her lips and being rewarded with a whimper breaking from her. I wasn't gentle. I was borderline cruel as I devoured her, demanding she respond, and she did. She moaned, core shoving against mine, arms going around my neck, and fingers digging in at the back. We were engaged in a war— who could take the most, give the most, last the longest without breath. One hand went to her lower back, pushing her even closer, while the other went to her hair, twining my fingers into the silky strands and pulling so her neck was exposed. I left my assault of her mouth to trail licks and nips down the smooth column, over her collarbone, and down to the swell my fingers had sought moments ago.

I bit the curve like it was the juiciest of apples, and she gasped, "Maddox."

My name on her lips, as well as her hand urging my head into her breasts instead of drawing me away, sent me over the edge. I inched aside the neckline of the sweater and found her just as I'd thought—bare. I growled at the sight, licking and sucking one nipple before going to the next. Her body pulsed against me, a little rocking motion my hips echoed.

I was two seconds away from shoving my pants down and pulling her onto the chair when my intercom went off, Amy's voice filling the room with regret. "Sorry to interrupt, Sheriff, but Trap's parole officer says he needs to speak with you immediately."

I growled quietly before reluctantly letting McK go and stepping backward. She looked like a goddamn dream. Tousled hair, pink skin, pebbled nipples. I wasn't going to survive McKenna Lloyd being in town. Not without losing myself completely.

It was that thought which brought me to my senses.

I couldn't afford to be lost.

I had responsibilities. I had Mila. McKenna would leave again, and now more than ever before, I wouldn't be able to follow her.

"Sheriff?" Amy's voice called.

I jammed my finger onto the intercom button and said, "Send him through." When I looked back at McKenna, she was righting her sweater with shaky fingers.

That's when the remorse hit me.

"McK, I'm…"

She shook her head. "No. Don't. We both kind of lost our heads there for a moment."

I hated the calm in her voice. I didn't want her calm. I wanted the breathy yearning I'd had not even a minute before. I wanted my face buried inside not only her chest but her legs. I wanted to taste the sweetness of her like I had once upon a time.

Instead, I picked up my office line and grunted, "Hatley, here."

Chapter Twenty-one

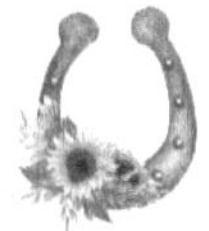

McKenna

EVEN IF I WANTED TO

Performed by Rachael Fahim and Brad Cox

Holy hell, I was shivering with need. It was rolling through me in waves I was having a hard time controlling even with Maddox on the other side of his desk and a phone in his hand. My body was begging me to straddle him in his chair and finish what we'd started.

It had never been this way with us before. In the past, we'd had a slow, sweet build that we'd lost ourselves to. This…this had been a tear-your-clothes-off, throw-you-on-the-bed kind of passion. The kind I'd doubted existed. With Kerry, I'd been lucky to climax before he was through. If I didn't, he told me I was too wound up that night. Moments ago, with Maddox, I'd been ready to come without him ever having gotten me completely naked.

I squirmed on the wooden chair across from him, forcing myself to take in my surroundings, to focus on anything but how his thick bottom lip moved when he spoke and how it had felt on mine. I concentrated on the plain tan walls and more black-and-white photographs I suspected were his, and when that didn't work, I started working my way through every bone in the human body.

When he finally hung up, we stared at each other for a long moment, and I wondered why he'd been talking with Trap's parole officer.

"Why—"

"Are you—" We both spoke at the same time and stopped with an uneasy laugh.

He waved a hand at me. "Please."

"Why are you looking for Trap?"

His jaw flexed as he debated telling me the truth. He got up, went back to the closet, and finished getting dressed. I could feel his eyes on me, but I refused to watch, knowing if I did, I'd only want to help him right back out of the clothes. Once he had his uniform on, he came and sat on the edge of the desk, legs inches from mine.

"Sybil is in town." He waited for my reaction, but I'd already heard the news from Rianne, so I just nodded, and he continued. "She screwed up the terms of her probation, and now I'm charged with arresting her and putting her in jail. I chased her up to the West Gears' Nest today, and…" He hesitated, rubbing his beard. "Let's just say, after the showdown, I have reason to believe Trap's life might be in danger."

I sat there stunned for a moment. Unsure what I was supposed to feel. Unsure what I actually did feel. I didn't love the man. Not in the way you were supposed to love your parents. Sometimes, I wondered if I could even love at all. If the capability had been ripped out of me with every hit and mark and bruise. *You loved Maddox*, my conscious screamed. And I had…or at least as much as a screwed-up teenager could love another human being.

"Did you arrest her?" I finally asked.

He shook his head. "No. She took off on an ATV with a member of the Gears. We're still looking. Now, it's your turn. Why are you here?"

I rested my hands on my knees, forcing my toes to be still. "Rianne…she told me about Mama and the threats she held over you regarding Mila's dad." I looked up, and his eyes narrowed in on me. I didn't know if he was upset with Rianne for telling me or just the fact I knew more than he'd wanted me to. I couldn't read him this way, so I just pushed forward with my logic. "I wanted to help. So, I called Trap to confirm he isn't Mila's dad and ask if he knew who Mama might have been with."

His eyebrows lifted, and he inhaled sharply. The idea of finding out who Mila's biological father was would be a sucker punch because Maddox was actually Mila's dad no matter whose DNA she had running through her. The love the two of them shared was undeniable and definitely more than I'd ever felt for either of my parents.

"Did you reach him?" he finally asked, voice deep and tortured.

I shook my head. "Some woman answered, but she said she could get him a message and would have him call me back."

"Give me the number," he said. The coincidence of us both looking for Trap on the same day was a weird twist of the universe, as if fate really was playing with us.

I still hesitated.

"McKenna."

"If I give you the number, you'll run it and have someone confront her, and then there's no way Trap will return my call."

"Trap's not Mila's dad, McK," he said.

"How can you be sure?"

"Just a gut feeling. He was damn pissed at Sybil when he found out what she did to you."

I fidgeted, not wanting to go there today, to relive more memories than I'd already been accosted with since coming back to Willow Creek. "Still…he might know who the father is."

I watched him consider this, and I imagined there was a war going on inside him. Did he want to know the truth or not? It could end up helping him…or costing him everything. The only thing it would do for sure was pull him out from under Mama's thumb.

"What did the parole officer say?" I asked.

"He hasn't been at his last known address for a while, and he wanted to know why I thought he might be six feet under because they have reason to believe he was involved in a bank heist."

My chest squeezed ever so slightly, and I was surprised, after just convincing myself I felt nothing for him, that there was even the slightest bit of sorrow at the thought of something having happened to my dad.

"I'm sure he's fine, McK. You know Trap. He has itchy feet. He's probably just riding the roads, thinking he has time before he has to check in again."

The intercom went off again. "Sorry, Sheriff. It's Willy now. He says he's missing tools again."

Maddox sighed and then answered back. "Did you tell him to check his truck? The last three times, that's where we found them."

"He said he did, sir."

"Where's Liam?" he asked.

"Out at the Travis farm, helping round up more escaped chickens."

I couldn't help it. I laughed. Chickens and missing tools. "Tough day at the office?" I said between chuckles, and, to my surprise, Maddox joined me.

"You have no idea."

He got up and headed for the door. He pulled on a pair of boots sitting by a coatrack, donned his Stetson, and then looked back at me. "I'll see you at home?"

That singular word did something to my insides, curling through me not with passion, but with something soft and fuzzy. Had I ever really had a home? Even when the Hatleys had tried to give me one, I'd protected myself from them, knowing I was going to leave. It had felt temporary, even when I'd felt the love and kindness they'd sent my way. *No one will ever want you enough to keep you*, Mama's voice returned to me. I'd heard it on repeat when I'd been staying with them. It had been ingrained in my veins that I wasn't enough for anyone.

I couldn't find my voice, so I just nodded.

He was halfway out the door before he looked back. "Don't let Mila convince you I let her have five cookies before dinner."

I smiled again.

"So, stay away from 'maybe'?" I teased.

He shook his head with a wry grin. "Absolutely no maybes."

And then he was gone, striding from the office with a confidence that didn't exactly surprise me but made me feel like I'd missed an important part of his becoming a man. As if the boy I'd known, who'd showered me with affection, had taken a turn I'd never seen coming. Maybe it was his law-enforcement training, or maybe it was just because he'd found his purpose and knew he was right where he belonged.

♫ ♫ ♫

When I got back to Maddox's house, Rianne and Mila were at the round dining table with Mila doing homework. I'd never done homework until I was much older because Mama would never have helped me. It wasn't until I could hide it from her that I was able to finally turn mine in.

"McKenna!" Mila jumped down and hugged my legs in a way that was starting to become addicting. She greeted her father the same way—full tilt, all joy. My heart flipped and turned.

"Guess what? Rianne made lasagna for dinner. Lasagna!" She skipped and twirled.

"You sure like food a whole lot," I said. Rianne snorted, and Mila just nodded.

She leaned into me and asked in a quiet, whispery voice, as if it was a secret. "Do you know what foods I don't like?"

I shook my head.

"Eggplant and Brussel sprouts. One time, Daddy tried to make Brussel sprouts like hash browns, and it made me throw up."

I laughed.

"Wait here!" Mila said, putting her hand up to me in a stop motion as if I was going to run out the door, and then she took off down the hall.

Rianne rose. "Her homework is done. Uncover the lasagna when the timer goes off, and cook it for another fifteen minutes before letting it rest for another fifteen. I have a book club meeting to get to. You'll be okay until Maddox gets back, right?" she asked, waving a hand in the direction Mila had gone.

I swallowed hard. I wasn't sure if I'd be okay. I didn't know what to say to my sister. I didn't know how Maddox would feel about us being alone. But I didn't say any of that. "I'm a licensed physician. I can handle any medical emergency, so I think I'll be okay," I said with a small smile.

Rianne laughed. "I don't think your medical degree can prepare you for Storm Mila, but you'll still be fine."

She patted my arm, hollered goodbye to Mila, who hollered it back, and then left.

I wondered again how Maddox would feel about this turn of events. My stomach twisted, but I wanted this, didn't I? Time to get to know her… A chance to fight for people in my life who had once cared about me so maybe I'd have more than one person in my corner.

"So, how was school?" I asked when Mila came back into the living room, pulling a little red wagon.

"Amazing!! Did you know turkeys were almost our national bird?" she asked.

My lips twitched. "I might have heard it at some time or other, but I forgot until you said it." I tilted my head toward the wagon. "What do you have in there?"

"My favorite things. If we're going to be best friends like you used to be with Daddy, you have some catching up to do. And—"

A ringing interrupted her, "Hey, Soul Sister" breaking out just like Maddox's ringtone. I looked around, but Mila didn't even question it. She ran to her backpack and grabbed a cell phone out of it.

"You have a phone?" I asked, shocked at a five-year-old carrying a phone around.

She nodded. "I have exactly seven numbers that I can call: Daddy, Nana, Papa, Rianne, Uncle Ryder, Auntie Gemma, and Auntie Sadie." She ticked them off on her fingers as she said them. "I can*not* get on the internet or buy anything." She said the last part as if it was the worst thing in the world. "I can't even play games like Missy can on hers. Daddy says it's only for mergencies."

"Emergencies," I clarified.

"That's what I said, mergencies." She answered the phone. "Dadddddy! Guess what? I'm showing McKenna all my favorite things, and Rianne made *lasagna*, which is almost as good as bacon, apple pie, craps, and cinnamon rolls but not quite."

She was quiet for a moment. "Okay, Daddy." Then, she stuck the phone in my direction. "Daddy wants to talk to you."

I took the phone, swallowed, and said, "Hey."

"I'm sorry that Rianne left already." He let out a huge sigh. "I thought I'd be home by now, but we pulled over the second truck full of stolen merchandise in almost as many days, so I'll be a few hours yet. I can call Mama or Dad to come and get her, and they'll keep her overnight."

That knife twisting in my sore heart made new marks. "You don't want me to stay with her?"

"No, it's not that…" He was quiet. "I just didn't want you to not have a choice."

A lump formed in my throat I had to clear before I could speak. "I'm absolutely, one-hundred-percent happy to be here with her."

And I meant it, from the bottom of my soul.

"One hundred percent, huh?" he said with a slight tease to his voice, and it eased my heart, remembering how Maddox had always loved his percentages. "Okay. She'll try to get you to let her stay up, but there's one more day of school left, so she needs to be in bed by eight."

"In bed by eight, got it."

"Two cookies at most."

"Two cookies. Check."

"Don't let her force you to wear tights, put on lipstick, or watch *Scooby-Doo* if you don't want to."

I let out a laugh at the thought of Maddox in tights with pink lipstick on. "I take it you're talking from experience?"

"Those secrets go to the grave with me."

The smile on my face grew, not only from the images of him the words had created but from the lightness in his voice and the fact we were talking without arguing. There wasn't the tension that had been there since I'd first arrived and he'd told me to get the fuck out.

That wiped my smile away. I was still leaving. If I could get my career back in California, I had to go finish it. What other choice did I have? But if my career was over… I shook my head. I didn't want to think about it tonight. I wanted to enjoy this moment with the sister I'd just discovered.

"Don't wait up," he said. "It'll likely be well past midnight before I get home."

Those words and images assaulted me with things I'd thought I'd given up wishing for after Kerry. I hadn't thought I'd ever want a home, or a partner, or someone coming back to me.

"See you in the morning, then," I said quietly.

"Wait," he said just as I was about to hang up. "Maybe I should have your number so I don't have to use Mila's once she's asleep."

"Oh. Sure. Of course."

I gave him my number, and my phone buzzed with an incoming text.

"Now, you should have mine, too."

I stared at the Winter County area code that hadn't appeared on my phone in a long time, heart slamming in my chest.

"Goodnight, McK," Maddox's voice was deep, as if he, too, was overwhelmed by the idea of having my number again.

"Goodnight, Mads."

♫ ♫ ♫

Contrary to what Maddox had said, I did wait up for him—just not in the living room. And maybe 'waiting up' was a bit of a stretch. It was more like I'd been unable to sleep as I tossed and turned, thinking of him out dealing with criminals like the West Gears. When the front door finally opened at twelve-thirty, I sat up in the guest bed, fighting the urge to go see if he was okay.

I heard his booted feet come down the hall, treading softly on the wooden planks but still making noise. He stopped in front of Mila's room, and I could imagine him peeking in at her to make sure she was okay, and then he continued down the hall, stopping outside the guest room. I fought another wave of desire to jump from the bed and into his arms. I clutched the comforter, twisting it in my hands and forcing myself to stay put.

I'd never felt this way when Kerry had gotten home late. I'd been annoyed if he'd woken me up, but now all I could think about was asking Maddox about his day, shoving my hands into his hair that was as silky and thick as I'd remembered it, and making him forget everything except us, our lips, and our touches.

I was delusional. I had to be half asleep.

When his feet continued down the hall, disappointment hit me low in the belly. But it was stupid to think he would have opened the door, even if I knew he desired me as much as I did him. It was stupid to wish for something I wasn't sure I could keep, because the last thing I wanted to do was start something that ended up with one of us hurt all over again. Do no harm… I had to remember my promise, even when Maddox's kisses tempted me to go all in, damn the consequences.

Chapter Twenty-two

Maddox

WANT IT AGAIN

Performed by Thomas Rhett

My body was exhausted, but my brain was still on alert by the time I got home. McKenna had left the porch and hall lights on for me, but the rest of the house was in darkness. I cursed myself silently for feeling disappointed. Had I actually expected her to be waiting for me as if we were more to each other than old acquaintances who'd shared a couple of heated kisses?

I looked in on Mila first. She was passed out, as always, Chester and Charlotte on either side of her. Her face was soft and peaceful, and my chest ached with how much I loved her. The steps I'd taken today…chasing down Sybil and Trap…it could threaten everything I'd built with her. But if I was honest, it could also set us free from threats that had hung over us the entire time we'd been together.

When I left her room, I stopped outside the guest room door, tempted to look in on McKenna as well. Would she be passed out? Golden hair spread out around her like Mila's? Would her face be soft and peaceful? I put my hand on the knob, debating. If she was awake, I could pretend I just wanted her to know I was home. I could ask how Mila had been and if they'd gotten along. When really, what I wanted to do was go in and finish what we'd started in my office. I wanted to strip her down until she was naked and squirming beneath me. I wanted to touch and lick and kiss every inch of her.

My body was no longer tired. It was as awake as my brain.

I forced myself away from the door and down the hall to my room. The cold shower did nothing to relax me, and my hand did nothing to assuage the ache I felt for her, an ache that had barely been hidden in the years she'd been gone and now had bloomed fully back to life. I'd always been an idiot when it came to her. Now, I was risking my little girl's heart as well as mine. I was risking some asshole being able to stake a claim on my daughter.

My heart clenched, and the hard-on I'd been sporting since standing outside McK's room disappeared. McKenna was right. I had to find Trap and see if he knew who had fathered Mila. If I could prove it was one of the West Gears, I doubted any judge in their right mind would grant them custody, not only because they were criminals but because they were transient, traveling between their headquarters here and another club farther south.

This brought a frown to my face. The Gears usually spent the winter down closer to Baton Rouge, and I wasn't sure what was holding them up this year. The second shipment we'd taken tonight was still nothing—appliances that had disappeared from a warehouse in Missouri—and yet, it felt like I was missing something that should have been screaming in my face. Something bigger than this was in the works, and it made the back of my neck itch, as if I had a reaper breathing down it.

When I finally climbed into bed, it was only to toss and turn through the wee hours until gray began to slice its way through the partially closed shutters. I gave up, putting on the uniform it felt like I'd just stepped out of and heading into the living area.

Rianne, Mila, and McKenna were at the counter, talking in hushed voices over plates filled with breakfast burritos. McKenna saw me first, eyes narrowing in as she assessed my face. I was sure I looked as bad as I felt, and the beard made me look even scragglier. I should get around to shaving it.

"Daddy!" Mila jumped down and ran to me, and I picked her up. She squeezed me as if I'd been gone a month. I held her tight, inhaling her scent, and kissed the side of her head before putting her down again. "I missed reading *The Day the Unicorns Saved the World* with you. McKenna tried her very best to do the voices, but she isn't as good as you. I told her she just had to keep practicing, which is what you tell me to do when I'm not so good at something."

"Breathe, Bug-a-Boo."

She stopped and inhaled sharply, and I found McKenna's gaze with mine. She was smiling, a soft smile, but this time, it was her real one, making her uniquely colored eyes glimmer and glow and the corners crinkle. It caught my breath, holding it captive until I thought I'd keel over.

"I left you a burrito in the microwave," Rianne said, and I reluctantly turned away from McKenna to look at our old teacher. I moved around the island to give her a side hug.

"Thanks. I don't know what I'd do without you," I told her.

"Starve," she retorted.

"We'd just eat at Tillie's every night. Right, Daddy? Or maybe at the Dairy Queen. Or maybe at Uncle Phil's, except I'm not really supposed to be at Uncle Phil's at night because it's for *grown-ups*," Mila whispered the last word at McKenna. "And Daddy says he and Uncle Phil don't always get along because Uncle Phil can be a *snake*."

McKenna laughed.

"Mila." I frowned.

"Oops. I wasn't supposed to say that. I overheard Daddy telling Auntie Gemma, and he says I'm not supposed to repeat other people's conversations even if I do have ears like a barn owl." Mila pattered away as she bounced from one foot to the other. "McKenna, did you know that owls can turn their heads almost completely around?"

McKenna nodded, but Rianne put a hand over Mila's mouth before she said anything else. "On that random fact, chick-a-dee, why don't you go get your coat and backpack on so I can take you to school, and your daddy and McKenna can have their own conversation."

I rolled my eyes, heading for the coffee pot and the food in the microwave.

Once Mila had pulled on her coat and backpack, she came running back to give me a goodbye hug and kiss. "Love you, Daddy!"

"Love you more, Bug-a-Boo. Be good. Learn a lot."

"I always do!"

Then she and Rianne were out the door, and silence settled down around us.

I sat at the island, leaving two stools between McKenna and me in order to stop myself from pulling her from it and kissing her good morning the way I wanted to. I couldn't let myself get used to this. To her. She'd likely be gone before the month was up.

"It must be hard," she said, and I tried not to choke as my fifth-grade-boy brain went to places it shouldn't.

I looked over my burrito at her and grunted out, "What?"

"Your schedule—sometimes seeing her at night, sometimes not."

I breathed out a big sigh, put the burrito down, and took a sip of coffee before responding. "Honestly, you've kind of seen my schedule at its worst. It's mostly an eight to five gig.

There isn't a lot of activity in Winter County that can't wait until morning."

She didn't say anything, and I risked a conversation I didn't really want to have. "You used to say you didn't want kids, but were you and the fiancé planning on having them?"

"Kerry. His name was Kerry, and he wanted them, but I didn't. We'd agreed to consider adoption but not until we'd both been in our jobs for at least five years."

"In other words, he thought you'd change your mind," I said.

She grimaced slightly. "Maybe."

"You have to work a lot of long hours yourself, right? You're in your third year of residency?"

She nodded, a haunted look returning to her eyes before she looked away.

"What field of medicine did you decide on?" I asked.

"Emergency medicine. I love the pace of the ER, the ebb and flow, being able to be there for people when it feels like the worst is happening," she said. Her choice didn't surprise me at all. She knew a lot about worst days, and I could absolutely imagine her wanting to make those better for others.

Her phone buzzed, and she ignored it.

"You have someone calling you a lot," I said, referring to the messages she'd received almost every time I'd been with her. "A boyfriend, maybe?"

She flushed. "I wouldn't have let you kiss me if I had a boyfriend."

My eyes fell to her lips, and they parted slightly under my inspection.

"I want to kiss you again." I was surprised to find the truth escaping me—a truth that seemed ridiculous after years of her absence and my panicked attempt to force her out of town. I still didn't trust her to stay. I didn't trust her to not hurt me and blow up my world, and yet, it was still true. I not only wanted to kiss her, I wanted to devour every inch of her. Notch myself in her so deep and so hard she'd finally forget about California, the ex, and anything but me and Willow Creek.

"Don't you have to go to work?" she asked, eyes sliding down my uniform and then toward the door.

I chuckled, stood up, and put my plate and cup in the sink. "Yes. And if I started kissing you, and there was no one like Amy around to interrupt us, I might never make it there."

My voice was deep and growly with barely contained desire.

Her phone buzzed again, and this time, she actually looked at it. Her expression changed immediately, fear slicing through her again as it had on Sunday.

I reacted on instinct, snatching the phone from her grasp.

"What the hell?" she exclaimed right as I read the text.

1-530-555-8220: Fucking fix this, bitch. Fix it, or I'll find you.

Fear and dread filled me. As if it wasn't bad enough that Mila and I had Sybil and the West Gears hanging over us, threatening our family, now there could be some unknown menace coming our way as whoever this was tried to find McKenna in Willow Creek. The piece of me that had screamed at her to get the fuck out the day she'd arrived raised its ugly head and made me want to scream it at her all over again. My number-one job was to protect Mila at all costs.

But then I looked at the fear McK was battling, and I saw the teen girl who I'd repeatedly shown up too late to save—the one with blood on her chin and terror in her eyes. And, suddenly, anger was the only emotion I felt. Not at her, but at this asshole who was threatening her, promising her violence after she'd spent an entire childhood being tormented by it.

I'd once promised myself I'd always be there to rescue her, or at least pick her up and hug her after she'd saved herself for the millionth time. And I hadn't. I'd let her go because it was easier to blame her for leaving than my inability to follow.

"You're right—what the hell?" I growled, and I wasn't sure who the growl was directed at—her, me, or the dick who'd sent the text. "Who is this? What is this?"

"Give me my phone, Maddox," she demanded, holding out her hand.

I didn't at first. Instead, I took my phone out and snapped a picture of the text before handing it back to her.

"Tell me why someone's threatening you," I insisted, trying to pull on the calm of my job and just ask for the facts. But inside, I was broiling. Inside, I wanted to smash a nameless, faceless person against a few walls.

"It's none of your business," she returned, pulling on the expressionless mask she was so good at wearing when the worst came at her.

"This…" I waved the picture I'd taken toward her. "This is why you're here. You're running? From who? For what reason? What could you have possibly done working at a hospital that would result in this kind of attack? Does the hospital know? What do the police say?"

I sounded like Mila, rambling out a series of questions one after the other, but my heart was pounding, and my chest was aching. My fight-or-flight instinct kicked in, and I was ninety-nine percent sure I was going to be knocking down doors and raising hell with people in California.

She sat back down at the island, elbows propped on the counter, and put her face in her hands. She looked…crushed. Lost and devastated, like she'd looked the first night she'd shown up, and I'd seen her crying in her car. I wanted to fix it. Needed to fix it. All those years ago, just like she'd said, I'd walked away without a fight, and there'd been no one there to protect her—some asswipe of a fiancé who'd abandoned her just as easily as I had.

I eased over to her, and when I rested a hand on her back, she jumped. She'd done that for at least a year after I'd first found her in the shed as a child. But later, she'd gotten used to me touching her in the random way friends would collide, had even touched me back at times. And when we'd finally kissed nearly nine years after the moment we'd first met, she'd never held back.

Now, who knew how long it had been since she'd been held. Adored. Cherished.

"McKenna," I said softly. "Please tell me."

She looked up from her hands.

"I did the right thing, and it ruined everything," she said.

Chapter Twenty-three

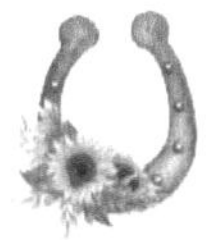

McKenna

Maddox looked so strong and determined, as if he could take the weight of my world and carry it easily on his shoulders, and it wouldn't be a burden to do so. I'd been an inconvenience my entire life. First to Mama, then to him and his family. I'd most certainly been dead weight to Kerry because I'd barely been able to contribute to our living expenses, whereas he'd had a trust fund and parents sending him an allowance every month. Of course, I never would have lived in the expensive condominium he'd chosen if I hadn't been with him, but still, I hadn't pulled my fair share.

The only time—the only place—I'd ever carried my own weight was in the ER.

There, I wasn't a burden. I was a protector.

The way Maddox was looking at me, though…as if he wanted—no, needed—to help me carry the load… God. It unraveled some knot I'd held tight in my chest for years. Maybe my whole life. It was his look, as if I was someone special who deserved to be loved, that had me crumbling.

Everything came tumbling out of my mouth in a rush. Layton. CPS. Being put on paid suspension. The texts I couldn't prove were from Dr. Gregory. The whole time I talked, his face got grimmer, tighter, until I thought his jaw might snap, and I'd have to wire it back together.

"You don't need to just take this," he said quietly when I finally stopped. "There are ways to find out the store he bought the prepaid phones from, if that's what he's using. We can get security tapes. At a minimum, you can file a restraining order."

I laid my head down on my arms on the island. The thought of doing all that, filing a report, trying to go after him… It all felt like…too much. What I really wanted to do was hide like I'd done whenever Mama was in a mood. The shed across the street had only lasted for a few years because she'd easily discovered it. But then there'd been the church, and Tillie's, and eventually, I'd been able to call Maddox on a cell phone I kept off unless I absolutely needed it, hidden behind a ceiling tile in my room.

"Let me help you," he said quietly, sitting down on the stool beside me, leaning over so his face was closer to mine resting on the counter. "This isn't like when we were kids, McK. I have resources, things I can do to make sure this guy stops threatening you."

Our gaze locked, and I wondered how, even after all these years, he could still read me so easily. Read my thoughts and feel my emotions. He'd said Mila was an empath, and even though they shared not an ounce of DNA, I wondered if she'd somehow picked it up from him, because he'd always felt deeply, carrying my hurts with him.

He'd been a beautiful soul at eighteen, and now, he was a magnificent man.

I moved ever so slightly, joining our lips. A simple caress meant only to be an enormous thank-you, not only for offering to help today but for all the times he'd wiped my blood from my body, put ice on my bruises, and helped me forget for a few hours how badly my life sucked. For giving his heart to me even though I'd stomped on it because I hadn't known how to keep it and still run.

The hand he'd had on my back moved up to my hair, tangling in it, and the kiss swiftly moved from a sweet thank-you into thundering need. I licked at the seam of his mouth, and he opened for me, letting me in where I continued to slowly explore every soft, wet corner, trying to give when I felt like I'd always taken.

He groaned, dragging me up and jerking the stool so I was tucked against him. His hands gripped my waist, thrusting our hips and cores together as he took command of the kiss, claiming me with the same fierceness I'd felt in his office. Long fingers slid under my T-shirt, softly caressing and sending a wave of glorious goosebumps across my skin that felt painfully raw. Every nerve ending ached to be touched by him.

His palm cupped my breast, and he inhaled sharply, lips moving against mine as he grunted out, "Do you ever wear a bra?"

I smiled. "Rarely."

"Jesus…" He pulled my top over my head, and I let him. Then, he just stared for a moment before slowly swirling his fingers around my nipples, which were taut and aching. "Even all these years later, these are the breasts I dream about."

He bent, licking and savoring one while his fingers worked the other. My body convulsed, my core rippling. It wouldn't take much to push me over the edge. I moved so I was straddling him, drawing him even closer as my hands found their way into his hair, and he continued to lick and suck and twist. My hips thrust, rubbing along the delicious length of him hidden beneath the zipper of his uniform, my yoga pants barely a barrier. A tortured whimper escaped me.

His mouth returned to mine, hands going to my ass, and his hips rocked into me, pushing against my core. I pulled free of his lips. "God, Mads, I'm going to…"

I shattered, shuddering and shaking around him. My eyes rolled back, and my entire body went limp, falling into him. He caught me, easily bearing my weight and kissing down the side of my jaw, sucking my earlobe, and igniting me all over again even as the last trembles of my orgasm were still rolling through me.

"You're so goddamn beautiful, McKenna. When you're stubborn, when you're running, but even more so when you're letting go and exploding from my touch." His voice was rough, almost hoarse, with the lust.

My hands slid down his chest, finding their way between us and stroking him through his pants. His forehead landed on my collar bone, breath coasting over my neck and chest, and I shivered again.

He pulled back, looking into my face, hands settling on top of mine where they stroked him, stopping the movements. "As much as I'd rather pick you up, take you to my bed, and not let you out until you've screamed my name several more times, I have to go to work."

"You're the sheriff. Can't you be late?" I asked, hardly recognizing my voice. It was full of desire and something I was afraid to name because it tied me to him in ways I'd once tried to sever.

"Normally, I'd say yes, but I've got a DEA agent coming in to meet with me this morning."

Regret filled me because I was making him late, because I'd taken the time to unburden myself and add another responsibility to his shoulders. No matter how much I told him now not to bother with Dr. Gregory and the texts, he wouldn't let it go. He'd add it to the list of things he needed to get done before he came home to his family.

I slid off of him, and he stood up, adjusting himself.

He caught my hand, drawing it upward, which forced my gaze to his. He placed a soft kiss on my palm, and I trembled again.

"I can see those wheels turning, McK. You're not a burden," he said, and my eyes widened a little because he had read my thoughts so perfectly. "This is my job. It's what I do. Let me help you."

I hesitated and then nodded.

"What can I do for you?" I asked.

His face broke out into the cockiest grin I'd ever seen on Maddox Hatley. It was sure and sexy and made my core clench tighter. "I'm sure we'll figure something out."

I laughed. "Is this how you conduct all your investigations, Sheriff Hatley? Quid pro quo?"

His smile remained, a chuckle escaping him. "Only with you, McKenna Lloyd. Only with you."

He leaned in, kissing the side of my head like I'd seen him do with Mila, and then stepped back. He walked toward the door, his steps awkward, and a laugh burst from me.

"Having trouble walking, Sheriff?"

He looked back at me as he placed his hat on his head, blue eyes glimmering. "Just wait, McK. You're going to be the one having trouble walking when I'm done with you."

"Promises, promises."

"And you damn well know I keep mine."

The door shut behind him, and my heart pattered with joy at the same time my body quivered with anticipation. Need. Want. Hope unfurled in my chest, and it didn't feel like the demon I'd thought it was. I didn't know exactly what would happen or how we could move forward, but I knew I didn't want to give him up again. I didn't want to give Mila up either. Maybe losing everything in California had actually given me exactly what I needed.

A trembling, scared thought peeked its way into my soul. Was there a way I could keep everything? Bring the best things from my past with me into my present?

I picked up my phone, opened the web browser, and searched how to get licensed in another state. I could at least figure out if it was possible, right? After I'd seen the steps it would take, I went onto the FREIDA site where doctors could find schools and hospitals accepting residents and looked for positions available in Tennessee. Just looking at the site hurt in multiple ways. Pained thoughts of taking a tiny step backward. Pained thoughts of not being allowed to finish at all. But then—almost worse—the beautiful, tortured idea of moving forward.

♫ ♫ ♫

I was just putting away the ingredients I'd bought for the one meal I could actually cook—tacos from ground beef and packaged sauce—when Eva showed up to drop Mila off from school.

"McKenna, McKenna, McKenna!" Mila said, running toward me. She was wearing a paper headband with a hand-colored turkey sticking atop it and was holding a goody bag with cartoon turkeys. "We did *not* celebrate Thanksgiving in school today because Mrs. Cody said it's wrong to celebrate the annexation of an entire race of human beings."

"Annihilation," Eva said, lips twitching.

"That's what I said." Mila rolled her eyes and turned from her grandmother to me. "But we *did* celebrate the *beauty* of turkeys. Mrs. Cody read a book that made me want to be friends with the turkeys and not eat them, just like the kids in the book. I've told Nana we absolutely *cannot* cook a turkey this week. I refuse. I will run away after I steal it from the house."

Eva chuckled. "How are you going to carry a frozen, twenty-five-pound slab of meat, Bug-a-Boo?"

Mila's mouth dropped open. "You froze him, Nana?! He's FROZEN?!"

Eva pulled Mila into her arms. "Remember the talk we had about the different types of cows on our ranch? The ones providing milk and the ones providing food?"

Mila nodded.

"And remember our talk about where bacon comes from?"

"I love bacon, but I still don't like the idea of killing pigs to eat it. I wish it wasn't so good," Mila pouted.

"Turkeys are the same, chick-a-dee. Humans eat plants and animals. As long as the animals are treated humanely, it's okay to enjoy the food."

Mila put her hands on her heart as she stepped away from Eva. "I don't know, Nana. I think I might become a vegetation just like Mrs. Cody."

"Vegetarian."

"Yep, that's what I said."

"You'd give up bacon?" I asked, inserting myself into the conversation for the first time. "I don't know if I could do it. Bacon is one of my favorite foods, too."

"It is?" Mila asked.

I nodded.

Her little face looked conflicted. "I need to think about this," she said. Suddenly, she stopped moving, eyes going wide before she took off at a dead run down the hall. "I have to go to the bathroom!"

The silence left behind her was, as always, loud.

Eva's lips twitched as she found my gaze with hers. "When I saw Rianne at our book club last night, she said you and Maddox seemed to be getting along well."

I tried not to let my face flush as I thought of the way we'd been tangled earlier on the very stool I was sitting on and the promise Maddox had made of making love to me until I couldn't walk. My chest ached, and my heart slammed against my rib cage.

Eva laughed. "The two of you were always like that. Combustible. I was half worried you'd end up pregnant before you could go off to college."

I lost the battle I'd been fighting, my cheeks fully turning red. "Wow…I don't even know what to say."

Her laugh died, and her eyes journeyed down the hall to where Mila had gone before they came back to take me in. "But there's a lot more at stake now, McKenna."

"I know," I said softly.

"I don't know why you came back to Willow Creek, and I'm not asking you to tell me all your secrets. Just tell me you're not going to walk away and not see them again for ten years."

There was not an ounce of anger in her voice, not even reproach, and I wondered why. I'd hurt Maddox, deeply, irrevocably. There was a chance I could do the same to her granddaughter, and yet, she wasn't holding my past over me. She just wanted to make sure I wasn't going to screw up the future.

"I very much want to stick around," I told her, feeling the strength of it in my blood. The research I'd done that morning I could put into action only if things in California went my way. If they didn't, I could still stay, but I'd have to consider an entirely new line of work.

Mila skipped down the hall with a paper in her hand. "I forgot to give this to you yesterday," she said as she handed it to me.

It was a stick-figure drawing of a man in a cowboy hat, a woman with what looked like a stethoscope around her neck, and a little girl who stood between them. Their stick arms had ball hands joined together, and above their heads was written *BFFs*. It hurt as much as it filled me with joy.

"I'm not that great of an artist yet. But that's Daddy"— she pointed to the man—"me, and you." She continued to point to the people. "You and Daddy used to be BFFs, which means all three of us can be BFFs now."

I hugged her to me tightly as, once upon a time, Maddox had held me, with an overwhelming sense of belonging rushing over me. I'd never felt it before. Not with the Hatleys. Not even with Maddox as a teen. Maybe because I'd never dropped my shield around them. But for whatever reason, the feeling slammed into me today. We could be a family. A family I'd never, ever had and never thought I needed or wanted, but it was all I could think about now—keeping them all.

"You know what my favorite part of BFF is?" I asked her softly.

She shook her head.

"The forever part."

She giggled, and when I looked up at Eva, her eyes were full of tears she brushed away. She patted my shoulder and headed for the door. "I'll see you on Thursday."

Mila wiggled out of my embrace and ran after Eva, hugging her legs. "Love you, Nana."

"Love you more, chick-a-dee."

Then, she was gone, leaving behind an air of warmth and love that I wanted to wear like a coat I never had to take off.

Chapter Twenty-four

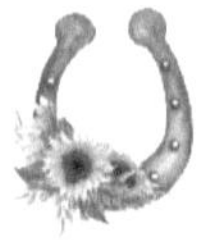

Maddox

When I got to the station, I sent Amy and Bruce off to track down information on Dr. Roy Gregory and the damn burner phone before going into the conference room where a DEA agent awaited me. Enrique Salazar was a medium-height, deeply tanned man with rows of muscles sure to make a heavyweight boxer jealous. He was dressed in a black T-shirt, jeans, and military-grade boots with tattoos covering almost every piece of skin peeking out on his upper body.

"What brings you to Willow Creek?" I asked him.

"How much do you know about the Lovato cartel?"

I frowned. "Out of Mexico, right? Rising fast and furious. Y'all have been chasing them along the border for a couple of years now."

He nodded. "They've been branching out, finding ways upstream. They've hooked up with small-time MCs and local gangs in an effort to stretch their wings and compete with some of the larger syndicates who already have their pipelines in place."

"You think they've been talking to the West Gears?" I said, the itchy feeling on my neck coming back.

"I've got pretty good intel that says they're way past talking. Your man, Chainsaw, has met several times with the Lovato family over the border. He's neck-deep into it. I heard you pulled over a shipment of appliances yesterday, is that right?"

I wasn't sure I liked how much of my business he knew, but I also wasn't going to turn down interagency help if it meant undoing the West Gears hold on my county.

"We did. Doesn't fit their prior MO at all, but it's the second haul in as many weeks. We took a look inside, but it's just appliances."

"Mind if I let my drug dog take a sniff?" he asked.

I said I didn't, and we headed out with his beagle to the facility behind Scully's station in the next county where we'd stored the semi-trucks with the stolen goods. It took barely a minute for the dog to start barking, and after we'd carefully pulled apart the appliances, we found ten kilos of cocaine hidden deep inside the working parts.

I wasn't sure if I was happy to finally have something solid or pissed that we'd missed it. Salazar and the district attorney spent the rest of the morning trying to get the two Gears we had in custody to flip on Chainsaw, and when they didn't, they added the drug trafficking to the list of charges already lined up on their arrest warrant. I was in the middle of arranging transport to the state prison, where they'd be held until trial, when Uncle Phil called.

The man was not my favorite relative. I wasn't even sure how he and our grandmother had come from the same parents. The way he looked at his female patrons made my skin crawl, but he'd never done anything overtly illegal or even morally questionable, so I just bit my tongue and avoided him as much as I could.

"What can I do for you?" I asked.

"I got a dead body by my dumpsters, so you can do your job and come pick it up before it scares the hell out of all my customers."

It took me a beat longer than it should have to process his words.

"Who is it? And how do you know they're dead?" I asked, grabbing my hat and hollering at Bruce to join me as I strode toward the door.

"The bullet hole in his head makes it kind of obvious," Phil said, and I swore there was a tremor to his voice.

"Shit. You didn't touch anything, did you?"

"I'm not stupid, Maddox."

"We're on our way. Don't let anyone near the scene."

When Bruce and I pulled up with our lights blazing, Uncle Phil was pacing by the dumpsters, looking decidedly green. When we joined him, we found Slider slouched against the brick, his eyes wide and soulless, with a gunshot wound at his temple. I didn't want to disturb the body before we had everything photographed, tagged, and bagged, but it was obvious he'd known his killer, because I could see the grip of his own piece peeking out from his waistband. He hadn't felt threatened enough to pull it.

Bruce called the medical examiner, who was also the chief of internal medicine at the local hospital, while I requested help from a few part-time crime scene folks we had on call for the rare times we needed more than the basics my staff and I could handle. Once they arrived and were thick into processing the scene, Bruce and I started canvassing the area.

We talked to the customers at the bar, businesses around Phil's, and knocked on doors. The duplex McK used to live in had a clear shot of the parking lot and rear entrance to the bar, but no one there had seen anything. At least, nothing they were willing to talk about. I was back outside, arranging a time for the autopsy with Doc Frank when Bruce radioed me from inside McFlannigan's.

"Sheriff, Sybil just walked in, sat at the bar, and ordered a two-hundred-dollar bottle of scotch. Ted wants to know if he should serve it? Want me to take her in?"

I lifted my hat, brushed my hand over my hair, and replaced it, all while wondering if this nightmare day was ever going to end. Hit after hit. Leave it to Sybil to be the cherry on the top of the cake.

"I'm on my way back in," I said, knowing Sybil would raise hell if anyone else tried to arrest her.

When I got inside, she was sitting in a dress that screamed money with jewelry dripping off her neck, wrists, and fingers. She looked and smelled like she'd just stepped out of a salon, and her entire attitude was so relaxed it was almost uncanny.

"Sybil," I said. "Surprised to see you just strolling in when you know there's a warrant out for you. Doesn't happen to have anything to do with Slider, does it?"

She raised a brow. "It's not my job to keep tabs on him, so why would I know where he's at?"

"That wasn't exactly my question, and I figure the laundry line in Willow Creek is short enough you've already heard I got his dead body out back. So, why don't you try again. Where'd you and Slider go after you left The Nest yesterday?"

"Slider dropped me at Stonemill Mall. After I was done shopping, I spent the night at the Heartland. Alone. Spent all day in their spa. They got surveillance cameras there, right? You can check it out, *Sheriff*."

My jaw ticked as it always did at the sneer she put on my title, but I wasn't going to rise to her bait. As far as I could tell, she was the last person to see Slider after they'd left The Nest, but it would be easy enough to check her story, just like she said. The mall and the hotel both would have cameras. It made me itchy again. Too convenient. Too tied up.

Did I believe Sybil was capable of murder? I couldn't be sure. She was evil, cruel, and violent, but she'd never taken anything that far before, and I'd never known her to carry a gun.

"I gotta take you in, Sybil. You're in violation of your probation."

She swallowed the scotch from the single glass Ted had placed in front of her, likely to placate her until I arrived. She didn't respond to me. She just slid off the stool, turned around calmly, and placed her arms behind her back.

Her silent acquiescence was eerier than her rants had ever been, and my skin continued to prickle as it had all day. I Mirandized her, cuffed her, and hauled her back to the station. She didn't say a word until I was sliding the holding cell shut.

Then, she looked up at me with a weird-ass smile and said, "I'm going to enjoy this."

I rubbed my beard, hating myself for giving in and asking, "Enjoy what, Sybil?"

"Watching everyone who's ever wronged me get what they deserve, including those little bitches I tore myself apart giving birth to."

My chest squeezed, anger flaring along with a healthy dose of disgust.

"Jesus, Sybil. Mila's a baby, and McK…" My throat bobbed. "She was just a kid when you hurt her."

"She was a selfish leech, an iron chain dragging me down below the surface. I had to stay in Willow Creek because of her! Trap left me because of her! If she'd never existed, I would have been able to go after him. I'd *still* be with him." Her calm veneer started to crack in the middle of her tirade. "I wouldn't have lost him to those other Gear whores. But no, he stuck me in that shithole duplex to raise a daughter neither of us wanted."

"You know what I think?"

"I don't give a flying fuck what you think," she said as she tried to pull herself back together.

"I think you would have lost him whether or not you'd had McK. I bet you got pregnant just to trap him," I said.

Her face paled, and her eyes went wide as if I'd uncovered her deepest, darkest secret. I gave her an ugly laugh because I finally knew the truth.

"He didn't want you, was probably leaving you, and you pulled one last stunt to try and tie him up. When it didn't work out the way you'd planned, you took it out on McK."

She rose and slammed a hand against the bar near my face. "You don't know shit. She ruined everything, and I'll ruin her and everyone around her, including you. I've kept a tally, and every single person who hurt me is going to regret it, including Trap, Chainsaw, and the West Gears."

Her words stirred up the vision I had stuck in my head of Slider's soulless gaze. If she was on a vendetta, had that included him?

"You kill Slider, Sybil?" I asked.

She laughed. "No. I didn't need to."

"So, you know who did, right? Who was he meeting with?" I asked, and I saw a flicker of something inside her cold eyes that might have been fear. "I might be able to get you a deal if you tell us."

"I don't want a deal. I'm happy right where I'm at. I'll watch everything burn to the ground, and then I'll walk out of here and start my new life."

I changed tactics. "You think Chainsaw is going to just let you walk away with whatever it is you're holding over him? I think you'll end up just like Slider."

"I'm not worried about Chainsaw," she said, but I could hear the false bravado in her tone. Then, she shrugged. "Besides, he won't be in charge long. I think I'm going to enjoy watching him go down next."

It was like an icy hand drifted down my back.

"What's that supposed to mean?"

She smiled an evil smile and then lay down on her cot without another word.

"If you've had a hand in this, Sybil, I'll personally see you locked up for the rest of your life."

She ignored me, humming that country song about a winning ticket.

I walked away, trying not to let her words and attitude affect me and wondering if I was more worried or less that she hadn't brought up Mila's father even once. I couldn't remember a discussion with her in the last four years when she hadn't held it over me.

Sybil knew something about what was going down. Chainsaw had sure as hell seemed in charge the day before, but maybe there was a war going on I didn't know about. Maybe it was with the Lovato cartel. Or maybe it was between the old Gears under Trap, who'd never really been into drugs, and the new Gears under Chainsaw, who were. Regardless, it was the last thing I needed, because a war meant more bodies ending up on the streets of Willow Creek.

The town and the people I loved were counting on me. I needed to get my head on straight and keep it that way. My brain was still whirling when I walked in the door well after midnight. I'd wanted to be home for dinner, but for the second night in a row, I'd missed it, just like I'd missed reading to Mila and finding out about her day—and McK's.

Thoughts of McKenna did nothing to help me stay focused on my job, sending my body into overdrive instead. Craving escape. Craving her.

As always, I ducked into Mila's room first. The kaleidoscope of shimmering rainbows surrounded me as I kissed her on her forehead. I retucked her blankets tight against her and stared down with my heart in my throat. I'd had to grow up fast when I'd taken her in, but I'd never regretted it, not even the tiniest bit. Every moment I'd had with her was the best moment of my life. She was pure joy. Heaven placed here on earth.

I closed her door and stopped in front of the guest room, just like I had the night before, but this time, emboldened by our heated kisses that morning, I turned the knob. The room was dark, only the hall light pushing at the black. McKenna was on her stomach, bare legs sticking out of the comforter and a tiny tank partially covering her top half. She had more skin showing than clothes or blankets. I ached to run my hand over the silky expanse, to tuck my fingers underneath it all and find her core that had come apart simply by rocking on me earlier.

But she was as passed out as Mila, and I had a feeling, from the dark circles under her eyes ever since showing up in Willow Creek, she hadn't been sleeping any better than I had lately. There was no way I'd take her peace even if it was to give her another kind. Instead, I closed the door and journeyed down the hall to my room.

My mind and emotions were a jumble—confusion over the feelings for McK which had resurfaced amongst the kisses and teasing we'd found in the last two days, frustration because I hadn't been able to spend my day chasing the asshole from California like I'd wanted, and anxiety over the West Gears, Chainsaw, the Lovatos and whatever the hell was going down with them. Layered over it all was the image of Slider's dead body. My life felt like a bunch of loose strings that needed to be tied together, and I was afraid if I missed one, everything would unravel completely.

Eventually, my brain and body finally shut down, tossing me into an uneasy slumber haunted by people running in the dark and faces I couldn't see, until Mila's tiny voice calling my name in fear jerked me from my dreams.

I yanked open the bedside drawer where I kept my gun in a lockbox only to realize there was no one in the room, and all my straining ears picked up was a sudden burst of laughter—Mila's and McKenna's—like two sets of windchimes echoing off each other or like the very first notes of your favorite song.

I pulled on a pair of sweats and padded out of my bedroom, down the hall, and into the kitchen only to stop suddenly at the sight before me. Mila was covered in chocolate powder from head to toe. It clung to her golden hair, turning it a strange shade of brown, and made her face look like a burlap sack. McKenna hadn't fared much better. She had it sprinkled all over her chest and the tiny tank top she wore over a low-hung pair of flannel bottoms. They both had stunned looks on their faces that turned into another round of laughter.

I inched forward, called by the infectious joy on their faces.

McKenna saw me first, and her smile disappeared. "Oh God, I'm so sorry. I'll clean it up."

"Daddy!" Mila launched herself at me, and when she hugged me, a little puff of powder burst between us that had me chuckling.

"What happened here, Bug-a-Boo?"

"McKenna and I were going to make chocolate-chip pancakes, and I thought she needed the hot chocolate, so I was trying to help, but the lid was stuck, and when I finally got it off, it imploded."

"Exploded."

"Right. Imploded."

Mila had her arms and legs wrapped around me like a little lemur as I slowly made my way toward McKenna. She looked upset, as if the mess was the end of the world. And maybe in her past, it would have been. Maybe in her current life, she lived neat and tidy, but I'd grown up on a ranch, with three siblings, and now I had Mila who routinely left disaster in her wake.

McKenna turned to the sink, wetting some paper towels. I pulled her hand from the water and drew her up tight against me with Mila still clutched to my chest.

"Good morning," I said, and I kissed McK's forehead before I even gave it much thought. Mila giggled, and McKenna's eyes went round, looking between my daughter and me.

"It'll just take a minute to clean it all," McKenna said, a little breathless, gaze landing on my lips and then journeying back up. I smiled, loving the way her look had lingered and knowing she wanted our kisses as much as I did.

I put Mila down, bending to meet my daughter's eye. "Go get undressed, start the water in the tub, and I'll be there in a minute to help you with your hair."

She sighed. "Fine. But do we still get chocolate-chip pancakes?"

I had a million and one things waiting for me at the station, but I was supposed to be off today. I'd planned on spending the first day of Thanksgiving break with my girl long before McKenna had shown up. Bruce would call if he needed me urgently. And sometimes, I needed to step away from a case in order for the pieces to glide back together, time and distance giving me the clarity I needed.

I tugged gently on Mila's loose braid and asked, "How about we go to Tillie's for breakfast, and then, after, I take you both to the ranch for a horseback ride?"

She stared at me for a minute before her face broke into an enormous smile. "That would be the *best* day *ever*!" She turned to McKenna. "Right, McKenna? Wait. Do you even know how to ride a horse? I know how to ride a pony, but

Daddy says I'm too small to ride the big horses on my own yet, even though Papa says Daddy was littler than me when he started riding."

"Mila. Breathe," I reminded her.

She took a breath as McKenna said, "Your Papa taught me how to ride, too."

Mila's eyebrows shot up. "You are sooooo like me! I mean, we look the same, and we like the same things. We're definitely going to be best friends."

McK and I shared a glance at her words, at the fact Mila had realized they looked alike. But neither of us said anything as Mila skipped from the room, puffs of powder going everywhere as she did.

As soon as she was around the corner, I turned back to McKenna, wrapped my arms around her waist, and drew her up close. She held herself tight but didn't pull away, and I didn't give her a second to start talking. Instead, I put my lips where they'd been aching to go since I'd walked out of the house the morning before harder than I'd ever been.

As soon as our mouths touched, her body softened, leaning into me.

She tasted like cocoa and hints of sweetness that had always been her. I licked her mouth, her cheek, down her neck, and along her chest, everywhere the dust had settled. I groaned at the sight of her pebbled tips through the thin tank, and I set my mouth on top of one, sucking through the fabric, inhaling chocolate and her.

She gasped, fingers digging into my shoulders, arching into me.

I reached behind her, tugged the pull-out sprayer from its hole, and flicked it on with my pinky. Then, I shot water all over her face and chest.

She screamed and blustered, pulling away. "Maddox!"

Water dripped from her hair, and her thin top was now completely see-through, clinging to her.

I laughed, enjoying the sight of her disheveled and sticky. God, I wanted her that way for other reasons. She reached for the faucet, trying to turn it off or grab it from me, and I easily kept it away, spraying her more and drenching us both in the process.

"You're on your own now," she said as she stepped away and put the island between us. "You can clean it up. I'm going to shower."

My laughter followed her as well as my gaze, taking in the way her hips swayed across the room. At the archway, she looked down the hall, as if making sure Mila wasn't there, then she pulled the tank top over her head, and my body, that had already been hard, jumped to full alert.

"Too bad I'm too old to have help in the bath," she said with a sultry smile.

I let the faucet go with a clang and set chase. She shrieked and took off down the hall with laughter bubbling from her lips, but by the time I got to the guest bath, she'd already closed and locked the door behind her.

"You're never too old for that kind of help, McK. I promise after I've made you too sore to walk, I'll give you a bath," I said through the door. She laughed, and I knocked on the wood. "Just remember, you started this."

"You're the one who sprayed me," she said.

"You're the one who tempted me," I told her.

"God, just go help Mila."

I chuckled, my entire body stiff with desire as I walked away, thinking about every single thing I was going to do to McKenna Lloyd and just how much we were both going to enjoy it.

Chapter Twenty-five

McKenna

LITTLE BY LITTLE

Performed by Joel Taylor

Seeing Shadowfax hit me with waves of memories and nostalgia. I'd expected the horse not to remember me, but after I put my hand out, he nuzzled and neighed, stepping closer and butting his muzzle into my shoulder just like he had ages ago.

My throat grew thick.

"Shadowfax is one of the prettiest horses at the ranch," Mila said. "I want to ride him, but Daddy says not yet. I do like Daddy's horse, too. Papa says for my eighth birthday, he's going to buy me my own horse and I can go with him to pick her out because horses and people find each other just like princes and princesses in fairy tales."

"Breathe, Bug-a-Boo," Maddox said, flicking his little girl on the cheek softly before turning to me. "You remember how to saddle him?"

"I remember," I said quietly.

Once we'd tacked up the horses, Maddox tucked several paper sacks he'd brought with him from Tillie's and placed them in the saddle bags he'd hung on Arod.

Tillie had been overjoyed to see us all together that morning. "M&M, thick as thieves again, I see."

Mila had picked up on it immediately. "M&M? Like the candy?"

"Yep, those two were inseparable," Tillie said with a nod. "Couldn't have one M without the other."

Mila had grown quiet before asking, "What do you call three M's? Because now there are three of us."

It had lodged another lump in my throat I wasn't sure I'd ever clear as Tillie considered her. "Well, I guess it would be M&M's because there are more than two kinds in the bag, right?"

"I'm definitely the yellow M&M," Mila said. "Because Nana says I have the most sunshiny soul she's ever seen."

Tillie had laughed. "That you do. That you do."

Mila had looked at us after Tillie had moved off and said, "Daddy, you'll be the blue M&M because of your blue eyes, and McKenna will be the green one because her eyes can look greenish sometimes. Have you noticed, Daddy?"

Maddox's gaze had met mine, locking me into place. "Yes, I've one-hundred-percent noticed. It's a good choice. Green M&M's have always been my favorite."

There was absolutely no scientific data to back the claim that green M&M's were some sort of aphrodisiac, but I still found myself flushing a thousand shades of red at Maddox's innuendo. I'd blushed more since coming back to Willow Creek than I had in what felt like a lifetime. I wasn't a blusher by nature. There wasn't anything about human anatomy and sex that I considered embarrassing. But Maddox's words…they weren't sex and anatomy. They were sweet compliments and sensual promises, and those I was unaccustomed to.

Now, as he held Shadowfax's reins for me while I mounted, my skin heated again as he caressed the back of my hand before stepping away. It was more than just a tender little touch. It was another torturous promise, just like the ones he'd spoken about outside the bathroom door.

I turned my gaze from his to Mila's as I pulled myself together.

She wasn't afraid of the horses at all. Instead, she stood with her hands on Arod's muscled shoulder while Maddox mounted. Then, he reached down to lift her easily up in front of him. His biceps rippled under the tight Henley he had on, and my gaze lingered on his bulging arms before looking up to his face. He winked and then tipped his hat down low over his eyes and urged Arod forward.

Shadowfax and I followed, and I watched as Mila and Maddox moved with the horse. There was something innately tender about the way she was wrapped in front of him, like he was protecting her from the entire world, and I guessed, in a way, he was. I could hear her chattering but not what she was saying because they were just a little too far ahead of me on the path. It was probably a good thing because I needed my complete concentration on learning the movements of a horse again, trying to remember all the things Brandon had ever taught me about riding and attempting to keep my hands light on the reins.

The sun was bright, but there was still a slight bite to the air that made me glad I'd done laundry while Mila was at school, so I had my thick green sweater and jeans on with my only pair of tennis shoes. I wished I had my cowboy boots—the ones I'd left at the ranch so Mama couldn't find them but then had taken with me to college only to promptly give them away in my efforts to forget Tennessee.

As we got farther away from the barn, I realized Maddox was leading us on the much longer path around the ranch to the hollow I'd visited. The route he was taking would make sure we didn't have to jump the creek. At the top of a small rise, Maddox pulled up, and I brought Shadowfax alongside Arod, looking down over the pastures and meadows. As far as I could see was Hatley land. Acres they'd almost lost during those tight times right before I'd left Willow Creek. But now, the freshly painted house, the fancy gate, and the half-dozen cabins behind the barn proved it was thriving.

"I'm glad y'all kept the ranch," I said.

"Y'all?" he teased with a wink. "Careful. Your Southern is going to start showing again."

I pushed my foot into his leg, and both horses danced in place at the motion.

"It's all due to Ryder," Maddox said. "At first, our parents were pretty wary of the idea, but he showed them the statistics on other ranches who'd become profitable again this way, and then, he went out and got the loans to oversee the renovations."

"And your parents? What do they think now?"

"They're happier than they've ever been. Mama gets to cook and fuss over our guests, and Dad loves teaching folks how to ride and fish. We've kept enough of the animals and crops to sustain the restaurant during season and have some small contracts with local farm-to-table restaurants in the off-season. Plus, there's still Mama's pies, which make a helluvalot more than you'd expect."

His voice was full of pride as he talked about his family. It was pride that was well earned. The Hatleys had banded together and saved their family land. What could be better than that?

"Do you still feel guilty about not working with them?" I asked quietly.

"Yes and no. I'm glad I stayed local to get my degree so I could be another pair of hands through the transition, but I don't love the business the way Ryder does. I love chasing bad guys and putting them behind bars."

"And chasing chickens and putting them in pens?" I teased, remembering what Amy had said the other day about Liam helping corral the escaped poultry.

He laughed. "Let's just say growing up on the ranch has given me the right experience to wear my sheriff hat."

"Daddy, let's go. I want to see if there's still a family of foxes down by the creek," Mila said, lifting her hand to his face. He kissed the palm.

"Okay, Bug-a-Boo. Shall we see if McKenna can keep up with us?"

Mila smiled, gripping the pommel as if she knew exactly what was coming. "Yes!"

He nudged Arod, and the horse took off at a fast trot that had Mila giggling. I patted Shadowfax's side, leaned low next to his ear, and said, "You ready to catch them, old fella?"

And then I was off, too, racing down the path after Maddox, the wind blowing through my hair, the sun shining, the air full of wet earth and grassy fields. My heart was light and happy, as if there was no weight on it at all. As if this was where I was always supposed to be.

We burst through the willow and oak trees near the top of the ridge above the hollow, slowing the horses to a walk before stopping them. Maddox slid down and then helped Mila off. I dismounted, and we left the horses to wander, knowing they wouldn't go far. Maddox pulled a blanket and the sack lunches from his saddle bags, and then, we used the roots of the trees as steps to climb into the little circle we'd always claimed as ours.

We spread everything out before piling onto the thick plaid wool, shoulders and thighs touching, while Mila dug into the sacks.

"Did your daddy tell you how we used to play pirates down here?" I asked.

Mila shook her head, biting into her sandwich and causing egg salad to squish over her cheeks in the cutest way.

"We'd pretend the creek was the ocean and that we'd sailed our ship into this secret cove so we could hide our diamonds the evil pirates were after. We'd sneak back in behind all the roots and bury our treasures," I said, pointing to the dark recesses of the tangled limbs.

"Are they still there?" Mila asked, eyes wide.

I chuckled but then thought of the jar full of my nightmares. It wasn't a treasure, but it was still there. "Most of it was food, so I'm sure some wild animal found it."

Mila pointed to the corner of the hollow near the creek. "That's where the mama fox had her babies. We only saw her twice, and Daddy thought maybe we scared her away, but I think she knows this place is safe. That we won't hurt her. What do you think, McKenna?"

"I think I always felt safe here," I replied, and Maddox's gaze locked with mine again. Heavy feelings, past and present, filled the air between us. Mila grabbed our hands and locked them together.

"You're okay now, you know," she said.

"Wh-what?" I asked, looking down at her.

"The pirates can't hurt you anymore." Then, she put down her sandwich and said, "I'm going to see if I can find any more gold in the creek!"

"One foot on the ground at all times, Bug-a-Boo," Maddox called after her.

"I know, I know!"

We watched her grab a stick and dig around in the water.

"She seems so...old for her age," I said quietly.

He didn't turn to look at me. Instead, he was tense, watching Mila as if he was going to have to go running to save her if she fell. It tugged at all those pieces deep inside of me that had once loved the way he'd looked out for me, too. There was a warm bubble that surrounded you when you realized Maddox Hatley was on your side, a safety net I'd tossed aside with a carelessness I'd forever regret.

"Rianne calls her an old soul," he said. "Mama calls her an empath. I think she's just lived a lot harder life than most. She may not remember it consciously, but her body does. Humans are geared to fight for our basic needs, and she had to fight harder than most."

I clenched my fist tight at the image he'd painted, hating Mama a little bit more.

"Daddy, I can't reach this one!" She turned back to us with expectant eyes.

Maddox went over, fished out a rock, and handed it to her before rejoining me on the blanket again.

"Is there actually gold in the creek?" I asked, surprised.

Maddox rolled his eyes. "That's all Ryder. He placed fool's gold in there and told her the fairies left it."

My heart snagged at the idea of the arrogant, playboy Ryder leaving fairy dust for his niece. "Wow, she really does have everyone wrapped around her finger."

He chuckled. "From the moment she showed up."

How much I'd already missed of her life hit me in the chest like a blow, and the ham-and-cheese sandwich turned to dust in my mouth. I shoved it back in the paper sack.

"Hey," he said, grabbing my hand. "You okay?"

"Mama…she made me miss one more thing," I said, frustration welling.

"You're here now. She can't make you miss anything again. Now, it's up to you."

We stared at each other, and I realized he was asking me what I was going to do. I knew what I wanted. I knew I wanted to stay, but I also didn't want to give up my career when I was so close to finishing it. I wanted my cake and to eat it, too. I wanted the issue with Dr. Gregory to disappear, my residency to be miraculously done, and for me to be able to find a job at the hospital here in town. But it felt like too much to ask of a universe who had barely granted me one small wish at a time. And it was too big of a conversation to have in the middle of the hollow with Mila playing next to us, so I just squeezed his hand, got up, and went to the creek to look for fool's gold with my sister.

Chapter Twenty-six

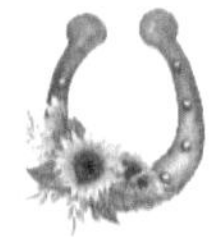

Maddox

I WANNA MAKE YOU CLOSE YOUR EYES
Performed by Dierks Bentley

The breeze picked up after we ate lunch, whistling through the trees and hollow, and making McKenna and Mila both shiver. We'd dressed warm, but not warm enough for nighttime, so as the shadows started to get longer and the sun started to sink, I knew it was time to head back.

"Can I ride with McKenna?" Mila asked, and my stomach knotted. I was always selfish when it came to Mila. I wanted all her moments, but I was also selfish in a different way now. I wanted Mila to worm her way into McKenna's heart and put down roots so maybe, just maybe, McKenna would have one more reason to stay.

"McK?" I asked. She knew I was asking for more than if she wanted Mila with her. I was asking was she ready for it? Could she keep them both safe?

"I'd like that. We'll have to ride slower than you and your dad, though, because I'm not quite the horseman he is," McKenna responded.

I helped Mila up in front of McK, and we made our way back to the barn, slow and steady, with them leading the way and me following. Mila chatted away the entire time, and I watched, fascinated, as McK's shoulders moved with laughter. My mama was right. Mila was the best kind of sunshine. Rays of joy that spread over everyone around her.

When we finally made it back, it was to find Sadie and Terrance in the barn. I tried not to overthink it when they broke apart as I opened the doors.

"I was wondering who'd taken my horse!" she said, coming over to nuzzle Shadowfax as I lifted Mila off, and McK slid down.

"I didn't know he was yours," McK said. "I'm sorry."

"Oh, don't be. We weren't going riding today, anyway. Terrance"—Sadie flicked the shoulder of the tall, red-haired guy next to her—"is afraid of horses."

I barely held back my snort, but Sadie must have caught it anyway because she glared. "Don't start, Mads. Otherwise, I'll be forced to tell McKenna about your monk lifestyle and lack of sex."

I put my hands over Mila's ears, felt my cheeks heat, and shot Sadie a glare. "Jesus, Sadie. Really?"

McKenna's lips were twitching.

Mila squirmed under my hold, and I removed my hands from her ears and said, "Go say hi to Nana and Papa real quick before we leave."

"Okay, Daddy!"

She skipped away toward the farmhouse.

"What have I said about talking like that around Mila, Sades?" I scolded.

Sadie leaned toward McKenna and talked out of one side of her mouth. "It isn't just Mila. He doesn't like any of us talking about sex. You should see the group chat with the four of us. It's like, 'Don't talk sex, don't mention sex, don't have sex,' all the time. I think he and Gemma almost wet themselves when I said Terrance and I had hooked up in the theater bathroom."

Terrance choked, and he and I exchanged a look that I turned into a glare.

"You do remember I can arrest you for public indecency, right?" I said, reaching over and tousling her hair.

She pushed my hand away. "It was absolutely, wonderfully indecent, too."

Terrance turned bright red and backed away from her toward the house. "I… I think I'm going to head back inside."

"Ryder and I thought we'd take you for a little car ride tomorrow, show you the sights. That all right with you, Terrance?" I boomed after him.

It was Sadie's turn to gasp, and she slammed her fist into my shoulder. "Knock it off."

"You started it by bringing him here in the first place," I told her.

She followed Terrance, leaving McK and me in silence. We rubbed down the horses, watered them, and tucked them into their stalls before heading toward the house ourselves.

"Sadie is…" McK trailed off.

"A firecracker. Just like someone else I know used to be." I looked down at her.

"I was never quite that…open," she said, and it took my smile away because she hadn't been. She'd teased and tossed out one-liners, but there'd always been a reserve to her that held her back from completely letting go. I wondered if it would still be there once I had her in my bed, naked and panting.

It was absolutely the wrong thought to have as I walked into my mama's kitchen.

"Daddy! I want to spend the night. Aunt Sadie is making pizzas and said I could design my own in any shape I want. I think I'm going to try and make a rainbow-shaped one with a puffy cloud hanging off the end."

I sighed. "You've already spent the night twice this week, Bug-a-Boo."

"Let her stay," Sadie said.

"Where's Mama and Dad?" I asked, looking around.

"Getting ready to go line dancing with the Abbotts. The rest of us are just going to hang out here. Mila will be fine."

"You won't be able to get distracted with…you know." I shot a glance over to where Terrance was on the couch with her other friends, a card game spread out on the coffee table in front of them.

Sadie rolled her eyes. "As if. Mama put me in Mila's room, and Terrance is staying over the barn."

"That doesn't mean shit. McK and I used to sneak out to the barn all the time."

McK made a garbled noise in her throat, and Sadie laughed. "I remember teasing you both about k-i-s-s-i-n-g-ing. That's kind of funny."

Thoughts of kissing McK were definitely at the forefront of my brain, but I still couldn't help feeling uneasy about leaving Mila with the college crowd.

"She'll be fine, Mads. You'll be here bright and early to help with Thanksgiving, anyway, right?"

"Daddy, pleasssssseeeeee?" Mila's eyes were wide, she had her hands in prayer mode under her chin, and she was still hopping from foot to foot.

"You'll miss spending time with McKenna," I told her in a last-ditch effort at finding a way out of this.

"I'm not worried. McKenna isn't going to leave us anymore," she said and then threw her arms around me, knowing I'd already given in. "I love you, Daddy."

She took off into the living room, demanding to know what Sadie's friends were playing.

"You sure?" I asked Sadie one more time.

"Oh, my God, yes! Just go before I throw the rolling pin at your thick skull."

I headed for the door with McKenna. Sadie's voice followed us out into the chilly evening air. "Have fun, you two. M&M sitting in a tree, K-I-S-S-I-N-G."

I threw a one-fingered wave back in at her, and she chuckled as the door slammed shut behind us.

McK and I were quiet on the ride back to town. It wasn't until we were nearly at the house that I realized I hadn't told McKenna about arresting Sybil and the threats she'd thrown out. I was shocked to realize I hadn't truly thought about any of it for hours. The Gears. Sybil. The threatening texts from Gregory. We'd had a peaceful day, and I wanted it to continue that way into the night, long enough for me to keep my promises I'd tossed at her earlier.

McK fidgeted, fingers tugging at her low ponytail.

"Where you at?" I asked as I pulled the Bronco into the garage.

"Nowhere, really," she said, unbuckling and climbing out.

I let us in the back door, flicking on the kitchen light. The counters sparkled from the extra cleaning they'd gotten that morning, trying to wipe away all the cocoa powder.

I dropped my hat on the counter, reaching for her arm before she could step too far away. I drew her into me, chests colliding. The scent of hay and horses, of grass and sweat, surrounded us, but also the chocolate still hanging in the air and the natural sweetness of McKenna.

My hand landed on her collarbone, surrounding her neck, sliding a finger up and down along her pulse point. "McKenna."

"Yes?"

"I think I'm going to have to break my promise." My voice was thick, desire already licking through me now that we were alone, now that I had her in my house with my hands on her.

"Yeah? Not sure you can perform? I mean, how long has it been, monk?" she teased, but she was nervous. Her teeth bit down on her bottom lip, and her pulse fluttered under my touch.

"Oh, I'm quite sure I can perform. But I think we need to put the bath before the sex in order to wash away the smell of the horses."

She pulled away, and I let her go. She took two steps backward, shot a glance toward the windows that were still shuttered, and then lifted her sweater over her head. She'd worn a bra today, probably because she'd known we were going riding, and I was slightly disappointed.

She took another step back and kicked off her shoes.

I followed. Every layer she took off, I echoed—shirt, shoes, pants—until we were in the hallway in just our underwear.

She hesitated on the final layers, standing there with her palm sliding over her stomach.

"Don't stop," I grunted out, my mouth watering and desire beating through me.

She tugged at the waistband of her underwear. "These? You want me to take these off?"

"I don't know, McK," I said, flicking at my waistband. "Do you want me to take these off?"

She licked her lips. I took a step toward her, and she didn't move back. I was close enough that I could reach out and pull the cup of her bra down, freeing her, watching as her tip hardened even more under my touch. I flicked the straps off, moving even closer so I could reach behind her and undo the clasp. "This made things uneven."

My palms surrounded her soft swells, fingers squeezing gently, and she let out a little whimper. I drew gentle circles around her peaks, and her breath grew ragged.

She dropped her hands to my waist, tugging at my boxer briefs, and I mirrored the motion on her panties. We played the same game we had moments before but removing each other's clothes instead of our own. A slide of a finger, a tug of cloth, tantalizingly slow movements with our eyes locked until both pairs of underwear dropped to the floor.

"How long has it been, monk?" she asked breathlessly.

"A while. You?"

She swallowed. "Since Kerry. I haven't really had time and sort of lost interest."

"What do you mean you lost interest?" I asked, sliding my hands around her waist and picking her up. She wrapped her legs around me, and I strode down the hall toward my bedroom.

"I was tired of doing all the work to barely get off," she said, and it sent ripples of anger and frustration through me. That she'd been with assholes who wouldn't take care of her. But knowing McK, she hadn't let them either. Knowing McK, she'd held up her barrier and refused them entry.

I kicked my bedroom door shut behind me and set her down on the bed. She was tall, only three or four inches shorter than me, and the bed brought her breasts to the perfect height, level with my mouth.

I took a moment to lick and savor each one as she ran her hand through my hair.

Then, I stopped and dropped to my knees, hands going to her ass, squeezing and massaging. "You want me here, McK?" I asked, moving so my breath coasted over her core and reveling in the fact her skin burst out in goosebumps.

"God, yes," she said with a soft moan.

"Then, you gotta promise me something."

"Anything."

That had me stopping, looking back up at her with a sure smile, loving that she wanted me this badly, wanted me so much to offer up anything.

"You can't hold back," I told her. "No wall. No shield. You drop it all, feel every goddamn thing I do to you tonight."

She swallowed hard but didn't deny the fact she normally kept up a barrier. She ran a hand over my cheek, fingernails scraping through the bristle of my beard, her pale eyes searing their way through my blue ones, leaving a golden mark behind.

She nodded, and I lost myself in between her legs.

She gasped and whimpered and pulled my hair, and I devoured her with licks and nips and fingers that twirled in and out. When her legs started to give out, I pulled her down onto the bed and resumed my feast, savoring every single touch and sound and movement until she was clenching around me and calling my name with that breathy whisper I adored. "Mads, God, Mads. Right there. Please…Mads…"

Then, she went over the edge, and I almost lost it with her.

I placed kisses up over her stomach, cherishing each breast one more time before my mouth found hers again. Our tongues slowly danced, in and out, pulsing as if they were other parts of us moving together. My hands explored every groove and valley, and hers returned the favor, squeezing and sliding over my muscles, my hips, my dick.

I shifted to the side table, pulling the drawer below my gun safe open and finding a string of condoms I'd never used in my house and wasn't sure why I'd placed there, but was glad I'd had the foresight to do so. I ripped the packet open with my teeth, looked back over at her, and stilled.

Her face was flush, eyes cloudy with desire, her hand slowly swirling around her belly button, legs spread, waiting for me to come back to her. Her ponytail lay over one breast so only a hard tip peeked through, and my heart lodged in my throat. McKenna was actually here, in my bed, ready for me, wanting me. I wasn't sure my bruised soul could handle it. I wasn't sure I would survive having her only to see her walk away again. But I'd take her—every way I could have her—until she left.

I settled back between her legs, kissing her again with deliberate, gentle thrusts of my tongue I wanted to repeat with my dick. But I wasn't quite ready to be inside her yet because once I was, it would only be a few minutes before it was over, and I didn't want it to be. Not yet. Not ever.

"Tell me you want this. That you want me," I demanded huskily as I kissed the corner of her lip, down her jaw, and bit gently on her earlobe.

She panted. "I want this. I want you, Maddox."

I drove into her, and she arched into me at the same time, as if somehow the two movements would bring us closer, blend not only our bodies but our hearts and souls, shedding the years we'd been apart, leaving behind the pain of absence, and somehow healing the wounds with the pure joy of being together again. Her legs wrapped around my middle, and I could no longer be gentle. I didn't want to be. I wanted to claim her with a raw fierceness. I wanted her to claim me back until she was incapable of ever letting me go.

I took her mouth with a growl as we moved together, biting and licking. I slid my hand over her body, in between us, demanding that every single part of her be present, that she let go and be completely with me.

"You feel so good, Mads."

"You're heaven, McK. My heaven."

She pulsed around me, crying out again, and I lost all control, my movements shaky and wild until I went over the edge into a bliss I'd never known, not even with her in our early days when we'd explored and touched and tried to bring each other pleasure. This. This was like leaving the world to journey through the night skies.

The journey was beautiful. Peaceful. Complete.

We rocked slowly to a stop, returning to the earth and the bed. I rolled, taking her with me, attempting to keep myself tucked inside her because I was unwilling to rend us in two again. She rested her head on my chest, playing with the dusting of hair there as my fingers slid back and forth over her shoulder.

"I thought you said we were going to take a bath first?" she teased.

I chuckled and finally moved away but only long enough to pick her up and toss her over my shoulder. She squealed, slapping my back as I headed for the giant tub I had in my bathroom for no reason other than Mila liked pretending she was a mermaid in it.

Now, it had a new purpose—an entirely grown-up purpose.

I set McK down on the edge, tossed the condom, and started the water.

She looked around the space.

"This feels like you. Much more than the other areas of the house."

I smiled. "I didn't let Mama or my sisters have any control here."

"They decorated for you?"

I shrugged. "They had a say. I wanted it to feel like a home and not some bachelor cave."

I stepped into the tub as it started to fill and held out my hand. She took it, climbing in with me. When we sat down, I pulled her back into my chest and reached for the soap, slowly working it over her skin leisurely, tantalizingly, tempting her to react. Her breath grew choppy again.

"God, I love the sound of you," I whispered into her ear, placing a kiss there. Hoping I'd be able to keep her. Hoping every sound and breath and look and touch would be mine forever.

Chapter Twenty-seven

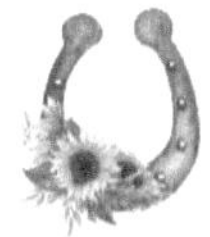

McKenna

BREATHE

Performed by Faith Hill

The first time we'd made love in the bed, it had shattered my soul. I'd left my barriers down, leaving me raw and open just like he'd asked me to. It had enhanced everything we'd done. Each touch had felt more significant. Each kiss and nip had found a new purpose.

In the tub, the second time we made love, it felt like another promise, one I was making to him in return. Forget the years and miles that had come between us. Live for this. These special moments, lost in each other.

"I'm on the pill," I told him as I'd straddled him in the water. "I'm clean."

His eyes widened as he got my meaning, and his dick pulsed between my thighs.

"I'm clean," he grunted, lifting me so I could come down on top of him.

The fullness I felt with him there…the completeness… There weren't enough words to describe it. Home. Family. Us.

The water sloshed around us, up and over the sides as we moved. Our pace was fast and furious, as if we were trying to catch up on years we'd missed. My heart was pounding, body soaring, tightening, quivering.

"Come for me, McK," Maddox said, fingers sliding between us, touching my tight bundle of nerves, and I did, quivering, shaking, calling his name again.

He followed, slamming into me with a growl and moan and something that sounded like a prayer.

I rested my cheek on his shoulder as our pace slowed and the water came to a stop. My arms around him squeezed, and he returned the motion, tightening until I let out a breathy laugh.

His stomach growled, and I chuckled more. He moved fast, dunking me under the water, and I came up sputtering and smiling. I attempted to push him under, but he was made of stone that didn't budge. He just gave me that cocky grin he'd never had in our past but did funny things to my insides.

I climbed out of the tub, grabbed the towel from the rack, and started to dry off.

Maddox stepped from the water, pulled the towel from my hands, and said, "Let me." Then, he began a tantalizing trail over my body with the soft cloth, fingers pushing and pulsing in all the right places until, somehow, impossibly, I was panting again.

"You keep going like that, and you'll be hungry all night."

"There's more than one kind of hunger, McK. This one…the one I feel right here…" He touched his chest. "That's waited too many years to be filled. My stomach can wait."

It was my heart exploding this time instead of my core. I'd promised I'd keep my barriers down, feel everything, and yet, I still wasn't ready for the sensation of losing my soul to him, of handing it over, knowing it would be impossible to get it back. But I wasn't afraid like I'd been anytime I'd gotten close to anyone before, because I knew the truth. Handing parts of myself to him meant I was giving them to someone who would not only cherish them but would do everything in his power to keep them safe.

I kissed him, hard and furious. He responded by picking me up and taking me back to his bed where we spent more hours finding our way back to each other.

♫ ♫ ♫

The only light we had on was the one in the hall, so when Maddox opened the refrigerator, his bare chest glowed. Even though we'd spent hours touching and devouring each other, I thought maybe I wanted to claim him right there in the kitchen all over again.

He had on a pair of gray sweats he'd finally relented to putting on when both our stomachs had growled so loud neither of us could ignore them anymore. I'd taken a T-shirt from his closet to wear, and I was basking in the scent of him surrounding me completely. Like grass and spice and the very best kinds of days.

"It looks like it's a mix-mash night," he said, looking over to where I sat at the island.

"A what kind of night?" I said with a confused frown.

"Leftovers. Little of this. Little of that," he explained as he pulled out a bunch of containers including the taco fixings I'd made, Rianne's lasagna, and what looked like tater tots.

He grabbed two plates and started crumbling things and layering items over the top of the tots almost like nachos, and I laughed.

"Wait…you're going to put them all together?"

"Just wait. You're going to love it. A little feast of flavors." He paused his movements, gaze locking on me. "Kind of like exploring you. Taste after taste. Sensation after sensation."

My thighs locked together. Sore and raw and yet still needy.

"Jesus, Mads. How can you make leftovers sound sexy? Sadie's completely wrong. You are definitely not a monk."

One eyebrow tipped up, the cocky grin returning to his face. "Just because I don't want to talk about my sex life, or my sisters', doesn't mean I don't know what the fuck I'm doing. Maybe you can drop a hint and get them to back off?"

I laughed. "No way am I talking about our sex life with them."

"I'll make it worth your while. Maybe you can embarrass them enough that they realize they don't want to hear about it any more than I do."

"Hmm. Worth my while, you say? Is there something more you can offer besides what we already did?"

He'd been coating the plates with a heavy layer of shredded cheddar jack, but his hand stopped, and he shot me an intense look. "That? That was nothing. I have plans for you, McK. I promised you wouldn't be able to walk, and I intend to keep my promise."

I laughed, but he just shot me another long look making my stomach flip in a completely delicious sort of way.

He put the plates in the oven and then sauntered over to me.

"We have twenty minutes. Think I can make you come again before then?"

"I don't know." I lifted a shoulder. "I've never had this many orgasms in one night. I'm not sure I have one more in me."

He picked me up, put me down on the island top, and pushed on my chest until I was lying back on the cool surface. He eased the T-shirt up and spread my legs. Then, cold liquid hit my skin. I shrieked, propping myself up on my elbows to see he'd swirled chocolate syrup along my thigh and stomach. He shot me a sinful smile before he dipped his head to run his warm tongue through it, licking the sauce and me and sending shock waves through every nerve.

"Holy hell," I said.

And I lost myself to his fingers and his mouth all over again.

By the time the oven beeped, I'd not only shattered again, he'd had time to clean me and the counter up. The grin on his face was even cockier than before.

My fingers found the corners of his mouth. "When did you get this?"

"What?" he asked, biting my finger softly before moving away, grabbing potholders, and pulling the plates from the oven.

"That cocky, sure grin."

He put the plates on the table instead of the counter, and I wondered if I'd ever be able to eat at the island again without thinking of what we'd done there.

He tucked my chair in for me and leaned down next to my ear. "Say it again."

"What?"

"Cocky."

I laughed. His hand went around my neck, squeezing playfully as his teeth nibbled on my earlobe. "Really, McK. Say it again."

"Cocky. Cocky, cocky, cocky."

He kissed me, wet and hard, before backing away.

"You're definitely not a monk," I said, my lips quirking.

And the laugh he let out filled my soul one more time. It was deep and free and utterly contagious.

I picked up the fork he'd placed by the plate and eyed the mound suspiciously.

"Trust me," he said, his voice a soft lure.

"If I throw up, it will end all our sexy times."

"You sound like Mila. You're not going to throw up."

He was already digging in, and I tipped my fork into the mix of food he'd piled together. The crumbled taco meat and lasagna over the salty tots was unexpected. But he was right. It was also good, a wild blend of flavors.

"Good, right?" he said.

"If I admit it, I feel like I'll be adding to this enormous ego you've somehow grown in my absence. I feel the need to take Sadie's side and humble you," I teased, but his face grew serious, and I realized I'd reminded him of what we were both trying to forget—how I'd been gone for a decade.

He cleared his throat and put his fork down.

"I arrested Sybil last night."

I lowered the bite I'd been about to put in my mouth.

"I'm sorry," I said quietly.

"Why are you sorry?" he asked.

"Because I know having to do it causes you an enormous amount of stress. Just like me being here."

"It was time," he said. "I was tired of feeling like I was at her beck and call. It was weird though. She didn't even mention Mila's dad. She just said she couldn't wait for everything to unravel…like maybe she'd already told him."

My heart moved into my throat. "Mads…" He gave me a sad, wry grin, and I slid out of my chair and into his lap, hugging him. "Whoever it is, he'll never be her dad. You're her dad. End of story."

He nodded, resting his chin on my collarbone, forehead tipping into my cheek.

"Should I try Trap again?" I offered.

"I don't know if he can help with the Mila situation, but I do think he might be able to add some insight into what's going on with the Gears. Sybil said Chainsaw won't be in charge long, and that sort of made me wonder if Trap was making moves to take the club back. I'd like a few minutes with him to get some answers."

I left my food behind, searched the floor for the jeans I'd tossed in our dance down the hallway, and pulled my phone from the pocket. There was another text from an unknown number I didn't even bother opening. I just pulled up the number I had for Trap.

The same woman answered as had the other day. "Hey," I said. "This is McKenna again, Trap's daughter."

"I passed your message on. That's the best I can do."

"Thanks. I just… It's really important. Is there any way you can get him another one? Explain it's urgent."

"Hold on."

I was pretty sure she muted me, and I suddenly wondered if she was with Trap, if he'd purposefully had her pick up so he didn't have to talk to me. It tore a little in a way I didn't think Trap was capable of doing to me. I'd never really let him in close when I was little, not only because he was rarely around but because I'd been afraid he'd see through me to what Mama was doing. I'd been terrified of what he would or wouldn't do. The nothing he'd done had almost been worse. He'd let the Hatleys take me without even a second glance.

In truth, I wouldn't have wanted to go with him, and maybe he'd known it.

"McKenna?" Trap's deep voice, scratchy and aged from years of smoking, actually tugged at my heartstrings even as he was ripping it out for having dodged my calls.

"Hey, Trap," I said. "Long time no talk."

He chuckled. "Yeah. Been a few years. You good?"

No, I wanted to say. No, my world had fallen apart. But then I looked over at Maddox sitting at the table, and I wondered if it had fallen together instead. The same thought that had hit me while riding with Maddox and Mila hit me all over again…like this was exactly where I was supposed to be.

"I'm in Willow Creek," I told him.

His response was immediate. "Ah, shit. I'm sorry, darlin'. I forgot to tell you I sold the place. I needed the money."

"It's not a big deal. I think you needed it more than I did," I said with a little laugh. He didn't respond, and I wondered if he felt any real remorse or just felt bad I'd found out he'd broken his only promise. "So, look. I have some questions I need to ask you—about Mama and the Gears. Did you know she had another little girl?"

"I heard something like that." His voice took on a wary tone.

"Do you know who the father is?" I asked.

"It sure as hell isn't me," he grunted out, and it felt like a slap. I winced.

"I figured," I said. It was what I expected, but the relief I felt at his confirmation was enough that I knew, somewhere in my subconscious, I'd actually wondered about it.

"Look. I can't talk on the phone about any of this, darlin'," he said, bite gone but the wariness still there.

"Okay. Can we come and see you?" I asked.

"Who's we?" he asked, even more hesitantly.

"Maddox Hatley and me," I said.

"The sheriff?" he snorted. "I bet he does have questions."

Silence settled down between us. I waited, almost able to hear the debate in his head. Finally, he responded, "Can you be in Knoxville on Friday?"

I covered the phone and repeated the question to Maddox. He nodded.

"Yes, we can be there."

Trap gave us the name of a diner where he'd meet us at ten in the morning and then hung up. I was suddenly bone-weary from the full range of emotions that had wound their way through me in the last few days. From the amazing, incredible, delirium-inducing sex Maddox and I'd had. From years of living with a tiny prick of hope that I actually had a father who would do something just for me, only to have even that slightest whisper dashed away. The demon called hope had scored another point.

Maddox was up out of his chair and surrounding me in his arms in two long strides. He hugged me to him tightly, kissing the side of my head, and I let the warmth and comfort of him and his embrace wash over me. I needed to stop hoping. I needed to just make what I wanted to happen come true.

There was nothing I could do about my career at the moment. I'd lose it, or not. But I could do something about this…about Maddox and Mila and the beautiful life I could have if I let myself be here. I just had to make the scary step. I had to come out of hiding, open my heart, and let them in.

Chapter Twenty-eight

Maddox

CHASIN' AFTER YOU

Performed by Ryan Hurd with Maren Morris

After the call with Trap, McKenna's mood shifted. The sensual teasing disappeared into a melancholy, as if Trap really still had the ability to impact her. I hated that almost as much as I hated some asshole threatening her. And yet, I was also glad the threats had sent her running in my direction. Even a month ago, I would never have said that, even to myself. I would have insisted McKenna being in Willow Creek would be the worst thing to ever happen to Mila and me, and now it was the thought of her leaving again that tortured me.

We cleaned up the kitchen together, and then I dragged her back down the hall to my bed, not willing to let her return to the guest room, not willing to let her go at all. I pulled her into my arms, her back to my front, and held on as if I'd never let go.

"I'm sorry he still can hurt you," I said softly.

She ran a hand up and down my arm. "Hurt's a strong word. Disappoint might be better. I shouldn't be, because I knew he never wanted me any more than Mama did. I've only talked to him a handful of times since I left. It's like having an uncle who lives across the country from you rather than a dad. Except, that would imply I have a family, and I don't."

"You have a family, McK. You have my family." My voice was thick with emotions behind it. The truth of it.

She flipped around in my arms so she could face me.

"I didn't really let you be one," she said. "Mama and Trap could hurt me so terribly when I hardly loved them, so I think I was terrified of what y'all could do to me when I loved you so desperately."

"We did hurt you. We let you go and didn't come for you."

She swallowed hard. "If you had, I would have been even crueler. I wasn't ready to keep you."

Her words hurt and healed all at the same time.

"And you're ready now…to keep us?" My voice was gruff and choked, full of an overwhelming sense of love I'd never lost but only buried. Our gazes were locked, and she didn't look away once. She brushed my jaw, and the beard I'd grown tickled as she rubbed it, but she didn't answer my question, and it stung, twisting my insecurities.

"When we were kids, I felt guilty for bringing my messed-up life into yours. Now, even though I've tried hard to straighten myself out, to be better, I'm a mess all over again," she said quietly.

"I could take it back then, and I can take it now," I said, and she closed her eyes. It hadn't been the right thing to say. It hadn't reassured her, so I tried again. "I don't see the mess, sweetheart. Do you know what I see?"

Her eyes opened back up, brows drawing together.

"I see this beautiful, resilient human being who didn't let the very worst kind of childhood hold her back. She lifted herself up, plowed forward with determination and a bit of stubbornness, and then took on a role where she could actually save others. Not some metaphorical 'save' bullshit either. You actually have people's lives in your hands. You had Layton's life in your hand, and you saved it. That's not a mess. That's nothing to be ashamed of. I'd be happy to stand right in the middle of everything with you, holding your hand and slapping everyone down who dares to say you're something less than the glorious heroine I see standing with a flaming stethoscope."

A little laugh escaped her. "Flaming stethoscope?"

"Well, a sword seems counterintuitive."

"Why don't you hate me?"

"I tried. It didn't work."

"The night I showed up here…I thought you did…"

"That was the fear for Mila talking," I told her. "But do you want to know what I did just a few days before, on your birthday?" Her eyes grew wide, and I continued. "I spent the entire day thinking about you, and when I was alone in my room, I jacked off to my memories of you, just like I had a million times before."

She stared for a long time, leaning in to kiss me tenderly, before saying, "A million times, huh? I bet you're pretty chapped. Maybe you should see a doctor about that."

And she worked her way down my body, tugging aside the sweats and putting her sexy as hell mouth to work in a way I'd never be able to forget, blonde hair swirling around my hips, wheat-and-sage-colored eyes darkening with lust. And all I could think was if I lost her again, there'd only be a shell of me left, but I was damned sure going to do everything in my power to keep her this time. Even if it meant chasing her down.

♫ ♫ ♫

When McK and I showed up at the ranch later than I'd planned the next day for Thanksgiving, the entire family sent knowing looks our way. McKenna blushed a pretty pink, reminding me of the flush that had coated her for hours the night before and made it almost impossible to stand in my parents' kitchen.

Mila saved the day, running in to hug me and then McKenna as if we'd been gone a year. In some ways, it felt like we had. I'd changed overnight, unlocked secret pieces of myself I'd kept aside because they'd only ever belonged to McK.

"Uh-oh, Ryder," Sadie said, bumping his shoulder with hers. "I think the monk might have finally lost his V card."

Ryder grinned, but Mama swatted at her with a kitchen towel, shooting an eye in Mila's direction. "Watch what you say, Sadie."

"What should his new title be?" Ryder asked, rubbing his scruff and trying to hide his smile."

"I have a title," I groused. "It's called sheriff."

"Sheriff Quick Draw."

McK's comeback was so quick it caused my head to twirl, and when I looked at the grin on her face, there was not one ounce of me that was upset, even as Ryder and Sadie burst out laughing. Instead, I headed toward McK. She squealed and ran, and I gave chase. When I caught her, I threw her on the couch and pinned her down with my weight as I jerked off her ankle boots and reached for her feet.

She was laughing and gasping. "Don't do it, Sheriff. I don't want to hurt you."

"Take it back, McK. Tell them the truth. Tell them what you were really screaming last night."

She shook her head, and I let my fingers slide down over her arch. I barely touched it, and she was already bucking and trying to escape with laughter still bubbling from her. My chuckle joined hers as I watched her squirm, remembering every single time we'd ended up this way as kids, including the time she'd knocked me so good I thought she'd broken my nose.

Mila ran in with a smile as wide as McK's as she watched us tussle on the couch. Not wanting to be left out, she crawled onto us, reaching for McK's stomach and getting her own tickles in.

"Stop…stop," McKenna breathed out between laughs. Mila and I shared a look and just picked up the pace of our fingers. "I'm going to pee my pants if you keep it up."

Mila immediately stopped, looking very serious. "It's okay. It happens to everyone, even grown-ups. That's what Daddy told me when I had an accident at the store and was afraid everyone saw, but they didn't because Daddy wrapped me in his coat and took me home."

"When you three have had enough of that horseplay, I could use your help in the kitchen with the turkey, Maddox," Mama said. Her words were a scold, but her face crinkled up in a huge smile, joy radiating from her instead of the worry she so often sent my way.

"Why can't Dad or Ryder do it? Aren't the oldest members of the family supposed to carve?" I asked.

"You know you have the best knife skills," she said. "They'll just butcher it."

I sighed, picking Mila up and setting her aside, then I looked down at McK, leaned in real close to her ear, and whispered, "You're going to pay for that later."

"Promises, promises, Mads," she said, eyebrow lifting, smile still wide and glorious.

"You know I keep my promises."

She caught her breath, her smile slowly fading as heat filled her eyes. I knew she was remembering the same thing I was—our night making love and how her legs had barely supported her as we'd showered this morning.

Her fingers landed on the corner of my lips and the smile I still wore, as if she was still amazed by it like she'd been the night before when she'd called it cocky.

Joy filled my heart. So much that it stayed with me the rest of the day, stayed until we had to leave so I could take over for Liam at the station, and he could enjoy the holiday with his family, too. It was how we did things around here, covering for each other, making sure no one had to sacrifice too much of their life for the job we already sacrificed a lot for.

Mila and McKenna were tucked together on the couch, watching *Scooby* when I came out of the bedroom in my uniform. McKenna eyed me up and down in a way that made me want to shed the uniform and haul her back into my bed.

"What would you be watching if Mila wasn't forcing *Scooby* on you?" I asked.

"*Buffy*," she said instantly, and I couldn't help the chuckle that escaped me, remembering just how much McK had adored the show when we were teens.

Mila caught on. "Who's Buffy? Can I watch it?"

I shook my head. "You'll have to wait a few more years, Bug-a-Boo. *Buffy* is more of a teenager show."

Mila rolled her eyes. "I'm going to be six soon. I'm not a baby."

"You won't be six for ten months, and six is not thirteen."

She counted on her fingers, got lost, and then frowned. "How many more years is that?"

"Too many," I said. "Give me a hug."

She jumped up and hugged me tight, holding on like she was never going to let go, and I liked that just fine.

"Early to bed tonight," I said. "You have Missy's birthday party tomorrow, and you don't want to be cranky. Rianne's going to take you, and Auntie Gemma is going to pick you up."

"Can't McKenna take me?"

"McK and I have to run an errand in Knoxville. We'll be gone for most of the day."

"A road trip?! You're taking a road trip without me?!"

I barely held back my laugh at her whine. "This isn't a fun trip. This is work. You'll enjoy yourself much more at the birthday party, trust me."

I kissed her on the side of the head and set her down. McK walked me to the door and kissed me softly on the lips—a habit I could quickly get used to.

"You'll be in my bed when I get home?" It was more demand than question.

She bit her lip. "You'll be tired."

"I won't sleep at all if you're not there."

She hesitated, and I tugged her to me, kissing her deeply, savoring and tempting and reminding her of how we'd spent the previous night lost in each other.

She laughed and pulled back. "Fine. You win, Sheriff."

She tapped the brim of my hat, and my chest filled with a well of emotions so deep it could drown me. Love I hadn't expressed because it seemed wild to say those words after ten years apart and mere hours together, but it pounded through my veins.

The truth was painfully clear. I'd never stopped loving McKenna Lloyd.

♫ ♫ ♫

The station was empty, the cells were empty, and even our dispatcher's desk was empty. I'd take any calls that came in tonight so my tiny staff could enjoy their Thanksgiving. Sybil had been moved to the women's jail while I'd been gone, and that filled me with nothing but relief. Hopefully, I was done with her.

When I sat down at my desk, I saw several reports Amy had compiled waiting for me there.

The first was the autopsy on Slider. No big surprise. He'd been killed with a nine-millimeter bullet, likely from a Glock or equivalent. The M.E. would know more once the lab had processed the mold he'd made of the wound. No defensive wounds, no other physical evidence. A dead end of sorts.

I pushed that report aside and opened the folder on Dr. Roy Gregory. Between Amy and Bruce, they'd talked to a host of different agencies in California to gather their facts. Before McK had filed the CPS report, he'd looked like an upstanding member of the community. It wasn't just his role at the hospital. He and his wife were also on the board of several charities in the area. Well known. Well loved.

But the district attorney was considering filing abuse charges, and Layton Gregory was currently in the custody of his maternal grandmother. Originally, at CPS's request, Dr. Gregory had removed himself from his residence, but the wife had allowed him back in after only a few days and then refused to let CPS inside the house. It was all within their rights but hadn't won them any points with the investigators.

Nothing would have come of the report McK had filed if it hadn't been for Layton. He'd run away when he'd realized his father was coming home. They'd found him with a friend, and he'd unburdened himself to the police officer and a child advocate, stating the abuse had been part of his life pretty much from the time he could walk. He'd said his mother had been hit as well, but there was nothing the law could do if she wouldn't leave him and report it herself.

Gregory was still fighting back, though. He claimed McKenna had made the false report in retaliation for a bad review he'd given her, and then her report had encouraged a rebellious son to make up even more lies.

The hospital had put him on paid leave just as they'd put McKenna.

If we could prove the burner phones with the threats were from him, it wouldn't solve anything, but I was eighty percent sure it would provide proof of his violent nature and could be added to the stack of circumstantial evidence piling up against him.

The fact his life was spiraling made him dangerous. A power-hungry, control freak like him would do anything to regain control, to prove he was as powerful as he thought he was. I was more relieved than ever that McKenna was thousands of miles away from the asshole.

I wondered if McK knew the kid had come forward. She hadn't said anything, but then again, I had no idea how she was being kept apprised of what was going on in Davis.

I went down a rabbit hole, hunting down the serial numbers on the burner phones calling McK and hoping the store had surveillance of some kind.

I was pulled from my search by a call from Agent Salazar.

"Hatley," I greeted.

"Want the good or the bad news?" he asked.

"I'm not sure I can take much more bad, but hit me with it first so I can revel in the good."

He laughed.

"Confirmed there are two high-level Lovato members in Tennessee."

"That's only bad for me if they're in Winter County," I said, rubbing my eyes and glancing at the clock. Bruce was due any second to take over for me.

"They're looking for the million or two Chainsaw owes them but hasn't paid."

"Fuck," I breathed out, and I wasn't sure why, but Sybil's jewelry and expensive clothes flashed in my mind. If there was missing money, the Lovatos would tear up my town trying to find it. "Your good news better be something about knowing where it is and having the Lovatos in lockup, or I'm going to think it isn't so good."

He gave a small laugh. "Good news is, if you let it play out, you might not have to worry about Chainsaw anymore."

A bitter taste filled my mouth as my stomach churned. It was bad enough that I wasn't sure I'd ever step in front of a bullet for Sybil, but what did it say about me that I wanted Chainsaw gone, too? What kind of officer of the law was halfway to glad someone might end up dead?

"You have a way to keep tabs on the Lovatos?" I asked.

"We do."

"You'll let me know if they show up on my doorstep?"

"Sure."

It didn't instill a bunch of faith. I knew the drill. He wanted the Lovatos. He'd do whatever was least likely to screw up his case.

"Thanks for the heads-up."

We hung up as Bruce was walking in my door. I spent a minute catching him up and letting him know about McK and my plan to go see Trap. His face was as grim as I felt when I walked out the door. We both wanted this shit as far away from our town and our families as possible.

There was no sign of the sun yet, and the black skies and quiet streets gave the town an otherworldly feel as I headed home. The heaviness of the job resting on my shoulders lifted just a hair as I remembered I had McK waiting for me in my bed. I could take the bad, the worries, if I got to get lost in her embrace at the end of each day.

But would I be able to keep her this time?

As always, as soon as I walked in, I looked in on Mila first. She was still sound asleep, but I'd only get maybe two or three hours of rest before she woke up and barreled into the room, bouncing on the bed. For the first time ever, I wondered if I should lock my door.

When I got to my room, McK was passed out on her stomach, legs spread, taking up a good chunk of my king-sized bed, and it made me smile. I ditched my clothes, kept my briefs on, and slid under the covers. She grunted, eyes fluttering when I slid myself under her so one of her arms and a leg were over my chest and thigh.

"Hey," she said sleepily, a small, gorgeous smile taking over her face as her lashes continued to flutter. "How'd it go? Wanna talk?"

I kissed her forehead. "Go back to sleep, McK. I'll be here in the morning."

But I had to wonder how many mornings I'd have left with her.

If Gregory was proven guilty, McK would get her job back. She'd be able to return to Davis and her residency. Where would that leave Mila and me? The thought of not having McK again shot a sharp pain through my chest that I kicked myself for. I had to have faith. I had to believe the words she'd said about her Hippocratic Oath and doing no harm.

I had to believe we'd found our way back to each other for a reason and that she wouldn't rip herself out of my world all over again. Then, the tightness in my stomach left because I knew the truth. Even if she did leave, I wouldn't just let her this time. I'd chase her down and convince her where she belonged was right here where she was loved most.

Chapter Twenty-nine

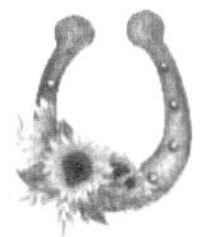

McKenna

Waking up in Maddox's bed for the second morning was still a shock and also nothing like it had been waking up with Kerry. Maddox and I were a tangle of limbs, blended so closely that, if he hadn't been so muscled from head to toe, I wouldn't have been able to tell where he left off and I began. With Kerry, we'd had our corners of the bed and only mixed temporarily before retreating to them again. "I can't sleep with your hot body touching me," Kerry had said.

And I was hot at night. I'd always been. It was why I slept in as little as possible. That had been another thing Kerry hadn't liked. He said it was "low class" to sleep in nothing more than underwear and a tank top. Maddox didn't seem to have a problem with it, as his hands were all over and under the skimpy pieces of clothing as I stirred awake.

His mouth was on my neck, and I'd just let out a little purr of approval when the door burst open. Mila was on the bed in two seconds flat, and Maddox had to put out a hand to catch her, otherwise he would have had some very injured body parts.

"You had a sleepover without me!" Mila cried out. "That's just mean. I love sleepovers. Nana says I give her the best back massage ever with my knees and feet. I don't even know I'm doing it."

"Good morning, Bug-a-Boo," Maddox said, squeezing her to his chest.

"Oh. Yeah. Good morning." She kissed his cheek and then turned and kissed mine. My eyes filled with tears of joy. "McKenna, we bought Missy *The Day the Unicorns Saved the World* and a stuffed unicorn, even though it isn't Chester or Charlotte or any of their friends because Daddy says they're improbable to find. Do you think that is going to be a good enough present? Because I told Daddy we should have bought her some more rainbow or unicorn things."

"Impossible, not improbable," Maddox said with a laugh. "And take a breath. I'm not sure McK and I are awake enough yet for this barrage of words from you."

Mila frowned. "What does barrage mean?"

"A lot."

"I'm hungry. Can we go to Tillie's again for breakfast because she always has bacon, and we don't have any bacon left. Rianne said we have to go grocery shopping to get more."

"We're not going to Tillie's again. Nana sent us home with leftovers."

Mila's little face mushed together. "I don't want turkey for breakfast, Daddy. I didn't even want to eat Bob last night."

"Bob?" he asked with a frown, and I realized he hadn't heard the conversation about the turkeys and her wanting to save them.

"Bob was a turkey, Daddy, and he just wanted to live a life on the farm with his family, and Nana *froze* him! *Froze* him, Daddy! Just think of how awful that would be."

"It's too early for this kind of talk," Maddox groaned.

I untangled myself from them and got out of bed with some reluctance, but I wanted to let him get some rest since he'd barely crawled into bed at three in the morning. Maddox eyed my scantily clad body as I pulled on a pair of yoga pants I'd flung on a nearby chair the night before.

"Come on, Mila, let's see if we can come up with something for breakfast while your daddy gets an hour or so more of sleep."

Mila bounced along the bed, sliding off and then skipping toward the door.

"I'm not going to be able to sleep now," Maddox said, voice thick as his eyes lingered over my butt.

I winked. "At least try. We don't need to be on the road until eight."

He groaned, but I didn't get a chance to respond before Mila was pulling me out of the room, chattering away about turkeys and unicorns and breakfast. It really was a lot to wake up to, but I loved every single second of it.

♫ ♫ ♫

It wasn't until two hours later, when we were in Maddox's work truck and heading for Knoxville, that I became nervous. I hadn't actually seen Trap since I'd left Willow Creek and he'd given me the key to Maddox's house. I hadn't talked to him in four years, and in that time, he'd been arrested, gone to jail, and been released. Our lives had spiraled even further apart than they'd ever been.

My phone buzzed, and I drew my eyes from outside the window and the Tennessee greenery to look down at it with trepidation. Relief flew through me when I saw it was Sally. I'd talked to her the night before while Maddox had been at the station, catching her up. She'd teased me about knowing all along that things between me and Maddox would go this way, and I'd laughed but wondered if she was right—if she'd been able to see the piece of me I'd been missing all along was really him.

> *SALLY: Good luck with your dad. But remember, he doesn't have any power over you.*

> *ME: How'd you know I was nervous?*

> *SALLY: Who wouldn't be? But also, because I'm your friend.*

> *ME: I'm lucky to have you.*

> *SALLY: It goes both ways, chica. Remember how you saved me from making the biggest mistake of my life with Grey?*

He'd been an intern who had so much charm that it felt magical, and he'd been sleeping his way through the staff at an almost mind-blowing speed. By the time he'd gotten to Sal, he'd sworn she was different, but I'd smelled snake. Unfortunately, I'd been right, and she'd caught him in one of the empty hospital rooms with a lab tech. I was just glad she'd gotten out before her heart had been completely broken.

> *ME: You would have discovered the truth on your own.*

> *SALLY: But I didn't have to. You protected my heart.*

> *ME: Because I love you.*

> *SALLY: Love you a gazillion times more than Angel loved Buffy, and maybe even more than Spike.*

My lips twisted upward.

"Everything okay?" Maddox asked, looking down at the buzzing phone, and I realized the only texts he'd ever seen me get were the ones from Dr. Gregory. I hadn't told him about the good parts of my life in California—the rare, tiny things, like my friend. So, I told him about Sally, everything she'd done for me, and how much I was going to miss her once she was gone.

"You really have nothing there for you," he said firmly.

"Except my job and my residency," I said, and I could tell the words worried him.

"How have you been keeping tabs on the hospital investigation?" Maddox asked.

"I have a lawyer through the hospital. That's only good if they determine my CPS report wasn't fraudulent," I said, my stomach twisting. "Why?"

Maddox shared what Amy and Bruce had found out about Roy Gregory and his family. I sat there, stunned, before I finally breathed out, "Layton… He's okay, then?"

"He's with his grandmother. That's all I know."

Some of the tension knotted in my chest whenever I thought of Davis and my last day at the hospital eased. Layton was safe—for now, at least. And he'd taken it upon himself to get out of the house where he was being abused. It was a good sign.

"What does this mean for Gregory?" I asked.

"I'm sure he'll negotiate something with the D.A. I doubt he'll serve time when everything is circumstantial. There's just the medical reports and the word of a teenage kid who doesn't like his parents. But if we can prove the threats he's made to you, we can probably make sure he doesn't ever practice medicine again and that he's slapped with a heavy probation sentence."

We both knew from the reality of my life how the story of proving abuse went. It wasn't that the police or CPS or even the courts weren't good at their jobs. It was the fact that the secrets were buried so deep and dark they couldn't be brought in the light enough for them to be proven, especially when some of the incidents were years old.

"The hospital's chief medical officer told me Gregory had an affair with the IT lady. That's how he tampered with my personnel file, so it looked like he'd written me a bad review when, in truth, there was nothing in my records," I told him.

Maddox's hands tightened on the steering wheel, and his jaw clenched.

"I'll pass the information along," he said.

I nodded.

"What will you do?" he asked. "If they clear you?"

I looked down, fidgeting with a string dangling from the artfully placed rips in my jeans—jeans I'd gotten on clearance, not wanting to spend a lot of money because I mostly spent my life in scrubs. I missed being in the loose-fitting clothes. Missed the action of the ER. The problem-solving. The camaraderie of the team who came together to help the people coming in at their worst moments.

"I'm still trying to figure it out," I told him the truth. I'd taken the first steps to see about getting licensed in Tennessee, and I'd even filled out a couple of applications for a new residency in the state, but I hadn't hit submit on anything. If I lost my license in California, there'd be no point in finishing any of it.

"I think you should call your lawyer," he said quietly. "Make sure they know you're waiting for a response from the hospital."

I nodded, but I was dragging my feet. I knew it. Maybe because I was afraid of the answers I'd find. Maybe because I wasn't ready to leave the little bubble Willow Creek had surrounded me in. I would have to go back to California at some point, but I also felt like it was a chapter I'd already closed, that these were the new pages I was writing on with Maddox and Mila and the Hatleys.

"Smile" came on the radio, and Maddox glanced at me, face bursting into an enormous grin.

The nostalgia hit me like a brick. Maddox and I, hair blowing in the breeze as we drove the Bronco out to the lake. The air was full of the scents of summer—wet earth, dry tules, bonfires, and sunscreen. The possibilities each day had held had seemed endless without Mama's drunken slurs hovering over me as country music blazed through Maddox's speakers. "Smile" might not have been the same silly pop song he had as his ringtone, but it was almost as ridiculous.

Maddox had never cared back then, and he didn't care now. He started singing, his grin growing, and I joined in. Our voices cracked and creaked because neither of us was musically inclined, but joy stirred through every note. It wasn't just the warm memories that sent happiness rippling through me. It was the sense of belonging I'd rediscovered here. I rolled down the window, letting the breeze in, stirring my hair and filling the cab with the scents of my childhood. It wasn't as cold as it had been earlier in the week, but it wasn't warm either. I didn't care. This glorious moment was all that mattered. Nothing before. Nothing after. Just the pure golden sunshine of our now.

♫ ♫ ♫

The diner where we were to meet Trap was in a part of Knoxville that didn't like cops, so the sheriff's logo on the side of Maddox's truck didn't win us any favors when we got out. The few cars parked in front of the place ranged from beefed-up muscle cars to ancient Toyotas looking like they should have been put out to pasture a century ago, but it was the slew of motorcycles that proved we were in the right place.

There was no bell above the door as we entered like there was at Tillie's, and no one greeted us with smiles or hellos as we walked in. The floors were caked with years of grease, the vinyl booths were cracked, and the scent of old oil hung in the air.

My stomach turned, and Maddox slid his hand into mine, squeezing it and reassuring me with just a touch. I was glad I wasn't there alone like I'd originally planned when I'd first called Trap. My eyes searched for my dad in the dim lighting filling the place. The dust-covered blinds were nearly closed, and the fluorescent bulbs in the ceiling were half burned out, casting a gloom over the room.

I finally found him in the farthest booth at the back with shadows surrounding him. Trap was as enormous as I remembered, but his face looked like it had aged thirty years instead of the ten it had been since I'd last seen him. His beard and hair were still clean and long, but there was as much gray in them as there was dark brown. The ever-prevalent bandana that had always covered his forehead and brows was no longer green but bright blue. He had on a leather vest over a red, short-sleeved T-shirt showing off the tattoos trailing over every available space on his arms. I knew, even though I couldn't see them, that he'd have on cowboy boots with spurs. The sharp edges were a weapon he carried with him just like the knife in his pocket and the gun I'd seen at his back most of my life.

Maddox had a gun, too. Even though he was dressed in civilian clothes, I'd seen him tuck a handgun into a holster at his back before he'd hidden it beneath a brown leather jacket. It made me feel skittish, the guns, the friction flowing through the room.

As we made our way across the diner to him, Trap's eyes narrowed in on my hands tangled with Maddox's. He was alone in the booth, no sign of the woman who'd been answering my calls, and he didn't get up when we approached. No hugs were coming my way for the long-lost daughter.

I slid in across from him, and Maddox joined me.

"You're lookin' good, darlin'," Trap said with a nod. Then, he turned his eyes to Maddox. "Sheriff."

Maddox tipped his chin in my dad's direction but didn't say anything.

Two men, also in leather with tattoos up and down their arms and grim faces covered in bushy beards, sat down in the booth across from us. Trap didn't acknowledge them, but I felt Maddox tense beside me, and when his hand landed on my knee, it tightened ever so slightly.

"You didn't need backup, Trap," Maddox said, his voice nonchalant and a complete contrast to how I knew he was actually feeling.

"I'm sure I don't. Just a chat between my daughter and me, right? But you can never be too careful."

"We just have a couple of questions," I said, nervousness skating over me.

"Phones on the table, and I need to make sure you aren't wired. Either of you," he said.

Maddox and I drew our phones from our pockets, laying them on the table face up, and one of the two men got up, running a device in our direction. He gave Trap a nod and then sat back down.

"Do you know who Mila's father is?" I asked.

"Mila is the little girl Sybil had?" he asked, as if needing the clarity, but his eyes were taking in Maddox.

"Yes."

"Why'd you do it?" Trap asked Maddox.

"Do what?"

"Take her in."

"Does it matter?" Maddox asked, voice calm when I felt like jumping up and running from the restaurant.

"Let's just say I need to have my curiosity assuaged before I engage in any exchange."

Maddox's hands clenched again on my knee beneath the table, and I set mine on top of it, running a thumb over his.

"I guess you could say she chose me," Maddox said, a hint of emotion peeking through his tone, showcasing the love he felt for Mila.

"And she reminded you of McK? You couldn't save her, so you were determined to save her sister."

"Maybe," Maddox admitted, and it did funny things to my heart and soul. The sweetness of it. The huge sacrifice he'd made for me when I'd basically told him to get lost. A lump formed in my throat.

"You took four years off my life," Trap said to Maddox, and I inhaled sharply.

"I wasn't the one showing off stolen rifles to everyone in Willow Creek. Not my fault I was the unlucky bastard who happened to be on duty," Maddox said.

"Wait. You're the one who arrested Trap?" I said, mouth falling open a little.

Trap chuckled. "Didn't tell you? That's interesting. Yep, your dear ol' friend here arrested me, made sure I got jail time, and then had the audacity to buy the damn house I'd saved for you. Pretty much dismantled every damn thing I had in Willow Creek."

If Trap expected me to be angry on his behalf, he'd lost any touch with reality. In fact, the entire thing had my lips twitching, making me want to laugh. Only in a small town like Willow Creek could all those things be possible.

Trap saw my attempt to hide my laughter, and his lips lifted in return.

"It is kind of amusing," Trap said, a rumble of a half-laugh escaping him as he tugged on the beard that almost reached his belt buckle.

Maddox's body loosened ever so slightly.

"If I had to guess," Trap said, "I'd say Chainsaw is the daddy. Sybil had been putting the moves on him for a while. They both wanted to make me jealous for different reasons. I think Sybil convinced him she knew more about me and my business than she did. The whole thing backfired on him though, because Sybil doesn't know shit about me. I was glad to wash my hands of her years ago. She'd been nothing but a bad omen since I picked her up, thinking she was legal when she was really only fifteen."

It was my turn to stiffen. Bad omen was what Mama had always called me. Had he hurt her by calling her it, so she passed it along to the person who couldn't strike back? The lump returned, growing until I wasn't sure I'd ever be able to talk around it again.

"Chainsaw says he wants nothing to do with her either," Maddox said.

Trap laughed dryly. "Anyone who gets a taste of Sybil wants to spit her back out."

As much as I hated Mama for the hell she'd put me through for years, I couldn't help feeling the tiniest prick of sorrow for her. That she'd lived a life where no one saw her worth. First in foster care, and then from the men she'd loved—or at least, she'd said she loved Trap. I wasn't sure she actually knew what the emotion really was.

For a long time, the lack of love and emotion had made me wonder if there was something wrong in her DNA that she'd passed along to me. I'd never really loved Kerry. I'd just wanted his life to be mine. But the man sitting next to me? The depths I felt for him? I knew it was love. Not only because I'd gladly give up my life for his but because bringing a smile to his face every day seemed more important than anything else I could do, including my time in an emergency room.

"What's Sybil got on him?" Maddox asked, returning my mind to the conversation.

"Chainsaw?" Interest flared in Trap's eyes. "Why do you think she's got something?"

"He was hiding her."

Trap tugged again on his beard.

"If she thought she was losing him, like she did with me, she might have tried the same bull, poked holes in the condom. And when the kid didn't work, tried to blackmail him into staying. Sybil ain't stupid. She's just unpredictable."

My stomach lurched as the reality of his words hit me. I was the result of a hole in a condom. My chest tightened, and tears hit the backs of my eyes that I refused to shed in front of Trap and his men. I bit my cheek, fisting the hand that wasn't in Maddox's. Trap's gaze landed on me, and it softened a little, a flash of regret wafting over him. "Sorry, darlin', that had to sting. Doesn't mean I ain't right proud of you and the life you've made for yourself. Doctor and all that shit. Even him." He tilted his head in Maddox's direction. "He's good for you. Can keep you safe."

My heart flipped over. I'd been responsible for my own safety for so long, keeping quiet and still so as not to make Mama mad, and running when it was the only choice open to me. I'd had to keep myself safe, but it was also true that Maddox had shown up and protected me in the only way a teenage boy could, by helping me flee when it was the only choice. Now, he wouldn't want to do either—run or hide. Instead, he'd help me face my demons without flinching.

"I heard a rumor about the Gears and the Lovato cartel. What do you have to say about it?" Maddox asked.

"Chainsaw has gone off his damn rocker," Trap said, the first real sign of anger entering his voice. "The West

Gears were never mixed up in cartels and drugs when I was in charge. We were just a gang of men, living our best lives. Freedom of the open road, enjoying our brief time on this shitty planet before it was gone."

"And stealing to support it," Maddox added in.

"You want help or you wanna talk ethics, pretty boy?" Trap asked with a grunt.

It was my turn to squeeze Maddox's knee.

"A big wig in the Lovato cartel is coming into town because Chainsaw owes them money. A mil at least, if not more," Trap said. When Maddox didn't respond, didn't even seem surprised, he continued, "Some say it's gone missing. I didn't know Sybil was in the picture, but if he's protecting her, it may be that she happens to know where the money ran off to."

I heard Maddox's quiet, "Fuck," and I turned wide eyes from Trap to him. "What?"

"I suspected it, yesterday, when we found…never mind. It just might explain the cash she's been throwing around town for weeks," Maddox said quietly, brows furrowed.

Holy shit. Mama had really done it this time. A million dollars. She had a million dollars of cartel money.

"Can you get me details about the meeting? When and where?" Maddox asked Trap.

Trap dragged a hand through his beard, untangling it. "Way I figure it, Chainsaw is going to end up dead when the cartel guys realize he can't deliver their money, which means I don't have to get my hands dirty taking back what rightfully belonged to me, if you see what I mean. You running in and stopping it don't serve me at all."

"I can have a talk with the D.A. and maybe drop your parole all together. You'd be a free man," Maddox offered.

"Parole ain't so bad."

Maddox got up, reaching back into the booth for my hand. I hesitated before letting him help me out, and I looked down at the man who was responsible for my being alive even if he'd never wanted me.

"The only thing you ever promised me was a safe landing place, and you didn't keep that promise," I told him, trying to stay as calm as both he and Maddox had been. I pulled on my doctor's voice and just stated the facts. Trap nodded but didn't say anything, so I continued. "If Chainsaw is the dad, we need him out of the picture. I don't wish him dead by cartel hands or anyone else's because I'm a doctor, and I save lives, not end them. I just want information about him and the cartel so he can be arrested and put behind bars so the courts don't feel inclined to give him visitation rights. You didn't save me when I needed you to, but you can help me save Mila. It's all I'll ever ask of you. This one thing."

Maddox squeezed my fingers tight, hearing all the emotions that had snuck into my voice as my little speech had gone on. I cleared my throat, regaining my calm as my father assessed me.

"Please," I added on, meaning it.

"I never understood why you were so damn happy to see me back then," Trap said quietly, regret in his eyes again. "I get it now… You were hoping I'd take you away. There's a special ring in hell for people who hurt kids." His voice was gruff, and I wondered, for the first time, about Trap's childhood. He never talked about it, and I'd never asked, but maybe…maybe the reason he'd lost his shit when he'd found out Mama was abusing me was because of his own messed-up past.

He got up, towering over me. He even had an inch or two on Maddox, who was no schlump. "I'll see what I can do," he said.

The two men opposite us also rose.

Maddox pulled me toward the door, creating more space between us and the three large men.

"Thank you," I said.

He nodded and watched us as we left.

Maddox opened the truck door for me, helped me in, and then shut it. When I looked back out the window, Trap and his two friends were standing outside the diner door, still watching. Maddox climbed in, turned the ignition over, and all but squealed the tires as he backed out and drove away.

I didn't know how she could still do it after all these years, but Mama had blindsided me again. I felt slightly beat up on the inside again, bruised and battered like I had all week, but also angry. I'd been a bargaining chip my whole life and hadn't known it. A last-ditch effort for her to keep the man who was slipping through her fingers. And I understood better than ever now why Trap had just put in a fleeting appearance as I'd grown up. Trap had been trapped. That ridiculous thought brought a gurgle of bitter laughter to my lips.

Chapter Thirty

Maddox

ALL THE TROUBLE

Performed by Lee Ann Womack

We were only a few minutes from the diner, Trap, and his men when my mind began whirling with the confirmation he'd given me about the cartel, the money, and Sybil. It meant hell was going to show up on my streets, and I had to figure out a way to keep it at bay without anyone getting hurt.

McKenna started laughing. It had a bitter, raw sound to it, and I glanced over at her, worried.

"Hey, you okay?" I asked.

She laid her head on the seat back, the laughter continuing to pour from her. The longer it went on, the lighter it got until my lips twitched as tears trickled from her eyes.

"Sorry," she said between chuckles, trying to get ahold of herself. She turned her head to watch me, and I had to keep glancing between the road and her, determined not to get us into a wreck as I found our way back onto the freeway. "That was just…like something out of a book. Or a movie."

She snickered some more.

"God, the entire thing… Mama and Chainsaw. Mama having stolen money from Chainsaw. Chainsaw tangled up with the cartel. How is this anyone's real life? Like, really? Does this shit actually happen?"

While she was still grinning and chortling, her words settled over me with an unease that had the hair on the back of my neck sticking up. It was pretty fucked up. But it also explained Slider's dead body. He'd helped Sybil escape The Nest. It was clear Chainsaw hadn't been hiding Sybil. He'd been keeping her there until she gave up the location of the money she'd taken.

I hit the call button on the steering wheel, and Bruce answered. "I need you to call the warden at the women's jail. Sybil needs to be in lockdown. I'm pretty sure—"

"Sybil's in the jail's hospital," Bruce cut me off. "She was stabbed this morning."

I glanced at McKenna, who was no longer laughing. She sat back up, eyes going wide. I jerked my gaze back to the road.

"Is she…" I trailed off.

"They think she'll make it, just a stomach wound, but someone was making a point."

"Chainsaw or the Lovato cartel. I'll fill you in when I get back, but I'd say one of them was responsible for Slider. When Sybil found out he was dead, she got herself arrested, thinking she'd be safe in jail, at least until the cartel took care of Chainsaw for her."

"Damn. I was hoping Salazar was wrong," Bruce said.

"I know, but Trap said pretty much the same damn thing."

"Shit. Okay, I'll call the warden back and tell him to get his eyes on any cartel members locked up there, and then I'll put out an APB on Chainsaw. See if we can wrangle him in for questioning."

We hung up, and I looked over to find McK staring out the window. I reached across the cab and squeezed her hand as I had back at the diner. "McK," I said quietly.

"How bad of a person do you have to be to not even care when your mama gets stabbed?" she asked softly. "To even wish…."

She shook her head, but her eyes were still trained out the window, refusing to look at me.

"She wasn't your mama, McK. She was your captor. Your tormentor. You wouldn't be human if you didn't want to see her pay for that."

"I'm a doctor. I'm supposed to cherish every life. What I told Trap about Chainsaw? It's true. I don't want to see him dead. I want to see him put away. But…Mama…"

I found a place to pull over, and McKenna finally turned to look at me. "What are you doing?"

I unlatched her seat belt and all but dragged her into my lap over the center console. She didn't resist. In fact, when she landed on me completely, she rested her head on my shoulder, face buried in my neck.

"She wasn't your mother, McK. She doesn't get to claim that title. You don't call Trap Dad. You need to stop calling her your mama. She's Sybil, and whatever the hell went wrong in her childhood—her life—doesn't justify what she did to you."

She nodded, nose nestled against me, breath coasting over my skin.

I raised her palm to my mouth and kissed it gently.

"You're a good person," I told her. "If you weren't, you wouldn't have guilt over your feelings."

"You don't even really know me, Mads. I've been gone ten years."

I twisted, tugging at her so she was forced away from my shoulder and I could hold her gaze.

"I know you, McKenna. I know you because as lame as you think my song is, you're my soul sister."

"God, I hope I'm not your sister," she said, lips twitching.

I chuckled. "You're right. It's the only part of the song that's wrong. Every other part is right. I know you. You know me. I love you. You love me."

"Psh. As if," she said, but she smiled, her full, real smile that took over her face and lit up her eyes, casting golden glows over everything around her.

"I can't wait for the world to see exactly what we are when we're together," I told her. "It's like that damn book of Mila's. At the end, we're pure magic."

She kissed me, slow and steady, with a promise I meant for her to keep.

We got lost in each other for a good fifteen minutes on the side of the road. It would have been longer if I hadn't been in my work truck, and we weren't in the bright light of day on the side of a highway. But it just made me more determined to get us home as quickly as possible so I could show her, one more time, all the ways we belonged together. All the ways we knew each other.

When I finally returned her to her seat and started the truck back up, my foot was heavy on the gas pedal, an urgency filling us both that needed to be fulfilled.

We were about ten minutes from Willow Creek when Gemma called.

"Hey, Gem Mine. Thanks for picking Mila up for me. Is she completely sugared out?"

Gemma's voice came over, shaky and slightly panicked. "Sadie picked her up for me because…it doesn't matter. But I'm back at the ranch now, and I can't find them."

"What do you mean?" I said, trying not to freak out, pulling on the shroud of calm my job required.

"Sadie's car is here, but it's weird. The doors are open, and her keys are still in the ignition."

My gut twisted, fear lodging in my throat. It was weird…but it didn't mean I should panic, except the hair raised on the back of my neck that was an eighty percent accurate measure of something hinky going down, said otherwise. I glanced over at McKenna, and I could see the worry coasting over her brows.

"Did you call their phones? Where's Terrance and her friends?" I asked, barely keeping my alarm at bay as my foot slammed even harder into the accelerator, a different kind of urgency filling me.

I took the next turn at speeds that made our wheels skid, and McKenna grasped the door handle with an audible gasp.

"Terrance and the others left to go back to UTK today. Sadie's staying until Sunday. And I tried both their phones, but neither of them is picking up."

Mila had her phone off a lot, which defeated the whole purpose, but I could still find it.

"I'm going to ping Mila's phone. Maybe she talked Sadie into taking Shadowfax out?"

"The horses are all here, too," Gemma said.

"Where are Mama and Dad? Ryder?" I asked as I scrambled to locate the *Find my Phone* app while still barreling down the road. McK grabbed the phone from me, flicking through the screens on the device.

"Livestock auction over in Cooksville."

Fuck.

"It says she's at the ranch," McKenna said, shoving the phone in my direction. It looked like her phone was right by the farmhouse.

"Gems, go out to Sadie's car and see if their phones are there."

It was quiet, but we could both hear Gemma's uneven breathing as she went out.

"Shit," Gemma said. "It's in her backpack in the back seat. I don't see Sadie's… Oh, wait. It's under the seat…like she dropped it."

I was no longer calm. I was fucking terrified. The hair on my neck was still standing up, my stomach was clenched tight, and all I could think was that I was seven minutes away from the goddamn ranch and my daughter. I forced myself to respond with a voice much calmer than I actually felt. "We're a few minutes out, Gems. I'm going to be there soon, but I'm hanging up so I can call it in."

Gemma sobbed. "Okay. God…I'm sorry, Mads…"

"This isn't on you, Gemma. They'll be fine. It's just a misunderstanding, I'm sure."

It wasn't a misunderstanding. I felt it in my bones. My daughter and my sister were in danger.

I hung up and tapped the radio I'd had turned down while we'd been out of the county, hating with every fiber of my being that I was going to use the code for a missing person in relation to my daughter. My voice shook as I filled in the names and details as best I could to the dispatcher. When it came to Mila's appearance, I hesitated because I couldn't remember what she'd been wearing that morning, and it was McKenna who filled in the information.

"Green leggings and a rainbow sweater," McKenna said.

Fuck. How could I forget what my child was wearing?

I could barely hear beyond the blood pounding through me. Only my training kept me going as I listened to the immediate response over the radio. Every law enforcement agency in a hundred miles as well as the fire department and search-and-rescue were gearing up and heading toward the ranch, but it was McK and me who arrived first.

I slammed my brakes in front of the farmhouse, next to Sadie's car, leaving black skid marks on the pavement. McKenna and I jumped out, and Gemma came running down from the back porch.

"Any sign of them?" I asked.

Gemma shook her head, tears pouring down her face. "What…what do you think happened?"

I stalked over to Sadie's car. "Don't touch anything," I barked as McKenna reached for Mila's backpack through the back passenger window. "Back away from the car," I told them both, and they did.

I scanned the drive, trying to see any trace of what had happened, but I wasn't a tracker, and there weren't any obvious prints.

A gunshot echoed through the air, and my body froze, heart forgetting to beat, lungs forgetting to breathe as dread filled me followed by a litany of curses and prayers. And then, I was in motion, running back to my truck and unlocking the rifle that hung in the gun rack. I threw the strap over my shoulder and raced in the direction of the sound while fingering the Glock I had tucked at my back.

It took me a second to realize McKenna and Gemma were both on my heels as I cleared the barn.

"Stay at the goddamn house. Let the others know when they arrive that shots were fired, and I've headed out," I hollered while not even slowing down.

I didn't wait to see if they listened. I just kept running, pulse slamming, chest aching. *Please be okay, baby girl. Please be okay.* The thoughts raced through me, making it difficult to stay clear-headed and calm as the situation demanded.

I jumped the fence instead of opening the gate, and I realized McKenna was still with me as she did the same. I slowed, not for her but so I could listen to anything besides the racing of my heart, hoping I'd hear something to point me in the right direction.

"Go back, McK," I growled.

"No!"

I didn't have time to argue with her. "I can't be worried about you, too."

"That was a gunshot, Maddox. If someone is hurt, I can help."

The thought of Mila or Sadie being wounded almost made my knees buckle.

Then, I heard it—a tiny scream followed by another gunshot.

I took off, heading in the direction of the creek. "Mila!" I screamed, not caring if I announced to the world I was there, just needing my daughter to know I was coming for her. Fucking let the asshole point his gun at me just so it would mean it wasn't directed at her. I knew what to do when faced with a gun. My tiny baby did not.

I heard the sirens in the distance by the time I hit the creek, and what I saw there had my stomach lurching and my knees quaking. Sadie was crumpled on the bank, and there was blood pouring from her. *Fuck, fuck, fuck.*

I slid onto the ground beside her with McKenna instantly at my side.

"Sads…Sadie, you with me?" I said, taking her hand. She was breathing, thank God. McKenna went into action, ripping at Sadie's pant leg where the blood was spurting from a hole in her thigh. My throat bobbed.

Sadie's eyelashes flickered.

"Talk to me, Sadie. Who has her? Where'd they go?" I demanded.

Sadie fought to open her eyes. "Gold…" she breathed out before she passed out.

"Fuck," I frowned.

"Go," McKenna said. "Go, I got this."

"McK…" I shook my head, trying to concentrate, trying to figure out what Sadie had meant.

"Gold, Mads. Fool's gold. The hollow. That's where Sadie probably told her to run."

Shit, she was right. My head was so clouded with fear and hatred for whoever had done this I wasn't thinking straight.

"Go!" McK yelled, and I did, leaving my sister bleeding on the shore with the woman I loved and hoping whoever this was didn't circle back around and finish what he'd started.

I was at a dead run until I got closer to the ridge above the hollow, then I slowed, ducking behind a tree, trying to assess the situation, forcing myself to focus and get my breathing under control so I didn't announce I was there before I was ready. A flicker of a blond-haired head showed above the ridgeline, standing in the dense copse of roots at the bottom.

"You little bitch," a voice hissed. "I don't have time for fucking hide-and-seek. Get your ass out here."

Chainsaw. It was his raspy, Louisiana voice, and my anger flared again as the knowledge hit me hard. He'd thought he could get to Sybil through me and Mila.

"If I have to go in there to get you, you'll be sorry." His voice was dark and menacing, but all I could think about was how proud I was of Mila for being smart enough to hide. The deep recess of cave-like tangles the roots made would keep her safe for a few minutes at least, hopefully giving me the time I needed to finish this.

I belly-crawled over to the edge, not wanting him to see me coming.

I laid the Remington rifle on the ground, lining up the shot with his chest. One bullet. He'd be done. Gone. Out of our lives. And I'd never have to worry about him again. My finger pulsed on the trigger as McK's voice rang through my head, *"I don't wish him dead."* I didn't either, but I'd been trained to stop a lunatic with a gun one way—a kill shot.

"Drop the gun, asshole, and get on your knees," I growled, trying to keep the fear out of my voice.

Chainsaw twirled, gun raised in my direction, but I knew he couldn't see much—the barrel of the rifle and part of my head, if he was lucky. Instead of keeping his gun pointed in my direction, he pointed it at the dark weave of roots. "I'll shoot her."

I didn't reply. I just watched his finger while keeping my aim on his chest. I didn't say anything, just waiting and watching for the moment I'd have to take the shot, because I knew with a hundred percent certainty that it wasn't going to end any other way.

"I just want my fucking money!" Chainsaw screamed. "Get Sybil to cough up the location, and I'll be out of this fucking town and this fucking state forever."

"Your first mistake was aligning yourself with the cartel. Your second was trusting Sybil," I said, rage rolling through my tone. "But your biggest fucking mistake was trying to take my daughter."

He let out a snarl and moved as if he was going to lurch for the roots, and I let the bullet fly.

He screamed, falling backward, body slamming into the ground. His arm went limp, and his gun went tumbling. I jumped to my feet, sliding down into the hollow. He wasn't dead, but it was luck from the way he'd moved more than my aim. The bullet wound gaped not far from his heart. He scratched his hands in the dirt, trying to search for the gun he'd lost. I slammed my boot onto his shoulder, and he screamed again. I pointed my rifle at his head as I kicked his gun away.

A scrabble of feet on the ridge had me pulling my Glock from my back with my free hand and aiming it at the top. Bruce appeared, his face white and sweaty. "Jesus, it's just me."

"Got cuffs?"

He nodded, joining me in the hollow. Chainsaw was cursing and swearing as we flipped him on his back, and Bruce started Mirandizing him. I slung my rifle behind me and made for the dark tangle of roots.

"Bug-a-Boo, it's me," my voice cracked. "You're safe, Mila. I'm here, baby."

"Dad-daddy?" Her terrified little voice about undid me, tears filling my eyes.

"Yep, I'm here, sweetheart. Come on out."

"I…I wet my pants, Daddy."

My throat bobbed. "It's okay, Bug-a-Boo. I think I might have also."

Silence.

I dug my shoulder between the roots, trying to figure out how the hell McK and I had ever fit, wishing I had my uniform on and the flashlight that was always with me. I could ask Bruce for his, but I didn't want him even glancing away from Chainsaw.

"Mila, you're going to have to come to me. Daddy's body is too big to play pirates down here anymore." I was trying to lure her out with a tease and soft voice, but my heart was slamming against my rib cage, fear deep inside me still. Fear that wouldn't go away until she was wrapped in my arms.

Movement at the edge of my peripheral vision had me turning my head to the right. She was crawling out from the back, on her hands and knees. And then she was there, and I was squeezing her, holding on tight. The berry scent in her hair was layered with her fear. My fear. I rocked her gently as she started to cry, and I did, too.

"I got you. You're safe. I got you."

"He was so mean, Daddy. He shot…" She trembled and cried.

"Auntie Sadie is going to be okay. McKenna is with her." I had to believe it was true. I had to believe my little sister hadn't lost her life because of an asshole using my daughter to get to me.

"McKenna's here?" Mila asked through little sobs.

I nodded. "Yep. And everyone from the station and the fire department and even Sheriff Scully and his men. They all came to see how you were doing. Wanna go see?"

She nodded.

I wasn't sure I could move, not only because I was wedged between some roots but because the fear and panic I'd barely kept at bay was washing through me, taking over my limbs. She was safe. I had her. She was safe.

As I scooted on my ass out, Mila held on tight, arms and legs locked to my body and face buried in my neck. When I could stand, I shifted so she wouldn't see the man on the ground or Bruce holding him there.

"You got this?" I asked him.

He nodded, face grim, and said, "I already called for EMTs. Liam is on his way out to help me."

I didn't respond. I couldn't. My feelings were still too huge. Too raw. Instead, I climbed out of the hollow with Mila wrapped around me so tight it almost hurt. She was trembling, and I didn't blame her. I was a mess of nerves as well, and I hadn't lived through her terror. A visceral hatred for Chainsaw washed over me again, almost making me want to go back and make sure there was no luck involved in my second shot.

Instead, I walked across the fields, only concerned with my chattering girl's silence.

"Are you hurt, Bug-a-Boo?" I asked, attempting to run my hands over her limbs the best I could with her attached to me.

"I skinned my knee," she said, voice wavery.

"Well, I think we can fix that up."

She finally looked up at me, eyes awash with tears trailing down her dirty face. Her clothes were filthy as well, torn in a couple of places, and I wasn't sure I was prepared to know why. Were they from the roots? Were they from him pushing her down? Bile hit my throat.

I reminded myself that I had her in my arms. She was safe. She was there. Everything else could be fixed. Relief trembled through my veins.

"You're crying, Daddy," she said softly, putting a hand on my cheek.

"I sure am."

She didn't respond. She just rested her head on my chest again, and I squeezed her tightly to me. We passed Liam and one of Sheriff Scully's deputies. Their eyes turned to relief when they saw Mila in my arms.

"She okay?" Liam asked.

I nodded, even though I wasn't entirely sure she was.

We just kept walking until I saw the creek where Sadie had been loaded onto a stretcher. Her arms were moving as she talked. More relief filled me. My sister was alive. There was a crowd of first responders around her and McKenna, who was wiping her hands on a cloth of some sort, blood staining it.

The stretcher had just disappeared over the hill when McKenna turned her head. As soon as she spotted us, she was in motion, running. She wasn't the only one who saw us, and applause burst out from the men and women who'd gathered to help me find my girl.

McK slammed into us, wrapping us in her arms as a sob escaped her. I moved my hands so I could hold them both. McKenna and I squished Mila between us, all of us crying and clinging to each other. I wasn't sure I was ever going to be able to let them go again.

Chapter Thirty-one

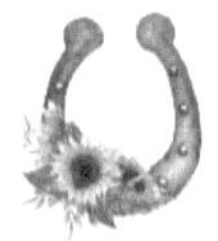

McKenna

THE HILL

Performed by Thomas Rhett

Holding on to Maddox and Mila, I let the terror and relief flow through me, coming out in streams of tears. Tears of joy at seeing them. Tears of sorrow for what Mila and Sadie had just gone through. Tears of anger because Sybil had caused another round of violence to show up in my world, and this time, I wasn't the only one who would be left with scars—emotional and physical ones.

"I kinda can't breathe, and you're always telling me to breathe," a little voice said.

I stepped back with a soft laugh erupting from me, and my gaze met Maddox's tortured one. I wasn't sure what he'd seen when he'd found her or what had happened, but Mila was safe, and that was what mattered most. I ran my hands over her legs and arms and back, checking for visible injuries.

"Auntie Sadie?" she asked somberly, turning a dirty, tear-stained face to me that about broke my heart.

"She'll be fine, sweetheart, just fine. They're going to be able to patch her right up at the hospital," I answered.

"You saved her," Maddox said, his voice deep with a flurry of conflicting emotions.

"I *helped* her, but from what I understand, Mila was the one who really saved her."

"Wh-what?" Maddox croaked out.

It could wait—the story Sadie had told me as she'd come fully awake while the EMTs were loading her onto the stretcher. I was sure Maddox would hear it many times.

We walked back to the farmhouse, catching up to the EMTs just before they placed Sadie into the ambulance. Gemma was hovering near her, face scrunched in worry with tears still pouring down. Both sisters turned pale faces toward us, and the same relief I'd felt coasted over them at the sight of Mila with Maddox.

Gemma hugged Maddox and Mila tightly, an anguished cry escaping her. Maddox squeezed her and then let her go as Sadie reached out a hand with a sob.

"Thank God…Mila…"

Maddox squeezed her hand. "She's okay, Sads. Now, we just need you to be, also."

"At least it wasn't my arm, Mads. I can still throw my darts. I'm going to put that fucker's face on my dart board and toss until there's nothing left. Who was he?"

I couldn't help the second choked laugh that escaped me since Maddox had appeared over the hill with Mila tucked to him. Maddox leaned down and kissed his sister's forehead all while Mila clung to him, head buried, more quiet than she ever was. She hadn't even reacted to Sadie's curse word.

"That was Chainsaw, one of the West Gears, and I'll help you destroy his picture with darts, but let's just concentrate on getting you healed first," Maddox said.

"I kicked him in the balls, just like you taught me," Sadie said. "Mila ran when I told her to, which was so smart and so brave, and I followed her after throwing my coffee in his face. But he was faster than I expected."

"Sads, you can tell me later. It doesn't matter."

"He dead?" she asked with a glower.

I turned wide eyes to Maddox as he shook his head. "Not when I left him with Bruce, but as I returned the favor he gave you by putting a bullet in his chest, there's no guarantee he'll make it. And if he does, he'll be going where no one will fuss over him while he heals like Mama and all of us are going to fuss over you."

"We need to get her to the hospital," one of the EMTs said. "They're prepping surgery now."

Maddox looked at me. "Will you ride with her?"

I didn't want to. I wanted to stay with him and Mila and make sure they were okay first, but I also couldn't deny him, not when he had to be feeling incredibly responsible for Sadie even when it wasn't his fault. I nodded, climbing into the back of the fire department's ambulance.

I looked back at the two people I loved most, clutching each other as if their lives depended on it, and my heart almost stopped.

"I'm gonna get her cleaned up, and then we'll meet you at the hospital," Maddox said as the door started to close.

I hated leaving them, but I swallowed hard and sent a telling look in Mila's direction. "Take your time."

The doors shut, and the ambulance rumbled to life.

"You don't have to come," Sadie piped in. "I think this very efficient EMT here has it all under control. Don't you, handsome?"

The EMT, who couldn't have been much older than Sadie, rolled his eyes as he hooked her up to wires and rechecked her vitals. The ambulance bounced over the driveway, making Sadie wince. She closed her eyes and kept them shut while I held her hand.

The EMT turned his eyes to me. "You did real good out there. Not every doctor can remain calm in that kind of chaos."

I'd given them my title as they'd shown up, telling them the best I could about the wound and the manual stats I'd taken while living the worst minutes of my life. Waiting for Maddox…not knowing what had happened to Mila…it had been beyond terror. The very worst kind of hell. My heart still hadn't returned to normal, and tears were threatening to fall again.

"I work in the ER," I said. "So, every day is pretty much chaos."

"Well, that explains it," he said with a wry grin.

I looked down at Sadie. Her eyes were still closed. I touched her cheek, and her eyes fluttered. "I think I'm going to take a nap." Her words were slurred, and I looked over at the IV he'd started with pain meds flowing.

"I think that's a great idea," I told her.

She was completely passed out by the time we got to the hospital, and I stood by while they unloaded her, following the stretcher all the way to the surgical doors. The EMTs were talking fast to the nurses and the doctor who'd come to greet them, rattling off what they knew about the situation and her numbers.

"This is Dr. Lloyd," he told them. "She's family but also probably saved her from bleeding out."

He gave me a wink and left. The doctor in charge glanced over me. "My name is Dr. James. We'll take good care of her, and I'll be out as soon as I can to tell you more."

I nodded, a lump forming in my throat, wishing I could scrub in and watch over the surgery but having to trust that this team knew what they were doing.

I found my way to a bathroom, washed my hands and face, and stared in the mirror. My body finally let go, shaking and trembling. Fear washed over me as my mind replayed Maddox's terrified face, the wild race to the creek…the blood. Sadie. My fear that Maddox or Mila would be injured…perhaps worse than Sadie. My relief at seeing them come over the hill.

It was a nightmare, but I was grateful to the bottom of my soul that everyone had come out alive. That they could be healed.

But I hated that this was tied to me…my family.

Was I really a bad omen? Had this all happened because I'd strolled into town while running, yet again, from people threatening me?

I shook my head. Mama— No, Maddox was right. She was just Sybil. Sybil had stolen the money from Chainsaw before I was even in town. That part of the story had nothing to do with me.

I took several deep breaths and smoothed my ponytail, all the while trying to will the tremble from my hands. When I looked down at the blood spattered across my sweater and jeans, it didn't help. Instead, a shiver ran up my spine. I was used to seeing blood on myself from the ER, but it was always on scrubs—and never from people I loved.

It was a long time before I felt like I could face the world again, but I finally emerged, asking at the nurses' station for directions to the family waiting room. When I got there, it was empty and quiet, a TV in the background playing some Disney cartoon on mute.

My phone buzzed, and I pulled it out, expecting it to be Maddox, and groaned internally when I saw another unknown number.

1-530-555-8225: Don't say I didn't warn you.

I almost wanted to laugh because what could he do to me? I'd just lived the very worst nightmare anyone could have with the people I loved being threatened. I could never imagine Roy Gregory coming after me with a gun like

Chainsaw had come after Maddox and his family today. Dr. Gregory used his fists and mental abuse to control people, and that was what he'd been doing to me, controlling me with threats like Mam—*Sybil* had.

For the first time since the texts had started, I responded.

> *ME: Keep texting me. I beg you to. Every message you send is a nail in your own coffin, proving Layton and me right. That you're nothing but a violent bully. You're not coming for me, asshole. I'm coming for you.*

I waited, but there was no response, and my chest filled with a strength I hadn't truly felt since that day he'd burst into the hospital room. I wasn't sure I'd ever felt this strong, not even on the day I'd left Willow Creek and…Sybil…behind. Maybe I hadn't felt strong because it had felt like running instead of fighting. If a tiny five-year-old could stand up to a man with a gun, I could stand up to a man wielding nothing more than threats.

I'd just put my phone away when the Hatleys burst into the waiting room. Eva and Brandon were at the front, faces drawn tight with worry. Gemma and Ryder were behind them, his arm around his sister's shoulders, holding her tight. Gemma looked like she was still a wreck, somehow feeling responsible for everything simply because she hadn't been the one to pick Mila up from the party.

Eva came right to me and wrapped me in a hug that felt almost as perfect as Maddox's. "Thank you…for being there."

My first reaction was my normal one—to stiffen. Back tight, fists clenched. Whenever Sybil had hugged me, it had been when she was putting on her world's-best-mama act, and the hug had always hidden a pinch or a fingernail sunk deep, warning me to stand still, to look like I was happy for her to be holding me. But the hug Eva was giving me felt stronger than any of the ones she'd ever given me before. It was full of real love—true affection—and I finally let go, wrapping my arms around her shoulders and squeezing back with a fierce protectiveness I suddenly felt toward all of them.

Brandon joined us, embracing us both. Tears littered my eyes that I barely held back.

"What do we know?" Brandon asked as we all moved apart, and Eva wiped her face.

I pushed aside my emotions, pulling on my doctor demeanor and willing my voice not to shake. "The doctor said he'd come out as soon as he was done with surgery, but she appeared stable and was talking to us before the pain meds took hold. I believe the bullet missed the femoral artery, but I couldn't tell what other damage may have been done. She could move her toes when I asked her to, and that's a good sign."

"Thank God you were there," Eva said.

My stomach twisted and turned. Would they feel the same if they knew Chainsaw might have come after Mila because of my mama? I swallowed hard, keeping my thoughts to myself.

Everyone sat down except me. Gemma rested her head on Ryder's shoulder, and Eva was tucked up against Brandon's chest. I ached to have my arms around Maddox and Mila. I wanted to know how she was doing, if she was still strangely quiet instead of wildly talkative, and if Maddox was crumbling.

I'd almost decided to get a ride back to the ranch or the house or wherever he'd gone, when they walked through the door with Rianne right behind them. Mila was still clutched to Maddox's chest, but they were both clean and in new clothes. Mila had Chester and Charlotte tucked under her armpits and a smoothie in her hands. I rushed over to them, hugging them tightly, and Maddox clasped me to him while Mila tugged at my ponytail.

The tears finally came. I sobbed, holding them to me as guilt and sorrow filled me…but also love.

"It's okay, McK. We're all safe." Maddox squeezed me.

We stood that way for what felt like hours but was probably mere seconds until he finally asked, "How's Sadie?"

"Still in surgery," I said, stepping back.

He pulled a backpack from his shoulder, and I realized, with a start, that it was mine.

"I put some clean clothes in here. I wasn't sure what you'd want, but…" he trailed off, looking down at my blood-covered ones.

"Thank you."

As the rest of the Hatleys came over to encompass Maddox and Mila in more hugs, I slipped away to change. I looked at the blood-stained clothes after removing them and then tossed them in the biohazard waste in the bathroom. Even if I could get them clean, they'd always remind me of this awful day.

Maddox had packed a pair of yoga pants and my UC Davis sweatshirt. Comfort. He'd known that was what I'd need. When I looked down at the logo on the sweatshirt, it felt like it belonged to someone else, someone who'd lived a life in California that had nothing to do with me, the Hatleys, or Willow Creek.

I'd barely returned to the waiting room and settled down into the chair next to Maddox and Mila when the doctor came out. His mask was down around his neck, and he had a serene expression on his face.

"She's lucky. It didn't break any bones or rupture the femoral artery, but the vein was nicked, and the femoral nerve was damaged. We've stitched her back together, but she'll likely have some loss of feeling in her thigh and maybe loss of movement. With physical therapy, she may or may not regain full range of motion. We won't know more until she's healed enough to get back on her feet. She lost quite a bit of blood, so it's going to take a while to recover. I don't want you to be alarmed if she doesn't seem like herself for several days."

Dr. James took a breath and looked us all over, but then his eyes landed on me as he asked, "Any questions?"

I didn't have any at the moment. There was nothing more he or I could do until Sadie's body healed itself.

"When can we see her?" Brandon asked, voice cracking.

"She's in recovery. As soon as she's awake and stable, they'll move her to a room. It could be an hour or more still, but one of the nurses will let you know when they've got her situated."

Ryder shook his hand. "Thank you."

Dr. James looked over at me. "I think it's Dr. Lloyd you need to thank. The number one cause of death from gunshot wounds isn't the wound itself. It's bleeding out because someone didn't know what they were doing. I've seen military medics freeze in the field the first time they're in combat. Dr. Lloyd didn't, and it saved Sadie's life."

My cheeks flushed at the compliment like they hadn't since I'd been back in medical school. It didn't ease the guilt I felt over this whole thing being tied to me, to Ma—Sybil, but at least I'd been there to try and fix it…to repair some of the damage before it had gotten worse.

After the doctor left, I sat in the chair next to Maddox, who had Mila pressed up tight against his chest just like he had when I'd first seen them coming back over the hill to the creek. Maddox looked down at her and then me, his frown growing as his girl remained quiet. She'd just lived through a horrific experience, and I wasn't sure she'd be herself for a long time. But this time, she was silent because she was asleep. Her breathing was slow and steady on his chest.

He spoke quietly, as if not to disturb her. "What did you mean, McK? That Mila had saved Sadie?"

Everyone's eyes turned to me.

"When Sadie came to, she said Chainsaw tackled her to the ground when he'd caught up to them at the creek. He aimed his gun at her, and Mila launched herself at him, biting his arm, which caused the bullet to hit her thigh instead of her chest.

"Fuck." It was Ryder who said the word, but I could feel the way Maddox was holding his breath. The idea of Mila running toward an arm holding a gun instead of running away from it was not an image he'd get out of his head anytime soon.

"How'd she get away?" Eva breathed out.

Tears journeyed down her face as she looked at the little girl.

I shook my head. I wasn't sure. I didn't know more than what Sadie had said.

Maddox reached with his free hand, pulling me closer, and I rested my head on his shoulder, looking into Mila's face as she slept. The bravest girl I'd ever known. Why had I never been that brave? Memories of my past assaulted me. All the times I'd taken Mama's abuse just standing there. The only action I'd ever taken was to run.

Maddox's cheek rested on my head, and eventually, I felt his body slacken. He'd fallen asleep, too. When I looked over, Gemma was asleep on Ryder, but his eyes were pinned to me, watching, assessing, trying to figure me out. I could almost hear the questions pouring from him silently. Was I going to stay? Was I going to hurt Maddox again? Would I hurt Mila? My only answer was to hold on to them tighter.

Chapter Thirty-two

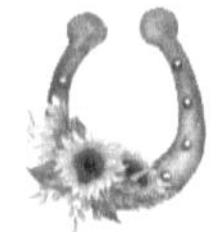

Maddox

WHAT WOULD THIS WORLD DO?

Performed by Maren Morris

I'd fallen asleep for a brief moment in the waiting room with Mila and McKenna wrapped in my arms. They were safe. We were all safe. Sadie was going to be okay. That enormous relief had led to exhaustion, and I'd drifted off, but a sharp sound in the hallway snapped my eyes back open. McK squeezed me tighter as she felt me stir. I looked down at her and then over to my brother. His gaze was dark and stormy. He was pissed, and I wasn't sure if it was at me or Chainsaw or the whole fucked-up situation.

A nurse came in, letting us know we could see Sadie, and we all headed down the hall to her room. She was pale with her leg splinted, monitors and tubes tucked around her, and when she saw all of us, she started to cry. It was as unlike my spunky sister as Mila's silence.

I'd tried to get my daughter to talk to me while I'd cleaned her up in the bath, but she'd just looked at me with big, tear-filled eyes, so I'd changed the subject. Instead of asking more questions, I'd talked nonsense about her unicorns and their friends.

Now, she was still conked out in my arms, and I was fine with that because if she was awake and wanting to run around, I might not be able to let her. I needed her close for a while longer.

Mama fussed around Sadie just like I knew she would, fixing the blankets and brushing Sadie's matted hair away from her face.

"He came out of nowhere when I got out of the car, Maddox," Sadie said. "I didn't expect it. I wasn't aware…"

"You were at the ranch, Sads. You shouldn't have had to expect an attack at your home," I told her, trying to make sure she didn't feel guilty. This wasn't on her. This was on me, my job, and fucking Sybil.

"When he caught me at the creek, I thought…" She shook her head, looking at my sleeping daughter with awe. "She saved me by biting his arm, and when he turned toward her, I grabbed his pant leg, trying to slow him down, but he kicked me…"

"You gave her enough time to get away, Sads. She hid where you told her to, in the hollow. You gave me time to get to her." My voice was thick. I wanted to stop talking about it. I didn't want to hear one more time how my five-year-old had thrown herself at a man with a gun and then ran for her life. My chest ached with a ferocity that made me lightheaded.

"Why don't you take her home?" Mama suggested. "She needs to be away from all these reminders that something horrible happened today."

She was right, and yet, I was reluctant to leave my family—the people who calmed me, loved us, and would protect her.

"Go. Really," Sadie said. "I'd rather her be in her room with the rainbows and unicorns than see me like this anyhow."

I leaned over and kissed Sadie's forehead. "Thank you for saving her."

"She saved me," Sadie choked out.

"Maybe you saved each other." It was McKenna who said it, and my gaze met hers. She was right. They'd done it together.

"Don't forget to eat," Rianne said as we headed for the door. "I left sandwiches in the refrigerator. They're all ready to go."

I nodded, but the thought of food made me slightly nauseated.

Dad and Ryder followed McKenna and me out of the room. Dad looked down at Mila and ran a hand over her blonde hair, saying softly, "I'll call you if anything changes, but just get some rest. Be together. Love on each other a bit. I have a feeling you all need it."

I clenched my jaw so I didn't cry again, like I'd cried when I'd found Mila.

Then, he walked back into the room. I waited, watching Ryder's jaw tick, knowing he had something he needed to get off his chest.

"What the fuck happened out there?" he demanded.

"Chainsaw came after Mila because he hoped I'd hand Sybil over to him."

Ryder's eyes shot to McKenna, and I shook my head.

"It had nothing to do with her."

I wasn't sure he believed me, and I didn't really have the energy to argue. My heart was already twisted up enough when I thought about how my job had put my family at risk and how it could continue to put targets on their backs. Assholes like the West Gears might always think they could use them as bargaining chips. I wasn't sure what to do about that, short of resigning, and that thought made my stomach flip, too.

"My shitty family bled out on you," McK said quietly.

I shook my head at her. "I have the best things in my life because of you...and Sybil."

McKenna frowned disbelievingly, and I realized she was going to hold tight to her own guilt regardless of what I said, just like I'd hold onto mine.

I started down the hall, and Ryder's voice halted me as he spoke to McKenna. "You staying or running?"

My eyes narrowed, unhappy at him for inserting himself into whatever was blooming again between McK and me but also loving him for trying to protect me.

"I'm not going anywhere," she said.

But she bounced on her toes in that nervous way of hers, and we both knew the truth. If things cleared up for her back in California, she had a life to go back to, a residency to complete. You didn't just walk away from ten years of hard work when the finish line was mere months away.

Ryder seemed to accept her answer though, because he turned on his heel and headed back toward Sadie's room while McK and I continued down the hall.

I hadn't driven to the hospital. At the ranch, Bruce had driven Mila and me to our house, and I'd ridden with her clutched to my chest instead of in a car seat. It wasn't safe, and yet, it felt like the safest place for her to be all at the same time. When we'd pulled up to the bungalow, Rianne had been waiting for us, the news of what had happened having spread like wildfire through Willow Creek.

She'd hugged us both, worrying over us, and completely understanding when putting Mila into the tub had almost undone me. I wasn't ready to let her go. As soon as she was clean, I'd handed her over, reluctantly, to Rianne to shower and change myself. Mila hadn't squirmed once or asked to be put down even when I'd taken her back from Rianne, and Rianne had driven us in the Bronco to the hospital.

Now, I stared at my vehicle and hesitated again. Holding onto Mila was the only thing saving me from a complete breakdown at this point.

McK took the keys from my hand. "I got this. Just sit with her."

So, we drove for the third time with her in my arms instead of in the car seat.

Mila stirred, her heart pounding, body stiffening, eyes panicking, as she called out, "Daddy?"

I squeezed her tighter. "I'm right here, Bug-a-Boo. Right here. You're safe."

She looked around, saw the Bronco and McKenna, and her little body relaxed. Before we'd reached the house, she was out again. Inside, I carried her to my bedroom. I wouldn't be able to sleep with her anywhere else tonight. McKenna came in behind me a few moments after I'd placed Mila in the middle of my king-sized bed. She plugged in several of Mila's nightlights that she must have grabbed from her room. I sat on the edge, staring at my daughter.

McK came over and sat on my knee, wrapped her arm around my neck, and watched her with me. "She's safe, Mads."

I nodded.

"You got to her in time," she said quietly.

"But what if…" God, my voice trailed off, tears hitting my cheeks. The terror I'd felt running across the ranch hit me all over again.

"You can't think about that. It doesn't matter. You *did* save her," McKenna said quietly.

I kissed her softly, a thank-you for the words but also for being there and saving Sadie from bleeding out. She kissed me back just as gently, as if she was afraid I'd break. Then, the kiss deepened, full of loss and anger and fear that came out in a stream of passion. She took every lick and bite and nip and handed them back to me, letting me rain my extreme emotions over her. When they finally eased, I looked down, and her mouth and cheeks were red from the ferocity with which I'd devoured her.

I rubbed a thumb along her bottom lip.

"Sorry," I said softly.

She shook her head. "No. Don't ever be sorry for showing me how you feel and letting me hold you up. Do you know how many times in our life you did that for me? Held me when I thought I'd break?"

"You never were going to break," he said. "You're too strong."

McKenna looked over at Mila. "She's the strong one."

I agreed. My daughter was strong, but her sister was also. They'd both faced horrors and walked away intact—at least physically. My heart twisted, wondering how this would affect Mila in the long run. If she'd have nightmares. If I'd eventually need to take her to someone to talk about them. She'd been way too quiet for too many hours now, and I hated that what had happened today might take her joy and chatter and change her into someone solemn and grim.

McKenna rose from my knee, hand rubbing along my jaw, and then asked, "Food? Rianne's right. We need to eat."

I looked over at Mila, stomach flipping at the thought of even walking out of the room without her. "I…I can't."

McK seemed to understand. "I'll bring it to you."

She left, and I toed off my boots and lay down on the bed, watching Mila breathe. My own eyes drooped as they had at the hospital. I struggled to keep awake, but it was a losing battle. The tidal wave of emotions dragged me under until there was only darkness.

♫ ♫ ♫

Giggles woke me, and at first, Mila's sweet laugh brought a smile to my lips. When my eyes slowly opened and I realized I was in my room with Mila's nightlights glowing around us, it confused me. Then, the entire day's events slammed back into my memories, tightening my chest, and I sat straight up.

McKenna and Mila were at the foot of the bed, a towel spread out with food all over it. Sandwiches, cookies, chips, juice boxes, and water bottles. A bed picnic of sorts.

Mila's little face was turned up with a smile, and relief washed over me, enough that it would have made my legs buckle if I hadn't already been sitting.

"And then, Missy said she'd never had a unicorn before and that unicorns were going to be her new favorite animal. And that I was her best friend. Do you think we'll be best friends forever? Because you and Daddy were best friends, and then you weren't, but now I guess you are again, right?"

Thank God…for her chatter. Suddenly, it wasn't Mila that needed to breathe. It was me because I felt like my lungs had stopped working. McK took in my expression, lips twitching as she responded, "Even though I told you the best part of BFFs is the forever part, I think your daddy and I sort of forgot it for a while, but now we've remembered, and forever it is."

Jesus. My heart wasn't going to be able to take it.

"Whatchya doing?" I asked, and Mila turned and smiled at me, jumping up and causing all the food on the towel to shift and dump over. McKenna chuckled as Mila launched herself into my lap.

"Daddy! We're having a bed picnic. Have you ever had a bed picnic before? McKenna says we can have a bed picnic all weekend. She even put a new station on your TV, and guess what?" She didn't wait for my answer. "It plays *Scooby-Doo*. As much as we want!"

"Did she now?" I said, running my hand over her hair and her arms, as if I could hardly believe she was here and whole and chattering away.

"You must be starving," McKenna said. "Come join our picnic."

Mila shoved herself from my lap and returned to the cornucopia of food. I eased over, stomach actually grumbling, and I picked up one of the wrapped sandwiches Rianne had left for us.

"That's peanut butter and jelly, Daddy. You don't want that. Remember, you don't like peanut butter. You need this one." Mila shoved another sandwich at me, sort of bouncing up and down on her butt on the bed. "It's salami, and I don't like salami. It tastes funny." Then, she froze. "I gotta go to the bathroom…"

She took off at a dead run for the toilet.

McKenna and I exchanged a small smile.

"She's…so amazing," I said, staring after her.

"Resilient. Brave."

"Just like her sister," I said softly, and McKenna flushed. "Should we tell her about you?" I asked.

McKenna's head tilted sideways as she considered it. "Not today. She's had too many big things happen. I don't want her finding out about me to be tied to this memory."

I leaned over the food and kissed her softly before leaning back again. "Resilient, brave, smart, beautiful. The whole package."

Her eyes lit up at the compliment, and I wondered if the ex had forgotten to tell her those things. It made me hate him a little bit more. But then I pushed him aside because he didn't matter anymore. We were all that mattered. Us and the future we were going to build together.

Chapter Thirty-three

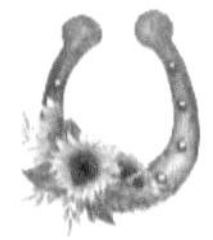

McKenna

FORGED IN THE FIRE

Performed by Caylee Hammack

My heart was full. Mila's and Maddox's faces were smiling again, and that eased the tension that had remained in my heart. It was amazing how resilient kids could be. I had a feeling she'd have nightmares at times, she might need to talk to someone who could help her process what had happened in her own way. But she'd been saved by her father, and that was what she would remember most—at least, I hoped so.

I was taking the food wrappers and empty bottles back to the kitchen when my phone rang. Dr. Gomez's name flashed across the screen, and my stomach twisted right back up into angry knots.

"Hey, Dr. Gomez," I greeted hesitantly.

"Good evening. I know it's rather late. Is this a good time for a talk?"

"Yes, of course."

"I went by your apartment, but no one answered," she said.

How long had it been since I'd been in California? It felt like years, but it had barely been a week. A week and my entire life had changed.

"Sally and I went out of town for a few days. Things were getting…heated."

"I'm sorry," she said softly. "I wanted you to know the hospital has officially let Roy Gregory go and filed a complaint with the medical review board asking them to revoke his license."

Relief flooded through me.

"Wow…I don't know what to say."

"It wasn't just the abuse charges pending against him now that Layton has come forward. We also have proof he altered your personnel file. From what we gather, yours wasn't the first file he'd asked Shirley to change."

"I'm grateful you believed in me enough to open the investigation to begin with."

"You did the right thing, Dr. Lloyd. I looked over your notes and reviewed the history you saw. If Dr. Gregory's name hadn't been tied to it, it would have been an easy call for me to make. With his name attached, I think I would have hesitated, but you didn't even blink."

"I know the signs really well," I told her, and it didn't stab at me as it would have even a few weeks ago. Somehow, being here, with Maddox and Mila, was helping me put the last remaining vestiges of my childhood trauma behind me.

"You lived it," she replied softly.

I took a deep breath. I'd never really talked about it with anyone but Maddox, Sally, and my therapist. I'd always been ashamed of the abuse and the role I'd played in keeping it a secret. But, like Mila today, I was a survivor. I'd been strong enough to live through it and still make something of myself. No one could ever take that from me. Not Dr. Gregory, not Trap, not even Sybil.

"Yes," I finally replied. "I lived it."

"I'll understand if you need a few days, but I'd like to be able to tell the ER when they can expect you back."

The knot in my chest returned as laughter burst from Maddox's bedroom.

"You're hesitating. You are coming back, right?" she asked.

"Honestly, I need a few days to figure it out."

"You're months away from finishing your residency. Don't let this stop you now. You're a damn good doctor. There are other Laytons in the world who need you watching out for them."

The compliment had me flushing just like with the doctor at the hospital. The realization finally hit me—my medical career wasn't over. I was going to get to finish what I'd started. Joy spiked, and as my eyes drifted down the hall toward the laughter again, I held my breath, wondering if I might actually be able to have my cake and eat it, too. Could I have all my dreams? The ones Mam—Sybil had tried to minimize, steal, and take away by telling me I'd never be anything and that no one would ever really want me? They'd been her feelings about herself, but she'd taken them out on me.

"I'm going to finish my residency," I told her. "I just don't know where."

"Ahh. I see. Well, under the circumstances, it's completely understandable. Let me know how I can help you make this happen. You've earned it."

We said goodbye, and I immediately called Sally to tell her the news. She screamed into the phone, shouting about justice and dicks who got what they deserved. Then, I told her everything else that had happened, and she got quiet.

"You need each other," she said.

I didn't respond because I knew she was right. We did. There would always be something missing in our lives if we weren't together.

"Don't walk away from it, McK. The job, your career…that can all be figured out. Love like what you have—lifetime, soulmate kind of love—it doesn't come around but once."

I thought of Maddox's ringtone and smiled.

She was right.

After we hung up, I floated back down the hall. I felt like the pieces of my life I thought had crumbled around me were actually being glued back together into a new shape, a glass jar becoming a stunning vase. Fate giving me this second chance.

🎵 🎵 🎵

We spent Saturday and Sunday mostly in the bed in Maddox's room. We left the house briefly to go and see Sadie at the hospital and to visit with the people who came by, dropping off food and care packages. But whenever the door closed behind us, we all returned to Maddox's room where we played games, snacked on the worst kind of food, and watched more *Scooby-Doo* than I'd ever known existed.

Mila was in heaven, loving the attention and the junk food and being together.

And slowly, Maddox was able to take his eyes off her for longer periods of time.

Sunday night, Mila looked at him and said, "Daddy, I need to go sleep in my own bed. Tomorrow is a school day, and you always say I have to be in my bed on a school night."

He hesitated, and I wondered if sending her to school, where she'd be completely out of his sight and control, would even be possible for him. I wasn't her parent, and I couldn't even imagine seeing her wave goodbye at the schoolroom door so soon after having almost lost her.

"Maybe you should stay home tomorrow," he said quietly.

"Daddy! No way! We are supposed to start our gingerbread stories tomorrow. We are going to work on them all the way until Christmas. Except, we can't celebrate Christmas because not everyone does. Did you know that, Daddy?"

He nodded and then added, "Gingerbread stories, huh?"

I reached over and squeezed his hand, trying to reassure him that he could do this, even though I wasn't sure I could let her go either. "She's going to be okay. The routine is good for her."

He stared at me for a long time, throat bobbing.

But he picked her up and carried her back to her room. I plugged in her nightlights and then squished into the bed with her as Maddox brought *The Day the Unicorns Saved the World* to his lap. Mila demanded I do the girl voices while Maddox did the boy voices, and she giggled as if nothing had ever gone wrong in her life barely two days ago.

When the story was done, Maddox and I got up, kissed opposite sides of her cheeks, and tucked her in so tight she could barely move. We said our I love yous and were headed for the door when her little voice stopped us.

"Daddy?" Mila asked.

"Yes, Bug-a-Boo?"

"I was really afraid the other day."

My stomach flipped, clenching tight.

"I know, sweetheart," he said, returning to her bedside.

"But I'm not anymore."

"You're not?"

"Nope, because you'll always save me."

Maddox cleared his throat, leaned down, and kissed her forehead again. "Always."

He walked over to the door where I was waiting for him and flicked on a baby monitor I'd never noticed being there. Mila sighed. "The baby monitor, Daddy? Really? I'm not a baby."

"No, you're not, but just like when you're sick, I can hear you this way if you need me."

She seemed to consider it for a moment and then just rolled over with Chester and Charlotte in her arms.

I grabbed his hand and pulled him back toward his bedroom. He flicked on the other half of the baby monitor tucked amongst the things on his dresser, adjusting the volume. I tugged at his belt loops, bringing our chests together. I lifted myself on my toes to kiss him. A soft, gentle kiss. It was all we'd been able to do for two days with Mila constantly at our sides. It had none of the heat and torture and passion that he'd kissed me with when we'd brought her home on Friday, or the sensual teasing kisses we'd had before Thanksgiving, but it was still full of love. Love and patience and caring.

Maddox put one hand behind my head, supporting me as he deepened the kiss with a nip of his teeth and a flick of his tongue. His other hand was at my waist, moving below the T-shirt, slowly tracing small circles up my rib cage, reaching higher and higher.

"As much as I hated the thought of her sleeping in her own bed, I've also been dying to do this again. To lose myself in you," he said, voice low and deep with desire.

I grabbed the hem of his T-shirt just as he lifted mine over my head. Our bare chests collided again. He massaged and thumbed my breasts as my hands explored his chest, his abs, the V-like indentation at his waist that led to the glorious things hidden beneath his sweats. We danced our way across each other's bodies with fingers and tongues, marking our souls with silent promises until we were quivering and shaking with anticipation and need. He lifted me on top of the dresser, spreading my legs and stepping in between them.

"I don't think I can wait even the two steps it would take to reach the bed," he grunted, mouth descending on a nipple as he plunged inside me. I let out a breathy whimper of pleasure, needing him just as much as he needed me.

We moved in uncontrolled movements, bodies slapping, breath becoming uneven. His hand slid between us, the rhythm of his fingers joining the push and pull of us in and out, and I let go, clenching and shaking, shuddering around him.

He lifted me again, denying his words by taking the two steps to the bed and sitting on the edge so I was straddling him. "I need you to take over," he said.

I rubbed my palms over his jaw, the beard having turned softer in the last couple of days as it filled out. His gaze met mine, a hungry need in it I would gladly sate. I moved my hips, using his shoulders as leverage, controlling the movements, increasing the pace, until he finally bit my shoulder and groaned while raising his hips to fiercely slam into me one last time.

He rolled us back onto the mattress so we were facing each other, bodies still aligned but no longer embedded in each other. I missed it already. Missed it and hated having to say things that might cause the distance between us to be more than physical.

"I heard from the hospital."

His hand that had been slowly running from my hip to the side of my breast and back down stopped. His gaze was no longer hungry. It was wary instead.

"Yeah? Was it good news?" he asked as he searched my face for my emotions.

"It was very good news. They've cleared me, fired Gregory, and filed charges with the medical board against him."

His throat bobbed. "That's amazing, McK. I'm really happy for you. Truly."

"Me too," I said.

His lips twitched a little. "You don't sound excited or happy."

"You know why," I told him.

"Because it means you're leaving," he finished.

He started to back away, and I reached out, grasping his cheeks in my hands and refusing to let him move or even look away. "It'll only be for a little while."

Then, I told him about the research I'd done on getting licensed in Tennessee and about finishing my residency somewhere in state.

His eyes closed, relief washing over his face like when he'd looked at Mila all weekend. Then, he kissed me again fiercely, possessively.

"I have to be honest," he said, voice deep and guttural. "I had images of using my cuffs to tie you to the bed."

I laughed, and he smiled, but then I turned serious again. "I don't know how long it will take. Dr. Gomez said she's willing to help me in any way she can, and I hate the thought of having to finish up where I'm at all the way through June, but—"

He put his fingers on my lips, halting my words. "I can do it, McK. I can do six or seven months if it means I'll get to keep you forever after that."

I wasn't sure I'd even be able to leave them, let alone stay away for months. "Just the thought of it kind of feels like someone is slicing off my skin."

"Skin grows back. It's hearts that don't."

I rested my forehead on his chest. "I'm just… Thank you for so many things. For being my hero, for being my sister's hero…and for giving me a second chance."

He slid his arms around my waist, tugging me tight up against him again. "Soul sisters, right?"

I laughed, and he swallowed it with his mouth.

I let myself revel in it. The feeling of completeness. The feeling of finally being home. The knowledge that, somehow, we'd put ourselves back together again.

Chapter Thirty-four

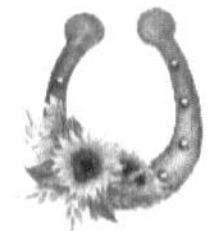

Maddox

Mila rebounded to her normal self in a way that spoke to the resilience of children…to her resilience. She spent the week chattering away about the damn gingerbread stories at school until I was seeing them in my sleep. She'd only had one nightmare since the incident. Her screams over the baby monitor had launched me into her room where I'd picked her up and carried her back to ours, settling her between McKenna and me where we'd both watched over her while she'd slept.

The tenderness on McK's face when she looked at Mila these days about undid me. I might even have been jealous if both my girls hadn't looked at me in the same way—with adoration and love. It felt like I'd gotten back a part of my soul that had been wandering aimlessly for years.

A little over a week after the worst day of my life, Mama and Dad threw a party at the ranch for Sadie, who'd finally been released from the hospital and was hobbling around with a splint and crutches, fiercely determined to get her full mobility back. The party was supposedly for her, but the truth was, we were really celebrating all the ways we'd saved each other that day.

The ranch was packed with an avalanche of family and townsfolk. The noise was loud and rambunctious in the very best way. Mila loved it, flitting around while being treated like the hometown hero she was, but McK retreated a little bit, reminding me of the very first time she'd come to a birthday party at the ranch. The chaos had sent her fleeing to the porch, and that was where I found her when I went looking for her now.

She was leaning against the rail, staring out at the mist swirling low above the ground. The day was cold with the promise of winter hovering in the air. McKenna shivered, and I pulled her up tight against me, our warmth blending together.

"Where you at?" I asked, kissing her temple softly.

"The D.A. from Davis called," she said as her hands found my biceps and squeezed. "Thanks to your lead, they found the store where the pre-paid phones were bought, and they had surveillance cameras that showed Dr. Gregory purchasing them. She wanted to let me know they're pressing charges."

She turned in my arms, fingers running along my cheek.

"Thank you," she said, and then she was kissing me, like she had all week, fierce and yet sad, as if each one could be our last. I tried not to let it snag at my insecurities because I could feel, in every touch and every word, her intention to return to me…to us.

She stepped out of my embrace, pulling something out of her back pocket that she clenched in her fist.

"Today, we've been celebrating how you, Sadie, and Mila all saved each other—"

"And you," I interrupted. "You saved Sadie, McK. And if you hadn't remembered the hollow and the fool's gold…" I swallowed hard, not able to think about the *if* for long.

She shrugged, passing over what she'd done that day. She continued as if I hadn't said anything. "I want you to know…you saved me, too. Not just with Gregory, not just when I showed up at your house thinking it was Trap's, but before…when I was little. The only thing that got me up and out of the apartment some days when I lived with Sybil was knowing you were waiting for me."

"McK," I grunted out, uncomfortable and overwhelmed.

She handed me a key chain. A broken heart that had half of the phrase "Best Friends Forever." She pulled the other half out of her pocket, and it already had her keys on it. "I know it's stupid and childish, but…this is the most important word." She pointed to the *Forever* on my half.

"One-hundred percent of the time McK. I'll always have your back. I should never have let you push me away that easily. I didn't fight for you, but I will every day for the rest of my life," I told her. "We're not just forever. We're forever and always."

She stared at me for a moment, tears filling her eyes that she brushed away. A small smile appeared on her lips. "Forever and always. You going to add that song to your sappy ringtones?"

I laughed. "Maybe."

And then I kissed her, proving the promise of my words with action.

♫ ♫ ♫

She left the next day. I'd wanted to drive her to the airport, but she had to drop the rental off, so Mila and I said goodbye to her at the house. My gut was in shreds. The last time McKenna Lloyd had left Willow Creek, I'd known she wasn't coming back, and now, even though she'd said she was, and I believed in the stupid forever and always we'd promised each other, I was still terrified something would change. That something would prevent her from returning.

"I drew this for you," Mila said, handing her a paper. "I still can't draw very well yet, and our unicorn horns look like we're wearing weird hats." The paper had three stick figures at the front with our names written over them, and then behind us in the sky was a bunch of faces with the names of my family, Rianne, and even Mila's friend, Missy. Below the three of us, it said *BFFs*, and at the top, in her imperfect kindergarten handwriting, someone had helped her spell out *The Day the Hatleys Saved Each Other*.

McK's throat bobbed, and a little sob escaped her as she pulled Mila into a hug that was tight and fierce.

"It's perfect, Mila. Just like you."

Mila giggled as McK reached over her head and kissed me like it was our last chance to do so, and that fear inside me, that she'd never come back, welled again.

I grabbed her by the back of her neck when she went to move away, gaze meeting hers.

"I love you." I infused it with every last ounce of love I felt in my heart.

"You're my favorite thing. My favorite memory. My favorite gift. My favorite person," she said, and it took my very worst memories of her saying those same words and turned them into the best. "In case you don't get what that means, I love you, too. So damn much."

"You have to put a dollar in the cuss jar, McKenna!" Mila said between us, and we both chuckled.

"Remind me when I get back, okay, Bug-a-Boo?" she said, and Mila nodded.

Then, my daughter and I watched her walk down the steps and get in the car and drive away as my heart nearly broke.

Mila skipped back into the house. "Daddy, you're sad for no reason. McKenna isn't leaving us. She'll be back."

God…to have that much faith.

♫ ♫ ♫

The next day, I was at the station when the call came in—yet another demand from Sybil Lloyd. Ever since she'd recovered from her stab wound, she'd been hollering to see me, and for a week, I'd ignored her. But now, she was raising such a fuss they were afraid she'd end up busting her stitches.

I drove to the jail to see her, but it wasn't because I gave a damn about her stitches. No, I went for a completely selfish reason. I wanted her to know she had no control over me or McKenna or Mila anymore. That her reign of terror was finally over.

When Chainsaw was in the hospital, they'd run a DNA test on him, and I'd gotten my proof—he was Mila's biological father. When he died on the surgical table, I said a big ol' thank you to the universe and didn't feel an ounce of guilt. Even if he'd lived, I wouldn't have had to worry about him in Mila's life because the bullet he'd put in Sadie's leg had been shot from the same gun that had killed Slider. He would have spent the rest of his life in jail.

Now, Sybil had nothing to hold over me, but I had a lot to hold over her.

She looked like hell when they brought her into the room and hooked the chain around her ankle to the floor by the chair. She looked even worse than the day I'd found her passed out in a sea of her own vomit with Mila screaming in the other room.

She crossed her arms over her chest, glared, and said snidely, "I've been asking to see you for days, *Sheriff*."

"I have one question, Sybil. Did you kill Slider or did Chainsaw?"

I already knew the answer, but I wanted to see her response. I wanted to discombobulate her and put her on the defensive like she always had me. Her mouth dropped, and then she put her arms over her chest, face turning squinty. "I had nothing to do with that."

"Are you sure? Because I think Slider threatened to give away your hiding spot. That you were afraid of losing your million-dollar payday."

Her jaw ticked. "I didn't kill no one. Slider was stupid. He went back to The Nest because he wanted his damn bike. I told him not to go. And what's all this about a million dollars?"

I pulled a bag up onto the table from where I'd had it at my feet. It was a worn, black duffel with a partially broken zipper through which piles of cash peeked out.

She let out a blood-curdling scream when she saw it, immediately reaching for it. "That's mine! Mine! Damn you."

I pulled it out of her grasp, shoving her back into her seat with a palm and tossing the duffel toward the door. It hadn't taken me long to figure out where she'd hidden it. It was the reason she kept coming back to McFlannigan's even when she knew it was as stupid as Slider going back to The Nest. She'd hidden the bag in the place her daughter used to hide—the shed out back.

"I fucking earned that!" she screamed. "Years of barely scraping by. Years of being at their beck and call and raising their fucking babies."

"Babies you were responsible for creating."

She acted like I hadn't even said anything. "Chainsaw is going to kill you, just like he killed Slider, once he knows you have it."

"Chainsaw is dead," I told her. "I shot him when he tried to use Mila as a fucking bargaining chip."

It shut her up. Fury and hate clouded her gaze, but she didn't have any cards left to play, and she knew it.

I rose. "The good news for me, Sybil, is I don't have any other reason to come see you again. Mila's mine. McKenna's mine. I don't know how a shitty-ass human being like you happened to create two bundles of joy, but they are…full of joy and love. No matter how you tried to beat and starve it out of them, they survived. They became bright, beautiful lights, and they're going to live long, happy lives because I'll make it my mission to make sure they do. While you…you'll die here, alone and miserable. Enjoy the life you reaped."

She screamed at me to come back, but I just walked out with the bag I would check back in to evidence when I got to the station. My heart was singing because I'd never have to see Sybil Lloyd again.

♫ ♫ ♫

Mila and I had just hung up from a video call with McKenna a few days before Christmas when she got sad and droopy. My chest twisted. I kept waiting for the storm to break, for her to have a meltdown because of what had happened, so my voice was slow and tentative when I asked, "What's up, Bug-a-Boo?"

"McKenna is going to be all alone on Christmas."

It made my gut twist and turn, too. I hated the thought of her being alone. McKenna's friend Sally had gone back to Davis only long enough to pack up her stuff and move in with her father on the Central Coast. Since then, McKenna had been putting in what felt like a thousand hours a week at the hospital. The work hadn't been easy, especially because a handful of the staff still believed Roy Gregory.

"She doesn't have anyone, Daddy," Mila continued. "We have everyone. Nana, Papa, Uncle Ryder, Auntie Gemma, Auntie Sadie, Rianne, Tillie, and Bruce, and—"

"I get it, sweetheart. We have the entire town of Willow Creek."

"She doesn't have any family."

My chest ached. McKenna and I hadn't talked again about when to tell Mila the truth, but it felt wrong to say McK didn't have family, especially when her sister was sitting in front of my eyes.

I pulled Mila to me and then took the leap. "We've talked before about how I found you when Sybil didn't know how to take care of you."

Mila nodded, brows creased as she said, "You and I were both sad and lonely, right? You said when you picked me up, it was like we both found our home."

Those had been my words. Words I'd keep telling her until she was old enough to finally understand what they really meant.

"Well, when I first saw you, I didn't know for sure who'd given birth to you, and yet, I still knew who you were."

Her frown grew. "I don't understand, Daddy."

"I knew who you were because I could see your sister in you."

She inhaled sharply. "I have a sister?! Where? Why don't I know her? Where are you keeping her?"

I smiled. "Breathe, Bug-a-Boo, and just think for a minute. Use that enormous heart of yours, and you tell me who you think your sister is. Someone you look like. Someone you already love and who loves you back."

Mila's eyes grew wide. "McKenna! *McKenna* is my *sister*?!" She jumped off of me, hopping from foot to foot, twirling around. She grabbed Chester off the couch and screamed in his face, "Chester! I have a *sister*!"

She came to a stop in front of me. "Daddy, you know what this means, right?"

My smile met hers, growing wide as I said, "We need McKenna to spend Christmas with her family."

"Yes!" She made the little victory move I hadn't seen her do in days and took off running toward the hallway. "Come on, Daddy. We have to pack right away." She stopped. "Nana and Papa are going to be sad because they say I am the joy of Christmas. But they have Uncle Ryder and Auntie Sadie and Auntie Gemma, and they will just have to be their joy this year."

I laughed, pulled up my phone, and searched for airline tickets as happiness and excitement filled me. I'd let McK go once and not gone after her, and even though I knew she was coming back, that this time things were different, it still felt right to go after her now. To make sure she never spent another damn holiday alone.

Chapter Thirty-five

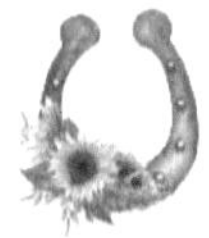

McKenna

DETOUR

Performed by Maren Morris

I sealed the last box with satisfaction and looked around my bedroom with a tired sigh. It was almost as empty as the rest of the apartment. The entire place felt cold and bare, like it had from the moment Sally had left for good, taking most of the furnishings with her. When I'd moved in, I'd only had my bedroom set, television, and a few odds and ends in the kitchen because almost everything at Kerry's place had been his, and he'd taken it all with him to Boston. It was a little sad to think I'd spent so many years in California and had so little to show for it. But in some ways, I was glad. It meant I could easily leave it behind to return to the people I loved.

During the last few video calls with Maddox and Mila, I'd had to get creative so they didn't see the state of the apartment and blow my secret before I was ready. I wasn't very good at keeping secrets anymore, especially not from Maddox, but the thought of surprising them on Christmas Eve had me giving it my best effort.

My phone rang, and I picked it up when I saw Sally's name.

"Hey," I said.

"I feel like I pushed you with all my soul mate talk. Are you really sure about this?" she asked, worry clear in her tone.

"Absolutely," I told her. In my heart, I knew it was the right thing. It was a setback, but it wasn't the end of my career. For a short period of time, I had thought I would never practice medicine again, so having to wait a few months to restart my last year of residency in Tennessee was nothing—not if it meant I could be with Maddox and McKenna in the meantime.

"You really love him." Sally sighed, relief from whatever misplaced guilt she'd had seeping into her voice, as if she'd actually been the one to force me in this direction.

"I love them both. But it isn't just that, Sal. I want to show Maddox he's worth giving up everything for when I wasn't willing to give up anything in our past. Besides, Dr. Gomez is pulling all the strings she can, so who knows if I'll even have to wait until July. I think she feels guilty that all of this went down on her watch."

"It means we'll be living, permanently, thousands of miles apart. The thought of you in Davis and me in Avalyn Beach was bad enough, but I still could have gotten to you in a couple of hours if I needed to."

"You can come and visit anytime and stay as long as you want."

I didn't want to presume I'd be living with Maddox, but I had a sneaking suspicion that once I showed up, he wasn't going to let me go. Just like after my first night in his bed, I'd never returned to the guest room.

All those thoughts thrilled me. Belonging to him—them—and having them belong to me, too. My joy at the thought of seeing Maddox and Mila again soared through me, just like the thought of being with the entire Hatley clan for Christmas did. I'd never looked forward to a holiday before.

This one was going to be special for so many reasons.

A knock on my door made me jump. I hadn't ordered food, and I'd given the final check to the landlord already, so there was no reason for anyone to be here. My thoughts drifted to the notes that had been scrawled across the wood before I'd left for Tennessee, but then I reminded myself I didn't have anything to worry about from Roy Gregory. He'd emptied his bank accounts, left his wife, and taken off to The Maldives where there was no extradition treaty and a good chance someone would hire him as a doctor regardless of the cloud hanging over him. If he stepped back into the U.S., he'd be arrested on a whole host of charges, including skipping bail.

"Sal, I gotta go. Someone's at the door."

"You want me to hold on while you check?"

"No, it's all good. I'll talk to you before I head out."

I was hoping to get as far as Reno tomorrow. If I drove at least ten hours a day from there, I'd make it in four, which would get me there just in time for Christmas Eve.

Another knock on the door brought me to my feet, heading from the bedroom out into the empty living space. All the blinds were shut, including the ones looking out onto the landing. I went over and peeked out, and my heart stuttered, dropping the blinds with a hand to my heart. Then, I looked again just to make sure they were real before my feet were flying to the door as my chest threatened to explode with love. I threw it open and stared at my two favorite people in the whole world.

"What? How?" The smile on my face felt so large I thought it might break my cheekbones.

"McKenna!" Mila squealed, tackling my legs and making me put a hand on the wall to stabilize myself. "Merry Christmas!"

I laughed. "It isn't Christmas!"

Maddox had looked worried when I'd first opened the door, as if I wouldn't be happy to see him. But now that I was grinning at Mila, his mouth started to tilt up, and then it broke into that gorgeous, stunning smile I loved to call mine—the one that changed his face from a bright star into a supernova.

He took one step inside, wrapped his arms around me, and his lips landed on mine. Heat, longing, and love rippled through my body, knocking all the nerves awake that had gone into hiding since I'd left them. When he started to move away, I fisted his T-shirt and held on, lips finding his again.

"You guys! You're squishing me. Remember to breathe," Mila's tiny voice said, and I laughed again, eyes finding Maddox's twinkling ones.

"Seriously, what are you doing here?" I asked.

Maddox shut the door behind him and looked down at Mila. "You want to be the one to tell her, Bug-a-Boo?"

Mila jumped from foot to foot and then screamed, "You're my sister!" My eyes filled with tears as I looked from her to Maddox and then back. "Did you know that?" she continued. "Because I absolutely did *not* know until we were talking about Christmas and how you were alone with no family, and then Daddy told me you're really my sister, and I said there is no way we can let you spend Christmas without your family, and—"

Maddox put his hand over her mouth. "I think she gets the point."

I knelt in front of her, bringing our eyes to the same height. "I didn't know I had a sister until I saw you at Thanksgiving, but now that I do, I can't think of anything I'd like more than to spend Christmas with you."

She wrapped her little arms around my neck and hugged me tightly before letting go and looking around the empty space.

"McKenna," she whispered. "Someone stole all your stuff."

I laughed again. "It kind of looks that way, doesn't it? But the truth is, the apartment is just packed up. All the boxes are in the bedrooms."

Mila raced toward the little hallway, looking into Sally's old room and then into mine. "Whoa," she said. "This place is a disaster." She turned back to us. "Daddy, where are we going to stay?"

When I turned to look at Maddox, he was frowning. "What's going on, McK?"

"You kind of ruined my surprise," I told him with a wry grin. "I was heading out tomorrow. I was trying to get to *you* before Christmas Eve."

Mila skipped back over. "You were coming home? But then I would have missed my first airplane ride ever, and we got to watch movies on the plane! Did you know you could do that, because I definitely didn't."

Maddox looked down at his daughter with an exasperated look I'd never seen on his face before. "Bug-a-Boo, I need you to go into McK's bedroom and give us five minutes alone."

"Are you going to kiss her again?"

"Maybe."

She giggled. "Okay, but tell me when five minutes is up because I still don't know how to tell time yet."

Then, she twirled down the hall.

"Is there anything she can get hurt on?" he asked.

I shook my head. "No, everything but the bed and my suitcases are pretty much packed."

He stepped closer, tugging the pocket on the front of my sweatshirt until I fell into him. "McK, what's going on?"

I put my arms around his neck, fingers tangling in the waves there.

"It's really rather simple. I didn't want to be without you, so I was coming home."

That word, *home*, slipped off my tongue, feeling strange and beautiful and right.

"What about your residency? Your license?" he asked, frowning.

"I'll start over next year."

He inhaled sharply. "McK…" Regret and worry coated his voice.

"It's nothing, Mads. Nothing. I'm lucky I still get to be a doctor after thinking my career was over, but none of it matters when I compare it to wasting even one more minute not being with you and Mila. I wasted ten years I could have been with you… I lost five years of Mila's life… I can't miss even one more day."

He kissed me again with a tangle of emotions that felt like hope and love and gratitude. The kiss should have felt familiar, as if we'd done it a million times before, and yet, it felt brand new. Like the first of many new ones because it was the first kiss of our new journey together. He pushed me up against the wall, hand sliding under my sweatshirt, cupping my bare breast. I pulled his long-sleeve T-shirt from his pants, palm grazing his back and reveling in the heat of his skin. Our tongues danced together, licking slow and deep, causing flames to curl through me and making my core throb.

"Has it been five minutes yet?" Mila yelled from the other room.

Maddox laughed and pulled back, thumb landing on my lips that felt blissfully raw from our kisses.

"How long do you think we can keep her in there before she realizes five minutes is up?" he asked with a slow smile.

"Daddy?" her voice rang out from the other room, and my chuckle joined his.

"I'd say you have thirty seconds."

"Perfect."

He kissed me again, this time without the hands or heat, but with a promise instead.

Mila came skipping back into the room.

"Daddy! Did you forget me? I told you to tell me when five minutes was up. And also, I'm hungry. And also, I'm not sure there's room for all three of us on McKenna's bed, so you may need to sleep on the floor."

He picked her up, swung her around, and said, "McKenna is coming home with us."

She rolled her eyes at Maddox. "I know, Daddy. She already said that."

"You know what that makes this Christmas, right?" he asked.

She put both her hands on his face and screamed, "Only the *best* Christmas *ever*!"

It was. Not just the best Christmas, but the very best life.

Epilogue

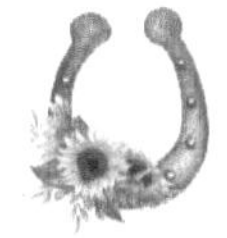

Maddox

ALL FOR YOU

Performed by Keith Urban

NOVEMBER 7th THE FOLLOWING YEAR

A year ago, I'd come home to my little girl and fallen asleep in an empty bed, thinking of the woman who'd gotten away. The one who'd ridden out of town and left this cowboy behind with a partially functioning heart and a slew of memories I didn't mess with. Today, my life and my heart were so full it was almost sinful, and McK and I were building brand-new, beautiful memories—brighter, deeper ones.

Only one thing was the same today as it had been last year, and that was me at McFlannigan's, wrestling Willy to the ground.

"I'm taking you to jail this time, Willy," I said as I cuffed his hands behind him and searched the ground for my hat. "And you owe me another goddamn hat."

Willy cried. "She's getting married, Maddox. To the suit."

"It's Sheriff Hatley to you, dumbass."

I helped him up and looked at my brother leaning nonchalantly against the bar, arms across his chest and a cheesy grin on his face.

I tipped my chin in his direction. "And you…thanks for the help, yet again!"

He shrugged. "They didn't elect me sheriff."

"I don't have time for this. I have to get back to the house," I said, pushing Willy toward the door.

I had plans tonight that meant I needed to beat McK home. She'd been lucky to find a hospital in the next county willing to take her on so she could finish up her residency, but it meant a bit of a commute. She said it didn't matter, that being here with us while she was lucky enough to do the job she loved was what was important, but I still didn't like it. I wanted her close because I was a selfish bastard when it came to my girls.

Ryder followed me and Willy out the door.

"You really going to do it tonight?" Ryder asked me as I tucked Willy into the back of my work truck.

I looked over at him, and there was concern in his eyes.

"Yep," I responded without a hint of nervousness.

He ran a hand over his stubble.

"Just spit it out, Ryder," I growled.

"I like McK. I like the dumbass, goofy smile you wear now that you're actually having regular sex."

I didn't rise to his bait. I just shrugged and asked, "But?"

He shook his head. "I guess you're just the better, bigger man because I would never give Ravyn a second chance."

"Like I've said a million times, what happened with McK and me was one-hundred-percent different than what happened with you and Ravyn," I told him.

While Ryder had sworn off anything to do with relationships after he'd had his heart torn apart, I'd always longed for what was missing in my life. Maybe because my heart knew what it felt like to be whole, and it had craved to be back in that state. With McKenna home, I felt like everything in my life was right again.

Ryder looked toward the back seat where I'd stashed Willy, sighed, and said, "Let him go. We both know what he's going through. And this way, you can get home quicker."

I hated that he was right. I opened the door, dragged Willy out, uncuffed him, and handed him off to my brother. "Make sure he makes it home."

"Thanks, Mads," Willy grunted out, wiping his face with his sleeve.

"It's Sheriff Hatley to you, dickhead."

Then, I rounded the front of the truck, got in, and headed the couple blocks to my house with my heart soaring and a smile already on my face.

When I opened the door, Mila came skipping over. Her skip was almost perfect these days. "You're home! Rianne and I were getting worried."

Rianne didn't look worried in the least.

"Go change," Rianne said. "We're just putting the final touches on everything now."

I grinned. "Thanks for helping."

Rianne smiled back. "I'm happy to do it. It's like a prophecy fulfilling itself."

"What?" I asked, lips twitching.

"Even in third grade, I knew you two were forever. I could see it."

I scoffed and headed down the hall, but I knew she was telling the truth. I'd known it back then, too. We'd just let ourselves get dragged apart by life, and our baggage, and our insecurities.

I was out of my uniform, cleaned up, and back out in jeans and a button-down in less than ten minutes, but it was still cutting it close.

I went out onto the back porch and stared at what Mila and Rianne had done. The rainbow of flowers I'd brought home at lunch covered every available space except for a little round table with a white linen tablecloth, candles, and three wrought-iron chairs painted white. Mila was spinning around in a dress covered with actual rainbows and holding a rainbow-colored bouquet. I wasn't sure if I'd be happy or sad when she outgrew them, just like it had been bittersweet the night *The Day the Unicorns Saved the World* had been replaced by *The Day the Dragons Saved the Universe*.

Rianne appeared at the screen door with a tray of food, and I held it open for her. She placed it on a side table as I thanked her again for everything. She patted my cheek and said, "Have fun and good luck—even though you don't need it."

Then, she hugged Mila goodbye and left just as McK pulled into the drive in the Bronco. She'd been using it since coming back to Willow Creek, and I'd finally gotten it fully restored so I didn't have to worry about it breaking down on her when she was coming home in the middle of the night after a long shift.

She drove right through West Gear territory every day, and if Trap hadn't taken the gang back in hand once Chainsaw was gone, I might have been more worried. But since moving back to Winter County, he'd made it abundantly clear he wasn't letting anyone hurt his daughter on his watch. He'd even been to dinner several times, and I wasn't sure which of us was more weirded out by it—the sheriff with the criminal he'd arrested sitting at his table or the gang leader breaking bread with the sheriff.

McKenna left the garage and headed for the front door like usual, not even glancing toward the back porch. She was on her phone, probably with Sally. The two of them talked almost daily.

Mila took off into the house, and I heard her scream McK's name as the door opened and could picture them colliding together in the way they did every time they were reunited. My lips twitched, happiness already filling my chest.

"You look pretty snazzy, Bug-a-Boo. When did you get that dress?"

"Daddy bought it for me when we went shopping. Come on, come on, we've been waiting for hours," she said.

Then, they were there with Mila all but dragging McK through the kitchen and toward the back door. I kind of felt bad she was still in her scrubs, face tired, hair pulled up in a tight ponytail, but if I'd told her to go get ready, she would have protested. She never wanted to do anything special on this day.

As McK stepped out onto the porch, her brow furrowed, bouncing slightly on her toes as she took in the romantic setting before landing on me.

"What's going on?" she asked.

"Happy birthday, McKenna!" Mila said, hopping about. "Daddy said you hate celebrating your birthday, and I said that was absolutely wrong and that we needed to change it. Isn't that right, Daddy?"

"Damn straight," I said, gaze not leaving McK's wary one.

"You owe a dollar for the cuss jar, Daddy, but not yet. We have other things to do." Mila turned to her sister and asked, "Dinner or presents first? I say presents, but it's your birthday, so you get to decide."

McKenna's face softened as she watched my daughter literally bursting with enthusiasm. "I guess…presents."

"Yes!" Mila made her little victory move and then pushed McK toward a chair. Once she was seated, my daughter handed her the first present. "This one is from me."

Mila had wanted to wrap it on her own, so it was pretty messed up, but McK didn't care about things like that. She actually looked like she might cry as she assessed the bulging corners and layers of tape. "I can see you wrapped it yourself, too."

"Of course!" Mila said. "I know I'm not good at it yet, but if I keep practicing, I can be as good as you and Daddy someday. Open it!"

The woman I loved with all of my naïve, teenage heart and my cynical, grown-up heart put together tugged at the tape until the wrapping fell off, and a jewelry-sized box appeared. McK shot me a look, but I just shrugged. It was a good distraction, doing Mila's gift first. It would throw her off a little.

When she opened the box, a silver bracelet sat on the velvet. One half of a broken-heart charm was looped onto it that had part of the phrase *Sisters are forever friends*. It was so similar to the key chain McKenna had given me that I'd known it would be perfect as soon as Mila had spotted it.

"Look, see, this is the other half," Mila said, shoving her foot up so McK could see the adult-sized bracelet wrapped around her ankle. "It doesn't fit yet, but Daddy said I could wear it here until I grow into it. Do you like it?"

McK pulled Mila to her, squeezing her tight and kissing the side of her head. "The only thing better is having my sister for real."

Mila giggled and then waved to me. "Your turn, Daddy."

I grabbed the other small package from the table. It wasn't wrapped, but it had a bow on it. I knelt before McK as Mila stood oddly still, quivering with anticipation.

"I feel like you've been a Hatley my entire life. You belonged to us the day you entered our lives, just like Mila did. And I know you've already promised to keep us forever, and that forever is the most important part, but I was hoping you'd also make it official by marrying us."

My breath caught as her face remained serious for way too many heartbeats.

She put a palm on my cheek and reached out for Mila with the other, drawing her closer to us. Then, staring deep into my eyes, she said, "We're a family, forever and always, with or without the official part, but there's nothing I'd rather do than claim my favorite people as mine in front of the entire town."

Mila squealed happily, and McK and I chuckled.

Then, I leaned in and kissed her. Once upon a time, when she'd driven away the first time, I'd thought she belonged to the world, but really, she'd always been mine. It had just taken a while for us to find our way back to each other. Heat licked through me with the sweet kiss, making me ache to deepen it, to devour her, to push my tongue in her mouth and my fingers through her hair, and bury myself inside her, but it would wait.

Mila hugged us, and when our kissing took too long, she pulled at our faces and said, "Breathe, you guys. Breathe."

I smiled that huge, sappy, goofy smile Ryder had mentioned was on my face all the time. Except, it wasn't just me smiling like that. McKenna's was just as big, and Mila's, too, as I tugged her so she was snuggled between us.

"You know what this means?" Mila asked, squirming in our embrace. "It means I have to write a new story. *The Day the Hatleys Got Married*! It's going to be epic."

"Why don't you go get some paper and start on it so you can give McK and me five minutes," I told her.

She sighed, moved away, and dragged her feet toward the door. "Okay, Daddy, but I know how to tell time now, so I'm going to be out in exactly five minutes."

The screen door slammed behind her.

I opened the velvet box and showed McK the ring I'd picked out. "I saved you from having one in an array of rainbow stones like Mila wanted. This looked more like you."

It was simple—a square-cut diamond with a pale-green emerald on either side that reminded me of the color her eyes turned when I was deep inside her and she was calling my name.

"It's beautiful, Mads." Her voice was a soft whisper on the ending letters the way only she did. The way I loved.

"I thought about taking you out, asking you when we were alone, but it—"

"Wouldn't have felt right," she finished for me. "No, I'm glad. Mila needed to be a part of it."

"Your birthday deserves to be filled with good memories, McK. And starting today, I promise they always will be."

She pressed her mouth to mine. I put my hand on the back of her head, deepening the kiss and tangling our tongues in a dance that was fierce and sweet all at the same time. I dragged her out of the chair and onto my knee, where I could feel her heart beat against mine and I could skate my fingers under her scrub top, working hard to keep us PG with Mila ready to bound back out at any second. Love flowed between us, growing with every nip and lick and soft moan until it flickered like the shimmering light of the candles, drenching us in their glow.

"I love you," she whispered.

"Forever and always," I whispered back.

"Five minutes is up. Can we eat now?" Mila asked at the screen door, completely ruining the moment and yet making it absolutely and completely right.

♫ ♫ ♫

Not ready to let the three M&Ms go yet?

Get a glimpse of them a few years later with this FREE BONUS EPILOGUE available with a newsletter sign-up.

https://BookHip.com/RKQHSRX

♫ ♫ ♫

Want more of the Hatley family? Ryder Hatley's happily ever after is coming in May 2024. Sign up for LJ Evans newsletter so you don't miss a thing.

But if you want to see what happens when **Maddox's sister, Gemma**, runs head on into an A-list actor who fall hard and falls first, keep reading right here right now for a first look at her **NOVELLA**:

https://geni.us/PerfectlyFine

SAMPLE

Perfectly Fine – A Novella

Chapter One

Gemma

SUPERSTAR

Performed by Taylor Swift

THE RED CARPET WAS BARE AS ETTA

and I left the theater, but I was still giddy from the dream-like experience of attending my very first movie premiere—a movie I'd had a teeny-tiny hand in making. I made Etta stop in front of the poster to take a picture. We hadn't dared do it earlier when the place had been teeming with the press, fans, and celebrities.

I stared at the selfie for a minute, overcome with strong emotions. It was almost impossible to believe that the woman with her blonde hair piled on top of her head, hazel eyes gracefully layered in makeup, and slim body clad in a black satin slip-dress was actually me. The dress, with its hemline ending barely below my butt cheeks, wasn't one I would have ever bought, but I was grateful to Etta for loaning it to me.

"I can't believe this is me," I said, looking at her with a cheesy grin before hugging her. "I never expected Wilson to invite me to the premiere. I'm just some low-life assistant, scuttling to get him coffee."

"An assistant who pulled a rabbit out of a hat with the yellow-stoned tiara you found in the middle of Nowhere, Tennessee!" she said as her tightly laced braids danced around her.

While I looked nothing like my normal self tonight, Etta was as gorgeous as always in purple satin that accentuated her deep-brown shoulders. She looked like a movie star, even if she had no desire to be one. Instead, her head was full of numbers and marketing schemes.

"The original tiara getting lost in transit was the best thing to ever happen to me," I said, gratitude filling my heart. "Look at me now! Living in Hollywood with you! Working at the studio with the Wilson Devney! I think

Great-Granny Mc would have gotten a kick out of her hoarding ways bringing me a step closer to my dreams."

"You're talented, Gemma. Your screenplay is absolutely going to find a home soon," Etta said.

I held my breath for a moment, thinking of all the queries I'd sent out. Rejection after rejection. But it only took one, and I wouldn't give up. Not ever. So what if right now I was barely scraping by? So what if I was living on a pull-out couch in Ella's one-room apartment? I was in Los Angeles. I had a fabulous new friend and a job where I got to see movie magic happen every day.

As Etta and I reached the curb, a black limousine pulled over in front of us. The window rolled down to reveal Wilson. His dark eyes were concerned, heavy eyebrows scrunching together in an ageless brown face.

"Etta! Gemma! What are you doing standing on the curb like you're waiting for a john to pick you up?" he groused, his booming voice carrying down the street.

My face flushed bright red, but Etta laughed.

"We're just waiting for the car we ordered. Don't get your panties in a bunch." Etta smiled.

The limo door opened, and Wilson waved us in. "Cancel it. There's plenty of room with us. Get in!"

Etta and I exchanged a look before crawling over Wilson's long legs into the back. It wasn't until we were seated that I realized it wasn't just Wilson and his husband in the car. My heart skipped about twenty beats before restarting at a wild pace. I inhaled sharply as my eyes met vivid, blue ones.

Rex Carter, A-lister and lead actor in *Wild River*, was in the flipping limousine with us! He looked magnificent in a black tuxedo cut and carved to fit every single chiseled muscle. The buttons on his jacket were open to reveal a black vest lined with silver threads that matched his silk tie.

The neutral palette blended in with his black hair and tan skin, making the royal blue of his eyes stand out even more.

I'd never understood the phrase "so handsome it hurt" until I'd come face to face with Rex in real life. But every time I was within a twenty-foot radius of the man, my chest exploded into a thousand pieces. It was ridiculous. The awareness tingling through my veins threatened to turn me into the drooling fan I'd promised myself I'd never be.

Rex's left eyebrow raised, the perfectly arched black curve going even higher as I continued to stare. He had indecently kissable lips that were quirked upward at the moment, smoothing out the tiny scar at the corner. His eyes strolled down from my face to my body clad in Etta's tiny dress before landing at the juncture between my legs and staying there for a beat. My face flared again as I realized that between climbing over Wilson and sliding down the seat to make room for Etta, the dress had scrunched even higher up my thighs. Rex Carter was probably getting a clear shot of my neon-pink underwear.

"So, what do you think, ladies?" Wilson asked. "Are we going to win an Oscar?"

Wilson rubbed his hands together in excitement. His blond-haired husband—also in a tux but looking nowhere near as devastating as the actor sitting next to him—put a large hand on Wilson's leg. "You know you are. Stop fishing for more compliments."

Wilson's laugh thundered through the car, and Rex's grin turned into a full smile that made my frozen heart squeeze tight.

"I'm not sure Gemma agrees," Rex teased, and I lost feeling in half my body not only because of the way he said my name, deep and guttural, but because he actually knew it. Sure, I'd worked on set for eight weeks while they'd been filming on location in my hometown, but we'd never had a single conversation.

Etta elbowed me, the sharp edge digging into my ribcage, and the pain finally broke my gaze from Rex's. When I turned to her, Etta was frowning.

"Gemma totally agrees. Don't you? Not only is Wilson going to win Best Director, but Rex is going to win Best Actor. There are no doubts. Believe me, I've nailed the winners with an eighty-percent success rate for five years," Etta said.

I cleared my throat, forcing my heart to beat again before finally speaking. My voice came out breathy and soft in a way that made me want to cringe. "Wilson has Best Director in the bag, but Rex has competition with Ben Winters."

Wilson chuckled, and Etta shot me a glare. I shrugged at her but refused to meet Rex's eyes as they bored into me. I wasn't going to lie just to stroke his ego. He didn't need it stroked…certainly not by me. Pink hit my cheeks again because stroking and Rex were definitely not words I should combine, even in my head.

"What?" I said, looking at Etta instead of the man making my pulse spike. "It's the truth. Ben's performance in *Deadly Escape* was riveting."

"Ouch," Rex said. The humor in that one word drew my gaze back to his face where his delectable lips quirked even more. I was saved from responding as the limousine came to a stop in front of Wilson's mansion in the Hollywood hills.

Wilson clambered out, reaching in to help Greg and then Etta out of the vehicle. Rex stepped out on the other side and put his hand back in the car to assist me. When I hesitated before accepting it, a rumbling chuckle broke from deep inside his chest that did all sorts of things to my core.

"I promise, holding my hand for two seconds isn't going to kill you," he teased.

I rolled my eyes. "You're ridiculous."

The moment my palm slid into his, shock waves rippled through me, zapping along my veins and making me falter. His other hand went to my waist to steady me, and the gentle touch lit me up like a roadside flare. I needed help. I needed to send an S.O.S. and hope someone would save me before I made a fool out of myself.

When I looked up into his face, towering above me even in my four-inch heels, his sexy smile had disappeared, and his eyes had turned stormy. His dark pupils were dilated, pushing his blue irises into tiny slivers.

Nerves had me biting the corner of my lip, and his gaze tracked the movement. His fingers on my waist flexed ever so slightly, easily digging into my skin through the barely-there dress.

Rex Carter was very, very wrong.

His touch could easily destroy me.

Chapter Two

Rex

NERVOUS

Performed by Maren Morris

MY HAND AND GAZE WERE STUCK on frozen on Gemma's soft skin. I caught a hint of pink tongue as she licked her lips before she sank her teeth into the bottom one. I had the overwhelming desire to pull both into my mouth. To devour them. To devour her. The severity of my reaction was a puzzle I hadn't figured out, even after eight weeks of filming with her on set in Tennessee. I'd had a hard time tearing my eyes from her when she'd been wearing jeans, T-shirts, and Keds, and now that she was in a tiny black dress barely covering anything, it was damn near impossible.

It took a wild amount of control to drag my hands from her, and I instantly longed to put them back, to bask in the warmth of our bodies joined. She shivered in the unusually cool November air, and I wished she was quivering from my mouth and hands on her instead of the temperature.

She was nothing like the women I normally dated, slept with, or had my arm around at events like this. I usually went for full-bodied, dark-haired women, and Gemma was the complete opposite. She had blonde hair naturally streaked with bronze, hazel eyes flecked with browns and greens, and small curves she'd hid well in T-shirts but were now on display.

As I turned away and headed toward the mansion, she whispered to herself softly. Words she didn't think I could hear but returned the grin to my face. "Idiot. You're an idiot, Gemma Hatley."

I was unspeakably pleased to find her fighting her attraction to me because she'd never once shown it during filming. She'd hardly acknowledged my existence, just like at the theater tonight. I was curious to know if it was a defense mechanism, or if there were other reasons she was resisting. Like my reputation as a Hollywood player who burned through women as fast as he changed roles. It was a mix of truth and fabrication because, for a long time, there'd only been one woman in my life. Thoughts of Mariah didn't bring me to my knees anymore, but the remnants of the pain remained even though it was more wounded ego than actual hurt.

As we entered the house, Gemma and Etta split off, winding their way deeper into Wilson's mansion packed with people in sparkling apparel and painted-on smiles. I ignored the crowd and the twinkling views from the mammoth windows set in a sea of marble and glass as I quickly found my way to the bar. I needed something to fill the ache left behind by Gemma's touch and the memories she'd unburied.

Once I had my brandy in hand, I turned to find myself surrounded by a slew of industry people—actors, actresses, directors, producers. They clamored to congratulate me, asking what I was working on even though anyone who was anyone already knew. The entire time, my eyes kept straying to Gemma. Her slinky black dress made me want to remove the thin straps with my teeth, push aside the hem, and explore with fingers and tongue what lay beyond the neon-pink panties I'd got a peek of in the car.

She made her way out the French doors to the terrace, and I yearned to go after her but forced my attention back to the auburn-haired, blue-eyed woman in front of me. Felicity Bradshaw was my costar in *Breakfast and Other Things*, and even though filming hadn't started yet, I was already tired of her. Maybe because I knew what she wanted, which was my name tied to hers not only for the benefit of the movie but because it would elevate her from the B-list she resided on. It made that dull ache of my past twist uncomfortably in my chest. I wasn't going to be anyone's fucking stepping stone again.

As gracefully as I could, I disengaged from Felicity and let my feet find their way outside. Gemma was leaning on the rail drenched in moonlight and staring out at the city lights sparkling below her. The breeze had picked up, and it sent tendrils of hair that had escaped her updo flying around her.

My body reacted to the stunning image she made, and it took almost a full minute for me to control myself enough to ease over to her. I propped my arms on the rail, and our elbows touched, sending an unexpected wave of heat spiraling through me.

"Ben Winters isn't going to win Best Actor," I said, breaking the quiet.

She looked up at me, eyes flashing, before she scooted her arm a little farther away. Her thick lashes blinked slowly, eyes darting to my lips and back. Then, her eyes crinkled at the corners as she smiled softly. "I didn't expect you to be so thin-skinned."

"I'm not," I told her. "Just stating a fact."

She laughed, and the soft sound flew through my veins.

"God, you really do have an enormous ego," she said, smile growing.

"It isn't the only thing that's enormous." I winked at her.

She rolled her eyes, ignoring the innuendo and launching into a whole string of reasons why Ben was a contender. It wasn't just his acting, she claimed. It was the script and the timing of the movie in the industry. Every comment she made was surprisingly insightful—smart and well thought out. We bantered back and forth a bit, me adding a few things I liked about Ben's movie but also sharing what I thought the film lacked.

The debate made her come alive, and soon, she was waving her hands and speaking with a passion that enthralled me, drawing me nearer until our faces were mere millimeters apart. Her eyes were alight, and her lips were curved upward as if the discussion was making her happy, and that simple idea rocked me to the core—the thought of her being happy with me.

I lifted a finger and touched the corner of her mouth. Her smile disappeared behind a tiny gasp as my thumb skated along her bottom lip. Lust and something deeper, a primal urge to make her mine, roared through me.

"These have been tantalizing me for weeks," I said as my finger came to rest in the middle of her mouth.

Her breath came faster, and her eyes returned my heated gaze, but instead of giving in to the feelings, she pushed my hand away. She turned back to the view of the valley spread below us, and a shiver went through her like it had when she'd stepped out of the limo.

"You're cold," I said, shrugging out of my tuxedo jacket and placing it around her shoulders.

She froze, looking at me from under lusciously long lashes. "What are you doing?"

"Being a gentleman," I told her, but the truth was, I didn't want to be a gentleman. I wanted to lead her into the guesthouse at the back of Wilson's estate, where I was staying, and devour her while the party raged around us.

She shook her head slightly. "No…what are you doing out here with me? Flirting. Making a play. I'm hardly your type, and I'm definitely not one to have a one-night fling with a celebrity just to say I did it."

The thought of having just one night with her twisted the same ridiculous primal feeling inside me. As if I knew, with an unheard-of certainty, that a few hours with her wasn't ever going to be enough.

I tucked her hair gently behind her ear.

"You don't seem like a one-night kind of woman, Gemma," I replied.

"I'm serious…Rex," she said, swallowing hard, as if saying my name was painful and beautiful all at the same time. "You need to go find someone else to hunt down. I don't want to be your prey."

I heard her no, and it filled me with regret. I wasn't like any of the assholes in my industry who'd force themselves. No meant no, regardless of the words used to express it, and she'd just told me to take a hike. Normally, I would have swiveled on my foot and taken off, but the sorrow her words brought me was so severe I couldn't leave. Not yet.

"I'm not hunting, Gemma. I've been drawn to you for weeks as if there's an invisible string tied around me, yanking me toward you. I think you're the huntress."

She closed her eyes briefly before opening them back up. "Don't throw lines like that at me."

I gave a small shrug, and my lips curled upward. "In the short time I've known you, you seem like someone who always speaks the truth. You did it with Wilson back in Tennessee. You did it tonight when it would have been easier to just agree that I'd win an Oscar. I appreciate that honesty. I like it. I like you. I'm not throwing lines. I'm giving you the truth right back."

She shook her head disbelievingly. "Is this payback, then? For me saying Ben was going to beat you? As if you have to prove to me you can act by convincing me you're into me?"

"I'm not acting with you. I *am* into you," I said and hated the stupidity of the words. Like I was thirteen and asking my first girlfriend out.

She still didn't believe me, and I knew I'd have to convince her. I put one hand on her waist, the other turning her chin to face me. My skin tingled and zapped. "I'd like to kiss you. I want to know if the insatiable need I felt by merely holding your hand was an anomaly or if it's everything I've been missing in my life."

She bit her lip again, but she didn't push me away. I risked pressing further, saying, "If after I kiss you, you want to throw my jacket at me and walk away, I'll let you and never bring it up again."

Our gazes locked, each of us searching the other for our inner truths. She seemed as wary as I was wounded. Maybe together we could find a place in the middle to actually be happy.

"One kiss," I promised.

She didn't protest, and I bent my head, gently placing our mouths together. A feathery touch that was not nearly enough, but I was determined to take it slow so I didn't scare her away. Her eyes closed, her cheeks flushed, and her hands circled my neck. When the soft tip of her tongue darted against my lips, it broke my tightly-held control, and I thrust into her mouth with a growl. She tasted like fucking heaven—sweet and mysterious. Her nails dug into my skin as I took command, licking, biting, taking what she gave and making it mine.

She moaned, and her body fell completely against me. The flames that had been brewing in my veins burst into an inferno. I tangled my hand into her hair, tugging until her head fell back, exposing her neck and allowing me to trail wet kisses down the silky length, licking the small hollow at the base before continuing downward. When I hit the silk pooling between her breasts, I slid my tongue underneath, finding her bare, and my already stiff dick grew impossibly harder. I sucked her nipple before biting softly, and she whimpered.

Suddenly, she pushed me away, and I felt the loss like a knife to my gut. She was flushed and panting as she adjusted the dress's neckline to ensure she was covered. Her eyes flashed to the French doors and the crowded room beyond them, but no one was paying us any attention. They were too busy mingling, networking, conniving to be the next big thing.

"Gemma," I said softly, grabbing her hand and twining her fingers with mine. "Don't run. Stay."

She swallowed hard, eyes traveling down my body, widening at the way my pants tented and then journeying back up. She was fighting some internal war between wanting me and needing to flee. Her jaw was clenched tightly, but her eyes were full of desire.

"I'm probably going to regret this," she said quietly.

My heart leaped, my dick rejoiced, and my arms pulled her back toward me, tasting her sweet lips again for a brief moment. Then, I turned and led her down the stairs at the side of the terrace, along the brick walk shrouded in shadows, and into the guesthouse.

As I closed the door and turned to take her in, hesitancy hit her eyes again. Caution that I needed to remove before I went further. The last thing I wanted was for her to regret this. I wanted her to ache for a repeat performance.

My hand slid along her collar bone, and her body quivered.

"Let me make love to you, Gemma."

I trailed kisses along her chest before slowly drawing the thin strap of the dress down with my teeth just like I'd imagined. I pushed the silky material over the small slope of her breast, kissing the swell before lavishing the tip with my tongue.

"Holy hell…" she whimpered, hand going to my hair and tugging.

"Say it," I growled. "Say I can make love to you. Say I can make you quiver until you scream my name."

♫ ♫ ♫

KEEP READING PERFECTLY FINE

RIGHT NOW ON AMAZON

https://geni.us/PerfectlyFine

Or get the eBook for FREE with a Newsletter Subscription

https://BookHip.com/KGWFHPP

Thank you for taking the time to read Maddox and McKenna's story inspired by a bunch of heartbreaking country songs like "Ain't Always the Cowboy," "Memories I Don't Mess With," and "If I Didn't Love You." I hope you adored watching two broken souls find their way back to each other, and I hope the mix of lyrics and story will burn a memory in your soul that you'll think about every time you hear one of the songs from now on.

If you like talking about music, books, and just what it takes to get us through this wild ride called life as much as I do, I'd love to chat with you about it in my Facebook readers' group, LJ's Music and Stories. Hopefully, you'll join, and our little group can help *YOU* through your life in some small way.

Regardless if you join or not, I'd love for you to tell me what you thought of *The Last One You Loved* by reaching out to me personally. I'd be honored if you took the time to leave a review on BookBub, Amazon, and/or Goodreads, but even more than that, I hope you enjoyed the story enough to tell a friend about it.

If you still can't get enough of me (ha!), you could also sign up for my newsletter where you'll receive music-inspired scenes weekly and be entered into a giveaway each month for a chance at a signed paperback by yours truly. Plus, you'll be able to keep tabs on the latest news in my book world, including **when Ryder Hatley's story will be available**.

Finally, I just wanted to wish you a healthy and happy journey through this carnival ride called life. May you live life resiliently with hope and love leading the way!

Acknowledgments

I'm so very grateful for every single person who has helped me on this book journey. If you're reading these words, you *ARE* one of those people. I wouldn't be an author if people like you didn't decide to read the stories I crafted, so THANK YOU!

In addition to my lovely readers, I'd be ridiculous not to thank these folks who've made this journey possible for me:

To my husband, who means more to me than I can explain in one or a thousand sentences, and who has never, ever let me give up on this dream, did everything he could to make it come true, and then CHEERED from the rooftops at even the tiniest successes. Here's to you being a "kept man" someday, my love.

To our child, Evyn, owner of Evans Editing, who remains my harshest and kindest critic. I'm so grateful to have you shaping my stories with me. I'm inspired every day by your courage and heart.

To the folks at That's What She Said Publishing, who took a gamble on me. I am, beyond words, honored to have you in my corner. I pinch myself daily to make sure it still isn't a dream. Thank you for all the great big things and all the teeny-tiny things you do daily to help me.

To my sister, Kelly, who made sure I hit the publish button the very first time and reads my crappy first drafts and still loves my stories anyway. I love you, sis.

To my parents and my father-in-law, who are my biggest fans and bring my books to the strangest places, telling everyone they know (and don't know) about my stories, thanks for making me feel like a rock star.

To the talented Emily Wittig, who made the perfect romantic cover I wanted for Maddox and McKenna, thank you for making it a reality.

To Jenn at Jenn Lockwood Editing Services, who is always patient with my gazillion missing commas, my hatred of the semicolon, and scattered deadlines, you're my Comma Queen.

To Karen Hrdlicka, who ensures the final versions of my books are beautiful and reminds me hyphens aren't always optional, thanks for reminding me that Webster's Dictionary still exists. Ha.

To the entire group of beautiful humans in LJ's Music & Stories who love and support me, I can't say enough how deeply grateful I am for each and every one of you.

To the host of bloggers who have shared my stories, become dear friends, and continue to make me feel like royalty every day, thank you, thank you, thank you!

To my dear author friends, including Stephanie Rose, Kathryn Nolan, Lucy Score, Erika Kelly, Avery Maxwell, Hannah Blake, Annie Dyer, Aly Stiles, and AM Johnson, who have shown me the friendships I've formed are more important than any paralyzing moment in this wild publishing world, you are a gift.

To all my ARC readers who have become sweet friends and always know just the right thing to scare away my writer insecurities, thanks for holding me up.

And I can't leave without a special thanks to Leisa C., Rachel R., and Leanne J. for being three of the biggest cheerleaders I could ever hope to have on this wild ride called life.

I love you all!

About the Author

Award winning author, LJ Evans, lives in Northern California with her husband, child, and the three terrors called cats. She's been writing, almost as a compulsion, since she was a little girl and will often pull the car over to write when a song lyric strikes her. A former first-grade teacher, she now spends her free time reading and writing, as well as binge-watching original shows like *Wednesday, Ted Lasso, Veronica Mars,* and *Stranger Things*.

If you ask her the one thing she won't do, it's pretty much anything that involves dirt—sports, gardening, or otherwise. But she loves to write about all of those things, and her first published heroine was pretty much involved with dirt on a daily basis, which is exactly why LJ loves fiction novels—the characters can be everything you're not and still make their way into your heart.

Her novel, ***CHARMING AND THE CHERRY BLOSSOM***, was *Writer's Digest* Self-Published E-book Romance of the Year in 2021. For more information about LJ, check out any of these sites:

www.ljevansbooks.com

FaceBook Group: LJ's Music & Stories

LJ Evans on Amazon, Bookbub, and Goodreads

@ljevansbooks on Facebook, Instagram, TikTok, and Pinterest

Books by L J

My Life as an Album Series

My Life as a Country Album — Cam's Story

A boy-next-door, small-town romance

This is tomboy Cam's diary-style, coming-of-age story about growing up loving the football hero next door. She vowed to love him forever. But when fate comes calling, will she ever find a heart to call home? Warning: Tears may fall.

My Life as a Pop Album — Mia & Derek

A rock star, road-trip romance

Bookworm Mia is trying to put years of guilt behind her when soulful musician Derek Waters strolls into her life and turns it upside down. Once he's seen her, Derek can't walk away unless Mia comes with him. But what will happen when their short time together comes to an end?

My Life as a Rock Album — Seth & PJ

A second-chance, antihero romance

Recovering addict Seth Carmen is a trash artist who knows he's better off alone. But when he finds and loses the love of his life, he can't help sending her a host of love letters to try to win her back. Can Seth prove to PJ they can make broken beautiful?

My Life as a Mixtape — Lonnie & Wynn

A single-dad, rock star romance

Lonnie's always seen relationships as a burden instead of a gift, and picking up the pieces his sister leaves behind is just one of the reasons. When Wynn enters his life just as her world is disintegrating, their mixed-up pasts give way to new beginnings neither of them saw coming.

My Life as a Holiday Album – 2nd Generation

A small-town romance

Come home for the holidays with this heartwarming, full-length standalone full of hidden secrets, true love, and the real meaning of family. Perfect for lovers of *Love Actually* and Hallmark movies, this sexy story intertwines the lives of six couples as they find their way to their happily ever afters with the help of.

My Life as an Album Series Box Set

1st four Album books plus an exclusive novella

In the exclusive novella, *This Life with Cam*, Blake Abbott writes to Cam about just what it was like to grow up in the shadow of her relationship with Jake and just when he first fell for the little girl with the popsicle-stained lips. Can he show Cam that she isn't broken?

The Anchor Novels

Guarded Dreams — Eli & Ava

A grumpy-sunshine, military romance

Eli's chasing a dream that he's determined to succeed at, no matter the consequences. He isn't looking for love, but when free-spirited singer Ava breezes into his world, he finds himself changing his tune.

Forged by Sacrifice — Mac & Georgie

A roommates-to-lovers, military romance

Mac is determined to change the world. A life in politics is his future. Georgie finally has her law degree in reach. When her family's past makes his future an impossibility, they have to decide just how much they're willing to sacrifice for love.

Avenged by Love — Truck & Jersey

A fake-marriage, military romance

Travis's focus is on his Coast Guard career and his brother's future. But once beautiful, comic-loving Jersey crashes into his world in desperate need of medical care, he offers a marriage of convenience to help. But what happens when convenience turns to love?

Damaged Desires — Dani & Nash

A frenemy, military romance

Nash is all about honoring a promise to his dead brother, so accepting a challenge from the long-legged force of nature tempting him isn't in the cards. Not if he wants to keep his only remaining friend and stick to the code he grew up on. Several dares later, he has to decide whether to continue hiding in his past or face a new future.

Branded by a Song — Brady & Tristan

A single-mom, rock star romance

Brady's come home to help the sister he left behind and find inspiration for a new album. What he doesn't expect is to discover his muse in a woman who's completely off limits and lost in the past. Can he help her find the strength to sing a brand new love song?

Tripped by Love – Cassidy & Marco

A broody-bodyguard, single-mom romance

Cassidy is juggling her restaurant, a tiny human, and unrequited love. There's no time for her ex to try and derail her. Marco is determined to bury the feelings he has for his boss's sister, but that doesn't mean he's going to let the sniveling father of her child steamroll her. What happens when a little white lie changes everything?

The Anchor Novels: The Military Bros Box Set

The 1st 3 slow-burn romances + an exclusive novella

Heartfelt reads full of love, sacrifice, and family. The perfect book boyfriends to kick off a binge read.

The Anchor Suspense Novels

Unmasked Dreams — Violet & Dawson

A second-chance, age-gap romance

Violet and Dawson had a heart-stopping attraction they were compelled to deny. When they're tossed together again, it proves nothing has changed—except the lab she's built in the garage and the secrets he's keeping. When she stumbles into his dark world, Dawson breaks old promises to keep her safe.

Crossed by the Stars — Jada & Dax

A second-chance, forced-proximity romance

Family secrets meant Dax and Jada's teenaged romance was an impossibility. A decade later, the scars still remain, so neither is willing to give in to their tantalizing chemistry. But when a shadow creeps out of Jada's past, seeking retribution, it's Dax who shows up to protect her. And suddenly, it's hard to see a way out without permanent damage to their bodies and souls.

Disguised as Love — Cruz & Raisa

A chemistry-filled, enemies-to-lovers romance

Surly FBI agent, Cruz Malone, is determined to bring down the Leskov clan for good. If that means he has to arrest or bed the sexy blond scientist of the family, so be it. Too bad Raisa has other ideas. There's no way she's just going to sit back and let the infuriating agent dismantle her world… or her heart.

The Painted Daisies

Interconnected series with an all-female rock band, the alpha heroes who steal their hearts, and suspense that will leave you breathless. Each story has its own HEA.

Sweet Memory

Paisley and Jonas's opposite-attract, second-chance romance.

The world's sweetest rock star falls for a troubled music producer whose past comes back to haunt them.

Green Jewel

Fiadh and Asher's enemies-to-lovers, single-dad romance.

He did it. She'll prove it. Her body's reaction to him be damned.

Cherry Brandy

Leya and Holden's opposites-attract, forbidden romance.

Being on the run with only one bed is no excuse to touch her… until touching is the only choice.

Blue Marguerite

Adria and Ronan's Hollywood-celebrity, frenemy romance.

She vowed to never forgive him... Not even when he offers answers her family desperately seeks.

Royal Haze

Nikki and D'Angelo's bodyguard, on-the-run romance.

He was ready to torture, steal, and kill to defend the world he believed in. What he wasn't prepared for… was her.

Perfectly Fine – A Hollywood, second-chance romance

He's a charming, A-list actor at the top of his game. She's a determined, small-town screenwriter hoping for a deal. They form an unexpected connection until secrets ruin their future.

Rumor – A small-town, rock-star romance

There's only one thing rock star Chase Legend needs to ring in the new year, and that's to know what Reyna Rossi tastes like. After ten years, there's no way he's letting her escape the night without their souls touching. Reyna has other plans. After all, she doesn't need the entire town wagging their tongues about her any more than they already do.

Love Ain't – A friends-to-lovers, cowboy romance

Reese knows her best friend and rodeo king, Dalton Abbott, is never going to fall in love, get married, and have kids. He's left so many broken hearts behind that there's gotta be a museum full of them somewhere. So when he gives her a look from under the brim of his hat, promising both jagged relief and pain, she knows better than to give in.

The Long Con – A sexy, antihero romance

Adler is after one thing: the next big payday. Then, Brielle sways into his world with her own game in play, and those aquamarine-colored eyes almost make him forget his number-one rule. But she'll learn… love isn't a con he's interested in.

The Light Princess – An old-fashioned fairy tale

A princess who glows with a magical light, a kingdom at war, and a kiss that changes the world. This is an extended version of the fairy tale twined through the pages of *Charming and the Cherry Blossom.*